Rabbi Benzion Firer

The • Twins

AND

THE LONG JOURNEY HOME

TWO-INTERLINKED-NOVELS-IN-ONE

FELDHEIM PUBLISHERS
JERUSALEM   NEW YORK

FELDHEIM PUBLISHERS
POB 43163, Jerusalem, Israel

208 Airport Executive Park
Nanuet, New York 10954

Distributed in Europe by:
LEHMANNS
+44-0-191-430-0333
info@lehmanns.co.uk
www.lehmanns.co.uk

Distributed in Australia by:
GOLDS WORLD OF JUDAICA
+613 95278775
info@golds.com.au
www.golds.com.au

Printed in Israel

Rabbi Benzion Firer

The
Twins

FELDHEIM PUBLISHERS
JERUSALEM   NEW YORK

My town

Once there was a town
which prayed a fervent prayer.
"Let my name be remembered," it asked.
"That is all I desire."

It told a well known story.
"I was the ancient home
of a holy and honored community.
I lived a rich, full Jewish life,
surrounded by my people.
My fame reached high places,
and my name was spoken with reverence and esteem,
for men of great stature lived within my walls.

"Men like the famous Reb Mendele,
his disciple Reb Hirsch,
and his son Reb Yosef.
Where are their graves today?
Any scholar will tell you my name
and then add,
'May their merit be a blessing to protect us.'

"Even the unlearned in my midst
were full of *mitzvoth*
as the pomegranate is full of seeds.
They bore the title 'Jew' with pride,
waiting impatiently for the Redemption.

"I loved all my sons —
the learned and the simple,
the great and the small.
I rejoiced in their joys
and was elated at their happiness.
I shared their suffering
and was stricken by their sorrows.

"My bitter end is well known.
In days of darkness,
a wild, barbaric people
ensnared my sons,
and with neither logic nor reason,
killed them all.
Young and old; suckling child and tiny babe;
men, women and children;
all were choked in the chambers of death
as the forces of evil
strove to exterminate
the people of Israel.

"When my sons disappeared,
I too vanished from the map,
my hopes dashed, my prayers unanswered.

"And now, my one remaining desire
is to be remembered.
With outstretched hands I plead:
Let my name be not forgotten!"

Upon hearing this plea, I was filled with anguish.
Would that I could fulfill it!—
but I cannot
for the history of my town is unknown to me.
Her years were already full without number
when I was just a boy;
her story was long in telling
before ever I felt her charm.
And when the Holocaust descended,
I was no longer there.
Before the slaughter began
I had been taken far away.
"I cannot fulfill your request," I wept,
and my town was silenced and sad.
But suddenly, her strength renewed,
she said,
"There is power in man's will,
and that which man truly wills
can be done!

"I have heard of your story—*The Twins*.
It is a tale of two orphans, brother and sister,
caught in the web of the Great Destruction.
Every Jewish town shared in its black devastation;
disaster and courage were equally mine.
Mention me in your story,
and I too shall be remembered.

"My claim upon you is a strong one.
For eighteen years, your father of blessed memory
was Rabbi here within my gates
and now his bones lie resting
in the ground beneath my feet.
You followed in his footsteps and filled his place,
teaching my people the Torah and its commandments.
Who then can I turn to if not you?"

"It is all true," I cry.
"And the story I have written
is your story too.
Let it therefore be a remembrance for you,
a sign that you are not forgotten."

And so, dear readers,
know ye all and remember,
the name of my beloved town was

    RIMANOV

May her memory be blessed.

                                              Benzion Firer

Nir Galim, 5726

◦§ contents §◦

◄§ I ▸► *Twins*

There was nothing out of the ordinary when twins were born to Yudel Glick. After all, his were not the first twins in Nachrovah, a city of several thousand Jewish families. However, as time passed, it was obvious that Yudel's children were unique.

They were brother and sister; Yudel called his son Chaim and his daughter Brachah. These names were special; they were not just picked from a book. Yudel chose them because they were the names of his father and mother who had passed away so long ago that he didn't even remember what they looked like. His father had served as a soldier in the army of Kaiser Franz Josef of Austria during the First World War. He had left home twenty-two years earlier when Yudel was only three, and he had never returned. Yudel's mother waited patiently for her husband year after year after year, until tired of waiting, she departed from this world. Yudel was sent from uncle to uncle, from his father's side to his mother's side, from his mother's side to his father's side and back again, until he finally grew up.

His family were all faithful, observant Jews, *chassidim*, although not necessarily of the same *rebbe*. Yudel, however, was outstanding. He was a *talmid chacham* and an enthusiastic *chassid*, and he was beloved by all for both his scholarliness and his *chassiduth*.

It was only a year earlier that Yudel had come to Nachrovah. His father-in-law, Reb Yisrael Reichman, was a learned and wealthy Jew, and Reb Yisrael's only daughter, Esther, was modest, pious, and beautiful. From the time Esther married Yudel, she radiated happiness. The young couple had no financial problems and could enjoy the best of both worlds. Yudel was rich in the world of Torah, and Esther's father was rich in the world of commerce. Thus Torah and wealth were united.

When the twins were infants, not even their parents noticed the great similarity between them. Tiny babies tend to change their appearance from day to day. However, after a while everyone began remarking on the striking resemblance. This resemblance increased as time went on and was the subject of widespread attention. If the twins had both been boys or both been girls, it would have been impossible to tell them apart, for they were like two drops of water. The only apparent difference was in their dress.

When Chaim reached the age of three, Yudel and Esther cut his hair for the first time and made a party in his honor. Then they brought him to the *cheder*. The teacher, seeing Chaim holding his father's hand and Brachah holding her mother's hand, smiled and said, "Are you trying to disprove the teachings of our Rabbis? They praised the Holy One, Blessed be He, and said that when a mortal king coins money, he makes each coin exactly alike. But God who in His greatness created all men in the likeness of Adam, nonetheless saw to it that no one man is exactly like another. Yet your two children are indeed exactly alike!"

Yudel smiled and replied, "Our Rabbis also told us the reason that people are different. Were two men to look alike, one might impersonate the other and steal his house or his wife. But this couldn't happen with a brother and sister."

"You are right, Reb Yudel," answered the teacher, savoring his reply.

"Ma'ase avos siman levanim." What happens to a father often happens to his son. Just as Yudel's father had been a victim of war before he reached the age of thirty, so did Yudel become the victim of a war before he reached the age of thirty. For the father, Chaim, it had been World War I; for Yudel it was World War II. Chaim had been drafted into the Kaiser's army, left home, and never returned. His death remained a mystery. But there is no mystery concerning Yudel and his family. Their story is told in the pages of this book.

♫ 2 ♫ *The Redeeming Angel*

When the Germans invaded Nachrovah after crossing the
Polish border at the end of 1939, they caused great hardship
for the Jews in the town. A year and a half later, they
enclosed three streets with barbed wire and built a ghetto.
Then, large signs announced that all Jews must move into
the ghetto. Any Jew found outside after twenty-four hours
would be liable for the death penalty.

The first to submit to this decree were the poor, simply
because they were more mobile. They had less to lose than
the rich, and the threat of death made a strong impression on
them. The richer households, however, were in no hurry to
follow the order. Some were more fond of their money than
of their lives, and some thought that their money would
solve any problem. Nor were they as meek as the poorer
people.

Reb Yisrael Reichman was among those who were in
no hurry to move to the ghetto. "Let's wait and see," he said
to himself. "Our Sages said that an evil decree is made to be
abolished."

It would be a pity to forsake a house like Reb Reichman's. Most of the things in the house could not be moved

because the Germans forbade the transport of furniture to the ghetto. Even if they were permitted to take the furniture, where would he put it? One thousand people could live in these three streets under normal circumstances; now five thousand Jews were being confined there. There was no room for the people, much less their furniture and other belongings. Reb Yisrael remained in his house and didn't move to the ghetto on the appointed day. He locked the door and stayed inside.

Reb Yisrael had a Gentile maid named Maria who had worked for him and his wife Leah for over twenty years. Maria had originally come to their house before Esther was born and later, she had been her nursemaid. Everyone trusted her and thought of her as part of the family. Now — in this time of danger — Reb Yisrael gave Maria the keys to the house and told her that if anyone knocked on the door, she should open it and tell them that the owners of the house had gone to the ghetto.

Reb Yisrael, his wife, Leah, their daughter, Esther, her husband, Yudel, and the twins, Chaim and Brachah, sat in the innermost rooms. Before long, heavy footsteps were heard at the entrance of the house, and a heavy knock was heard on the door. Maria opened the door and found herself face to face with German soldiers, who asked if there were any Jews in the house. But she couldn't understand what they were saying. One soldier knew a little Polish and asked in her native tongue, "Are there any Jews in this house?"

Maria immediately turned and pointed towards the innermost rooms. "In there," she said.

When the Germans entered the rooms and found Reb

Yisrael and his family, their eyes gleamed. With terrifying shouts, they drove the Jews from the house.

Thus, Reb Yisrael and his family arrived in the ghetto, empty-handed and barely alive. Reb Yisrael had lost his gamble. All he had with him was a little money in his coat pocket. He brought even less than those who had practically nothing to bring in the first place

From the very beginning, life in the ghetto was no life at all. Those who had nothing began to starve on the very first day. Those who had money or valuables began to starve a few days or a few weeks later, depending on the amount of wealth they possessed. Reb Yisrael and his family were fortunate enough not to go hungry the first week, but he had to pay whatever price was asked in order to buy bread for his family. By the second week, he had joined the ranks of those who had nothing, and hunger entered his household.

Hunger tends to tease a man and to paint pictures of food before his eyes so that wherever he turns he sees a loaf of bread before him. The whole world seems to revolve around a loaf of bread. So it seems — but only to those who are weak in spirit, not to those who are strong. The latter are also hungry and need bread, but even in times of trouble, they know that man does not live by bread alone. Their need for bread does not blind them; they are still aware of the importance of other things in the world.

Yudel and Esther were strong in spirit. They did not give in. They could be deprived of their bread, but not of their will, and their will was not to lose their share in the World to Come. Bread could be stolen from them, but not their Torah, and as Jews they had to study Torah even when they had no bread. The Torah would help them gather strength until the wicked of the world were destroyed. Without Torah, a Jew would fall into despair.

After several meetings were held in the ghetto, it was decided to organize groups of boys and groups of girls to teach them Torah. Esther was chosen to teach the girls. She was an intelligent woman who had read many books, and few women could compare their education to hers. No one was more worthy of teaching the girls than she. Encouraged by Yudel, Esther agreed to accept the task. She would be a fitting helpmate for him. Both of them would be involved in the same work, since he would teach the boys and she the girls.

Esther's pupils were about nine or ten years old, but Esther frequently took her daughter, Brachah, to the class although she was only six. Brachah was an intelligent girl; she may not have understood everything, but whatever she did grasp would be a blessing for her. But there was another reason Esther took her. She was afraid to leave Brachah at home alone. Jewish children needed the best protection possible from the Nazis. Yudel was too busy to stay home, and the other parents were also away. They spent long hours each day in line, waiting to receive the little food that was offered. Esther was less concerned about Chaim. Although he was the same age as Brachah, he was quicker, more daring, and did not require as much supervision.

One day, Brachah accompanied her mother to the dark schoolroom cellar. It took a few minutes to see inside. There were some shaky benches and a long table made of rough boards, but few books. Esther would tell the girls stories of *kiddush haShem*—of Jews who had been martyred in the past. She taught them prayers and blessings—almost all by heart. Brachah sat quietly and listened. She didn't understand everything, but she understood that she was not to disturb her mother. She sat on the floor in a corner, curled up and withdrawn, waiting for her mother to finish the lesson.

The girls sat and listened attentively to their teacher, Esther. She was a gifted storyteller. As she spoke, the scene would come to life before the eyes of her audience. It fed their souls and made them forget their thirst and their hunger.

Suddenly Esther heard something. She stopped talking for a moment and listened carefully. She wanted to continue teaching so as not to worry her pupils, but she feared that her voice would be heard outside and would lead to trouble. So she continued to speak, but in a whisper. This quietness only served to add suspense to her words. The girls' eyes, burning like hot coals, were glued to Esther's mouth.

The sounds outside grew louder, and the noise increased as it came closer and closer. Esther's heart began to beat faster. She tried to continue talking in order to calm the girls, but she could not hide her own tension. Her voice began to shake. Then, she became silent. Better not to speak at all than to speak in a quaking voice. Esther waved her handkerchief and extinguished the candles burning on her table. Within a few moments harsh knocking was heard at the door. Those inside the cellar held their breath and did not answer. They were all experienced. They knew that crying and pleading would be of no use to them now. They would have no effect on the hard hearts of the Nazi soldiers.

But sometimes silence could fool them, and so they sat in absolute silence.

But this time, it was to no avail. A few kicks at the door with spiked boots, a few knocks with the butts of their rifles, and the door gave way and burst open. In the entrance stood a German soldier, and behind him were two Poles with ribbons on their sleeves and guns in their hands. Esther, who stood at the head of the table opposite the door, ran the length of the cellar and placed herself between the intruders and the girls. She knew that she could not save anyone whom the Nazis wished to hurt, but her sense of responsibility for the girls forced her to place herself between the two. Perhaps this was a mistake on her part. No one who entered the cellar from outside could see anything in the darkness inside for quite a while. Perhaps in the silence, they would have assumed the room empty and would have retraced their footsteps. Now that Esther had acted, they knew the cellar was inhabited. One soldier took a flashlight from his pocket and focused it on Esther's face. She stood proud and upright, her eyes ablaze, deeply afraid, but brave. She too had been influenced by the stories of *kiddush haShem* — of martyrdom — that she had so recently told, and she was ready to act accordingly.

The German looked around at the group of girls and hesitated for a moment. Esther was afraid they would all be arrested, so when the soldier finally turned to her and commanded her to follow him, she rose quickly, before he could change his mind. Now the girls could run home safely, and when danger would threaten her alone, she would figure out what to do. She took her daughter's hand in her own and followed the soldier.

As she passed the street where she lived, little Chaim was standing at the window. He saw his mother following a German soldier. His tiny, thin body trembled at the thought that the soldier was taking his mother to the place where they kill Jews, a place he had often heard of in the conversations of the adults. Quick as an arrow, he ran down the stairs and stood at the gate as his mother walked down the other side of the street. Chaim wanted to scream "Imma!" but he didn't. Perhaps he was so frightened that his voice left him; perhaps he wasn't sure the soldier was really taking his mother away. After all, it could possibly be just a coincidence that his mother was walking behind the soldier, and if he cried "Imma," the soldier would turn around and notice her.

Chaim stood still and didn't call out. Terrified, he watched his mother as she held Brachah's hand. At that moment, Esther stopped for a second, picked Brachah up, and ducked behind the closest gate. The soldier continued walking for a few steps until he realized that the Jewess was no longer following him. He turned around and saw that she had disappeared. He stood still and looked around, his eyes bulging from the strain.

When he looked to the right and saw Chaim, he mistook him for the child who had been with the Jewess. With one jump the soldier entered the gate of the house where Chaim was standing and began to chase after his victim. He opened all the doors of the rooms on the ground level and then went up to the second floor. Nowhere could he find her. He ran crazily downstairs to catch the child and find out where his mother had fled, but now he couldn't find the child either. He thought of asking passers-by, but was ashamed of his failure. After a few minutes of seething anger, the soldier clenched his fist and left.

Those few minutes were centuries to Esther. She had hidden in the stairway opposite her house and couldn't believe that she had been saved. If the soldier had entered the building, he would have found her immediately.

When Chaim told his mother the story, his voice shaking with fear, Esther realized that Chaim had been the angel sent from heaven to rescue her. Although Chaim's clothes were different from Brachah's, the Nazi had not noticed. He had seen only their faces, and so he had been misled. If honest people couldn't differentiate between Brachah and Chaim, how could a person whose sight was distorted by evil tell the difference between them?

~§ 3 §~ *Deportation*

Life in the ghetto became harder and harder. Worry about food was no longer the only, or the most important, worry. People were afraid for life itself. The Germans no longer had time to wait for them to starve to death. They had begun to murder people whom they did not need. Much slave labor was needed, but only the strongest were chosen for this, and they received work-cards as their payment. The weak, who could not do heavy work, were considered parasites whom the Nazis were loath to support. They were superfluous. Why should people who were of no benefit to the Nazis continue to live? They were sentenced to death.

Since it was not possible to kill everyone at once, anyone without a work-card lived in perpetual fear. At any moment, he might be picked up and sent off to the place of no return.

Yudel had no work-card, but not because he was weak or unable to work. On the contrary, he had a sacred mission which he was not willing to forsake: Yudel taught Torah to innocent, starving Jewish children.

Esther had no complaints over her husband's decision. Although a work-card would undoubtedly have made their family more secure, she could not ask her husband to submit to forced labor in order to receive the card. They both agreed that if everyone worried only about himself, who would worry about those who needed help? And who would worry about the things a work-card could not buy? A work-card could provide a measure of bread and a measure of security, but it could not provide Torah or wisdom, so Yudel remained in the cellar with his pupils, without a work-card. He placed his trust in God and was no more anxious than those who did possess the much coveted cards.

One night, there was no sleep for the Jews of the ghetto. Bitter cries could be heard from many houses as mothers cried for their sons and wives cried for their husbands. People were being taken away. The Nazi messengers of death had come for those who had no work-cards. They loaded them on trucks which transported them to an unknown destination, a place of no return.

The people without cards were like fish caught in a net: There was nowhere to run. The ghetto was enclosed by electrified barbed wire, and no one could leave without permission. It was also very difficult to hide. The messengers of death had a thousand eyes. They could find the smallest hiding place. And there were so many more people than there were places to hide. A precious few did manage to conceal themselves, but the majority sat despondently and waited for a miracle to save them.

Even in those houses where the angels of destruction had not yet arrived, people were aware of what was happening. Anything happening at one end of the street was known to those at the other end, for ghetto houses had many ears. There was no privacy in the ghetto where several families lived in every room, each squeezed into its own tiny floor space. The house where Reb Yisrael Reichman and Yudel Glick and their families lived was also very crowded. It was crowded when everyone stood up and even more crowded when they lay down. There were so many men, women, and children that it was hard to find anyone.

As the Nazis drew nearer to each house, the hearts within held less and less hope of salvation. When the danger was far away there was always the chance that the Nazis would fill their quota of victims before reaching them. But when they came closer, there was little hope left. Even so, people continued to hope against hope until the end. People have an inborn will to live, and this causes them to anticipate all kinds of possible miracles and to keep their hope alive.

In the house where Reb Yisrael Reichman and Yudel Glick lived, there were those with work-cards and those without. Reb Yisrael and Yudel were among the latter. Most rooms contained both kinds of people. Those who held work-cards were both fortunate and unfortunate — fortunate in that their lives were not in danger, but unfortunate in that the jealous eyes of their desperate brothers were fixed on them, as though this tragedy were their fault. Yudel was not jealous of those who had work-cards. He could have had one himself, if he had wanted, and one who has made a choice of his own free will does not blame others for the consequences.

Yudel was also less afraid than the others. The Torah that he taught Jewish children had made him immune to panic and had strengthened his spirit. He couldn't explain why he wasn't afraid. After all, he also wanted to stay alive

Nevertheless, he was not overcome by fear, as were many of the others. Yudel sat silently. Esther, too, did not speak. They were prepared to face the fate from which there was no escape. There was no trick that could save them. They could only wait and see what would happen. Esther's eyes met Yudel's from time to time. They understood each other without uttering a sound. They looked at Chaim and Brachah who were curled up in a corner of the floor in their worn-out, tattered clothes. Tears gathered in Esther's eyes. Yudel pressed his lips together and locked his compassion inside his heart.

The noise drew nearer to their house. A large van stood downstairs, half-full of frightened, degraded human beings, an armed soldier guarding them. When the Nazis entered the house, a tumult arose. Even those who had proper work-cards were unnerved. Seemingly, there was no reason for them to be afraid; nevertheless their hearts were not free of fear. They recalled the Rabbinic saying, "Once the Angel of Death is set loose, he does not distinguish [between men]." It is dangerous to get too close to the Angel of Death, even when he is coming for someone else.

Because of the noise, Chaim and Brachah awoke, lifted up their small heads, and looked with puzzled eyes at the adults. When Esther saw her children sitting up, she said to herself, "The similarity between these two attracts too much attention. If a Nazi catches sight of them, he may be tempted to play games, and the games Nazis play with Jewish children are too cruel." Esther took Chaim's hand and brought him into the next room, appealing to the people there to allow Chaim to remain for a while. The people in the room couldn't understand why she had brought them the boy; but since they pitied this unfortunate woman whose father and husband were both without work-cards (unlike themselves), they complied with her request without asking unnecessary questions.

Chaim felt out of place in this room. He stood bewildered. There was no one his age, and most of the people were unknown to him. He had nothing to do here. It was someone else's room, not his. Why had his mother brought him here? Where was he to go? Where should he sit? In his great bewilderment he stood by the door.

When the Nazis opened the door, they knocked Chaim over. He was hit badly but did not cry. He knew there was no point in crying. He stifled his sobs and didn't make a sound, but he had no strength left to get up. As he didn't get up immediately, one of the Nazis kicked him to the side so as not to block the entrance. Chaim, with his last ounce of strength, pulled himself up from the floor. Another dirty look from the Nazi was enough to send him, shrinking, into one of the corners of the room. The Nazis checked the work-cards of the members of the room, found them all in order, and left.

This particular building had three rooms to the right of the main entrance and three rooms to the left. The Nazis had gone through the first and second rooms to the right. Then they entered the third room where two Jews with no work-cards were taken outside. A few heart-rending sobs accompanied those who left, but immediately stopped. Probably the woman who had cried had fainted. The men who had been taken out tried to explain something while still in the hall, but their captors were not interested. The captives did not submit easily. They had nothing to lose in any case, for you can only die once, so they tried to resist. Finally, the Nazis dragged their victims down to the van and returned to the house to finish their work.

They approached the room of Reb Yisrael Reichman and his son-in-law, Yudel. As they opened the door, Brachah was facing the doorway. When the Nazi who had knocked Chaim down looked at her, he said to his friend, "We were here already," and they left the room.

After the noise died down and they knew that the danger had passed, Esther brought Chaim back to their room. Leah embraced her grandchildren, Chaim and Brachah, and smothered them with kisses. Esther said, "These two children are Good Angels who were sent into this world to bring salvation. And something which has already happened twice will surely happen again when the time is ripe." After a moment of silence, she added, "Please God, may it be this way." Reb Yisrael quickly answered, "Amen." Yudel, who was absorbed in his thoughts, made no reply.

It must be added here that Esther's blessing was not in vain. It came true many years later, although she herself did not live to see it.

◦§ 4 §◦ *The Apostate*

In Nachrovah there lived a Jew, Yank Shmendrikovitz, who had converted to Catholicism. At his *brith milah* he was named Ya'akov ben Shimon, but when he changed his religion, he also changed his name.

Shimon, Yank's father, had not been an Orthodox Jew. In his youth, when he first heard the news of the Emancipation, he had stroked his beard and exclaimed, "We are saved! Now the Gentiles will no longer murder Jews. The Redemption has come." From that day on, Shimon was one of the "enlightened." He desisted from study of the Oral Law and concentrated on the Written Law, so as not to be different from the Gentiles, for unlike the Oral Law, the Written Law is studied by priests. He also began to study foreign languages, and he trained his hand to write from left to right.

Of course, he was not a Gentile — he was of the Jewish faith — but he thought that if Jews were as similar as possible to Gentiles it would help to unite them. "If Gentiles and Jews dress the same, speak the same language, and read the same books, they will eventually open their hearts to one another. The Gentiles will come to love the Jews."

Of course, when Shimon said "love," he did not mean it literally. He had learned *gemara* in his youth and was familiar with the Talmudic maxim, *Tafasta merubeh, lo tafasta* — "If you grasp for too much, you will retain nothing." One had to be realistic. He knew that the Gentiles would never love the Jews, but it would be good enough for him if they didn't hate them. It would even be good enough if they would only hate them secretly, but not show it openly.

In order to show the Gentiles that he, Shimon *hamaskil,* ("the enlightened"), was willing to meet them halfway, he began to skip certain sections of the prayers. In the *Shemoneh Esreh* (Eighteen Benedictions), he no longer prayed, "Return mercifully to Your city, Jerusalem," or "Let our eyes behold Your merciful return to Zion." He said, "If the Gentiles have given us the Emancipation, we must be just as patriotic as they are. The land where we Jews live now is our homeland. We must love it and not pray for any other land."

Shimon wore a short frock coat, cut off his *peyoth* and trimmed his beard so that it was just like his Polish neighbors'. He considered himself a Pole of the Jewish faith.

He enjoyed studying Hebrew grammar and composing prose in the holy tongue, but he spent most of his time trying to learn foreign languages and reading foreign literature. Not that he was terribly successful in his efforts. Polish words just didn't come out of his mouth as they did from Yanovsky's. There was something in his throat that held them back. Nevertheless, he could exchange a few words with Gentiles when necessary.

If he himself was not overly successful in his efforts, he wanted his only son, Ya'akov, to speak like a Gentile from birth. When Shimon sent Ya'akov to a Polish school, his dream came true. Ya'akov spoke Polish even better than his Gentile friends, and Shimon was extremely proud of him.

"You see?" he said to the Jews of Nachrovah. "When a Jew wants to, he can even speak like a Gentile. It just takes a bit of effort."

The Jews of Nachrovah were busy trying to earn a living and had no time to stand and listen to the opinions of Shimon *hamaskil*. If they did listen, they had no time or patience to answer him back. They kept their distance from him. They felt he was different from them, and somehow this frightened them.

When Ya'akov graduated from elementary school, his father sent him to the Gymnasium. There, Ya'akov did his lessons even on Shabbath. In elementary school, Shimon had asked that his son be excused from classes on that day, but he didn't dare ask for such a thing in the Gymnasium. If the Gentiles were good enough to accept his son as one of their own in the Gymnasium, he wasn't about to make a fool of himself by discussing Jewish things like Shabbath with them. They would only laugh at him.

When Ya'akov finished the Gymnasium and wanted to register at the university, a few Gentiles tried to stop him. But they were unsuccessful, for he was an outstanding student, and they were forced to open their halls of learning to a scholar of his caliber.

Upon Ya'akov's graduation from the university, he decided that his Judaism was a hindrance. Even though he wasn't part of the Jewish community and didn't practice any Jewish customs, the Gentiles considered him a Jew. Ya'akov said to himself, "It is impossible to go on being a Gentile to the Jews and a Jew to the Gentiles, not belonging anywhere. If I am a Gentile to the Jews, I may just as well become a Gentile to the Gentiles." And he converted to Catholicism.

At that time, his father was no longer alive. Ya'akov wondered what his father would have said to him. Would he have been sorry or not? But now he was free to do as he pleased.

After Ya'akov had converted, he married a Catholic woman whose name was Marussa. She was from a wealthy family, had a good education, and a warm heart. Their wedding took place in the Catholic Church according to all the Catholic rules and regulations. Many guests had come from the bride's family, but none from the groom's. A year later, their baby daughter was born and christened Yanka, after her father.

Years passed, and Yank was appointed judge of Nachrovah. This was the reward for his conversion. No Jew had ever been a judge, not in a Jewish town, and certainly not in a Gentile one. But Yank was no longer a Jew and thus could become a judge. The Jews of Nachrovah were displeased. They would have preferred to stay away from Yank and to ignore the existence of an apostate in their midst, but now they couldn't, for he was their judge. They often had occasion to come to court with complicated problems of inheritance, or disputes between neighbors, which ended up in the Polish courts. Of course they would first approach their rabbi to hand down a decision according to the Torah, but there were those who would then appeal to the Polish courts if the rabbi's decision was not in their favor.

And disputes between Jews and Gentiles obviously went to the Gentile courts. No one had asked the Jews of Nachrovah if they wanted Yank Shmendrikovitz to be their judge. Judges were appointed by the government, and the government was run by Gentiles.

Yank Shmendrikovitz was also vice-mayor of the town, in charge of local affairs. The Gentiles had elected him. The Jews had voted for someone else, but the Gentiles were a majority in the town and their votes were decisive. In Jewish affairs Yank was very cautious. He did not want to harm the Jews. He didn't hate them, but he was afraid to stand up for them because the Poles would have said that he was not a good Catholic. Therefore, he took care not to express an opinion.

When the Germans invaded Nachrovah and the Jews' troubles began, Yank was not affected. At first, he was treated like any other Gentile, and he remained at his post. Either the Nazis were unaware that he was a convert, or at that time converts were still considered worthy of being Gentiles. But a short time later, Yank and his family found themselves in great trouble.

One day, after the Nazis had erected the Jewish ghetto, three Gentiles came to Yank's house. One was a German officer and the other two were his Polish assistants. When they asked if this was the residence of Ya'akov Shimeonovitz Yank was so astounded by the question that he could not answer.

Marussa saw that her husband was speechless, so she answered for him, "My husband's name is Yank Shmendrikovitz."

The Poles smiled, and one said, "Where is his certificate of conversion?"

Yank hurried to his desk drawer, and taking out the certificate, which was always close at hand, he thanked God silently that he could prove he was a Gentile. He held out the certificate to the German, who passed it on to an assistant and commanded him to read and translate it into German. The Pole did as he was told.

When he had finished, the German said to Yank, "If so, you were born a Jew and are a Jew now. You must move to the Jewish ghetto."

Yank replied, "On the contrary, this document certifies that I am a Catholic because I converted to Catholicism."

"Once a Jew, always a Jew," the German answered. "Hitler does not permit the Jews to deceive the Christians. Conversion is a Jewish invention to escape the Jewish fate. A Jew remains a Jew even if he has converted to Christianity."

Yank had nothing to say. His face turned white. "I will move to the ghetto with you," said Marussa gently.

"You are a Christian," the Nazi answered, "and you may remain at home."

"Nevertheless," Marussa answered, "I will follow my husband to the ghetto, together with our child."

The Nazi looked at Yanka and said, "The little girl is half-Jewish. She also belongs in the ghetto." That very day, Yank, Marussa, and Yanka moved to the Jewish ghetto.

When Yank entered the gates of the ghetto, a few Jews were standing nearby discussing their troubles. Their faces were serious, their eyes fearful. When they first caught sight of Yank, they made way for him to pass. They may not have liked him, but he did command their respect. As a judge and vice-mayor, he must be treated honorably and according to Polish custom, for he was an apostate and no longer a Jew.

But a moment later, they grasped the irony of the situation. Yank in a Jewish ghetto? What a funny sight! If they hadn't seen it with their own eyes they would never have believed it. One of the group turned to Yank and asked, "Pan Shmendrikovitz, what are you doing here?"

"I was sent here," Yank replied.

"But why?" asked someone else.

"I don't know why myself," said Yank.

"Perhaps it was a mistake," volunteered a third person.

"I certainly think it was a mistake," answered Yank.

"Surely you could have made them understand their mistake, Pan Shmendrikovitz?"

"How I wish I could have made them understand their mistake. The whole world has gone crazy." Thus ended the conversation.

The Jews saw Marussa's weary face, the baby in her arms, and they pitied her. She was not responsible for her husband's actions and should not have had to suffer for them. Yank went his own way, and the Jews went back to discussing their own troubles.

Yank suffered even more in the ghetto than the Jews did. "What do I have in common with Jews?" he asked himself. He neither practiced nor did he know anything about Jewish customs. It was just as if he were born Christian. He was a Catholic through and through. He went to church; he had had a Catholic godfather at his baptism; his Catholic friends had given him many presents and had praised him highly for his courageous act. How could he be called a Jew?

These thoughts gave him no rest. At first he tried to avoid all contact with the Jews. He said to himself, "This is all some kind of insanity. It will pass and everything will be as it was before." Accordingly, he did everything he could so as not to be considered a Jew later. Because he couldn't find an apartment all to himself and was forced to live in a room with several Jewish families, he was brought to despair. He would have been able to tolerate life in the ghetto for a while had he not been together with so many Jews. He erected a wall of silence around himself and talked to no one. Hour after hour he walked the streets, absorbed in his own thoughts.

But after several days, Yank began to realize that his behavior was not wise. Every person must be a part of some group. If the Gentiles were now unwilling to accept him, then he must be friends with whichever Jews were willing to accept him. It was impossible to live in the ghetto and not consider oneself a part of the ghetto. It would be unwise and would gain him nothing. Little by little, Yank began to befriend his neighbors. Not that he considered himself one of them, but he allowed himself to talk to them. Nonetheless, more than once he caught himself saying, "we Jews."

Yank did not work and he had no work-card. He had no need for such a card to obtain food, for he had plenty of money and could pay whatever prices were asked. Nor did he think that he was going to stay in the ghetto for long. The Catholic Church would surely intercede in his behalf. They would not permit good Catholics to remain in a Jewish ghetto. He didn't need the work-card to protect his right to life, either. Even if his certificate of conversion had not kept him out of the ghetto, it would certainly keep him from being sent away to the mysterious place where the Jews were sent. After all, he was a Catholic.

The night that the Jews without work-cards were carried away, the Nazis also visited the house where Yank Shmendrikovitz lived. When they entered Yank's room, he did not panic, and when they asked for his work-card, he took his conversion certificate and showed it to them. The German took the document, examined it carefully and said, "This is not a work-card."

Yank replied, "It is a certificate stating that I am a Catholic."

"What is a Catholic doing in the Jewish ghetto?" asked the German.

"This document shows that I have converted to Christianity," said Yank.

"What were you before that?" asked the German.

"Before that he was Jewish," replied Marussa.

The German laughed and said, "Once a Jew, always a Jew. If you have no work-card, then you must come with us!"

Marussa cried out, "Jesus, help us!"

The German looked at her and asked, "What do Jews have to do with Jesus?"

"I am not Jewish," Marussa cried, showing him her certificate.

The German asked, "If you are Christian, what are you doing in the ghetto?"

Marussa pointed at Yank and said, "This is my husband."

"Well," the German answered, "since we are taking your husband, you may leave the ghetto."

They took Yank from the room and left Marussa sobbing. Yank was thrown into a truck already crammed full of Jews, and the Nazis continued their work.

~§ 5 ~ *Esther and Marussa*

Esther renewed her teaching in a different place. She did not return to the old cellar, for the Nazis were liable to visit there again. The first time they appeared, a miracle took place, but who could count on a second miracle? One is not permitted to depend on miracles. Esther threw herself more and more into her holy task. She now taught a second group, thirty teenage girls about seventeen or eighteen years old. Esther was not much older herself, but she was wiser. She had been blessed with much wisdom which she gladly shared, and the more she taught, the wiser she became. She was known as an outstanding teacher. The girls were deeply attached to her, and Esther was deeply attached to them. There was great love between them.

She taught Jewish history, where sorrow and hope were intermingled. Sorrow — because Jewish history contains many chapters of blood and tears and much tragedy. Hope — because what was happening now in the ghetto was not new; history was repeating itself.

Esther did not teach from history books. There were many mistakes in the books. Truth and imagination were intertwined, and it was hard to differentiate between them.

Esther taught from memory. True, she did not remember everything by heart. She couldn't say exactly on what date and in which place a certain incident had happened, but she did not attach much importance to the exact date or month or even year. She didn't attach much importance to the place either—it could be a bit to the north or a little to the south, further to the east, or slightly to the west. What was important was an *understanding* of the events which had occurred. She made history live, until it seemed to the girls that each event was happening now, for the first time.

Esther spiced her lessons with the stories of our Sages in the Talmud and Midrash, stories of glory and heroism. For the first time the girls heard of the heroism of other girls their own age, girls who knew how to defend their honor and how to mislead and trap the evil people who tried to ensnare them. The girls' eyes shone. Pride filled their hearts. It was good to be the sisters of such heroines.

Esther also became a mother to her girls. Their natural mothers were so engrossed in worrying about the fate of their daughters in the ghetto that their judgment was clouded, and they had little strength left for understanding their daughters. Esther wasn't worried, so she understood the needs and doubts of each girl. She did all she could for them. If one of the girls was sick, Esther would stand at her bedside and feed her with whatever food she had found. Everyone in the ghetto knew that she obtained much support for her selfless, God-fearing work. She had ways of getting things that no one else could get, both medicine and food. Many people wondered at this and asked how she managed such things. But wondering did not change the facts.

Not all of Esther's girls came from religious homes. One girl, Chavah, who came from a non-observant home, was outstanding in her intelligence and sensitivity. Why had her parents sent her to study with Esther? Because they had drawn nearer to Torah in the ghetto. The hopes they had pinned on the Gentiles were dashed, and there was no longer any reason to imitate them. In the ghetto, they repented and drew closer to God. Before they were sent to the ghetto, they had hidden many things connected with Judaism from Chavah, in order to save her from the suffering of the Jews. "The less she knows about Judaism, the better," they had reasoned. When this failed and they were thrown into the ghetto together with all the other Jews, they changed their minds. Now they wanted their daughter to know everything that other Jews knew. If she was just as Jewish as other Jews, she should know herself. It is not good for a person not to know who he is.

But for three days, Chavah had not come to the cellar. For three days, Esther said to herself, "She must be busy with something else and hasn't had time to come." On the fourth day, Esther went to look for Chavah. She found her lying in bed. Chavah had been sick for three days but was now beginning to feel better. Her father and mother were not home.

Esther sat down at the foot of Chavah's bed and asked what she could do. Chavah said that a doctor had examined her and prescribed a certain medicine, but her parents couldn't find it. They were still out searching for it. Chavah pointed to the long white paper on the shelf above her head, on which the doctor had written the prescription in Polish.

Esther took the prescription, looked at it and said that she would try to find the medicine.

While Esther and Chavah were talking, they heard sighs from the corner of the room. Esther turned her head and saw a young woman lying in bed. Esther questioned Chavah with her eyes, and in a whisper, Chavah told Esther about Marussa. When her husband had been carried off by the Nazis, Marussa's head had begun to reel, and now she was unable to get out of bed. Esther knew the story of the apostate, as did all of Nachrovah, but she knew of his wife only by name. Cautiously, she approached the sick woman's bed and asked how she was feeling. Instead of answering, Marussa sighed.

For three days Marussa had been lying in bed, eating remnants of food. She was pale and weak. There was no one to take care of her. Her husband was gone and the neighbors kept their distance. Marussa understood why her neighbors kept away and did nothing for her. She was an intelligent woman and understood that the Jews were not very fond of the Poles. The Poles had become allies of the Germans and did all they were asked to — and even a little more — to torment the Jews. This angered the Jews greatly. The Germans had robbed the Poles of Poland, yet the Poles were still eager to cooperate with the Germans in tormenting the Jews.

Jews had lived in Poland for more than a thousand years and had helped the Poles build Poland. Now the Poles turned on them and murdered them. Marussa herself had not collaborated with the Nazis. She had suffered from them. Despite his Christianity, they had abducted her husband, thrown him into the ghetto, and sent him to some unknown destination. Nevertheless, the Jews were not fond of Marussa. She too was Polish. Whatever the Poles had done was ascribed to her. If more Poles had been like Marussa, perhaps the Jews would not have blamed her. But most Poles abused the Jews, so the Jews hated all the Poles.

Marussa was an intelligent woman and understood the Jews' feelings. When Esther approached her and asked how she was feeling, Marussa didn't answer. She was sure that this woman didn't know who she was. Were she to find out, she too would keep away. The fact that Esther spoke to her in Polish, not in Yiddish, didn't prove that she knew who she was. Many Jewish women in Poland spoke a foreign language instead of their mother tongue.

When Esther again repeated her question, Marussa understood from her tone of voice that this young woman must know her identity. She must have heard from Chavah. This time she replied and told Esther her story. When she had finished, Esther asked why she didn't leave the ghetto if she had permission to leave. Marussa pointed to a bundle on the right side of her bed, a baby curled up asleep in a pile of clothes. "Whose baby is this?" she asked.

"She is mine," Marussa answered. "Her name is Yanka." Esther understood, and asking no further questions, she promised to bring back food and medicine. It was known that Esther never made promises she could not keep.

Esther returned to Chavah. She sat with her a few more minutes, and then, before getting up to go, she took Chavah's hand and held it for a while. After she let go, she took it again, repeating this a number of times. Esther didn't know what made her do this. Perhaps she had a premonition of some future event. Finally, Esther wished Chavah a speedy recovery and went home.

⋅§ 6 ৶ The Ordeal

When the early risers in the ghetto left their houses at sunrise, they saw notices in large print ordering them to appear at a line-up at nine o'clock in the morning in the empty square behind the former site of the synagogue. The synagogue had been burnt down by the Germans with the Poles' assistance, but the square nearby could not be uprooted. It remained in its place. Children and old people were excused from this assembly, the notices said. It was prohibited to bring anything along to the square. The news spread like wildfire throughout the ghetto. Fear filled the air. The ghetto dwellers had learned from experience that no assembly was for their benefit. Each assembly resulted in the deportation of a large — or sometimes huge — number of the assembled to an unknown destination. This destination was dreaded by all. There were many ideas concerning it, but no one dared to speak them aloud.

A tumult arose. People tried to hide, but only a very few succeeded. With every minute the alarm grew, the panic increased. Thousands of human brains were searching for a way out of the trap — in vain. They all knew they could not escape; nevertheless, they tried until the very last minute.

Zero hour was quickly approaching. It was eight o'clock. They had one hour to assemble.

Some people decided to take their children with them. True, the children were not required to attend this torture. But where could they leave them? Sometimes they had to stand in the square for hours. Besides, the children might also bring good luck. A woman with a child or babe in arms might arouse mercy more than a woman alone.

Esther and Yudel were also going to take their children with them, but at the last minute they decided it would not be wise to take them both. They were too identical and might attract the attention of the Nazis, who enjoyed playing cruel games with Jewish children. Only one child should accompany them. Chaim would go with them and Brachah would stay behind. But with whom? Could they leave Brachah with her grandparents? No. Neither Reb Yisrael Reichman nor his wife was old enough to be excused from the assembly. Since every family wanted to stand together so as to know what was happening to their relatives, the grandparents would be standing next to Yudel and Esther; if Brachah stood with them, she would also be near Chaim.

Just then, Esther had an inspiration: Marussa! Marussa would not be at the assembly. She was a Christian and her baby daughter was excused from the line-up because this time all children were excused. She could leave Brachah with Marussa.

When Esther and Brachah entered Marussa's room, Marussa recognized Esther immediately. She lowered her eyes, unable to face Esther. She knew about the assembly and was ashamed that she was privileged to be excused from this dreaded ordeal. Marussa also knew that the Poles were of great help to the Germans at the assemblies, and she was ashamed of this too.

When Esther told Marussa why she had come, Marussa raised her head and looked gratefully at her. Now she need no longer be ashamed of remaining alone in her room while all the ghetto dwellers were forced out of theirs. She would remain not only for her own good, but also to watch over a Jewish child. Her appreciation was apparent as she took Brachah's hand and showered her with kisses.

Esther kissed Brachah on the mouth and left, uttering words of thanks to Marussa. Yudel, Chaim, Reb Yisrael Reichman and his wife, Leah, were waiting outside at the gate. When Esther came out, the five of them went to the assembly.

Thousands of men, women, and children were standing in the square. It was a summer day. The sun had already risen high in the sky and had heated up the air. There was a tense silence. After a little while, a ring of S.S. soldiers with Polish assistants surrounded the square. The dread increased. Reb Yisrael Reichman and his family stood close together. Esther held Chaim's hand. He was still small and he didn't have an adult's understanding, but his fear was as great as that of the adults.

Just then, Poles with official guard bands on their sleeves entered the square. They roughly pushed all the people to the right side of the square. Then they arranged them in rows. The left side of the square was empty. Next, a Nazi with stars on his shoulders and a rubber club in his right hand began to stride up and down the rows. He pulled out a person from here and one from there, and with his cudgel, he motioned to them to go to the left side.

While this was going on, each person was preoccupied with himself, watching only to see if anyone from his own family was being taken. No one paid much attention to the group that was forming on the left. Those from whom a member of the family had been taken were gripped by hysteria and saw nothing. When the S.S. officer had finished his work and left the rows, everyone turned to look at the left side of the square. One hundred frightened young girls, around seventeen or eighteen years old, had been chosen to stand apart. A ring of S.S. officers and Poles surrounded them.

A wave of revulsion passed through the assembled Jews. This was intolerable. Here and there the choking sounds of mothers' cries could be heard. Fists were clenched and unclenched. Something must be done. But what? Older men and women started towards the group of girls. But they were chased away and beaten by rubber clubs.

Feverishly, her eyes burning, Esther searched the group of girls. At one end of the group stood twenty of her students. They were all standing together. They had not been taken from one place but had been drawn together to one place. Esther felt as though fiery coals scorched her heart. She knew that she had only a few seconds in which to act. Soon they would take the girls away. While Esther's eyes were fixed on her students, her eyes met Chavah's. Esther read both despair and a plea in Chavah's eyes. Esther could no longer remain in her place. She removed her hand from Chaim's and moved to her left.

Yudel noticed immediately. He stretched out his hand to take hers and to restrain her, but then he took his hand back. While Esther hurried through the empty space separating the right side from the left, she heard the horror-stricken voice of her father, but she didn't turn her head. She could not allow herself to waver. Any slight hesitation might spoil everything.

Esther stopped a short distance from her students and stood still. When the bodyguards saw a young woman approach deliberately, without the outbursts of those who had preceded her, their curiosity was aroused. One of them asked what she wanted. Esther answered that she wanted to join the group on the left. The guard smirked and said, "As you wish. You are a bit older than the rest, but you may come too."

The circle of guards opened, allowing Esther to join the group. Tears formed in the eyes of Chavah and her friends, tears of happiness. In every tragedy there must be some small reason to rejoice. Esther approached her students and they clung to her. They didn't know if she would be able to save them, but at least it would be easier to bear the terror and dread in their hearts if she was with them.

Esther tried to compose herself but did not succeed. Her heart shook within her. She knew what a great responsibility she had undertaken for the girls' fate. Would she have the necessary strength? Is one permitted to believe in oneself?

The people who watched Esther scorned her. Some thought she had gone out of her mind. Some thought she was a fool who didn't understand what was happening. All thought of her as a poor, unfortunate woman who had sealed her own sad fate.

Soon the order to disperse was given, but no one moved. German guards and Polish assistants pushed their way into the crowd, chasing them out of the square with wild cries and brutal beatings. The square began to empty out, little by little, until the last person was chased away. That person was Yudel. He wanted to see Esther as long as he could. Their eyes met time after time. His eyes full of caresses, Yudel gave his assent to Esther's act. She rejoiced in this; it made things much easier for her. They would share the responsibility together. She was not alone.

After Yudel had been chased out of the square, Esther looked around. The group of girls had formed into several lines, and she entered one of them. They began to march, a ring of guards surrounding them. They left the ghetto and passed the market square where many people were standing about. Today was Sunday, and they had just left church. The Poles watched the strange procession wonderingly.

The girls arrived at the train station where five cars were ready, waiting on the rails. The girls were subdivided into five small groups, about twenty in each group. The Germans had commanded them to divide themselves up, but they didn't interfere with the process. Each girl could choose her own group. Esther and her students comprised one full group. They entered the third car.

One of the guards brought food to the car, good food, the likes of which hadn't been seen in the ghetto for a long time. White bread, butter, sardines and steaming, fragrant coffee. As the guard left the car he told them that the trip would take about five hours. Then he locked the door from the outside, and the train began to move along the tracks.

A deathly silence filled the car. The girls didn't utter a sound. They knew it was now time for their revered teacher to speak. Esther had increased in stature sevenfold. Of her own free will, she had volunteered to share their fate, leaving behind everything dear to her. They felt that they were as precious to her as her own father and mother, children and husband. Who could have imagined such self-sacrifice? Such a thing was beyond their comprehension. She must be an angel, not a human being.

Esther sat on the floor in the center of the car, the girls in a circle around her. She looked into their eyes to see how much fear was in them. To her great joy she saw tranquility instead. Peace of mind is much better at a time like this than fear. Esther began to tell them inspiring stories about outstanding Jewish heroines of the past. They were brave, courageous girls and women who had acquired the right to enter the World to Come in one act. Among others, she told them of the following incident:

Once there were four hundred boys and girls who were taken captive by the Romans for immoral purposes. When they realized what would be demanded of them, they asked each other, "If we drown ourselves at sea, will we merit the World to Come?" The oldest of the group quoted the verse, " 'God has said: From *Bashan* will I return [them]; I will return [them] from the depths of the sea.' *From Bashan will I return* refers to those who are saved from the lion's teeth (BaSHaN — *bein shinei aryeh*); *I will return* [them] *from the depths of the sea* refers to those who drown at sea." Upon hearing this, the girls all jumped into the sea. The boys inferred the following lesson from their act: "If girls, who are frequently taken captive (for such purposes) could do such a thing, how much more are we required to do so." And they also jumped into the sea. (*Gittin* 57)

Chavah commented, "How good to have someone great among us to teach us. But what can even a great person do if there is no sea nearby?"

The girls all looked at Chavah, waiting for an answer to the question each one had asked herself. Esther didn't say a word. She pulled out a small bag that had been hidden under her clothing. In it were tiny seeds as white as shrouds. Sighs of relief welled up from the girls' hearts. Some of their faces showed a faint smile of victory. Esther heard the sighs, saw the smiles, and her heart filled with an overwhelming love for her students who would not fail the test. Without a word, Esther gave each girl one seed. Each one held the seed in her right hand as though it were an angel of redemption. They caressed the poison with a tremor of holiness. Joy mixed with fear filled their hearts. Now, if they could muster the strength, evil would have no more control over their lives. Now they alone would control their own lives. They had not felt this way for a long time.

Esther rose from her place, went over to a corner of the car where a bucket of water and a cup stood. She wet her fingers with the water, returned to her place, and began to recite verses of *viduy*—the confession before death. She didn't remember the whole confession of Rabbenu Nissim by heart, but what she did remember was sufficient to purify their hearts. The girls repeated each verse after her. After the confession, they recited *Shema Yisrael* and took upon themselves *ol malchuth shamayim*, the obligation to serve God.

Once again Esther arose, went over to each girl, kissed her on the forehead, and received a kiss in return. Then the girls themselves arose and kissed each other. When all had returned to their places, Esther raised her hand and put the poison in her mouth. All followed her example. Not one hand trembled during this act. Esther said, "You have done well. Avraham Avinu's hand did not tremble either when he took the knife to sacrifice his son Yitzchak."

Then Esther adjusted the kerchief on her head, straightened her dress, and lay down on the floor. Her body was on the floor, but her head was in the lap of one of the girls. All did likewise, each one's head resting in another's lap.

The train's engine went faster. It emitted impatient gusts of air. It sounded as if it wanted to run away from the heroines it carried, but it was unsuccessful. The girls in their car followed behind the engine, as if to say teasingly, "We have arrived at our destination first." When the engine despaired of winning the race it slowed down and finally stopped and was silent. The door to the third car was opened, and the food was found untouched.

◦§ 7 ◦ Brachah Leaves the Ghetto

The Sokolsky family were Gentiles who did not hate Jews. Mr. Sokolsky was a building contractor who made a good living and led a comfortable life. Until the war he was quite satisfied with his life. He also basked in the honor accorded to his son-in-law, Mr. Shmendrikovitz, who was both judge and assistant mayor. Besides his daughter, Marussa, he also had a son, Stashek, who was a medical student at the University of Cracow. From time to time, Stashek would come home for a visit, and he too added to his father's prestige.

When the Germans threw Mr. Shmendrikovitz into the Jewish ghetto, Mr. Sokolsky's luck changed. Now that the Germans had made it permissible to spill Jewish blood and the Jews were of little value to the Poles, Mr. Sokolsky lost his status. The greatest shame of all was that even Marussa lived in the ghetto, together with all the Jews. Mr. Sokolsky, who had never been an anti-Semite before, now began to love the Jews less. "They always bring trouble," he thought to himself. "Without them, would anything be missing from my life? If Yank Shmendrikovitz had not captured Marussa's heart, this tragedy would never have happened to my family. Wherever there are Jews, there are troubles."

Stashek was even more ashamed than his parents. Mr. and Mrs. Sokolsky were no longer young, and neither were their friends. Older people don't change much from day to day. True, their friends did ridicule them after Yank Shmendrikovitz had been declared a Jew in every respect and had been thrown into the ghetto, but they did not cut off their ties of friendship. Mr. and Mrs. Sokolsky could also spend most of their time at home and thus retain a quiet dignity.

But Stashek was young, and a young person goes out with friends. Stashek's friends were anti-Semites. They had hated Jews even before the German invasion of Nachrovah; now they hated them seven times more. When Stashek's friends spoke disparagingly of Jews, Stashek would try to remain indifferent, but he did not succeed. He would blush, and his friends would look at him with open derision.

In those days there were two topics of conversation among Stashek's friends. They always began talking about the need to set up an underground to fight the Germans, and they always ended up talking about the German war against the Jews. When they talked about the underground, Stashek would also take part in the discussion, but when the talk turned to the Jews, Stashek felt uncomfortable, as though he too were Jewish and they were talking about him.

The Sokolsky family discussed the matter and decided that Marussa must be persuaded to return home. Once Marussa was out of the ghetto, the Sokolsky family name would no longer be dishonored. Everyone would know that Marussa was no longer Yank's wife, and they would forget their former relationship. Marussa could leave Yanka with Yank, to prove that she had severed all ties with him. Of course they were aware that Marussa would not want to leave Yank, and even if she could be persuaded to leave him, she wouldn't want to leave Yanka, but there was no harm in trying. A drowning man will clutch at any straw.

Who would go to Marussa? Stashek. He would persuade her to lift the shame from her father's house and to correct her mistake. Until now, they had been careful not to visit the ghetto so as not to give people any additional opportunity to look down on them, but now there was no choice. If Stashek would not go, who would?

When Stashek arrived at the ghetto gate, he was allowed to enter. If Jews were allowed to enter, then certainly Poles could do so. But only Poles were allowed to leave. Stashek didn't know where his brother-in-law lived, and he began to question passers-by. But he couldn't get a clear answer. Some pretended not to hear the question, and some heard but answered that they didn't know. Every Pole was suspect to the Jews in the ghetto. No Pole ever came to the ghetto to do anyone a favor, only to cause trouble. Even those who knew Mr. Shmendrikovitz and where he lived hesitated to pass on this information to a Pole. Mr. Shmendrikovitz was indeed an apostate, but the Gentiles considered him a Jew, and the Jews did not wish to cause him harm. Stashek was dressed in a student's uniform, and this increased their suspicion even more, because most Polish students were known to be anti-Semites. Stashek was angry and perplexed. "That's just the way Jews are," he said to himself. "They are not at all polite. They won't even help a man find his sister. They could help but they won't. They won't even cooperate in such a simple thing as telling you where so-and-so lives. They are all liars. The Jews are a strange people. It's no wonder that the Poles don't love them."

Finally Stashek met a Jew who stopped and listened to his request, and since this Jew knew that Mr. Shmendrikovitz had been taken away by the Germans, he told Stashek where the house was. When Stashek opened the door, he found Marussa. She and her brother stood facing each other, so surprised that they even forgot to smile; they finally recovered and shook hands. Marussa gestured to a shaky chair for Stashek to sit in and asked how her parents were feeling. Stashek gave a noncommittal answer, while examining all corners of the room, which at that hour was empty. He was insulted. His sister was living in a room not fit for any decent human being. Filth like this was possible only with Jews. Everything here was neglected. Neither the floor nor the bedclothing were clean. All the furniture was faded and peeling. "When people say that Jews are not clean," he thought, "there is truth to it."

Stashek paused until he had succeeded in hiding his anger and then he asked, "Where is Yank?"

Marussa lowered her wet eyes and said, "They took him away."

At that reply Stashek could have jumped out of his chair from sheer joy, but he forced himself to sit still. "And where is Yanka?" he asked.

"Yanka went for a walk with Brachah," answered Marussa.

"With whom?" he asked.

Marussa told Stashek about Esther, and Stashek asked.

"What do you think made that Jewess do such a thing?"

Marussa answered, "She probably lost her senses from so much suffering."

"Perhaps she came to her senses and became light-headed," suggested Stashek.

"If you had known her you wouldn't say such a thing," answered Marussa.

Stashek replied, "Even those who think they know them, don't really know them."

"Whom are you calling 'them'?" asked Marussa.

"The Jews," answered Stashek. Marussa looked at him but didn't reply.

Just then, the door opened and Brachah entered, holding Yanka's hand. Stashek picked Yanka up and put her on his knees. Then he pulled a chocolate bar out of his pocket and gave it to her. Marussa took the chocolate away from Yanka and broke it in half. She gave half to Brachah and half to Yanka. Stashek looked at Marussa but said nothing.

Then Stashek put Yanka down, gave her to Brachah, and told the girls to go outside for a while. When they had left, he said to Marussa, "Let's get to the point."

"What point?" she asked.

"To the reason for my visit."

"I thought you came to see me," said Marussa.

"I did, but I also came to ask why you don't leave," said Stashek. "If Yank is no longer here, why are you staying?"

Marussa replied, "I did want to leave already, but I'm afraid that they won't let me take Yanka out."

"I'll take Yanka," said Stashek. "If they see her in my

arms they won't dare to stop me. She even looks like me. The guards at the ghetto gate will think she's mine."

"But," asked Marussa, "what will happen to Brachah?"

"Brachah is Jewish and should be handed over to the Jewish Committee," answered Stashek.

"No," protested Marussa. "I won't give her to anyone here! She was given to me, and it's my responsibility to take care of her. It's dangerous for her to remain here."

"But where will you keep her outside of the ghetto?" Stashek asked. "Father won't permit her to enter our house. People ridicule us and treat us as if we were Jews. We must forget the past and not give anyone the opportunity to disparage us any more. And the law prohibits keeping Jews in any house outside the ghetto. If the Germans found out, we would be in danger."

"I'll put her in the convent, but I must save her life," Marussa answered. "Here she is in danger. If no one has come to take her back from me, that must mean that none of her relatives are alive, and I must take responsibility for her."

Stashek asked, "And what if they don't allow her to leave? Will you remain here because of her?"

Marussa reflected for a minute and then answered, "I will do what I can, but no more than that. If her own people, the Jews who guard the gate, don't allow her to leave, it will be their own fault. I will have done my share."

Stashek didn't continue the discussion. He silently prayed that the Jews at the ghetto gate would not let Brachah out and would save his family from this new trouble.

That very day, Stashek, holding Yanka in his arms, and

Marussa, holding Brachah's hand, all left the ghetto. The Jews at the ghetto gate did not detain them. Stashek's uniform and his and Marussa's Slavic faces served to obscure Brachah's Jewish eyes from the ghetto guards.

Stashek's prayers were not answered.

Yudel didn't go home. He couldn't bear to see the suffering of his in-laws. Furthermore, he didn't want to disclose Esther's secret to them. Perhaps they still held some slight hope of seeing her again, and he couldn't bring himself to extinguish this hope. Neither did he go to bring Brachah back from Marussa. Brachah would only ask about her mother, and he didn't know how to answer her questions. He therefore thought it better to wait a few days until Brachah was used to not seeing her mother. Chaim didn't ask about his mother. He wanted to, but when he looked into his father's face — suffused with suffering — he didn't ask.

Yudel went to Shimon's house. Shimon surpassed Yudel in both age and strength. Yudel had learned much Torah and that had worn away his physical strength. Shimon, on the other hand, was strong, and though he himself had learned little Torah, he held in high esteem those who had.

Shimon used to live on the ground floor of Reb Yisrael Reichman's house, outside of the ghetto. Whenever he would meet Yudel while passing by the gate, he would greet him loud and heartily. He didn't honor him for the sake of his father-in-law, the landlord, but for his own sake, because he was a *talmid chacham*.

In the ghetto, Shimon was no longer a tenant of Reb Yisrael Reichman who now had no house of his own. Actually, no one here had a house of his own. Even those whose present dwelling had once been their own no longer owned these homes. All the houses had been expropriated and belonged equally to all the homeless. Everyone had his own floor space in a room shared by a number of families.

Yudel went to Shimon's room. Shimon had also witnessed Esther's deed. He understood why Yudel couldn't go back to his father- and mother-in-law. He couldn't bear to see their suffering.

Shimon received Yudel warmly. He divided his floor space in two and bestowed one half on Yudel and Chaim. Shimon was a widower who had no children. He was also a carpenter—not an ordinary carpenter, but one with hands of gold and dexterous fingers which could build anything his eyes could see. In the ghetto, Shimon had received a grade A work-card, so his position was secure.

A week after Esther was taken away, Yudel went to fetch Brachah from Marussa, but no one was there. When he asked where Marussa had gone, the neighbors told him that she had left the house three days ago with a Polish student, holding Brachah's hand as they went. At first, Yudel was heartbroken.

"Apparently," he thought to himself, "Marussa left the ghetto and took Brachah with her after hearing of Esther's deed." But after thinking it over, he decided that perhaps Brachah was much safer outside the ghetto. When he, too, was able to leave the ghetto, he would go and take her from Marussa. Nevertheless, Yudel was unhappy. He tried to convince himself that it was all for the best, but he found no peace of mind—neither that day nor in the days that followed.

If he left the ghetto, he would get Brachah. But what would happen then? Would Brachah find her place among the Jewish people again? Yudel suffered greatly because of his daughter, in addition to the pain he suffered because of his wife. It would have been too much for any other man to bear, even for someone as strong as Shimon, but Yudel bore all that suffering within himself.

Yudel had many close friends in the ghetto, but Shimon was not one of them. Why then had he gone to Shimon rather than to one of the others? Yudel's heart told him that now was the time for him to stay close to Shimon, and his heart did not deceive him. Shimon was a simple person. He wasn't immersed in Torah, and neither was he an expert in other areas, but he was a proud Jew.

Whenever a Gentile would attempt to make fun of the Jews, Shimon would stand at the gate, ready to defend their honor. Once, when some Polish hooligans had thrown stones at the windows of the synagogue during the Prayer for Rain, Shimon had come out wearing his *tallith* and had smashed their bones, putting a few of them to bed until the time for the Prayer for Dew six months later. Shimon used to say, "It is good to hear the voice of Ya'akov in the synagogue, but not in the Gentile marketplace. In the synagogue one honors God with words, but in the marketplace one must honor Him with strength. When one fights the Gentiles, it is a *kiddush haShem*." Shimon would have liked to fight in the ghetto, too, but he didn't know how to go about it. Nevertheless, he didn't give up.

One day, Shimon came home from work and found Yudel sitting and meditating. He asked, "What are you thinking about, Yudel?"

Yudel answered, "There is no lack of subjects for meditation in this ghetto."

"There is no value to such thinking," answered Shimon. "Something real must be done."

"What do you mean?" asked Yudel.

Shimon replied, "Come with me and we'll speak about action."

Yudel answered, "Talk has no substance either."

"You're right, Yudel," said Shimon. "Then let us not waste our words and not lose time. Let us act."

Yudel and Shimon left the room. Chaim remained at home with a few other people. When Yudel and Shimon arrived at their destination, others were already there. They were in a dark cellar whose only door was hidden from the outside by an old clothes cupboard. They pushed the cupboard to the side, opened the door, and entered the cellar. Then they returned the cupboard to its place, locked the door from the inside, and were well-hidden.

The discussion began. Shimon was one of its leaders. He began by saying, "After the incident with the girls, the time has come to do something." Everyone looked at Yudel and lowered their eyes.

"Are we all agreed?" asked Shimon.

Zechariah the butcher nodded his head.

"Well, Shimon, what has to be done?" asked Berel the porter.

Shimon looked Berel in the eyes and answered, "We have to get out of the ghetto." Then he added, "That is why we are here now—to figure out how to get out of the ghetto."

One of the group, whose face Yudel could not see because he sat further back in the darkness of the cellar, said, "Even if we find a way to get out, where can we go? All the Poles outside the ghetto are looking for Jews to hand over to the Gestapo."

"We can escape to Yanovsky forest, east of Nachrovah," said Shimon.

Another person shook his head and said, "Until we go, we won't know how to escape. Only after we've left will we know how we did it."

Shimon answered, "Nevertheless, we should know where to start."

Zechariah the butcher added, "Our Rabbis taught, 'If one rises up to kill you, kill him first.' We have to get rid of the guards at the ghetto gate, and then we can escape from the ghetto and flee to the forest. Not all of us together, like a herd, but each man for himself. Even if they pursue us, they won't catch everyone. Those who will get to the forest will get there, and those who don't make it will suffer no more. Endless suffering is worse than the end."

One of the group objected. "But Jews guard the gate. Shall we harm them?" This question was not answered.

Shimon turned to Yudel and asked, "And what does the Torah say about such a case?"

Yudel answered, "Every Jewish person is commanded to do all in his power to save his own life. We must escape from here and trust in God Almighty to send good angels to help us on our way."

Shimon asked, "Yudel, you said 'us.' Are you coming with us?"

Yudel answered, "Yes, I will go with you."

Shimon asked, "And will you take Chaim with you?"

"Yes," Yudel answered.

Shimon thought a bit and said, "We cannot leave here empty-handed. A man in the forest with no weapons is helpless. We must prepare weapons before we go." By the time they left the cellar it had already grown dark, and each man went his own way.

The next day, a Jewish *kapo* (policeman) approached Shimon at work and summoned him to Mr. Shefler, the head of the Jewish Committee. On his way to the committee office, Shimon stopped off at his home and found Yudel there. "I came to see if you were at home," said Shimon. "Perhaps you'll come with me to Mr. Shefler?" Yudel thought for a minute and then agreed.

When they entered the committee building, they saw many people and heard much crying. They entered Mr. Shefler's office, and he invited them to sit down. He looked into Shimon's eyes and said, "We hope that our troubles have come to an end. Jews will no longer be sent away. We have only to sit quietly and wait for the end of the war when we will be able to leave the ghetto. Meanwhile we must be careful not to endanger everyone in the ghetto by hasty actions."

Shimon heard but did not answer. He was shocked. How did Mr. Shefler learn of their plans? Was one of his group an informer? As Shimon made no reply, Mr. Shefler asked, "Why don't you answer me?"

"There was no question to answer," said Shimon.

Mr. Shefler saw that Shimon would not disclose his secret, and he stressed, "Anyone who dares to act without the approval of the Committee will be severely punished."

Then he turned to Yudel and said, "You are a *talmid chacham.* Tell me, does the Torah endorse endangering the community to save an individual?"

Yudel answered, "If it is for the good of one individual, it is certainly forbidden, but if it is for the good of many, then it is also for the good of the community. But I don't understand what you're talking about. I only came here with Shimon because I am his neighbor."

Mr. Shefler rose. "You may go now," he said. Then he turned to Shimon and added, "Remember, I warned you." Yudel and Shimon left the building.

It must be noted, in defense of Shimon's group, that none of them had turned informer. His own behavior those past few days had aroused suspicion. He was distracted and disorganized, always busy, but doing nothing. Anyone who looked into his eyes could read his thoughts. Shimon couldn't disguise the burning desire in his mind and his heart. He himself was the unwitting informer.

Mr. Shefler didn't depend on the warning he had given Shimon. He said to himself, "If Shimon does take action and tries to escape from the ghetto, Germans or Poles had better be standing guard at the gate, and not Jews. Otherwise they will blame me for cooperating with the runaways and my life will be worthless." For several days, only Poles guarded the ghetto gate, as Mr. Shefler had requested from the authorities. The reason he gave for this request is unknown to us. We followed behind Shimon and his men and paid no attention to Mr. Shefler.

One day, Shimon and his group took action. A few dozen young and not-so-young Jews, carrying weapons and accompanied by a few children, reached forest. Yudel and Chaim were among them, but Zechariah the butcher was not. His suffering reached its end before he reached the forest. In the struggle between the escapees and the guards, there were several casualties, and Zechariah was apparently among them. The escapees took some comfort in the fact that there were also casualties among the guards. Which side suffered greater casualties is not known. Those who escaped were too busy to stop and count the casualties at the gate.

Happiness and sadness were both in Brachah's eyes. One minute her eyes smiled; the next moment they were on the verge of tears. She could not yet grasp the great change that had taken place. She was now in the company of five girls. Three of them were her own age, and two of them were about three years older. All of them wore clean clothes and whole shoes. She was also dressed in new clothes after the old clothes in which she had arrived were taken from her. Everything here was clean. In one room there were as many beds as there were girls. Six. Low chairs and tables were in a second room. Brachah was very comfortable sitting at such a table.

Marussa had brought her here this morning and had spoken to a middle-aged woman. The woman had listened to what Marussa was saying, all the while looking at Brachah. Brachah didn't understand what she was doing in this place, nor did she know who this woman was. When Marussa finished talking, the two women came over to Brachah. Marussa patted her head, said, "You will be very happy here, my child," and left. Then the other woman also caressed her and said, "From now on, you will stay with me. Call me Maria."

Brachah didn't know this Maria. She wasn't the same Maria who had worked in her grandfather's house. When Marussa had brought her here, Brachah thought that she was being taken to her parents, but now she saw that Marussa had not brought her to her father and mother, but to Maria. Maria wore a gray dress and a white apron. Her eyes were not dark like the eyes of most of the ghetto women. They were blue. Her hair, too, was not dark but light. She looked very much like Marussa. Perhaps they were sisters. Who knows...

Brachah stood and watched the girls, and the girls gazed back at Brachah. No one spoke. After a while, Maria broke the silence, turned to the girls, and said, "You have a new friend. Her name is Brachah. Come and talk to her. She too will be here with us." Then she left the room.

When Maria had left, the girls approached Brachah and asked, "Who brought you here?"

Brachah answered, "Marussa brought me."

The girls asked, "Who is Marussa? Is she your mother?"

"No," said Brachah. "My mother's name is Esther."

Sarah, the eldest of the girls, asked, "Where is your mother?"

Brachah answered, "In the ghetto."

Sarah said, "Don't be afraid, Brachah. We also come from the ghetto."

Brachah wanted to ask where she was, and who Maria was, but she didn't. She was too shy.

At 10 AM the girls went out to a yard which was enclosed by a tall, spiked fence painted green. You could see the street through the fence, but the spikes were dense so that from afar it was impossible to see into the yard. Well-dressed people walked up and down the street, and children played in the yards of the houses opposite. How different it all was from the ghetto! Brachah had never seen people dressed so well. Her heart rejoiced in what her eyes saw, until she remembered her mother and father and became sad. She also remembered Chaim and was jealous of him. Chaim was with Abba and Imma, so why was she here and not with them? There was no one to ask. The girls who were here with her surely did not know where her parents were.

Soon Maria called the four younger girls into the room. She sat them down at the low tables and handed each one a copybook and a pencil. The new copybook and pencil were for Brachah. The other three girls had been here for several weeks already, and Maria had begun teaching them to write a few days before.

Maria set up a small blackboard opposite them, and in white chalk she showed them how to write "father" and "mother" in Polish. She wrote beautiful, big, round letters on the board, and the girls tried to copy what Maria had written. The three other girls had some experience and had acquired some skill, but Brachah was trying her hand for the first time. She had never seen letters like these. In her parents' home she had seen books with completely different letters. Brachah knew how to speak Polish, because she had spoken to Maria who had worked in Grandfather's house. But she had never before seen letters like these.

Brachah tried to copy the two words. She wrote them anew on each of the twenty lines on the page. Each line looked better than the previous one. It was hard to read what she had written on the first lines, but the last ones were quite legible. For one hour the girls sat and wrote. When Maria announced that the lesson was over, they gave back the copybooks and pencils. Maria would return them at the next lesson.

While Brachah had been writing she had been absorbed in the work and hadn't thought about what she was writing. Now that she was finished, she began to think of the words, and tears came to her eyes. She had written "father" and "mother," but they were far away from here. Did they know where she was? Why hadn't they come to take her back from Marussa? Were they sick? Were Grandfather and Grandmother also sick? Was everybody sick? But when Brachah looked at the eyes of her friends and saw no tears, she dried her own tears and calmed down. The younger girls went out to the yard again, as the older girls came back in. Apparently they too were learning how to write.

At twelve o'clock the girls were called to dinner. They sat at the same tables at which they had written their lessons. A young woman whose dress was just like Maria's served them. Brachah looked at the food with amazement. She had not seen such food for a long time. White bread. Hot soup with meat. She was overwhelmed with happiness. Her mother had taught her to recite a *berachah* whenever she ate anything, so in a loud, joyous voice she said the appropriate *berachah* over each type of food. The girls looked at her, a bit startled. The young woman blushed. She looked at Brachah for a long time and finally left.

During the meal, the girls all talked with each other at

once. By now, Brachah knew all their names. Sarah was the oldest, and Rivkah came next. The three younger girls, Chavah, Leah and Rachel, were Brachah's age. They told Brachah that they had come from the ghetto a few weeks earlier. Sarah also knew why they had come. She said that there had been rumors in the ghetto that the Nazis were about to send away the children, and so their mothers had arranged to have them taken out of the ghetto, but she didn't know how. She did know that there were also boys in a similar house for boys.

Brachah asked Sarah, "If the Nazis were really going to take away the children, then why didn't they take me?"

Sarah answered, "Not everything they say in the ghetto is true. But perhaps it is true, and if they have not taken them away yet, they will do so tomorrow or the next day." Brachah was glad to be with the girls, where she would not be taken away.

After dinner the girls were told to lie down and rest for an hour. When they got up, they went to the yard. On her way out, Brachah noticed that the house contained several more rooms. In the corridor she met more women dressed just like Maria. She was a bit surprised that everyone wore the same clothing, but she liked the idea.

At night, before going to sleep, Maria told the girls that it was time to say their bedtime prayers. The five girls formed a line and then knelt on one knee, facing a corner of the room, the palms of their hands pressed together. Brachah looked at the corner and saw, above her friends' heads, a picture of a woman holding a little boy. Above the picture burned a small lamp which shed a dim light on it. Brachah wondered why she had not noticed the picture during the day. She looked at it again and saw that both the woman and the child in her arms were very sad. She said to herself, "His mother must be taking him out of the ghetto before the Nazis come to take him away."

Just then, Maria came up to Brachah and asked, "Why aren't you praying, Brachah?"

Brachah answered, "Before I go to sleep I recite *Shema Yisrael*."

Maria said, "You must pray before the picture." Brachah couldn't understand the connection between the *Shema* her mother had taught her and this picture, but in order to satisfy Maria, she stood beside the girls facing the corner. Maria said, "Kneel on one knee." Brachah tried, but she couldn't do it. She had never stood on one knee and one foot. Maria helped Brachah to kneel, and then she too knelt down and began to pray. The girls repeated each verse after Maria.

Brachah didn't know the prayers that Maria was saying. She knew what her mother had taught her by heart, and that was easier for her. Brachah knelt on one knee, faced the picture, and whispered, "*Shema Yisrael*," "Hear O Israel the Lord our God, the Lord is One." She didn't look at the picture because Imma had taught her to close her eyes while reciting the *Shema*, and you can't look at a picture with your eyes closed.

This incident was repeated the next morning. Brachah knelt on one knee before the picture and recited the *berachoth* that her mother had taught her to say every morning, her eyes closed. All the girls repeated what Maria said, but Brachah recited what she remembered of her mother's prayers.

Every day, Maria told the girls the name of the day. On Shabbath, she told them that it was Saturday. When Maria called the girls in for their writing lesson, Brachah was amazed. She knew that Shabbath was not like all other days. Certain things are not permitted on Shabbath, and writing is among those things. It is even forbidden to hold a pencil in one's hand. She wanted to ask Maria about this, but she was embarrassed. When Maria handed Brachah her copybook and pencil, Brachah took them weakly. Maria wrote on the blackboard in white chalk, "Tomorrow is a holiday," and the girls began to copy these words.

Brachah didn't know what to do. Imma had told her that it was forbidden to write on Shabbath, but Maria, who also knew what was forbidden and what was permitted, had told her to write. Brachah wrote "Tomorrow is a holiday" with shaking hands. That day, all the letters that Brachah wrote came out crooked. After the lesson, Maria collected Brachah's copybook but couldn't read it. The letters were so crooked they were illegible. Brachah had written much better yesterday. What had happened to her today?

At dinner, while Brachah was still preoccupied with the writing, another strange thing occurred to her. Why had Maria written, "Tomorrow is a holiday"? Was tomorrow really a holiday? Tomorrow was Sunday. Today, Shabbath, was a holiday, not tomorrow. This business with Maria was very puzzling. Brachah knew that Sarah and Rivkah were older than she and knew more than she did. In the yard, she therefore approached Rivkah and asked her about the writing. Rivkah looked at Brachah and laughed.

"What are you laughing at?" Brachah asked.

Rivkah answered, "Maria is a Christian, not a Jew. All of them here are Christian." Brachah looked into Rivkah's eyes but couldn't understand what Rivkah was saying. What were ghetto children doing with Christians?

Brachah's puzzle was not solved. On the contrary, it grew more confusing. When Rivkah saw that Brachah didn't understand her, she added, "You are still young. When you grow up a little, you'll understand everything." Brachah left Rivkah, full of sorrow that she would have to wait until she grew up before she could understand. Who knew how long that would take!

The second and third Shabbath, Brachah also wrote in a much poorer handwriting than she had during the rest of the week. Maria thought about this and discussed it with the other nuns. Brachah perplexed them. One of the nuns said, "Perhaps the Jews in the ghetto set some magic spell on her so that she would be unable to write on their Shabbath. The Jews always practice magic on the Christians."

The nuns were very much afraid when they heard their friend's opinion. If the Jews could control someone in the convent with their magic, who knew what other things they might do? But the nuns believed in Jesus and comforted themselves that he would protect them from Jewish magic.

◆§ 10 ᚱ᛬ *Yudel's Mission*

Those who escaped from the ghetto of Nachrovah were the first to reach Yanovsky forest, but not the last. A few dozen Jews from the neighboring Temyonovah ghetto also escaped to the forest. The head of their group was Peretz the redhead. In peacetime he had been a tin worker and had prayed at the workers' synagogue, "Yad Charutzim." On Shabbath afternoons Peretz used to sit in the synagogue and listen to Reb Naftali the Dayan tell inspiring tales from the Midrash and Ein Ya'akov. When the stories were very sad, tears would well up in Peretz's eyes, as he shared the troubles of the Jewish people. When the stories were happy, he would stroke his red beard with visible enjoyment and rejoice with Israel.

Peretz was put into the ghetto with all the other Jews of Temyonovah, but not for long. On the very first day, he began plotting his escape. He dreamed of being one of those who arose to save the Jews in times of distress. He had always been jealous of these heroes when he heard about them from Reb Naftali the Dayan. He often thought to himself that if he had lived in the days of Bar Kochba, he would have joined his army. It was too bad there was no such person nowadays. On one hand, he held it against Bar Kochba for disappointing the great Rabbi Akiva by making Jewish boys cut off their thumbs to test their bravery, but he was also proud that such a person was Jewish. He admired his courage and bravery.

In the ghetto, Peretz felt that his hour had arrived. True, he was not as strong as Samson, nor was he a soldier like Bar Kochba, but every person is capable of doing something. What exactly he would do to save Israel he didn't yet know, but he did know that it would be easier to take action outside the ghetto than inside it. No prisoner can free others from jail. In order to free others, he would first have to free himself.

Peretz did in Temyonovah what Shimon had done in Nachrovah. He, too, with a few dozen other Jews, escaped from the ghetto, but his method of escape was different. He spent a few weeks digging a hole in the ground to make a tunnel from his room in the ghetto near the barbed-wire fence, to a deserted lot on the other side of the fence. Two other Jews helped him, but he did most of the work. The others got very tired after digging just a bit. Peretz was actually no stronger than they were, but sheer will power overcame any lack in his physical strength. When the tunnel was ready, Peretz revealed his secret to a few dozen members of his synagogue. One dark, cloudy night, when a storm had chased the Gentiles off the streets and pouring rain washed away all footprints, Peretz and his men left the ghetto for the street, and from there they continued to the forest.

After a short time, Shimon from Nachrovah and Peretz from Temyonovah became fast friends. They were happy to find each other, and they could help each other share the responsibility for the lives of the few dozen Jews, including several women and quite a few children. Peretz's own wife and twenty-year-old son had also come with him. Shimon and Peretz organized the camp in the forest. Since it was summer, the rainy season, and the women and children had to be protected from the rain, they cut branches from trees and built huts. The huts were not real houses; heavy rain could penetrate them, but at least they afforded protection against light rain. It felt good to have a roof of branches thick enough to hide the stars over their heads. The huts also afforded privacy. No man, and certainly no woman, wants to live in the street. A person needs four walls of his own.

Shimon and Peretz also accepted the responsibility for supplying the people in the forest with food. This was a job no one else could have done. They were familiar with the neighboring villages and would leave the forest every night, heading for a different village each time. They would knock on one of the village doors, and a farmer or his wife would open the door and stare open-mouthed. Opposite them stood two bearded "Jids," each one holding a rifle. The farmers wouldn't ask any questions — they would be too astonished to talk. Shimon would say his piece, and shortly after, Shimon and Peretz would leave, carrying with them sacks of food — bread, potatoes, and vegetables. Sometimes they paid more and sometimes less. When their money ran out, they didn't pay at all. Some of the farmers recognized Shimon and knew that this "Jid" could turn them into a pile of bones, even without a rifle, so they fulfilled his request for food quickly.

Shimon and Peretz knew that all these Poles were Jew-haters who could not be trusted not to betray them to the authorities. Therefore, they warned the Poles that anyone who told tales would meet a bitter end. Before the Germans could reach the Jews in the forest, the Jews would find out who had betrayed them and would punish that informer. The Poles knew that these were not mere threats, and they were careful. So far no one had said anything to the Germans; they didn't even talk about it among themselves. Each one kept his secret in order to protect his own life.

The partisans did not forget that their main purpose in escaping to the forest was not just to save their own skins, but to take revenge on the Nazis. Since they could not defeat them in face-to-face combat, they would do so by cunning and trickery. This was part of war. Among the weapons Shimon and Peretz had managed to smuggle out with them was a small amount of explosives—not a lot, but better than none at all. Now they had to make good use of it. The largest number of Nazis possible must be killed with this precious bit of explosives. Shimon and Peretz racked their brains until they hit upon an idea.

Nachrovah was the seat of the local Nazi headquarters. The headquarters building had formerly been the home of Reb Shloimeleh, the head of the Jewish community. When the Germans invaded Nachrovah, they seized the house. Reb Shloimeleh, displaced and dispossessed from his home, wandered from one place to another, until he and all the other Jews finally ended up in the ghetto. Now his house was marked as the partisans' target. It was the seat of all the plans hatched against the ghetto dwellers and must be blown up, together with the Nazi officers who occupied it daily. This building was the source of the death decree issued against thousands of guiltless Jews. The partisans knew that one act alone would not suffice to uproot all of the evil they were witnessing. Persons even more wicked might replace those who were killed, but every small victory over evil weakens its power to some extent, and revenge in such cases is very sweet.

Shimon called a meeting and announced the decision which had been reached. He asked for a volunteer to carry out the mission. It was clear that only someone from Nachrovah was eligible, someone who knew the town and all its pathways. Many Jews from Nachrovah volunteered, including Yudel Glick. Shimon chose Yudel. He could be counted on not to let them down. If necessary, he would even sacrifice his life.

The date was set for the following evening. At night, the Nazis left their headquarters one by one until only a few officers remained on duty. Therefore the act would have to be carried out at the beginning of the night.

At that time the British were bombing the German airfields, one of which was close to Nachrovah. To prevent the enemy from locating the airfield, it was necessary to enforce a blackout for several kilometers around it. Thanks to this blackout, Yudel would be able to approach Reb Shloimeleh's house unnoticed and to leave a small pitcher of explosives against the back wall. Yudel didn't understand the mechanism inside the pitcher—Shimon and Peretz had built the bomb. All Yudel knew was that he had to lean the pitcher against the northern wall of the house at 9:00 PM;

half an hour later, the explosives would work automatically. During that half hour he had to get back to the forest, at the entrance of which he would hear the explosion.

That night, Yudel couldn't fall asleep — but not because he was afraid of his mission the following evening. After all, no one had asked him to volunteer. No, it was the natural reaction of one who was about to carry out an important mission and couldn't take his mind off the act. While Yudel, his eyes closed, was picturing himself carrying out his task, he suddenly saw a circle of young girls. He narrowed his eyes to watch the circle and saw that they were dancing a dance the likes of which he had never seen before. They all moved simultaneously, as if they were one person, not many. He looked at their faces and saw that they all looked alike. This seemed a wondrous thing to him. Twins could be identical, but not strangers. The girls were singing, "Nevertheless we have not forgotten Thy Name." They repeated this verse over and over. Yudel racked his brain trying to remember the words preceding this verse. Finally he remembered: "We were as sheep brought to slaughter — to kill and wipe out, for blows and for shame." The last words echoed in his mind. For shame. For shame. For shame.

After he had thought of the verse he looked at the girls' faces again, and his heart stopped. The face of one of the girls now looked like that of Esther. His Esther. He saw that Esther was much taller than the other girls. She led them in the circle, and they all followed her.

When Esther passed by, she suddenly turned towards him, looked at him, and stopped walking. They stood opposite each other. She looked at him and he at her. After a silence, Esther smiled and asked him, "Where is Brachah?" Yudel didn't know what to answer. Esther's face saddened, and she said, "Brachah must be saved." Yudel knew it was his fault—he had not gone to get Brachah back from Marussa—and he lowered his eyes.

When he looked again, he no longer saw Esther. He saw Brachah sitting on the dome of a church, her tiny hand holding on to the cross in order not to fall off. Yudel stretched out his arms so that he could catch her when she let go of the cross. At that minute he felt someone hit his arm and he woke up. He was terribly upset by his dream. For a long time he couldn't compose himself.

Finally, he made a decision. He would find Brachah, come what may. She was in Nachrovah with Marussa, not far from where he was. He must find a way to locate Marussa. He knew where her father's house was. He must go there. Of course, he realized that this was dangerous. If he were seen in a Polish house, the Poles would inform on him to the Nazis. But he must not abandon Brachah. Perhaps, after his action the next day, the Poles in Nachrovah would realize that the Jews of the forest knew how to take revenge, and it would be less of a risk to be seen in a Polish house. In the future, perhaps they would not dare to inform on the Jews.

When dawn broke, Yudel got up. He washed his hands and recited the *berachoth* over the Torah. Then he put on his *tallith* and *tefillin* and prayed with great devotion. He tried to take his mind off his dream, but he was unsuccessful. It had set his soul afire. All that day Yudel was distracted and could find no peace of mind.

An hour before dark, he took the pitcher with the explosives and started out for the city. He had to be at the edge of the forest exactly at nightfall in order to reach the headquarters at the appointed time. Shimon accompanied Yudel part of the way and showed him exactly what to do. When they parted, Shimon wished Yudel success. Yudel thanked him weakly. He had not yet recovered from his dream of the night before.

In order not to arouse suspicion, Yudel wore farmer's clothes. His pitcher was covered with a lid and might have contained milk or fruit. His beard was concealed by a scarf, as he would not allow it to be cut off. After sunset, he left the forest and followed a dirt trail. By the time he reached the town, it was pitch black. It was the end of the month, and there was no moon and no stars, only a cloudy sky.

Yudel arrived at the headquarters exactly at nine o'clock. He walked behind the house on the northern side. There was no entrance there, and no one ever passed that way. He put the pitcher down quickly, leaning it against the wall, and immediately left the site. Now he had only to return to the forest, east of the town.

As Yudel passed Catholichka Street, he heard a familiar voice call, "Abba!" Yudel trembled. He stood still and looked around to see where it was coming from. To his left he saw the convent, a cross rising from its dome. Could Brachah possibly be in that building? No, it must be his imagination. All day he had been so preoccupied with his dream that now he imagined he heard Brachah's voice. But whether the voice was real or imagined, his heart was filled with boundless suffering.

As Yudel stood there, a man came up to him and asked whom he was looking for. Yudel mumbled some kind of an answer which did not satisfy the questioner. He grabbed Yudel's arm and said, "Come with me." As they were walking, the Pole examined Yudel carefully. "You are not one of us," he said.

Yudel didn't answer. He was so absorbed in his own thoughts that he didn't even hear what the Pole had said. As they came closer to headquarters, Yudel suddenly remembered that the building was about to be blown up. He tried to resist and to run away from the Pole. He was not afraid for his own life, but he had to take care of Brachah and Chaim. But the Pole was stronger than Yudel and forced him into the building. A German officer asked him his name and occupation, but before Yudel had a chance to answer, the entire house was lifted up into the air and then fell back down. In its place, there was now a pile of stones, with all the contents of the house buried underneath.

Echoes of the explosion reached the forest. The partisans rejoiced at Yudel's success. Now they knew that he had carried out his mission faithfully. They waited impatiently for his return so that he could tell them all about his feat. But hour after hour passed and Yudel didn't come. They began to worry.

The next day, several Poles reported that they had left the building shortly before the explosion occurred, and as they were leaving they had seen a Jew forcibly brought into the building. When the partisans heard this from one of the village farmers, they knew that Yudel would never return to the forest.

Peretz was envious. He said, "Yudel died just like the mighty Samson. Samson prayed, 'Let me die with the Philistines,' and Yudel prayed, 'Let me die with the Nazis.' What a beautiful death. What a beautiful death," Peretz repeated over and over.

When Brachah cried out "Abba," Sarah jumped out of bed and went over to her. She took Brachah's hand in her own and said, "You must have been dreaming, Brachah."

"No," Brachah answered, "I wasn't dreaming."

"Then why did you cry 'Abba'?"

"I saw my father passing by the house," Brachah answered.

"How could you see your father passing by the house while you were lying in bed? Even if you were standing by the window, you couldn't have seen him pass by. It's dark outside."

"I don't know how I saw him, but I saw him."

"You were dreaming, Brachah, and you thought it really happened."

Brachah didn't answer. She closed her eyes and fell asleep, and Sarah went back to bed.

At prayers the next morning Brachah refused to bow down before the icon in the corner of the room, even when Maria ordered her to do so. Maria couldn't understand what had happened. Every day Brachah behaved just like all the other girls — why was today different? Maria asked Brachah, but Brachah didn't answer. Instead, she looked at Sarah and kept her silence. Maria understood that there was some secret between Sarah and Brachah. She decided to investigate — not now in front of all the girls, but later. After breakfast when the girls had gone out to play in the yard, Maria summoned Sarah to her room and began to question her about Brachah. Sarah told Maria about Brachah's dream while Maria listened, bewildered. Earlier that morning she had heard about the Jew who had been carried off to the Gestapo headquarters just a few minutes before it was blown up. Everyone realized that this was the man who was responsible for the deed. He had died a hero's death. Even though he knew what was about to happen he had not attempted to save his own life by telling the Germans. According to Sarah, Brachah had cried "Abba" shortly after the girls had gone to bed. Bedtime was before 9:00 PM. Had that Jew really passed by the convent? If so, was he Brachah's father? Even if he were Brachah's father, how could she have seen him while she was lying in bed?

Maria's head was filled with questions to which she could find no answers. It was all very mystifying. She told the story to the other nuns, and one of them said, "The Jews have practiced their witchcraft on Brachah. Her soul must be saved. She must be treated very severely. Her stubborn refusal to bow down and pray is not her own; it represents the will of all the Jews in the ghetto. Even now in the ghetto, the Jews continue to deny Jesus, and they suffer for their heresy. There is no hope for them. God has cursed them. But some few can be saved. Brachah can be saved. However, we must treat her very severely." She repeated her opinion over and over until Maria was convinced of its truth.

From that day on, Maria stopped smiling at Brachah. Her tone of voice turned Brachah's bones to ice. During writing class, Maria continuously found fault with Brachah's work and rebuked her for not doing as well as her classmates. The five girls who had been Brachah's friends saw that Maria was angry at Brachah, and they too withdrew from her. They feared that Maria would be angry with them if they remained friends with Brachah. Maria did everything for them. They needed her and wished to stay in her favor.

Brachah wept alone. She felt that her heart would break. She had no one to talk to. The children laughed and played with one another, but shunned her. Brachah withdrew into herself. She pressed her lips together, determined to remain silent. She did not answer Maria's questions. She did not bow before the icon. At prayer time, she recited the *Shema*, morning and evening, her eyes closed and her head upright. Her father's image never left her. She knew that he would not want her to bow down before the picture of the mother and child. He had never told her so explicitly, but he himself had never done so, and she would not either. When her father's image was before her eyes, he was always smiling, not like Maria and all her friends. Whenever Brachah's heart grew cold and lonely, she would close her eyes and see her father smiling at her, and she would feel warm and happy.

Brachah grew pale; from day to day she seemed to shrivel. She ate almost nothing and withdrew deep into herself. Who knows what might have happened to Brachah had Marussa not come. Marussa saved her body, but not her soul.

Since Marussa had left the ghetto and returned home to her parents, she hardly ventured outside. She couldn't bear the scorn that she had brought upon herself. Is there any greater shame for a Christian woman than to marry a Jew? Even now, when Mr. Shmendrikovitz had disappeared, Marussa's shame had not lessened. Marussa was aware of what people were saying about her, and she avoided them. She even began to doubt herself and to wonder if it really had been wise for her to marry Yank. Even so, she was furious at her countrymen for siding with the Germans — Poland's eternal enemies.

And she could not understand why the convents should welcome Jewish children from the ghetto if they mocked her for marrying a man who had converted to Christianity. Weren't the Poles contradicting themselves? Marussa sat at home and spun her thoughts into a thread which grew longer and longer.

Then suddenly, Marussa's status changed overnight. When the Poles heard of the explosion at the Gestapo headquarters they could not help but be impressed and full of admiration for the heroic act. With one blow, a Jew had wiped out dozens of German officers and workers and had paralyzed the work of the headquarters for a long time to come. All the documents which the Germans had worked so hard and so long to amass were lost, and the confusion and loss of information which this caused would cost the Germans many precious months of work.

The Poles began to respect the Jews. They did not often praise them, but their silence reflected their envy. Soon after, Marussa began to venture outside her house. When her former friends met her now, they lowered their eyes. She had gained their respect, and they no longer mocked her. Although she was a Christian, just as they were, they looked upon her as a Jewish heroine. It was as though she herself had carried out the heroic act in the headquarters, or as though the Jew who did so were her brother.

It was then that Marussa came to the convent to visit Brachah. She had been in a good mood and had thought of her. When Marussa heard of Brachah's dream, her heart skipped a beat. And when she heard of Brachah's sad plight since that day, her heart fell within her. She asked to see Brachah, and Maria went to the courtyard to summon the girl. As she was about to enter the room, Brachah caught sight of Marussa. For a moment, she was confused and stood rooted to the spot. Then she let out a great cry and ran to Marussa. Marussa caressed the excited girl and hugged her with all her might. She sat Brachah on her lap and stroked her head until she calmed down and stopped crying.

Marussa signaled Maria to leave the room, and when they were alone, she asked Brachah many questions but received few answers. Finally Marussa said that Maria was a good woman who wished to help Brachah, and that Brachah should obey and try to love her. She, Marussa, would come now and then to visit; meanwhile Brachah should behave like all the other girls. They had all come from the ghetto and were no different from her. Marussa might have continued talking to Brachah for a long time had not Maria interrupted them to announce that it was time for the writing lesson. Marussa rose, kissed Brachah goodbye, and promised to come again soon.

From that day on, Brachah obeyed Maria and behaved just like the other girls. She even knelt on her knee before the picture of the mother and child.

Although no one discussed what had happened to Yudel in front of Chaim, Chaim understood. He read in their eyes what they would not say aloud. At first, he wanted to ask why his father hadn't come back to the forest, but in the end, he didn't. He was afraid to hear the answer which he already knew. Shimon befriended Chaim and took him under his wing, and Chaim gave his silent assent. In their free time, Shimon would sit with Chaim and talk to him so that he would not be so lonely.

Once, Chaim asked Shimon about his sister, Brachah. Since the day they had left their house in the ghetto for that fateful line-up behind the burnt synagogue, he had not seen Brachah. He had no idea where she was. As long as his father was with him, he had not asked about her because he was sure his father knew where Brachah was and was taking care of her. But now that his father was no longer with him, Brachah began to dominate his thoughts, so he asked Shimon about her.

Chaim assumed that Brachah had remained in the ghetto, and when the war was over, they would be reunited. He was amazed to hear that Brachah had left the ghetto with a Christian woman and was now in Nachrovah. He couldn't understand how Brachah could be in the town when he and the other Jews in the forest were not allowed there.

At first he was jealous, but later, he began to worry about her. Wasn't it dangerous for a Jewish girl to remain in Nachrovah outside the ghetto? He began to see Brachah in his dreams. Each time he saw her he rejoiced, although he knew that these were merely dreams. He began to realize that now, since his father and mother were gone, no one but he would worry about her. He didn't yet know how he could help her, but he did know that he must not forget her, and so he rejoiced to see her. These dreams would prevent him from forgetting her.

Chaim had several different dreams about Brachah. Sometimes he would picture her sitting at a table and eating a rich meal—white bread with butter and other foods whose names he had forgotten. He hadn't eaten such foods for a long time, and he was happy to see his sister eating them.

Another time he saw her standing at the window of a nice house, her eyes searching for someone. Her face was sad and her eyes red from crying. He shouted to her with all his strength to let her know that he saw her, but she neither saw nor heard him.

Chaim did not always remember his dreams the next day, but he always remembered that he had seen Brachah, and this was sufficient cause for him to rejoice. Chaim also told himself that if he remembered her, she must remember him, and so he was not alone in the world. Someone was thinking of him. Of course, Shimon thought of him and took care of him, but Shimon was not his relative. It was good to have a sister who thought of him.

Chaim would lie for hours, his eyes closed, trying to picture Brachah. At first he would not succeed. Only after his intense efforts had worn him out, and his skinny body was covered with sweat, would Brachah appear to him in a dream. People wondered at his strange habits, as most children do not usually lie idle for hours at a time.

When he was on his feet, Chaim was quick and daring. Shimon had taught him to be brave. He assigned him to guard duty far away from the camp towards the city. Chaim stood at his post fearlessly, listening for suspicious sounds. This guard duty was an innovation, begun after Yudel's exploit, as the partisans were afraid that the Germans would attempt to attack them. Shimon did not assign Chaim to guard duty from any lack of able-bodied men, but in order to train him not to be a coward. Guard duty gave Chaim pride and self-confidence. It also strengthened his feeling that, as a strong, mature person, he would be able to help his sister.

Peretz also befriended the orphaned Chaim for the sake of his father. To Peretz, Yudel was like one of the great heroes he had heard of in Reb Naftali the Dayan's stories. Shimon took charge of Chaim's physical needs, and Peretz took charge of his education. Although Peretz had little formal education and there were no Torah books in the forest, he taught Chaim all that he remembered of the wonderful tales of Reb Naftali the Dayan. He told him of Rabbi Akiva ben Yosef and his followers and of Bar Kochba and his army. He told him tales of Eretz Yisrael and of Yerushalayim, the Holy City; of the *Beith haMikdash*, the

Holy Temple that was twice destroyed; and of the *Kothel baMaʻaravi*, the Western Wall, which remains standing to this day.

Chaim absorbed all of Peretz's stories. His favorites were the stories about the Baʻal Shem Tov. Peretz described the palaces which the Baʻal Shem Tov and his followers found in the forest one Friday just before sundown, when snow buried the whole world and the horses were unable to draw the carriages and their passengers to their destination before Shabbath. While listening to this story, Chaim would imagine that he and all the Jews of Yanovsky forest were the holy Baʻal Shem Tov's disciples. His eyes closed, he would see himself in the palace. Chaim was especially fond of Peretz because of these tales, which both comforted and inspired him. Peretz also enjoyed his role as storyteller. Although the stories were not new to him, they took on new life as he told them. He had always listened to others speak and had never realized that he himself was gifted. Now, as he became aware of his talents as a storyteller, each tale, as he told it, appeared in a new light to him.

One day Shimon posted Chaim on guard duty about two kilometers from the camp. He was told to listen for suspicious sounds from the direction of Nachrovah. Chaim had done this many times before. When on duty, he never allowed himself to sink into reveries about Brachah or muse over Peretz's tales, but he would concentrate on listening.

Why that day was different was a mystery to Chaim. He had always been able to stand for hours, but today it was hard for him. He sat down and leaned against a tree trunk. It was a quiet noon. The thick forest protected Chaim from the sun's rays. Chaim, like all the children in Yanovsky forest, was weak. He saw white bread and butter only in his dreams, and even then it was Brachah, not he, who was enjoying them. What he ate—black bread and potatoes cooked in their skins—was not enough to sustain his small body. All he drank was water, which was sometimes not fit for drinking. Apparently he was too weak today to stand up. Today, he didn't even have the strength to sit for long, so he stretched out on the ground. Lying down, one could press his ear to the earth and hear even better than sitting or standing. The earth is the ally of the oppressed. It exposes the footsteps of those who pursue them.

Chaim lay on the ground contentedly. He had not slept on a pillow for a long time. To him there was nothing sweeter than to lie on the ground. He recalled how Ya'akov Avinu, may he rest in peace, had slept on a pillow of stones when fleeing from Esau. If Ya'akov could sleep on stones without complaining, then Chaim would surely not complain, because the ground is much softer than stones.

After a while, Brachah appeared before his eyes. She was standing in the yard of a nice building and looking about her. Chaim came close to her, wanting to surprise her, but when he got very close he was stopped by a wall. Chaim walked the length of the wall, searching for the opening, but he couldn't find it. He was amazed. In front of him was a high wall; nevertheless he could see Brachah. But how could mortal eyes penetrate a wall? Chaim tried to catch Brachah's eye. If he succeeded, she would show him how to reach her.

For a long time he stared at her unceasingly so that she would turn around and look at him. Once he had heard from adults that staring at someone causes him to look back in response. He was sure that she would see him, and he was right. Brachah turned around and looked straight into his eyes. At that moment, Chaim was about to ask Brachah how he could reach her, but her look frightened him. She gave him such a cold stare that he froze.

How could Brachah not recognize him? Even if she didn't recognize his face, she must recognize her own. Weren't they as identical as two drops of water? She must know who he was, but in her anger, she was refusing to smile at him. He had no idea why she should be so angry. After all the time that he had devoted to her, she had spurned him. Chaim gestured to Brachah to come towards him but she didn't move. She stood where she was as if she didn't see him. Chaim's heart was broken. Brachah had rejected him. He had tried to rescue her and she had rejected him! What a fool! How ungrateful! He wasn't really angry at her, for she seemed so very young. Perhaps she didn't understand. Nonetheless, he was extremely hurt.

Suddenly, Chaim heard a loud noise. He turned his head in all directions to identify its source. It seemed to be coming from all sides at once. Chaim turned his attention back to Brachah, but she had disappeared. To his astonishment, the house and the yard had also disappeared. His attention was drawn back to the noise, which grew increasingly louder. He began to be afraid. Now he was happy that Brachah was no longer there to hear the noise. She would have been frightened. Chaim suddenly remembered that Shimon had stationed him there to notify him of any suspicious sounds. He wanted to run back to the camp, but someone was holding his hand. He tried to withdraw it but was too weak.

When Chaim finally opened his eyes, he saw many people around him. Frightened, he jumped up. The people looked at him with curiosity and asked him his name and the location of the Jews' camp in the forest. Chaim didn't answer their questions, but they understood why and didn't interrogate him any further. They tried to reassure him by saying that they were Poles, not Germans. Chaim himself had realized this, as he knew Polish and understood their conversation, but this was small comfort to him, for he knew that the Poles also hated the Jews. Chaim felt terrible. What would he tell Shimon? He had not carried out his orders. He had failed to do his duty and was ashamed of himself.

The men took Chaim with them and continued on their journey eastward into the forest.

Yudel's bravery had lowered the self-esteem of Stashek and his friends. Cowardly Jews had performed a heroic deed, while they, the Polish patriots, had not yet accomplished anything worthwhile. All they had done so far was talk endlessly about the need to take action against the Germans. They also envied the Jews their new popularity and respect. They hated the Jews and couldn't bear to hear other Christians praise them. At last, when they could find no other alternative, they decided to follow in the Jews' footsteps and take to the forest to fight the Germans from there.

During that period, Stashek was much more at ease among his friends. In their efforts to salvage their own honor, they stopped deriding the Jews. Now that Stashek no longer had to bear the jeering looks of his friends, he could relax.

They set the date for their venture to the forest for a week from Sunday. Why Sunday? On Sunday, the Christian day of rest, people would take long walks, in and out of town. The group planned to simply walk out of town towards the forest. Once they entered the forest, they would be at war with the Germans. It was much easier to reach the forest in the daytime, during a leisurely walk, than to flee there at night.

That week, they stocked up on everything that a partisan might need. They prepared pistols, explosives, and food for a day or two. They also had a few rifles, but you can't carry a rifle when you're out for a walk. Antek would bring the rifles at night, in a wagon covered with straw. He would drive up to the edge of the forest, and they would pick them up there.

They were in high spirits all week. Now they would not need to be embarrassed by the heroic deed of that cursed Jew. They would show everyone in Nachrovah that the Poles are braver than the Jews. The Jew's accomplishment was an exception to the rule, but they would perform many such deeds. It may be said in their praise that all week they waited impatiently for Sunday to come. They became more and more envious of the Jews and impatient to redeem themselves from the disgrace of inaction.

On Sunday morning they went to church. They listened to the priest's sermon, enjoining them to cooperate with the authorities. His words disturbed them a bit but were quickly forgotten. They prayed hastily. Their knees touched the church floor, but their hearts were already in the forest.

After leaving the church, they all gathered at a friend's house and drank a substantial toast to their success. Their jubilance swelled, both because of the strong drink and because of their imminent departure to Yanovsky forest.

As they drank they discussed their venture. One of the group wondered if they should ally themselves with the Jews in the forest or keep their distance from them. A friend answered that they must keep away from the Jews. If they were to cooperate, no one would know afterwards who had carried out the heroic acts they planned to perform.

In the afternoon they split into several innocent looking groups. Each group walked around town, then out of town, and finally into Yanovsky forest. They remained at the edge of the forest, however, not penetrating deep inside, for they didn't want to meet with the Jews. Towards evening Antek brought the things they had not carried with them on their walk, and the Polish partisans set up camp.

Now the Poles in the forest did just what the Jews had done several months before. They put up huts. It was much easier for the Poles than it had been for the Jews. The Jewish camp included women and children, while the Polish camp was comprised of men only. There was another difference. The men in the Jewish camp were not all young—even Shimon and Peretz were not so young anymore—while in the Polish camp they were all young.

Several days passed and the Poles began to plan their action against the Germans. So far they had not accomplished anything. Whatever action they had taken was in the villages. The food they brought with them was gone in two days' time, and they began to steal into the villages at night for supplies. In this they were more successful than the Jews. They were blood brothers to the Polish farmers and were highly regarded by them, so that unlike the Jews, they did not have to resort to threats in order to obtain a little food.

But the Poles' complacency was short-lived. The Germans dispatched new officers to Nachrovah to replace those killed by Yudel. They found another house in place of the one that had been destroyed, and they once again began to take action against Jews and against Poles who collaborated with Jews.

The Germans had heard rumors about partisans in the forest, and they feared that actions such as the explosion at the German headquarters would be repeated. As their fear grew, they decided to surround the forest and capture all those hiding within. If they succeeded, there would no longer be any threat of danger, and they would be able to continue exterminating the Jews undisturbed.

One morning the Poles heard suspicious sounds coming from the edge of the forest. Listening carefully, they realized that these were German voices, not Polish ones. They looked at one another and estimated the risk. Quickly, they took down their huts, packed their belongings, and began to move deeper into the forest.

Truth to tell, they panicked unnecessarily. The danger was not imminent, for the Germans were afraid to enter the forest. They wanted the partisans to come out to them. Outside the forest, they had the advantage. They possessed tanks and planes, whereas the Jews and Poles only had rifles and pistols. Inside the forest, the Germans lost their advantage. They therefore tried to scare the partisans out of the forest by raising a great ruckus nearby. Had the Poles not run away, the Germans would probably not have attacked them. But the Poles, not realizing that the Germans too were cowards, fled deeper and deeper into the forest.

As they cut further into the forest, they found Chaim asleep on the ground, his hands and legs stretched out and his face turned towards the town. They recognized him as a

Jewish child, one of the group of partisans. This meant that they must be close to the Jewish camp. Stashek looked at Chaim and wondered silently, "That face is familiar. Where have I seen it before?" He couldn't remember. "Perhaps with my sister Marussa? No, Marussa had a girl with her, not a boy." Stashek took hold of Chaim's hand and gazed at him for a long time, trying to remember where he had seen him before, until finally he gave up. When Chaim woke up he took his hand away from Stashek, frightened and upset.

The Poles made no attempt to talk to Chaim as they walked. They knew he would not answer their questions, because he didn't trust them. That's the way the Jews always were. They lived on Polish soil but distrusted their Polish overlords. It was not for nothing that the Jews were disliked. On the way, Stashek kept glancing at Chaim, trying unsuccessfully to remember where he had seen him. Still racking his brain, he arrived with the others at the Jewish camp.

In the camp, no one heard them coming. The Poles had walked in silence, each one contemplating the imminent confrontation with the Jews. When the Jews first saw their guests, they recognized them and did not panic. They realized that these were not German agents. Shimon, the commander of the camp, took a few steps towards them. He was the first to greet them. The Poles returned his greeting, smiling like old friends who were meeting after a long separation.

Shimon waited for the Poles to speak first. They were the guests so it was up to them to state the purpose of their visit. The Poles, about thirty of them, spread out in a wide formation. Yashek, who was their commander, stepped forward and offered his hand to Shimon. Shimon took Yashek's hand and shook it heartily. Yashek stated that they had come to the forest to fight the Germans. Since the Jews were also at war with the Germans, the Germans were their common enemy, and it would be advantageous to combine their strength to fight them. Shimon nodded his head in agreement and with a generous gesture invited the guests to enter the camp.

Shimon's eyes searched the group of Poles, looking for Chaim. Where was he? How was it that he had not seen them coming? How had the Poles not seen Chaim? All this time Chaim had stood behind the line of Poles. He was greatly afraid and even more embarrassed. When Shimon finally saw Chaim hiding behind the Poles, he heaved a sigh of relief. He called Chaim to him and smiled at him benevolently. Chaim was very pale and his whole body quaked, but when he saw Shimon's smile, he felt better. Relieved, he began to weep for joy.

◆§ 14 ◈ *Cain and Abel*

Gradually, the two camps developed friendly relations. Suspicions faded and were replaced by mutual trust. People tend to believe what is most convenient for them, and at that time it was most convenient for both the Poles and the Jews to live together as friends, not as enemies.

It was the end of summer. Winter was just around the corner for Nachrovah, Temyonovah, and for Yanovsky forest between them. In the winter the temperature would fall far below zero and everything would freeze over. Anyone wanting to survive would have to provide himself with some means of defense against the cold. In Nachrovah and Temyonovah, people fought the cold by sealing themselves in rooms heated by wood furnaces; in the forest they would flee underground.

In the partisans' camp they dug caves. Even though they lived in one camp, there would be separate caves for Jews and for Poles. There was no formal decision about this, but it was taken for granted. People are most comfortable among their own kind. Poles like to talk about certain topics in one language while Jews talk about other topics in another language. Peretz's stories, for instance, would not be appreciated by the Poles. Since the Jews and Poles were not going to live together, each group dug its own cave.

The fact that they were not digging together did not disturb the friendship between the two groups of partisans. It was taken for granted and did not arouse anger or hatred. The Poles' cave was ready first. Thirty pairs of young Polish hands could work much faster than those of the Jewish partisans. In the Jewish group, the women and children did not participate in the digging, and many of the men were not so young. When the Poles had finished their own cave, they helped the Jews. Everyone was in high spirits, and mutual help was the order of the day.

The winter would bring both cold to the world and warmth to the caves. The snow covering the ground above the caves would protect and insulate them against the cold. The digging took several days, during which time they did nothing else. When they were finished, they remembered that they hadn't come to Yanovsky forest to dig caves, but to fight the Germans, and they began to think.

The Poles were especially anxious to act quickly as they had already been in the forest for a few weeks and had not yet accomplished anything. They knew that their towns-people were waiting to hear of their exploits. The Poles are a proud people whose reputation is very dear to them. They were eager for their countrymen to hear of their bravery. The Jews were also eager to take action against the Germans. They had no need to justify their escape to the forest, but they knew that in weakening and defeating the Germans they would be saving their own lives.

The group commanders sat and debated what course of

action to take. After hearing various proposals, they decided in favor of what seemed to be the best one: Not far from the forest ran the railroad tracks which were used by various trains, including those which transported German soldiers eastward to the Russian front. They would find out exactly when the transport would pass by and blow it up.

This idea was not original; such exploits had already been reported in the papers. Although the newspapers were censored and incidents such as these were played down by the Germans, people read between the lines and were quite impressed. This would be an easy mission for the partisans of Yanovsky forest as the railroad ran the length of the forest less than two kilometers away. It would be simple to blow up a train passing by in the middle of the night. Two partisans had only to reach the tracks under cover of darkness, place explosives on the tracks, and return to the forest before the explosion.

Vachek and Paltiel were chosen to carry out the deed. Vachek had studied engineering and would set the time for the explosion. Paltiel would help him and would also carry the explosives to the tracks. Yashek ascertained the train schedule from one of the station workers. The train would pass through the forest at two o'clock in the morning, a convenient hour for terrorist action. At one-thirty Paltiel would bring the explosives to the train tracks. Vachek would supervise their placement, attach a string about five meters long, and a minute before the train was about to pass, he would light the string and retreat quickly. There would be just enough time for him to run a few meters away and hide behind a small hill nearby. Then, during the commotion following the explosion, the partisans would be able to retreat back into the safety of the forest.

Why had Shimon seen fit to choose Paltiel? He was strong, a porter by trade, and could carry the explosives easily. Shimon also thought that it was wise for any Jew accompanying a Pole at night to be stronger than the Pole. This would prevent the Pole from being tempted to harm the Jew, and it would enable the Jew to protect himself. Paltiel, a simple, good-hearted Jew who trusted everyone, did not follow Shimon's line of thought. He was simply proud to have been chosen for the task and happy to do something to help others.

The next day Vachek and Paltiel prepared themselves for action. Vachek prepared the explosives, weighed them, and measured the string, while Paltiel stood and watched. His part was less complicated. He was only Vachek's porter and aide. At one o'clock in the morning Vachek and Paltiel left the camp, a package on Paltiel's shoulder and a rifle in Vachek's hand. At one-twenty-five they reached the edge of the forest. There they stopped for a few seconds and listened in all directions. All was still.

They walked towards the tracks, without a word. Silence is appropriate at such a time. At one-thirty they arrived at the railroad tracks. Vachek tapped Paltiel on the shoulder, and he set down his package. They both stood and listened attentively. The silence was undisturbed. Vachek put his mouth to Paltiel's ear and whispered to him to pull the package another few steps. Then he took the package from Paltiel and motioned to him to wait behind a small hill.

Paltiel walked to the place Vachek had indicated and sat

down on the ground behind the hill. Vachek remained near the tracks. Paltiel had to wait only half an hour for Vachek, but it seemed to him a million years. When would the train come? Paltiel strained his ears and imagined that he heard the train coming. His heart began to pound. But minutes passed and the train didn't come. Paltiel was greatly disappointed. The same thing happened a second time. The third time that Paltiel heard the train coming he didn't believe it. But when he saw a bright light from the west, he knew that this time it really was the train. His heart stopped. Every second was endless. He lay flat on the ground. Just then he felt a hand tap him, and he knew that Vachek had arrived and that in less than a minute there would be an explosion.

Paltiel was completely gripped by the excitement of the impending explosion. Suddenly his ears were deafened by a powerful blast that shook the world. And just when a great light from the explosion lit up the entire area, Vachek pressed the trigger of his gun and shot Paltiel in the heart.

If Paltiel managed to let out even one groan, it was swallowed up by the noise of the explosion. After that Vachek took off his cap and shot two holes in its visor. He replaced his cap and started on his way back through the forest.

The partisans in the forest had heard the mighty blasts and were overwhelmed with happiness. They had succeeded! Many people had remained awake to wait for the explosion, and others got up now to welcome the heroes. There was no doubt that the train had been blown up. Even in the forest they had heard it passing, and the echoes of the explosion had testified to a powerful impact. When explosives blow up without destroying anything, they do not cause such powerful echoes.

Half an hour later, Vachek reached the forest. Those who saw him cheered in his honor. Shimon was among the first to welcome him. His sharp eyes anxiously searched for Paltiel's shadow, but in vain. Shimon's heart beat faster. He approached Vachek and asked excitedly, "Where is Paltiel?"

Vachek answered, "I assume Paltiel will come in a few minutes."

"What do you mean 'in a few minutes'? Didn't you come back together?" asked Shimon.

"Germans were standing guard on top of the trains, and when they saw us they began to shoot. Each of us ran in a different direction," Vachek answered, removing his cap and showing them the visor. "There is no doubt that Paltiel will come in a little while. Perhaps he is hiding some place, or sat down to rest a bit."

Vachek's words did not convince Shimon. They left him in great despair. If Paltiel didn't come, what would be the fate of the other Jews living side by side with the Poles in the forest?

Paltiel didn't come.

The Poles saw how upset the Jews were over Paltiel, but they were not disturbed. They were happy that the exploit had been successful and that now the townspeople would praise them for their bravery. They even perceived the Jews' distress as a sign of weakness not befitting the brave of heart. They didn't see how anyone could mourn one man's death at a time like this. Even in times of peace, death did not greatly disturb them, and certainly not in wartime.

Vachek, who kept his secret to himself, tried to pretend to be sorry that his comrade, Paltiel, had not returned. But grief cannot be feigned. Vachek's attempts were not only unsuccessful; they almost gave him away. Anyone who witnessed Vachek's strange "grief" wondered. But Shimon didn't wonder; his suspicions were now confirmed. Vachek's attempts at concern only increased Shimon's grief.

But the Poles' elation over their triumph was short-lived. That very evening Yashek and Stashek went to the village to bring food and to bask in the glory of their victory. They wanted to hear what was being said in town about their exploit against the military transport.

Instead of feeling glorified, they were frustrated and

disappointed to hear all the farmers speaking about the bravery of the Jews. A Jew had been found murdered near the railway tracks, and according to all the signs it was he who had laid the explosives on the tracks and blown up the train and all its passengers. One farmer even knew that the Jew had a loaded pistol in his pocket. The farmers were awed by the bravery of the Jews. This was their second great achievement. According to the farmers, Nachrovah was like a beehive with everyone talking about the feat of the Jew who was found dead near the railway tracks.

When Yashek and Stashek returned to the forest and told their countrymen what they had heard in the village, the Poles were deeply disappointed — Vachek most of all. He had brought this shame upon his own head. If his comrades knew his secret, they would be furious with him. He had ruined their good name. Now people would say that the Poles had done nothing against the Germans, especially in contrast to the Jews.

Shimon and Peretz also went to the villages to get food, and they also heard of the bravery of the Jew who had blown up a military transport. Shimon thought to himself, "The price of Jewish honor is very high. Only by dying can a Jew gain esteem." It cannot be denied that this did bring Shimon some small measure of comfort. "Paltiel's sacrifice was accepted," he thought. "He has brought honor to the Jews of the forest and shame to the Poles. If Paltiel cannot be brought back to life, at least his death should be avenged. And even if revenge cannot be fully realized, the honor he has brought the Jews in Gentile eyes is in itself a kind of revenge on the Poles."

The tension between the two groups of partisans heightened. The Poles were angry that the Jews had stolen all the credit. Poles do not easily waive a claim to honor. It is too precious to them. It was not the Jews' fault that people spoke highly of them, but this made no difference. Anger needs no logical justification. It is always justified in its own eyes. Nor is it overly modest; nor does it hide for long. On the contrary, it seeks any excuse to burst out into the open.

Someone who needs an excuse for his anger can always find it—anywhere, any time. Nothing is easier, and the Poles soon found an excuse to release all their pent-up anger against the Jews. This is what happened:

The Poles had often seen Peretz talking privately with Chaim. At first they paid no attention, but gradually their curiosity was aroused. How long could an adult talk to a child? Once Stashek took Chaim aside, after he had left Peretz, and asked him what Peretz had been talking about. A kind of friendship had grown between Stashek and Chaim since that time that Stashek had found him asleep in the forest and had spoken to him softly. Stashek often remarked that he had already met Chaim before, but he couldn't recall when or where. This also brought the two of them together. Chaim told Stashek that Peretz had been telling him stories. Surprised, Stashek asked, "What kind of stories?"

"Peretz was telling me about Bar Kochba," Chaim answered.

"Who was Bar Kochba?"

"He was a Jewish hero who fought against the Romans who destroyed Jerusalem and burnt down the Holy Temple," answered Chaim.

All the Poles listened to the conversation between Chaim and Stashek. Among them was Vachek. Vachek jumped up as though bitten by a snake. He ran over to Peretz, who was then talking with Shimon.

"What kind of stories have you been telling the boy?" Vachek asked Peretz.

"What difference does it make to you?" replied Peretz.

Vachek said, "It's wrong to tell children lies."

"What are you talking about?" asked Peretz.

Vachek answered, "The stories about Bar Kochba are lies."

"How do you know they are lies?" asked Peretz.

"The Jews have no heroes," stated Vachek.

Shimon broke in, "They certainly do! They have always had heroes, and even today there are Jewish heroes."

"Who are the Jewish heroes of today?" challenged Vachek.

Shimon answered, "Chaim's father and Paltiel are heroes."

Shimon's reply hit Vachek where it hurt the most.

"Paltiel a hero?" he thought to himself. "I, Vachek, did the bulk of the work in exploding the train, and Shimon has the nerve to call Paltiel a hero?" The blood rose to his face. He screamed with all his might, "Jews are cowards who make themselves out to be heroes. They steal the honor of the Poles. There is good reason to dislike them." Then he raised his fist and was about to punch Shimon in the face, but Shimon was quicker, and he struck Vachek forcefully.

No one knows what might have happened next had not Peretz come between them just in time. Peretz knew that

Shimon, while fighting with a Gentile, would not let up until the Gentile was in danger of his life. Here in the forest, this would endanger all the Jews. Peretz placed himself between the two enemies and scolded them softly until they both agreed to give up the fight. The Poles, who had been watching the incident, pressed their lips together and swallowed their anger. All that day and the next, tempers ran high among the partisans. Little by little the storm settled outwardly, and only the hidden rancor in their hearts remained.

One day, the partisans heard many voices outside the forest. They were sure that these were the voices of Germans who had come to capture them. They knew that the Germans would not sit quietly by after the operation against the military train. Silence would mean surrender and would constitute an invitation to the partisans to repeat the operation. The partisans were gripped by fear. Face-to-face combat with the Germans would be very dangerous. After all, the partisans were a small group with only the poorest and smallest number of weapons. The Germans, on the other hand, had an unlimited stockpile and could send an unlimited number of soldiers to the forest. This new threat made the partisans forget about the fight between Vachek and Shimon. Now was not the time for matters of that sort. Now they must all unite to prevent the Germans from penetrating the forest.

All day long the next day, the partisans waited for the Germans to enter the forest. They prepared themselves for face-to-face combat and didn't even leave the forest to find food. Much to their astonishment, although the voices outside had not ceased, the day passed and not one German had been seen in the forest. That day, they also heard planes fly low over the forest, and there was the sound of shooting to the east, not far away. They wondered what was happening. If the planes had come to drop flares into the forest, why hadn't they done so? If the shooting was directed against the partisans, why did it sound as if it were outside the forest?

Another day passed without food from outside. People were getting hungry. Perhaps the Germans were blockading the forest in an attempt to starve the partisans out. But in that case, what did the planes and shooting have to do with the blockade? One more day went by, full of endless questions but no answers.

Then Yashek and Shimon sent some men to see what was happening. The men advanced slowly to the edge of the forest, not in a group, but singly, each one separated from the other by several hundred feet. Peretz was one of them. When the partisans got very close to the edge of the forest, they saw innumerable Germans, all coming from the east and proceeding westward.

The men ran back to the camp to tell what they had seen, but it was still puzzling. Was it possible that the Germans were really fleeing for their lives — away from the eastern front? It seemed that they were.

When the partisans heard the report about the German retreat, they let out cries of surprise and began to move towards the road. Everyone went to see the miracle. Hearts beat quickly and feet were light. Yet they walked silently. Although they had no doubt that the Germans were really fleeing, they still had not overcome their surprise, and so they could not fully express their happiness.

They reached the edge of the forest and with their own eyes saw the long lines of German soldiers clearly retreating in panic. Their eyes filled with tears, blurring their vision. They wiped away the tears, and their hearts lightened at the wonderful sight. They tried to see where the lines of retreating Germans began and where they ended, but they couldn't. The lines moved like waves in an endless sea, with neither beginning nor end.

They gave up trying to measure the long lines stretching endlessly in both directions, and concentrated on the Germans passing close by them. Looking closely, they saw fear in the Germans' eyes. The Germans, in turn, saw strange people standing along the edge of the forest, and they were afraid of being shot. Even the guns that they carried could not protect them from the fear in their hearts. Fear which no gun can banish accompanies fleeing soldiers.

When the partisans saw just how fearful the Germans were, they were ashamed that they had not thought of attacking them. They had been standing there like little children absorbed in watching an interesting film. Of course, it was dangerous to shoot from such a short distance. Although the Germans were afraid, they would undoubtedly defend themselves if attacked and would cause casualties among the partisans.

The partisans retreated to the forest. They sent the women and children back to the camp, and only the men remained at the site. Hiding behind trees close by, they began to fire bullets at the rows of marching Germans. The Germans panicked. Some tried to return fire, but they couldn't hit the partisans who were protected by the trees. There were many casualties among the German ranks, until they finally realized that the area was unsafe and began to detour around it. Shortly afterward, the march along the forest stopped altogether.

Now the partisans could only watch the Germans moving towards Nachrovah, out of reach of their rifles. There was no point in trying to pursue them. In the open field, the Germans would have a great advantage both in numbers and in weapons. It would be preferable to wait in the forest. Perhaps a few more Germans, not realizing the danger, would chance to pass by.

With time on their hands, they left the forest to examine the victims who had fallen on the path. They estimated a total of several hundred. Satisfaction filled their hearts. Now it couldn't be said that they had done nothing in the forest. The hundreds that they had felled were an accomplishment to be proud of.

As they were looking at the spread of German corpses lying on the ground, it seemed to Shimon that one of them was alive. He went up to the "corpse," touched his hand, and pulled him this way and that, until the "dead man" opened his eyes and looked straight into Shimon's. Shimon commanded him to stand up and he did so. All the partisans came running to watch the show. They surrounded the German, whose leg was slightly wounded. He stood forlornly, his eyes bulging. The partisans were astonished. They had never before seen such a wretched German. They were accustomed to proud, self-assured Germans, whose whole appearance proclaimed that the world was created for them alone. They had never seen a frightened German whose whole appearance proclaimed subjugation and humiliation. Standing and watching the German filled their hearts with joy. This sight alone gave them great satisfaction.

Finally, they remembered that they had to do something with this German. Yashek asked him where the soldiers were going. The German didn't answer. Yashek spoke Polish, and he, the German, couldn't understand what was being said. When he didn't answer, Yashek kicked him so hard that he fell over. Shimon remarked to Yashek, "There is no doubt that a kick like that befits a German, but he didn't understand you." When the German got to his feet, Shimon repeated Yashek's question in Yiddish, which is similar to German. The Nazi understood part of it and guessed the rest. He answered that they were fleeing from the Russians who had been pursuing them for several weeks.

From his tone of voice, it was obvious that he admired the Russians for their strength. When Shimon translated the German's answer into Polish, Stashek said, "He is a fawning bootlicker! He wants to butter us up so that we'll let him live."

Shimon answered, "It's not just bootlicking; it's also admiration. Germans admire strength. They will serve anyone who is strong."

The partisans tried to decide what to do with their captive. There was no doubt that he deserved to be killed. The only question was what type of death he deserved. The German looked into their eyes and read their thoughts. He became very nervous. He looked at the Poles, pleading for mercy with his eyes. Then he remembered the Jews among them. He had spent a lot of time learning how to recognize the Jews. His officers had also told him that Jews were soft-hearted cowards and that there was no need to fear them.

Now, when he noticed Jews among the Poles, he turned to them to save him. If they were soft-hearted, they would not be able to refuse his pleas. He looked at Shimon and was startled. He saw before him a Jew, fitting all the signs and stereotypes he had been taught, but this Jew's eyes showed no signs of a soft heart. Shimon looked into the German's eyes and read his thoughts. All the hate that had accumulated in Shimon's heart welled up in his eyes until it nearly pierced the German's heart. The German saw that he would get no mercy from this Jew. Apparently his officers had lied to him about this, just as they had lied when they had promised a fast victory over the Russians. Yes, they had fed them lies, deliberately misled them. From between clenched teeth, he let out a juicy curse. For whom? He himself didn't know.

Shimon said, "He should be hanged."

Yashek replied, "There'll be time to hang him later."

Shimon asked, "And what do you plan to do meanwhile?"

Yashek answered, "Let's have a little fun with him first. It's not every day that a German falls into our hands."

"What kind of fun?" asked Shimon.

Yashek replied, "Let's kill him limb by limb until hanging is unnecessary. We'll hang him later, as a decoration."

Shimon said, "We are not like the Germans who enjoy that kind of fun. A murderer must be put to death, but the death penalty is not for fun."

"The Jews are soft-hearted and can't stand to watch someone fluttering between life and death," said Yashek. When Shimon saw that Yashek would not give up his "fun," he left.

Shimon and his men stood a short distance away and spoke about the Germans' retreat. They said, "The end of the war is near. The world will again return to normal, and this nightmare will finally pass away. The Jews will leave the ghetto and return to their homes, and perhaps those who were taken away will also return to Nachrovah and Temyonovah. They must have withstood much torture and suffering, but time heals all wounds. Even their suffering will eventually cease." They sighed over so-and-so who had died or been killed. They sighed over the deaths of Yudel Glick, and Zechariah the butcher, and Paltiel the porter. Shimon was reminded of Brachah, who must be brought back from Marussa. Someone would have to take care of Chaim, now that his father had been killed. Who knew what had happened to his mother? If Reb Yisrael Reichman was still alive, he would care for his grandson. But who knew if he was still alive?

An hour later, Shimon and his men returned to the Poles and saw the German hanging from a tree. They didn't ask what the Poles had done to him. Shimon looked at the German and said, "Hanging befits a German like a cockscomb befits a rooster." The Poles looked contemptuously at the Jews who had not taken part in the German's death.

∽§ 17 ৡ∾ *The Empty Ghetto*

After the Germans evacuated Nachrovah, all of the partisans left the forest, and the Jews immediately returned to the ghetto. But the ghetto was empty. Not a single living soul was there. The houses were empty both of people and of any personal belongings. This was very strange. The partisans knew that the Germans' custom was to abduct the Jews, but not to touch the little that those Jews left behind them. Nor did the Germans permit the Jews to take with them more than the absolute minimum that was necessary for survival. Then what had happened to all the odds and ends that every house is full of, even in the ghetto? In many apartments only the four walls remained. Some of the houses had missing doors and windows. Here and there even the woodwork had been removed.

The Jews were deeply pained at this sight, and they were very anxious about the fate of their brothers. Shimon suggested, "You stay here in the ghetto, and Peretz and I will go to ask the Poles where all the Jews are."

In every house, the Poles opened the door only a crack. Through the crack Shimon and Peretz asked the tenants about the Jews of the ghetto, and through the crack they received their reply. Not all the householders gave the same reply. Those who were noncommittal said they didn't know. Those who were open and honest said, "All we know is that the Jews were deported from the ghetto by the Germans."

Shimon asked, "Peretz, my brother, why don't the Poles allow us to enter their houses? Are they afraid we'll burn their houses down with our fiery breath?"

Peretz answered, "They're afraid of the 'evil eye.'"

"Why are they more afraid now than they ever were before?" asked Shimon.

Peretz bent over and touched the sidepost of the door with his fingertips. When Shimon looked down to examine the spot that Peretz had touched, he saw a slanted stripe where the paint had faded. There had once been a kosher *mezuzah* in that place, guarding a Jewish home. Peretz put his hand to his mouth and kissed his fingertips. Shimon did the same. Tears were in both their eyes.

Peretz said, "If the Poles even took things which had to be uprooted from Jewish houses, they must certainly have taken everything that wasn't nailed down. That's why they don't want us in their houses. They don't want us to see those things."

At that moment, Shimon was reminded of Brachah. "Come, Peretz, my brother," he said. "Let's go find Yudel Glick's daughter."

As they passed one of the houses, Shimon stopped for a minute and looked at it. Peretz asked, "What do you see in this house that attracts your attention?"

Shimon answered, "I see something new here. This house never had a courtyard before."

Peretz examined the hedge around the yard and said, "You call this a courtyard — but I would call it a graveyard." Shimon looked at him quizzically as Peretz pointed to one of the stones in the hedge and said, "This is a gravestone." Shimon examined the stone and saw that it was straight and wide at one end, narrow and rounded at the other. He knew that Peretz was right. Shimon and Peretz went to the gate, looked inside and saw that Hebrew letters had once been engraved on the inner side of the stone. It was impossible to read the inscription, for the letters had been chiseled away, but there was enough left to see that they had been in the holy tongue.

When they reached Mr. Sokolsky's house, Stashek walked out of the door. Surprised to see him there, Shimon exclaimed, "Oh, it's you!" He hesitated a minute and then asked, "You were in the house. Did you see Mrs. Shmendrikovitz there?"

Stashek answered curtly, "This is my father's house. There is no one here by that name."

Surprised at his answer, Shimon objected, "It may be your father's house, but I was told that Mrs. Shmendrikovitz lives here."

"Who told you that?" asked Stashek.

Shimon answered, "The person who told me is no longer alive. He was Chaim's father. His daughter is in Mrs. Shmendrikovitz's care." Suddenly, Stashek had an insight. The riddle of Chaim, which had bothered him for so long, was solved.

Stashek paused a minute and then said, "Apparently the Jew who told you that was mistaken; if not, then he misled you. The Sokolsky family, not the Shmendrikovitz family, lives here. Now get out of here, Shimon, and don't disturb us."

Shimon measured Stashek from the soles of his feet to the top of his head, and said to himself, "Vachek was not the only one. They are all Jew-haters." Like many of the Jews of Nachrovah, he had never heard the name Sokolsky. Perhaps this was Yank's fault. Everyone had called Mr. Sokolsky "the father-in-law of Mr. Shmendrikovitz," until few Jews were familiar with the name Sokolsky. Shimon and Peretz left, their hopes of finding Brachah dashed.

Since they found no Jews in the ghetto of Nachrovah, they went to look for Jews in the ghetto of Temyonovah, but both towns had shared the same fate. Nor did the Poles of Temyonovah open their doors to the Jews more than a crack, through which they stared with wicked, bewildered eyes. The Jews who had returned from the forest gave up trying to find Jews from the ghetto. Apparently, the Germans hadn't wanted to leave any behind to tell what they had done to them.

There was still one glimmer of hope. Although there were no Jews left in the small towns, perhaps they could find some in the big cities. The cities offered more opportunities to hide and so to remain alive, and many more Jews had lived in the big cities; possibly a few had managed to survive. But even if they found no Jews in the cities either, they would never return to Nachrovah or Temyonovah. No Jew could live side by side with Poles who shut their doors in his face and wouldn't allow a Jew to pass their threshold. What would happen if they did find other Jews was also an open question. They only knew that if they did locate other Jews, they would do whatever these Jews did.

The group remained in Nachrovah and Temyonovah only one day. The next day, they decided to set out for Cracow. Cracow had been one of the oldest and most important Jewish communities in Poland. It was impossible to imagine Cracow without Jews.

But before leaving, the Jews went to take their leave of the dead. The Germans couldn't have banished the dead; at least *they* must have remained in their places. But when they reached the cemetery, they saw that they had been mistaken.

The Germans had also banished the dead, for even though they remained in their places, their places were unidentifiable. All the gravestones had been uprooted. With no stones on any of the graves, who could tell where anyone was buried? Grass grew over the graves, covering the dead from the eyes of the living. The living stood there, wanting to bid farewell to the dead, but not knowing what to say in parting. Should they ask for forgiveness for leaving them behind with the Poles? Heaven and earth were witness that they did so against their will, not voluntarily. They could not live together with such evil people. They also had to continue their search for the Jews from the ghetto — perhaps some of them would need their help.

Peretz stood up and said, "I have something to say to the dead." All turned their eyes to him. "In the cemetery of Nachrovah, righteous men and women of good deeds rest in peace. When the redemption comes, speedily in our days, and the *Mashiach* arrives, the dead of Nachrovah will come to Eretz Yisrael through special paths and will be resurrected.

"I beg of you, the dead of Nachrovah, in God's Name, not to forget to bring with you to Eretz Yisrael—Yudel Glick, and Paltiel the porter. They died *al kiddush haShem*, to sanctify God's Name, even though they were not privileged to be buried here with the other Jews in the cemeteries of Nachrovah and Temyonovah."

"We must all recite *Kaddish* over the Jews of the ghetto whose graves are not known," said Shimon. "And we must recite *Kaddish* beside all the graves which have been desecrated." Everyone stood up. Shimon took Chaim and stood the child beside him, saying, "Chaim is an orphan and must recite with everyone else." The men stood together and, in a loud voice, said the prayer. The women and children answered, "May His great Name be blessed forever . . ."

◄§ 18 §► *A Hero's Death*

When the Jews reached the railway station, they found it teeming with Poles. When their eyes met, the Poles read much suffering in the eyes of the Jews, and the Jews read much contempt in the eyes of the Poles. They waited a long time for the train as in those days nothing worked very efficiently. After the chaos of a war in which everyone was against everyone, it was not simple to restore order.

When the train arrived, the Jews all tried to squeeze into one empty car, together, but they could not all fit. Some of them had to crowd into the next car together with the Poles. The Jews all squeezed into one corner by themselves, so as not to be together with the Poles whose eyes reflected their displeasure. The Poles were angry and disappointed to see so many Jews board the train. When the Germans had left Nachrovah, the Poles were sure that there were no Jews left in the world. They assumed the Germans had murdered them all, but now they saw that many Jews had remained alive. They had never dreamed so many could be saved. Their disappointment made them bitter, but they didn't dare express themselves out loud. Poland was under a new regime, and the hated Russians were now on Polish soil.

Perhaps the Russians would not look favorably on open enmity towards Jews. It was better not to take chances, better to wait and see.

The train began to move. From time to time it stopped. The Jews looked through the window in their corner, searching for Jews among the crowds waiting in the station. No, there were no Jews among them. Although some passengers got off, more and more boarded at each stop, so that the cars became more and more crowded. As more Poles entered the car, the Jews were pushed even tighter into their corner. A heavy silence rested on the car, such as exists between two enemy camps who must be careful not to reveal anything to each other.

What could the Poles talk about in those days, if not about the war that was over? And how could they talk about the war without mentioning the Jews? But they were too uncomfortable to talk about them in their presence. With the opinion of the new regime as yet unknown, it was too dangerous to say some things out loud. And the Jews certainly would not talk about themselves in the presence of non-Jews. So each one kept his thoughts to himself. On the other hand, in the car where the Jews were alone, they spoke freely.

Shimon was in the car with the Poles. He wanted to be where the danger was, and there was less to worry about in the Jewish car than in the mixed car. Shimon knew how the Poles felt about the Jewish survivors, and he was prepared for anything. Some Pole might be unable to restrain himself and might come to attack one of the Jews. It was necessary to have someone among the Jews ready to fight back.

In normal times, the trip from Nachrovah to Cracow took five hours, but at that time it took six. There were fewer cars and more passengers. The passengers delayed the train in their efforts to squeeze into the already packed cars. Between one station and the next, the train traveled with breakneck speed, as if trying to make up for the delays.

It was noon. The sun beat down on the cars as the train slowed down. The Jews thought they were approaching a station and squeezed next to the window to see if there were any Jews in the station. But when they looked outside, they saw that the train was stopping in the middle of the fields opposite a small forest. Five young Poles entered the car of the Jews and commanded all the Jews to get off the train. The Jews, their hearts full of fear, didn't move. The Poles began to push them roughly towards the door. In a few seconds all the Jews in the car were standing on the tracks below.

When Shimon looked through the window of his car and saw the Jews from the adjacent car getting off, he was puzzled, and he quickly joined them. At that moment the young Poles got off and commanded the Jews to march towards the forest. Shimon, fearing tragedy, knew it was time for him to act. In a split second, he raised his hand and lowered his fist onto the skull of one of the Poles. The Pole managed to let out an "Oy" and fell to the ground. The other four Poles were so surprised, they lost their ability to think. They had expected tears and pleas for mercy from the Jews, but never blows. After all, this was not the first time they had taken Jews off the train.

Shimon knew that one was no match for five, not even

one like him, and that even if Peretz, Yonah, and the others came to his aid, there were a hundred times more Poles on the train. He would have to act quickly and not give the Poles time to think. He raised his hand again and repeated what he had done the first time. One more Pole buckled and fell. The remaining three Poles fled to the forest.

Shimon motioned to the Jews to return to their car immediately. He himself was the last one to remain on the tracks. Just then a shot was fired from the forest, and a bullet entered Shimon's head. As he fell onto the tracks, a terrifying shriek was heard from the steam engine. The train began to move, as if, terrified by Shimon's courage, it was trying to flee.

No complaints were possible against Peretz and the other Jews who had not come to Shimon's aid. Everything had happened so fast that Peretz and the others couldn't grasp it. When Peretz finally realized what happened, he sighed and said, "Happy are you, Shimon. You died a hero's death and saved a whole Jewish community. Woe to that man whose hour has not yet arrived." By "that man," Peretz meant himself. He envied Shimon and was sorry not to have been found worthy of a similar fate.

Preoccupied with their own sorrow, none of the Jews paid any attention to the reaction of the Polish passengers on the train. But we, as bystanders, noticed. When the Jews were ordered off the train, the Poles pushed their heads out the windows, broad smiles on their faces. They rubbed their hands together in eager anticipation. The minute Shimon went into action, their smiles disappeared and they clenched their fists, waiting to see what would happen. When the train left with the Jews aboard, they pulled their heads back into the cars, a disappointed look on their faces.

Before the train arrived in Cracow, Peretz said, "We must fulfill Shimon's will." They all looked at Peretz, not knowing what he was referring to. Peretz explained, "It was Shimon who said that we should recite *Kaddish* together in the graveyard of Nachrovah in memory of the Jews of the ghetto. Now we must recite *Kaddish* together, for him."

All the men, including Chaim, stood up and recited *Kaddish*, and all the women and children answered, "May His great Name be blessed." This time there were no tears in their eyes; instead, their eyes were filled with fear.

When the train reached Cracow, the Jews of the forest got off and, to their great joy, saw that there were other Jews in the train station. These Jews looked neither like partisans nor like ghetto Jews, but like pre-war Jews. But there was no time to speculate, for these strange Jews surrounded them, greeted them with warm smiles, and took them away from the station. Later, the partisans found out that these were Jews from America and from Israel.

These members of the Jewish Rescue Committee brought the partisans to a house where they had prepared everything the refugees could possibly require. They exchanged their torn clothing for new clothes. They fed them a hot meal and gave them clean beds where they might rest from the hardships that had been their lot for years.

Chaim was not the only orphan in Cracow. There were many children among the survivors, orphaned of both father and mother. The Rescue Committee grouped all the children together, apart from the adults. A child's world is different from that of an adult, and it is not wholesome for children to have no corner of their own, to always be in the company of adults. In the children's house, they resumed their studies.

The Jews of Nachrovah and Temyonovah knew that this was only a temporary station. The Rescue Committee had come to evacuate them. The soil of Poland was too soaked with Jewish blood for Jews to remain there. The remnants of the Jewish people were being gathered together in order to sail abroad. They had their choice of many possible destinations, but the most popular were Israel and America. Each person was free to choose his own destination.

Most of the Jews of Nachrovah chose Israel. Peretz chose Eretz Yisrael because it was the home of the Maccabees, Rabbi Akiva, and Bar Kochba. Others chose it because their relatives, killed by the Nazis, would be there when the dead were resurrected. For many of the partisans, this was a source of great comfort.

The orphans and the children of parents who had chosen to move to Israel were the first to be sent to Israel. Children were given preferential treatment because they needed to return to school and they had less strength to withstand suffering. The children were sent on their way by Jewish Agency and Rescue Committee representatives. The Jews of Nachrovah also accompanied them to the train station. Chaim was one of the children in this first group. After Shimon's death, Peretz had "adopted" and looked after him. Now, Peretz accompanied Chaim to the train station, going along as far as he could, and planning to meet him in the holy city of Jerusalem.

On Sunday there were no classes in the convent. It was a day for recreation. The six Jewish girls never left the building to walk in the streets of Nachrovah. They only played in the yard. Through the fence they could see children running in the street, but they didn't ask why they were different from the other children. Their ghetto days had made them realize that they were different. It was a fact they simply took for granted.

One Sunday, Sarah, Rivkah, and Brachah were playing hide-and-seek together. Inside the courtyard surrounding the convent building were a few small service buildings behind which they could hide. Brachah leaned her head on the fence separating the yard from the street, her eyes closed until Sarah and Rivkah would hide and she would go to look for them. Suddenly, Brachah was startled to hear her name spoken. She opened her eyes and saw two men walking past the fence. They had already taken a few steps away from her. She looked at them and realized they were Jews. Both had beards, one black and one red. Their old worn-out clothes testified that they were from the ghetto. Brachah was bewildered. Why had they mentioned her name? Who were they? Was one of them her father? She wanted to cry "Abba," but she was afraid that if she did, Maria would be angry with her.

Sarah and Rivkah waited and waited for Brachah to come and find them, but in vain. Finally, tired of waiting, they left their hiding places and went to look for her. At the entrance to the building they saw Brachah standing in her place, not even trying to find them. Coming up to her, they asked indignantly if she had forgotten they were playing. In a voice shaking with excitement she explained to them that her father had just passed by. Sarah laughed and said, "Brachah, you are just daydreaming."

Brachah answered, "He mentioned my name."

Rivkah said, "You think about your father so much that you imagined he passed by."

"But he wasn't alone," objected Brachah. "Another Jew from the ghetto was with him. The other one had a short, red beard."

At that moment, Maria came into the yard. When the girls saw her, they stopped their conversation. Maria had sharp eyes and saw that they were telling secrets. Curious as to what they had been talking about, she thought it might be important for her to know what had been said. She came over to them and asked them, but the girls didn't answer. Sarah looked at Brachah as if to say it was up to Brachah to answer the question. Maria's curiosity was aroused. Apparently this was an important secret. She asked them again what they were talking about, but in place of an answer, Brachah burst into tears. Maria was taken by surprise.

In a stiff, dry voice, she turned a third time to Sarah, the eldest of the three, to tell her what was happening. Sarah's eyes turned towards Brachah's, and Maria read in them an apology. Then Sarah turned to Maria and told her of the newest incident with Brachah. For a minute, Maria was taken aback. She knew that Jewish partisans had indeed come back from the forest and were walking around town. Two of them could have passed by. Could one of them have been Brachah's father? But hadn't Brachah's father been killed over a year ago in the explosion of the Gestapo headquarters? Either Brachah had been mistaken then, or she was mistaken now. Perhaps this was all witchcraft as Tzorerkeh had told her then.

Knowing that she had to say something, Maria scolded the girls for talking nonsense and immediately returned to the convent. Inside, she told her friends of the incident with Brachah. Sinavkeh advised, "The girls should be kept inside and not permitted in the yard. There are Jews all over town, and perhaps they are looking for the girls." Tzorerkeh agreed with Sinavkeh. Maria went out to the yard and called the girls into the house. Today they would play inside. The girls lowered their eyes, knowing that this was their punishment for talking nonsense.

The following Sunday, Maria told the girls that they would go for a walk through the town. The girls broke out in exclamations of astonishment. They had never dared to hope for such a thing. How wonderful! A minute later, Rivkah hesitatingly asked Maria, "Really, Maria? — or are you just joking?"

Maria repeated herself in a holiday tone of voice, "Today — and not only today, but every day from now on — the girls may take walks and play in the streets of the town, not only in the yard." The girls were overjoyed. They didn't know what had caused the change, and they didn't want to ask. Whatever it was, was for the good. In the afternoon — in just another two hours — they would walk through the streets.

At dinner, the girls had no appetite. Their great expectations made them forget about food. Maria understood and did not rebuke them for eating carelessly.

At 2:00 PM, the six girls left the convent. Two nuns, Sinavkeh and Tzorerkeh, accompanied them on their walk. Maria didn't go with them this time. When they were in the street, the nuns paused, and Sinavkeh asked the girls, "Where do you want to go?"

The girls looked at each other and didn't answer. Sinavkeh repeated the question. Brachah whispered, "Perhaps we could go to the ghetto."

"Very well," answered Sinavkeh. "Let's go to the ghetto. Anywhere you like."

The girls stopped chattering and walked silently beside the nuns. Their hearts were beating strongly. What would happen if they met their fathers and mothers in the ghetto? After a long silence, Sarah stopped for a minute, turned to the nuns, and asked in bewilderment, "Will we be allowed to leave the ghetto? I know that no one is allowed to leave the ghetto."

Sinavkeh and Tzorerkeh smiled, and Tzorerkeh said, "Now everyone can leave the ghetto." Sarah didn't quite understand. If it were now permitted to leave the ghetto, why hadn't her father and mother come to get her?

Nevertheless she didn't ask any more questions. She realized that this was a very complicated matter which was not easily understood.

As they drew near the ghetto gate, they saw that it was open and unguarded. The girls looked at it cautiously, not comprehending how the ghetto gate could be left unguarded. They walked down the main street of the ghetto, Katlinskah Street, looking searchingly in all directions. They saw no one. They walked up and down a few more streets and still saw no one. Rivkah asked, "Can we go into the houses?"

"Certainly," answered Sinavkeh, "let's go into the houses. We'll go wherever you want." They went into one house, a second house, a third. All the houses were empty.

As they passed one house, Sarah jumped up and called out happily, "This is our house! I want to go into our house." They all went into the house. It was deserted. Not a living soul was inside. Sarah asked Sinavkeh in a desperate tone, "Where are all the Jews?"

Sinavkeh answered, "Come girls, let's leave this house. Outside I will explain everything."

Once outside, Sinavkeh and Tzorerkeh sat the girls on a pile of stones near the house. Tzorerkeh pointed to the pile they were sitting on and said, "This pile is all that remains of a house that was destroyed in the war between the Poles and the Germans. Before the Germans fled, the Poles bombed this house and destroyed it. Many houses were destroyed during the war and many people were killed. There are no more Jews in the ghetto because before the Germans fled, they killed all the Jews."

Tzorerkeh's speech frightened and confused the girls.

"Where are my father and mother?" asked Sarah.

"And mine?" asked Rivkah.

"And mine?" asked Brachah.

Tzorerkeh repeated, "I don't know where your fathers and mothers are. I only know that the Germans killed all the Jews they found in the ghetto."

"That's not true," said Brachah. "I saw my father near our house on Catholichka Street last Sunday."

Sinavkeh answered, "Maybe it wasn't a Jew that you saw, and if it was, perhaps he wasn't from Nachrovah. It certainly wasn't your father. There are no Jews from Nachrovah left."

Brachah answered, "There were two of them, not one. One was my father."

Tzorerkeh said, "Brachah, you're talking like a baby." Brachah was embarrassed and said nothing further.

Sarah asked, "Why did the Germans kill all the Jews?"

Tzorerkeh answered, "This was their punishment from Heaven."

"For what?" asked Sarah.

Tzorerkeh answered, "This was their punishment for denying that Jesus was the Messiah."

When Tzorerkeh mentioned Jesus, Brachah knew that she was talking about the little boy in the picture with his mother. She couldn't understand what the Jews wanted from the boy. Such a poor, little boy. Brachah was sorry for him and ashamed of her parents for denying him. She didn't understand what the word "denying" meant, but when Tzorerkeh had spoken about it, Brachah had understood that it was something bad. They certainly didn't like him — but why, she didn't understand.

After that, the girls returned to the convent. At night, when they kneeled before the picture of the mother and the child, they couldn't look at the child's eyes. They felt guilty. Their fathers and mothers had denied him. At that moment they forgot that their fathers and mothers were among the Jews that the Germans had killed, as Tzorerkeh had told them today. The girls only remembered that their parents had denied Jesus and they were sorry for it. They lowered their eyes and couldn't look at the picture.

From that day on, the girls went wherever they wanted to in the streets of Nachrovah, and they played outside with all the other children. They were also given new names. Brachah was called Barbara.

One day, Maria announced that today the girls would be baptized as Catholics. They were overjoyed. They didn't know what baptism was, but they knew that afterwards they would be different than they were now, and they were curious to know just how they would be different. They also knew that after baptism they would no longer have to be ashamed of the Jews denying Jesus. They would be able to look straight at the picture and not have to lower their eyes during prayers.

The girls were brought to Nachrovah's Catholic church. Many people came to see the young Jewesses baptized. Marussa was among them. She felt personally involved, for it was she who had brought Brachah to the convent, and she was proud of herself. This accomplishment would help obliterate the bad reputation she and Yanka had acquired.

Catholics knew how to forgive. If she could show that she was a good Catholic, all would be forgiven, even her marriage to Yank.

The ceremony was short. As there were no other Jews left in Nachrovah, it no longer seemed so important to dramatize it. The priest sprinkled the girls with holy water and recited a prayer. When the girls left the church, old ladies kissed them. Marussa gave Brachah a present and asked Brachah to accept her family name. From now on, her name would be Barbara Sokolsky. The girls knew that now they were Catholic, not Jewish. They were different. Truth to tell, they were a bit disappointed. Somehow, they had thought that being different would be more exciting.

◄§ 20 ֍ *Chaim in Eretz Yisrael*

When Chaim reached Eretz Yisrael, he was placed in a Youth Aliyah school where Torah and other religious studies were taught. Chaim threw himself into his studies and in a short time his teachers noticed his talents. His intelligence and diligence gave them great hopes for him. The teachers appreciated his talents, but they esteemed him even more for his diligence. Talent is a gift fom God; one cannot choose to be talented. But diligence is a matter of choice. It is a habit which is acquired and retained only through hard work, and one who works to achieve it is worthy of esteem.

Chaim's teachers thought his diligence was due to his desire to make up for what he had missed in the ghetto and in the forest. We know that there was also another reason. Chaim had not forgotten Brachah. He hoped to find Brachah when he left the forest, but now that he was in Eretz Yisrael and Brachah was still in Nachrovah, how would he ever find her? This caused him great pain. To take his mind off Brachah and to lessen his pain, he immersed himself in his studies.

During the day, Chaim could forget about Brachah by fleeing to his books. But at night, in bed, he couldn't take refuge in his books, and memories of Brachah would torment him. He knew that he would not be able to help her while he was still young. Shimon was gone and there was no one to advise him. No one here knew the slightest bit about what had happened in Nachrovah. Maybe Yonah would come and bring him some news about Brachah. Maybe he would find her in Cracow. Of course, this was not very probable. Brachah had remained in Nachrovah, so how could Yonah find her in Cracow? Nevertheless, maybe a miracle would happen. Maybe Brachah would come to Cracow and Yonah would see her walking down the street. However, Chaim knew that Yonah was not Shimon. Even if he found her in Cracow, he might not know how to bring her to Israel—but Chaim wanted to believe in some miracle. He didn't want to give up his sister.

Maybe Peretz would find her and bring her to Eretz Yisrael. Peretz was as astute as Shimon. True, Peretz didn't know Brachah, for he was from Temyonovah, not from Nachrovah, but Chaim knew that he and Brachah looked very much alike. Anyone who knew him would recognize Brachah.

Often, Brachah would take pity on her brother and visit him in his dreams. She would smile at him, and he would feel that she, too, was waiting for a miracle. But sometimes she would look at him mockingly as if to tease him and say, "You'll *never* find me again!" Then Chaim would wake up greatly distressed. Would he really never find her? Those were the times when Chaim would hurry to school and drown himself in his books to relieve his distress.

When Chaim had arrived in Israel he had been placed in

third grade. Now, only three years later, he was about to finish eighth grade. By the end of the school year he would be *bar mitzvah*. The principal of the school, Mr. Avichail, was preparing a joint *bar mitzvah* celebration for five of his students. They had no fathers or mothers to care for them, and so various institutions were taking care of their needs.

There was much to do. Five good pairs of *tefillin* must be bought, and a dinner, which cost even more than the *tefillin*, must be held. The boys also needed new clothes. As they were the guests of honor, everyone's eyes would be on them and if they didn't have nice clothes, they would be very embarrassed.

Mr. Avichail received some generous donations, bought what was needed, and made all the necessary preparations. But he did not work alone; all the teachers helped him. Chaim's teacher, Mr. Melamed, taught Chaim his *bar mitzvah* speech. Of the five boys, Chaim alone would present a speech. The other boys were not as advanced as Chaim nor were they as talented. It was hard for them to make up for the years they had lost in the ghetto.

Many people were invited to the party: the local rabbi, representatives of the institutions, and many guests. Chaim must be well prepared, both for his own sake and to uphold the school's honor. Mr. Melamed was lucky; it was easy to teach Chaim. After one or two rehearsals, the boy knew the whole speech by heart.

The day of the party arrived. Rows of tables and chairs were set up along the whole length of the school auditorium. The head table stood along the east wall. The five boys would sit in the middle and the local rabbi, a man of imposing appearance, would sit at their right with Mr. Avichail at their left. The hall filled with guests, and every seat was taken. Pupils of the school — some before and some after their own *bar mitzvah* — sat at a separate table.

Mr. Avichail rose and delivered the opening speech. He welcomed the rabbi and the other guests. Then he introduced Chaim who would deliver the *bar mitzvah* speech on behalf of all the *bar mitzvah* boys. Chaim rose and began to recite the speech Mr. Melamed had taught him. Mr. Melamed stood behind him, holding the text of the speech, ready to prompt him if, God forbid, Chaim forgot a line. There was no need to expect any trouble, for Chaim had an excellent memory, and the teacher knew that Chaim knew his speech backwards and forwards. Nevertheless, it didn't pay to take chances. Chaim was still young and could not be depended on completely.

Chaim began his speech according to the text. He spoke in a loud, clear voice, and Mr. Melamed followed his words in the text with great satisfaction. Suddenly, Chaim deviated from the text. Mr. Melamed, surprised, tried to correct him. He began to whisper more and more loudly, but Chaim didn't pay any attention. Mr. Melamed nudged Chaim gently to return to the written text of the speech. He was afraid that Chaim would get lost completely and would not know how to end the speech, and what could be worse than that!

But Chaim continued to deliver his own speech. When Mr. Melamed lost all hope of returning Chaim to the written text, he began to listen to what Chaim was saying. Apparently the boy had prepared his own speech independently, and Mr. Melamed found that it was a pleasure to listen to him. When Chaim finished, there was much applause. He had made a great impression. Even what he had read from the text had become his own, because he had put his own heart and soul into it.

Next, the rabbi spoke. He praised the *bar mitzvah* boys, and he praised Chaim's speech. Mr. Avichail was quite pleased that the speech Mr. Melamed had written found favor in the rabbi's eyes. After the rabbi had finished talking, Mr. Melamed—a modest person—told Mr. Avichail the whole story, and Mr. Avichail related it to the rabbi. He was quite impressed. "Really?" he said. "Why, that's unbelievable!" Chaim was sitting in the middle, two boys to his right and two to his left, and did not hear the conversation between the three men. If he had, he might have blushed.

The following year Chaim entered a *yeshivah* in Jerusalem. Here he found great opportunities for his diligence. In school there had been fixed hours for each subject, which the pupils had to follow. The *yeshivah* was different. Here no one objected if he kept to one subject for many hours. Chaim began to devote himself to the study of *gemara*, to dive into the deep waters of the Talmud. His talents found a fertile field as his memory recorded page after page. When he learned one page, it did not make him forget the ones he'd learned before. All the pages stood in order before his eyes, even with his *gemara* closed. He was able to connect one page to the other and to bind many pages into one in his mind's eye.

During those days he almost forgot about Brachah, not only by day, but even by night. His brain was always occupied with Torah thoughts, even upon retiring, and these left no room for anything else. Nevertheless, it cannot be said that he forgot her completely. On the contrary, he tried now to keep himself from forgetting her. Once, he had fled to his books in order to relieve his heartache and to forget about Brachah for a while. Now he had to purposely remind himself of her. He must remember her. Perhaps the miracle which would reunite them would still occur.

The older he grew, the better he comprehended Brachah's tragedy. When he was little, he had longed for her because she was his only sister. Now that he was grown, he realized that Brachah was in danger, not physically but spiritually. A Jewish girl surrounded by non-Jews was liable to forget her God. Even if she remembered, how could she remain Jewish? How could one lone girl retain her Jewishness in a completely Gentile world?

Now he knew that both his father and his mother had been murdered by the Nazis. He had heard about his mother's conduct, and he understood that his father had also agreed with her course of action. She had died *al kiddush haShem*, to sanctify the Holy Name.

Would Brachah, whose mother had died because she was a Jew, become a Christian? Could there be any tragedy greater than that? Would Brachah, whose father had been so learned — a real *talmid chacham* — and more righteous than most, assimilate among the Christians? No, it was impossible to accept. Although he did not yet know what to do to save Brachah, he knew that he must not despair. His heart told him that he would find her yet.

His hopes were not without basis. In the *gemara* he had

learned about an incident that had happened to the daughter of Rabbi Nachunya the well-digger. (Rabbi Nachunya dug wells for the Jews who came up to Jerusalem during the holidays, as Rashi explains.) "She fell into a deep well her father had dug. Men came to tell Rabbi Chaninah ben Dosa. The first time they came, he said 'Shalom.' The second time, he said, 'Shalom.' The third time, he cried, 'She has come out.' He asked her, 'My daughter, who took you out?' She answered, 'A ram came along, led by an old man.' They said to him [to Rabbi Chanina], 'You are a prophet.' He answered them, 'I am neither a prophet nor the son of a prophet, but I know that if a righteous man does a *mitzvah*, his children cannot be hurt by it.' " (*Yevamoth* 121)

Chaim thought, "The same is true of Brachah. She will not forget that she is Jewish. She will not fail in that very thing for which both her mother and father died." He was convinced that Brachah would remain part of the Jewish people, but he didn't yet know how.

Brachah also grew, both in age and ability. She graduated from school with honors. She was a devout Catholic, more devoted than her Catholic friends who had been born into their faith. She felt that it was up to her to receive absolution for the sins of her heretic parents and that she could achieve this by her devotion to Christianity.

A few weeks ago, the bishop had inquired about Sarah, whose name was changed to Silvana. She had a brother who had survived the war and gone to Eretz Yisrael. The Chief Rabbi of Eretz Yisrael had come to Poland to request the bishop's aid in returning Sarah to Judaism. Silvana was shocked. She didn't want to return to the heretic Jews. She wanted to be a Catholic. Barbara, however, was left in peace. She took this to be proof that her brother also was killed by the Germans.

She was happy that none of her Jewish relatives came to disturb her. Nevertheless, she couldn't forget her father and mother. She wanted to, but she couldn't. As if to make her angry, they kept appearing before her eyes.

Barbara tried not to look in the mirror. When she looked at herself, she was reminded of her mother. She looked just like her. Frightened, she would look at her own eyes and see that they were black, just like her mother's. They were Jewish eyes. How happy she would have been had she been able to exchange her dark eyes for blue ones, like those of Marussa or Maria. She had been given Marussa's family name, Sokolsky, but she didn't look at all like them. What good was a Polish name if her eyes betrayed her?

Of course she didn't hate her mother. Her mother had been born Jewish, and no one could blame her for not being a Christian. But she, Brachah, didn't want to be like her mother. She was a Christian, not a Jew, and she wanted to look like one.

· Years passed. Barbara successfully completed the Catholic Theological Seminary. What would she do now? This question troubled her and her teachers. After much discussion they came to the conclusion that she should act as a missionary to the Jews.

Because she looked Jewish, Jewish children would believe her more easily. She was very devout, and her talks would be most effective because they came straight from her heart. And most important of all, she must gain absolution for the sin of having been born Jewish. She could do this by bringing the children of heretics into the Catholic Church.

For years there had not been such a golden opportunity to save the souls of heretics. All the Jewish communities had been utterly destroyed by the Nazis, and the few Jews who survived were suspended between heaven and earth. They could not find their place. None of their former Christian homelands were willing to take them back, so they wandered from place to place until many of them sank into despair. If the Church were willing to help them, they could be ready to believe in Jesus. People will pay any price to find sustenance and peace.

Barbara began to work as a teacher in a mission school. She spoke to desperate, unfortunate women with no bread to feed their children — women who had wandered from place to place searching for husbands who had been lost in the stormy war. These women could be persuaded to enroll their children in the institution where Barbara taught. When Barbara saw the fear in these women's eyes, she would speak softly to them and reveal her secret, that she too had been born a Jew. She spoke in Yiddish, and this reinforced their trust in her.

The question must be asked, how had Barbara managed to remember her Yiddish after so many years among the Christians? In her dreams, she had spoken only Yiddish with her brother Chaim. Her dark eyes also spoke for her. Both Barbara's eyes and her message helped these women — and men, too — to take the step they so dreaded. The Holocaust had caused confusion in many hearts, and had implanted the seeds of disbelief. One word for or against could be decisive — and this word was often provided by Barbara.

Barbara was not alone in her work. What she did in one place, Silvana did in another. Possibly Rivkah, whose name had been changed to Cariba, was also employed as a missionary. Barbara knew that each one of her old friends from the convent was in a different place, but she was too busy to keep in touch or even to follow their activities.

At that time, a convention of priests and monks was

held to discuss recent events in the Holy Land. The Jews had proclaimed their own state, and when the seven neighboring Arab countries had tried to conquer the country, they had been defeated by the Jews. Now the country was in Jewish hands.

The Christian priests and monks were apprehensive as to what was taking place in the Holy Land. In their Sunday sermons they had always preached that the Jews were cursed and doomed to wander all their lives because they had denied the Messiah and crucified him. Now, with a Jewish state, there was no need for them to wander any longer. What would the priests say in their Sunday sermons? The priests also feared that all the boys and girls who had converted to Christianity during the Holocaust would begin to reflect about recent events in the Holy Land, and sinful thoughts are the greatest sins of all.

Some of the priests and monks were almost in despair, but to others the picture was not so bleak. "On the contrary," they said, "in the State of Israel, the mission can accomplish more than anywhere else. Everywhere else the Christians hate the Jews, and even Jewish converts do not have an easy time. When the Germans invaded the countries of Europe, they drew no distinction between Jews who had converted to Christianity and those who had not. Even converts were banished to the ghetto together with all the other Jews and sent to concentration camps with them.

"Anti-Semitism strengthens the Jews' ties to their religion. In the Holy Land, the situation is different. There, the Jews have their own state. There are no Christians to hate the Jews, so the Jews will accept the New Testament willingly, if the missionaries only find the proper way to present it to them.

"Many Jews in Israel have not yet found their places. Their state cannot offer all of them housing, food, and employment. If someone else offers these things to them, they will follow him. It is also possible to utilize the Church's connections with other countries to aid Jews in emigrating from the Holy Land. The great advantage to this is that it means one more Jew who believes in Jesus and one less Jew in the Holy Land."

This opinion gained wide circulation. Perhaps because they truly believed in it or perhaps because it was the only alternative to failure. It is human nature to do everything possible to avoid failure. By a great majority, the priests decided to embark on a great Christian mission to the Holy Land. The Holy Land in the hands of heretic Jews would endanger Christianity and its teachings. If successful, the mission would save the Jews from heresy, and the Holy Land from the Jews. The mission, which even in normal times did not suffer from a lack of funds, made special efforts to assure an unlimited amount of money for this particular campaign. They wanted to make sure they had sufficient money to attract people whose suffering had passed all limits, and there was no lack of such Jews in the Holy Land.

The clergymen pored over their lists of missionaries, choosing the most successful to be sent to the Holy Land. When they reached Barbara's name, they paused to consider whether it would be wise to send her or not. On the one hand, Barbara, with her Yiddish speech and Jewish eyes, would draw many Jews who might otherwise hesitate to convert. On the other hand, Barbara herself might return to her people once she saw that they had a state of their own.

After weighing the alternatives, they decided to send her. There was no real danger that Barbara might return to Judaism. She was a devout Christian—heart and soul—strong enough to draw other Jews after her, and not to be drawn after them. When they reached Silvana's name, they weighed the matter well and decided not to send her to the Holy Land. Silvana was not Barbara. She was not as serious and could not be relied upon so completely. She might well change her mind if she changed her residence.

When Barbara was informed of the decision to send her to the Holy Land, she was very happy. She couldn't understand why, but she was. She wondered what there was to be happy about. What difference did it make where she was working for the mission? Was saving a heretic's soul in Poland any less important than saving such a soul in the Holy Land? Nevertheless, she felt elated.

But she had little time to think about this. In a few weeks she was scheduled to leave Poland. The major arrangements, such as the trip itself, were to be taken care of by the Church, but she had many minor details to arrange for herself.

Before her trip, Barbara paid one last visit to Marussa. She had Marussa to thank for bringing her to the convent in Nachrovah and for the gift of the name, Sokolsky. She wanted to bid farewell to Marussa, and to Yanka, who had grown into a young lady. Marussa greeted Barbara warmly. When she heard that Barbara was on her way to the Holy Land as a missionary, she became reflective.

"Marussa, what are you thinking about?" Barbara asked. "I am happy, but you seem to have second thoughts."

Marussa answered, "You have been given a sacred task. I hope you are successful." Truth to tell, Marussa couldn't tell Barbara what she was thinking. She was filled with doubt as to whether it was really wise for the Church to send Barbara to the Holy Land. She, Marussa, didn't have much faith in converts. She knew that her Yank had been a convert; nevertheless he had not believed in Jesus. Who knew if Barbara's heart was true to her mouth, and even if she was sincere today, who could guarantee that she wouldn't change her mind tomorrow? Marussa, however, told Barbara nothing of the thoughts that ran through her mind.

Barbara bid farewell to Marussa and Yanka. As she took Yanka's hand, she looked into her eyes and felt a twinge of jealousy. Yanka, whose father was Jewish, nonetheless, had Polish eyes. How fortunate for her! Marussa and Yanka accompanied her to the street, said goodbye again, and returned home.

When Barbara was left alone, she stood still for a minute, deciding where to go. Then she turned towards the ghetto. As she passed the house where she and Chaim, Abba and Imma, and her grandparents had once lived, she stopped for a minute and gazed at the house. It had been changed completely — repaired and repainted. She had a great desire to see the house from the inside, but other people lived there now. What would she tell them when she entered? She wanted to go away, but desire to see the house from the inside was too strong. She found an excuse and went in.

When she entered, she apologized to the old woman she found there for disturbing her. She said she had simply made a mistake and confused this house with another. Before she left, she looked hastily around the room in which she was standing. She looked at the corner where she had lived in her ghetto days. She seemed to see a little girl. Looking into the little girl's eyes, she recognized herself. How different she was today! After apologizing to the old woman again, she left the house, but the little girl was still before her eyes. She began to walk fast, to chase the picture of the girl from her mind, but she was unsuccessful. She felt uneasy. This little girl was Jewish, but she herself was Catholic. She was not that little girl grown up. No, now she was someone else entirely.

৵ 22 ৵ *Barbara in Jerusalem*

It was Barbara's second day in Jerusalem. She had joined the teaching staff of the mission of St. Paul's Convent, where she would also live. On her first day she had rested up, after the long trip by land and sea from Nachrovah, and had not even left her new home.

On the second day, she went out to see the city. She would not begin her work for a few days. First she must get to know the people and learn how to differentiate between the different Jewish ethnic groups by their facial characteristics, language and clothing. She also needed to refresh her memory of the square Hebrew letters which she had forgotten with the years. Most important, she had to feel at home before beginning her work. In order to persuade others, she must first gain confidence in herself—which she could only do by being familiar with her surroundings.

Barbara didn't go out by herself. Paulina—also a teacher in the mission school of St. Paul's Convent—went with her. Paulina was from Germany, but they spoke French together. They had both learned the language at the Christian Theological Seminary.

On Yaffo Street, Paulina pointed to men with long

coats, sideburns and beards, and said, "Those are Jews." Paulina knew that Barbara came from Poland. In Poland after the war, there were very few Jews, and the few who had remained did not look Jewish. The fear which had been implanted in their hearts during the Holocaust had remained, and they tried to hide by looking like Poles.

Probably, Paulina reasoned, Barbara had never before seen a Jew with a beard and *peyoth* and a long coat in the summer. Barbara looked at the men Paulina had pointed to, but didn't say anything. Paulina looked into Barbara's eyes and saw that she was preoccupied. She didn't know if she had even heard what was said to her, or if she had noticed the men.

At that minute a tall young man with a coal-black beard passed by them. Barbara stopped in her tracks, turned her head, and looked him. When he entered one of the houses, Barbara turned around and resumed her walk. Paulina asked, "Why did the sight of that young man make you turn around? He's not the only one who looks like that. Here in Jerusalem there are many more like him. They are among the greatest heretics of all." Barbara looked into Paulina's eyes but did not answer.

Paulina continued, "Barbara, you are as white as chalk. What happened? Did that Jew frighten you? There is no reason to be afraid of them. They won't do anything to us. They do hate the mission, but they won't harm us. The law forbids it. There is even talk that this city may no longer remain part of the Jewish State. This city is holier to us than it is to the Jews, and we will not relinquish it."

Paulina continued to talk for a long time, forgetting

that in the beginning she had asked Barbara a question which had not yet been answered. Paulina saw that Barbara was absorbed in her thoughts and attributed it to the fact that she was overwhelmed by the strange-looking people she had seen.

From Yaffo Street they reached Me'ah She'arim. They passed a one-story house which had a window open. Through the window came the melodious sound of someone learning *gemara*. Barbara stopped not far from the window. Paulina said, "That is how Jews study the Talmud. They don't study it; they sing it. Did you ever in your life see a man reading a book as if he's in prayer? Strange people. The Talmudists are the greatest heretics of all. There is hatred of the Christians in the Talmud. You know that in Spain, and later in Germany, the Christians burned the Talmud. Even so, it has survived until today; the Jews will not abandon it. I myself have never studied the Talmud, but I have heard from pious Christians that it is full of treachery and heresy towards Christianity."

Barbara stood and listened to the joyous voice of the Jew learning *gemara*. Suddenly, she felt sick. Leaning against Paulina, she said, "I am dizzy. I can't stand up." Paulina held Barbara and looked around for a taxi to return to the convent, but there was none. Near the house was a bench. Paulina supported Barbara, and with great difficulty, Barbara dragged herself to the bench and collapsed. Paulina was frightened by the look on Barbara's face. The voice of the Jew still reached their ears. Barbara leaned her head on Paulina's shoulder and said, "I feel a bit better. Let me just sit here for a minute."

In a while Barbara stood up and said in a slightly shaky voice, "Come, Paulina, let's go home." But before they left, she walked to the window of the house and looked into the room. Suddenly the voice stopped, and a young man with a big book in front of him looked up, surprised to see a young woman standing at the window. Barbara was frightened by his bewildered look, and she quickly drew away.

As they left Me'ah She'arim, Paulina commented, "Apparently you've never heard a Jew studying Talmud. Was it such a novelty that you had to go up to the window to see? I have heard them so many times that it no longer interests me."

When they returned to the convent, the nuns and teachers wanted to ask Barbara what she thought of the city, but when they saw her pale face, they asked no questions. No one could understand what had happened to Barbara Sokolsky.

After Barbara retired to the room she shared with Paulina, the nuns asked Paulina about Barbara. But Paulina knew no more than they did. She said, "Apparently Barbara was overwhelmed by what she saw. The new impressions had a bad effect on her." At suppertime, Paulina went to the room to see how Barbara was feeling and to bring her to the dining hall. Barbara asked to be excused. She couldn't join them for supper as she was dizzy and wanted to rest until the next morning. No, there was no need to summon a doctor. She was sure that it would pass. Paulina wished her good night and left the room quietly.

That night Barbara saw many things. As soon as she shut her eyes, she found herself standing near a low house with one open window, a sweet joyous sound emanating from it. This time, when she went up to the window and looked inside, she saw her father. Yes, it was her father. She recognized him immediately. His beard was black, his face gentle and pale. She wanted to cry "Abba" but she didn't. She was afraid he would see her and be angry with her. She didn't know why he should be angry with her, but she was afraid just the same. But then her father looked out the window and saw her. He stopped learning. The wrinkles in his high forehead relaxed, and a wide smile spread across his face. "Come in, Brachah," he said. "Why are you standing outside? It's cold at night in Yerushalayim. Inside it's warm. Come, Brachah. Come into the room."

Barbara was ashamed to look into her father's good eyes, and she turned her head to the right. There she saw her Imma. Her face was very beautiful. Barbara looked into her mother's eyes. Black eyes. Barbara sighed. Why didn't her mother have blue eyes like those of Maria and Marussa? Her mother's eyes were velvet, soothing, but so very sad. Why were they so sad? She couldn't bear to look at such sad eyes.

She turned her head to the left. There stood Chaim, grown up, tall and good-looking, a black beard adorning his handsome face. When their eyes met, Chaim asked her, "Why don't you come into the house, Brachah? Didn't Abba tell you to come in?" Barbara heard the angry note in Chaim's voice, angry because she had not listened to Abba. Barbara was not hurt by Chaim's anger. He was no older than she, and she didn't have to listen to him. After all, they were the same age.

Just then someone grabbed her shoulders. Barbara

trembled. She wanted to scream but was so afraid she couldn't utter a sound. She turned her head around and saw Grandma Leah. Her grandmother smothered her face with kisses and then entered the house. Barbara watched her.

Suddenly Barbara realized that Chaim had left the room to fetch her and bring her inside to Abba and Imma. Panic-stricken, Barbara fled as fast as she could. She ran so fast she grew short of breath.

Barbara pulled the blanket off her head and inhaled deeply. Shaken, she looked around the room and tried to remember where she was. Her dream was still very much alive. She closed her eyes, trying to recall every detail, but when she looked through the window again, the room was empty.

No Abba, no Imma, no Chaim, no Grandma Leah. Her eyes searched the corners of the room—perhaps she would catch sight of them even if they were hiding from her. In one corner, Chaim was sitting before a large book and studying. Barbara cried, "Chaim."

Chaim lifted his eyes from the book and looked at her. He said, "It's not nice, Brachah, it's not nice. Why didn't you come inside to Abba and Imma? You only have one father and one mother. If you run away from them, you will lose your footing in this world. You shouldn't run away from your brother, either. Why did you run away?"

Just then Brachah heard footsteps and knew that they were coming to get her, to bring her to Abba and Imma. She was so frightened she began to scream.

Paulina touched her lightly and said, "Barbara, why are you screaming?" Barbara opened her eyes and saw that there was no one there but Paulina. "You must have been dreaming, Barbara," said Paulina.

Barbara nodded, "Yes, I was dreaming."

Paulina held Barbara's hand tightly and said, "Dreams are full of nonsense." Then she left the room and Barbara got up.

All that day Barbara was absorbed in reflecting on what she had seen in town and later in her dreams. She knew that she must overcome her emotions. These emotions were signs of weakness, and must pass quickly. They had come to her through her encounters with Jews, but she must remain stalwart and strong. She was a Catholic, not a Jew. She must forget her parents and her brother. They had remained Jews, denying Jesus. She had been sent to the Holy Land to redeem sinful souls from heresy and not to become preoccupied herself with sinful thoughts. She must not allow herself such sinful longings. No, she would not allow these heretical thoughts to enter her heart. She would be strong. She would fulfill her mission faithfully. In a few days, Barbara recovered and began her work as a teacher in the mission school of St. Paul's Convent.

The remnants of the Jewish communities of Nachrovah and Temyonovah remained in Cracow and waited. A few immigrated to America, but most of them wanted to immigrate to Israel. The British Mandate was in force in Palestine, and few Jews were permitted to enter the country. Young orphans were allowed to immigrate, so Chaim could enter but Peretz and Yonah had to remain in Cracow.

Time passed, and some of the Jews from Nachrovah who had not been with the partisans in the forest reached Cracow. The Jews from the forest surrounded them and asked where they had been taken to and where they had spent the remainder of the war. The ghetto Jews told the partisans the following story.

One day the Germans took all the Jews from the ghetto and commanded them to start walking. They walked until they reached the forest. Then they were commanded to dig a long, deep ditch. The Jews dug the ditch, not knowing what it was for. When the ditch was ready, the German commander summoned Mr. Shefler, the head of the Jewish Committee. Mr. Shefler approached the commander and stood at attention before him. The commander said, "I would like to thank Mr. Shefler, head of the Jewish Committee, for his faithful service on behalf of the German cause. All the Jews must follow Mr. Shefler's example." Mr. Shefler blushed at the commander's words and saluted him. The commander smiled and said, "Now Mr. Shefler will do as I command him, and everyone else will follow his example."

The officer commanded Mr. Shefler to stand at the edge of the ditch, facing the ditch. Mr. Shefler quickly followed the command, but the other Jews were in no hurry to do likewise. The commander began to scream at them at the top of his voice.

Some of the German soldiers and their Polish assistants began to hit the Jews on the head with the butts of rifles and to push them towards the ditch. A number of people, especially women and children, were killed during this attack. Those who were not killed were forcibly pushed to the edge of the pit. Those who remembered the *viduy*—the confession before death—by heart, recited it aloud. Those who couldn't recall the words thought about it in their hearts.

Suddenly a shot was heard. When they turned their heads to see whom the Germans had shot, they saw Mr. Shefler fall into the pit, face first. A great tumult arose. Most people were rooted to the ground, in terror, but some started to run. Those who didn't run away fell into the pit, one by one, after Mr. Shefler. Those who fled hid in the forest. Most of them survived for only two or three days at most. No one can live on air, and they dared not approach any settlement to get provisions.

But a few Jews survived for another two or three days, until the Russians entered Nachrovah. Then these Jews, whose souls were just about to depart from their bodies, were permitted to return to town. When they were well enough to stand on their own feet, they left Nachrovah in search of their brethren. They wandered from place to place until they ended up in Cracow, where they met Peretz and Yonah and the rest of the Jewish partisans, and told them their story. After Peretz heard the story of the ghetto Jews, he told them the story of the Jewish partisans.

Among the Jews who had come to Cracow and who listened to the stories of the ghetto Jews and the partisans were two men on whose left arms were tattooed blue numbers. The ghetto Jews and the partisans looked at the numbers questioningly. They had never before seen religious Jews with such tattoos. The two Jews told them, "We have come from Auschwitz." When the other Jews heard that, they were even more puzzled. What kind of answer was that? The two Jews with the tattoos then stood up and told their story.

They had been abducted from Nachrovah during one of the Germans' night excursions and had been sent to Auschwitz. Upon their arrival in Auschwitz, they met a population of thousands, almost all of them Jewish. Very few people died in Auschwitz. They were murdered before they had a chance to die. They were murdered very quietly. The voice which goes from one end of the world to the other when a soul leaves a body was not heard in Auschwitz. Hundreds of people were locked into a room. After a short time, when the door was opened, they were all found dead.

The dead were cremated in huge furnaces built especially for that purpose, and only their ashes remained.

This does not mean that everybody was murdered in the same way. In Auschwitz people were murdered by all kinds of cruel and terrible methods, but the gas chambers were the principal method.

The Jews listened to this story and lowered their eyes in pain and embarrassment — pain over what had happened to their martyred brothers, and embarrassment that they had told their own stories first. Compared to the story they heard from these two Jews, their own stories were like children's tales.

In Cracow, the Jews of Nachrovah found Jews who had been neither in Auschwitz, the ghetto, nor the forest. These Jews had been more fortunate. When the Germans and Russians divided up Poland between them, they found themselves living on the Russian side of the border. The Russians did not go so far as to put the Jews into a ghetto, but they did not trust them. They suspected the Jews of favoring the Germans, and so they exiled them all to Siberia. There, far away from the border, the Jews could not constitute a threat to Russia. The Jews from Siberia were unaware of what the Germans had done to their brothers in Nachrovah and Temyonovah. After the war, they were allowed to leave Siberia and to return to Poland, which had meanwhile been reunited in a pro-Russian Polish regime.

When the Auschwitz Jews heard the tales of the Jews from Siberia, they smiled and said, "We wish we had been with you. The cold of fear is much worse than the cold of snow." It was easier for the Jews in Russia to be afraid of dying from lack of food and lack of strength, than it was for the Jews in the ghetto to die of fear. You can only starve to death once, but you can die of fear many times.

On the other hand, when the Jews from Siberia heard the stories of the other Jews, they said, "We believe you, for we know you are honest, upright people and would not lie. Nevertheless, it's hard to accept what you have said. You must have exaggerated. Is it possible that such things as you have told really happened?" The other Jews tried, with little success, to prove to them that these things really had happened. The Siberian Jews listened patiently, but were not convinced. "Much of it is exaggerated," they said to themselves. It took a long time before they could really believe that there had been such a Holocaust.

The soil of Poland was soaked with Jewish blood; Jewish survivors could not remain there. The American Rescue Committee and the Jewish Agency transferred them to other countries — to France, Italy and, surprisingly, to Germany. Even though it was the Germans who had actually murdered the Jews, they had murdered more Jews in Poland than anywhere else in the world, thanks to Polish cooperation and encouragement.

When the State of Israel was proclaimed, the Jews from Auschwitz, the ghetto, the forest, and Siberia were finally permitted to immigrate to Israel. Those of them who had not already gone to America, now went to Israel. Every day a few more left. Those who didn't go immediately made their preparations. Preparations for *aliyah* are also a kind of *aliyah* because through these preparations their spirits rose even before their bodies made the actual physical *aliyah*. As time passed, almost everyone emigrated. A small group decided to remain in Poland and Germany, for reasons which remain beyond our comprehension.

When the immigrants arrived in Israel, they were housed in canvas tents and tin and wooden shacks and were given food. Quite some time would pass before they would receive permanent housing and jobs to support themselves. Houses must be built, and housing for all the Jews of Nachrovah could not be built in a day. Some of the immigrants complained, "After all we went through, the least we deserve is houses, not tents."

But Yonah told them, "Houses don't sprout up like mushrooms after the rain. They must be built, and that takes time. If you start today, you won't finish today. In a short time each one of us will have his own house, or at least a part of a house. Even in Nachrovah not everyone had his own home." When the Jews of Nachrovah heard what Yonah had to say, they realized he was right and stopped complaining.

Those Jews who were not working left their tents and shacks to explore the land and to see the Jewish state. The sight of signs hanging over storefronts printed in the holy tongue brought them back to life. In Nachrovah these letters had only been engraved on stone monuments for the dead; here they were engraved over the shops of the living. Passing a schoolyard, they saw crowds of children. When they listened to fragments of their conversation, they could understand very little. Yonah said, "From the little that I can grasp, I gather that they are speaking from their *siddurim* and *machzorim*. How nice that the children of Israel speak the language of the prayers of Israel." Each new thing they saw gave them cause to rejoice and forget their own problems.

Peretz also immigrated to Israel. He also toured the country, but he gave the dead precedence over the living — visiting them first. He went to Modi'in where the Maccabees were buried. Then he went to Jerusalem, where the members of the Sanhedrin were buried. After that, he went to Tiberias and Safed where the sages of the Mishnah and Talmud and other outstanding, righteous Jews were buried. He stood with awe and admiration beside the caves where Israel's heroes and great men were buried. Everything that he had heard from the stories of Reb Naftali the Dayan came to life. Stories could not be seen or touched, but graves can be both seen and touched.

After he had fulfilled his duty to the dead, he went to visit the living. He visited Tel Aviv, Haifa and other places. He couldn't grasp much of what he saw. Many things were very different here than in Nachrovah or Temyonovah. He saw teenagers who looked just like their Polish counterparts in Temyonovah. When he heard them talking to each other in the holy tongue, he was astounded. When he was told that these boys were Jewish, he exclaimed, "How wonderful that in Eretz Yisrael even the *goyim* are Jewish!"

After Peretz had seen the country, he remembered Chaim. He had been Chaim's guardian since Shimon's death, and now it was his obligation to locate him and look after him. He had heard from the Jewish Agency representative in Cracow that Chaim was studying in a *yeshivah*. At that time there were not many *yeshivoth* in Eretz Yisrael so it was quite easy to find him. After trying one or two places, Peretz found Chaim.

❧ 24 ❧ *Yank Shmendrikovitz*

Living together in canvas tents and wooden or tin shacks had united the Jews of Nachrovah physically and emotionally. When they finally received permanent housing, they separated, each one making his home in a different place.

In the beginning, they were so happy with their new houses that they thought of nothing else. But after a while, they began to miss the company of their *landsleit*. Nachrovah, the town they had known, no longer existed, but they couldn't forget it. It stood before their eyes even now, just as it had been before the Holocaust. They saw all the Jews of Nachrovah together in the synagogue. They saw all the Jewish houses and shops clustered around the market place, which was bustling on weekdays and quiet and peaceful on the Shabbath and holidays. They couldn't forget, nor did they want to. Living together, it had been easy to retain the feeling of Nachrovah. Each individual contributed his share, and the sum total of all their memories and recollections brought Nachrovah back to life.

Now that they had each gone their own way, they began to miss Nachrovah. Peretz had cursed Nachrovah and likened its fate to that of Sodom and Amorrah, but it was not the Jewish Nachrovah he had cursed; it was the Polish town, built upon the ruins of Jewish Nachrovah.

Peretz suggested, "Let us hold a convention of all the Jews from Nachrovah in Eretz Yisrael once a year. The sight of our *landsleit* will remind us again of Nachrovah." Peretz himself was from Temyonovah, but from the time that the Jews of the two cities were united in the forest, the towns themselves were considered as one.

The tenth of Teveth was chosen as the date for the convention of Jews from Nachrovah. This date had been designated by the Israeli Chief Rabbinate as the date upon which *Kaddish* would be recited for all Jews murdered by the Nazis. It would be appropriate for all the Jews of Nachrovah to recite *Kaddish* together for the martyred of their town.

Long after each meeting, memories of Jewish Nachrovah would remain before their eyes, as if the town were still there, and they would recall it lovingly. The Poles had succeeded in banishing the Jews from Nachrovah, but they could not succeed in banishing the memory of Nachrovah from its Jewish survivors. This annual meeting became an institution for the Jews from Nachrovah, held in a different place each year. It was their way of keeping the town alive.

But each year fewer and fewer people came to the convention on the tenth of Teveth. They did not forget their city, Heaven forbid. But each year the Angel of Death visited another few Jews whom the Nazis had not succeeded in wiping out. Their children, who were born in Israel, didn't attend the conventions. They had never seen Nachrovah and had no memories to relive.

One year a new member appeared. A gray-bearded Jew of about fifty entered, took a chair, and sat alone in the back of the hall. Observing him closely, it was obvious that he didn't understand what was being said, even though he was listening intently. Everyone was puzzled by this new guest. Usually Jews of one town do not attend the conventions of another. Was this Jew from Nachrovah? They glanced at him out of the corners of their eyes in order not to embarrass him, but no one could recognize him. They queried each other, but no one knew who he was.

There was something else which puzzled them. When they all rose to recite the *Kaddish*, he also rose. But he did not say a word. This was beyond comprehension. How could a Jew attending a memorial meeting listen to everyone recite *Kaddish* and not join in?

During the meeting, no one approached him. There was still the possibility that someone in the audience would identify their strange guest and inform the others. By the end of the meeting no one had. Finally, Yonah approached the guest. Before asking his name he gazed wonderingly into the man's face, which seemed familiar. The guest returned his gaze with a smile. Seeing that Yonah could not recall his name, the guest said in Polish, "Don't you remember me? I am from Nachrovah. My name is Ya'akov Shimeonovitz."

Yonah could not recall anyone in Nachrovah by that name. When the others saw Yonah talking to the guest, many of them approached, and stood in a circle surrounding them. Yonah turned to the circle and asked, "Do any of you know Ya'akov Shimeonovitz of Nachrovah?"

Someone asked, "What was his father's name?" The

guest answered with a smile, "My father was Shimon the *maskil.*" He pronounced the last word with a Yiddish accent.

His answer elicited shouts of surprise, "Mr. Shmendrikovitz, Mr. Shmendrikovitz!"

The guest said, "Don't call me Mr. Shmendrikovitz. Call me Ya'akov Shimeonovitz."

The circle did not disperse. Ya'akov Shimeonovitz stopped smiling. He rolled back his shirt sleeve and showed them the number tattooed on his left arm. Then he began to talk. Yes, he had been in Auschwitz. With his own eyes he had seen men, women and children brought into the gas chambers. With his own eyes he had seen them cremated afterwards. He had also seen people murdered in various other ways. In those days he had asked himself, "How could Christians, whose religion preaches mercy, do such cruel things?" Then he had examined his own heart. Realizing that he didn't believe in Jesus at all, he returned to Judaism. His own life had been saved miraculously, and he was one of the few who had survived the camps.

Ya'akov stopped talking and waited for questions. He knew that the Jews of Nachrovah had a great deal to ask him. When asked why he hadn't returned to Nachrovah, to his wife and daughter, after leaving Auschwitz, Ya'akov replied, "I did return to Nachrovah. When I entered my house, my wife and daughter weren't at home. Only Stashek, my brother-in-law, was there. When Stashek saw me he grabbed a knife and was about to kill me. I fled from the house and never returned. I know that Marussa will never return to me, nor will she give me Yanka. I wrote to her afterwards, while I was still in Poland, and I also wrote from here, but I have never received any response. She doesn't want to answer me." He paused and then added, "Or possibly Stashek never showed her my letters." He sighed and added again, "I made a great mistake in my life. Now I am left with nothing. I don't believe in Christianity, and I don't know anything about Judaism. I don't even know how to say *Kaddish*. I have lost both worlds."

The Jews of Nachrovah saw that Ya'akov Shimeonovitz had truly repented. They tried to forget the hard feelings they had held against him in their hearts all these years, and to replace them with a bit of love. Someone asked, "Mr. Shimeonovitz, why didn't you ever come to our meetings before?"

Ya'akov answered, "I never came before because I was embarrassed. Everyone wants to be seen at his best, not his worst. Do you know why I came today? I came because I had a dream. In my dream, my father appeared to me. He had a beard — not the short little beard that he had during his lifetime, but a long, Jewish beard — with a *tallith* around his shoulders and *tefillin* on his head.

"When he saw how amazed I was to see him with a long beard, *tallith*, and *tefillin* — things he never wore while he was alive — he smiled and said, 'Ya'akov, my son, I made a big mistake in my life. I thought Jews could live together with Christians. I didn't know the Christians. I made a mistake. You, who know them, flee from them if you want to live. Go to the Jews. Your place is with them.' When my father disappeared I opened my eyes and recalled the dream. That very day I read in the newspaper that the Jews of Nachrovah were holding a convention today, and so I overcame my embarrassment and attended. Now I feel better. I have fulfilled my father's wish."

When Ya'akov finished talking, the circle quietly dispersed. Ya'akov went home to his one-room flat with Peretz accompanying him. On the way, Peretz spoke to Ya'akov about Brachah and asked him if he would write one more letter to Marussa asking, incidentally, about Brachah. Perhaps this time Brachah's merits would guide the letter to Marussa's hands and help both of them. Ya'akov listened to Peretz and promised to fulfill his request, even though he himself had lost all hope of finding a way to Marussa's heart. Peretz gave Ya'akov his own address, said goodbye, and returned to his own home, which was also in Tel Aviv.

Ya'akov kept his promise. The very next day he sat down and wrote to Marussa, repeating everything that he had written in his previous letters. At the end of the letter he added a question about Brachah, the daughter of Yudel and Esther Glick. Did Marussa have any idea where she was today?

One afternoon, a month later, Ya'akov returned home from work and found a letter in his mailbox. Looking at the envelope, he recognized Marussa's handwriting. With trembling hands, he opened the envelope. In his excitement, his eyes were momentarily blurred, so that it took a few moments until he could read.

My dear Yank,

When I saw your handwriting, I almost fainted. I had always believed that you were no longer alive. When I recovered, I read and reread your letter, and even now I still cannot believe in my good fortune. This is the only letter I have ever received from you since your abduction from the ghetto of Nachrovah. The previous letters you spoke of never reached me. I miss you very much. I will do all I can to come to you in the Holy Land.

Yanka has written a few words at the end of my letter. Much has happened to us. My parents passed away a few years ago. Stashek is married and lives in the left wing of the house while Yanka and I live in the right. Three months ago Stashek and his wife went abroad to study and they have not yet returned.

With great longing and hopes to see you soon,

Marussa

P.S. Concerning Brachah, I can only tell you that her name was changed to Barbara Sokolsky, and she immigrated to the Holy Land about a year ago.

M.

Dear Father,

My happiness knows no bounds. I have been reborn. Now I have a father. I am studying and trying to be a good student. I will help Mother try to come to you soon, with all my might. Be strong and well and wait for us. We will surely come.

Your loving daughter,

Yanka

That very day, Ya'akov went to tell Peretz about the letter. Peretz read the lines about Brachah and was overcome with surprise and happiness. Early the next morning he traveled to Jerusalem to tell Chaim that his sister Brachah was in Israel.

Chaim was now learning in the famous *yeshivah*, Yeshivath haMathmidim. When Chaim heard Peretz's news, he closed his *gemara* and went with Peretz to the offices of the Jewish Agency. They wanted to look through the list of Polish immigrants and see exactly when Barbara Sokolsky had arrived in Israel and where she was now. But no such name appeared on the Jewish Agency list. Chaim was terribly disappointed. Peretz immediately returned to Tel Aviv to ask Ya'akov to write a second letter to Marussa, asking for the exact details of Barbara Sokolsky's immigration. Meanwhile Chaim returned to his study of *gemara*. His hope had been strengthened. Brachah was alive and in Eretz Yisrael, and with God's help, he would find her yet.

Why didn't Marussa write Yank that Barbara Sokolsky had not immigrated through the Jewish Agency, but rather in the service of the Catholic Church? Perhaps she didn't write about it because she too was a Catholic and didn't want to disturb the Catholic missionary activity. She was obligated to answer the question about Brachah truthfully, since Brachah had been entrusted to her care, but she was not obligated to reveal the secrets of the Catholic mission.

There were four members in the Feldsher family: Marcus, his wife, Rosa, and their daughters, Sabina and Coralla. Marcus was a little over forty, and Rosa was a little under forty. Sabina was twelve and Coralla ten. They had only been in the country for a few months. The Jewish Agency had found them in one of the refugee camps in Germany and had put them on a boat to Israel.

Before the war, the Feldsher family had lived in Pihokovah, a small town with a small population, many of whom were Jews. The non-Jews were farmers, and the Jews were merchants or craftsmen. Marcus was a barber whose services were needed by all. Every Jew in Pihokovah had to have a haircut before the holiday, and some shaved their beards or had them trimmed every Friday in honor of the Sabbath. Non-Jews also needed a barber once in a while. Of course, Marcus couldn't get rich by being a barber. It is doubtful if he could even have supported himself at all had he not had a few other skills on the side. On Sundays and Wednesdays he dealt in medicine and bloodletting for a few important householders. He could have done this on Fridays too, but on Fridays, he was busy with haircuts and shaves and had no time for anything else.

And any Jew who was kept awake by a toothache during a long winter night, and who was reminded of the saying of our Sages, "Man would have been better off had he not been created," would rise with the first crow of the rooster, gather up his courage, and wake up Marcus to take care of his tooth. Marcus was not in favor of prolonged treatments. He would hide a tiny set of tongs in the sleeve of his white coat and would tell his patient to recite, "Open your mouth and let your teeth shine."

Marcus would then act quickly and the Jew would cry "Oy!" Before he could cry "Oy!" a second time, Marcus would smile and show him his tooth caught in the tongs, as if to say, "There is no more reason to cry 'Oy.'" Truth to tell, Marcus did not really deceive his customers. Everyone in town was aware of Marcus's method of treating toothache. Nevertheless, when the time came, everyone was willing to be deceived. Apparently it was easier that way. It took too much courage to look straight at the tongs. From all of these occupations, Marcus managed to eke out a respectable living.

He was not very stringent in his observance of the *mitzvoth*. As a matter of fact, he was as lenient as he could be. He had sinned by shaving off Jewish beards and had repeated this act so many times that other prohibitions also seemed permissible to him. But every Shabbath and holiday he came to the synagogue. There he had a seat among the important householders, and this in itself sufficed to draw him there. Compared to the pharmacist, Pan Isaak, Marcus was extremely religious. Pan Isaak attended synagogue only once a year, on Yom Kippur, while Marcus came every

Shabbath and holiday. Since he was more "Jewish" than the pharmacist, he was not called "Pan."

During the war, Marcus and his family suffered much. After the war, Marcus saw that many Jews were immigrating to Israel, and he thought, "What shall I do in a Poland without Jews? My whole livelihood depends on Jews. The Poles don't let blood or have toothaches. My place is among the Jews." He acted accordingly and immigrated together with the others to Eretz Yisrael.

Marcus received a two-room apartment and, after much effort, a store in the neighborhood shopping center to open a barbershop. At first he blessed the Jews and their state, but he was soon disillusioned. He couldn't make a living from his trade in his neighborhood. All the men worked outside of the neighborhood, and if they needed a shave or a haircut, they would get one near their place of work. Neither did the Jews in the neighborhood have time to let blood. Anyone who had a toothache would go into town to an expert dentist who would treat the tooth for several months before extracting it.

Greatly disappointed, Marcus went to the Jewish Agency office and complained to the clerks that he had been misled. Had he known what the situation was, he wouldn't have come. The clerks answered him, "You're not the only one with complaints. Many people are dissatisfied. Many have complained before you and surely many will complain in the future. Do what everyone else does."

Marcus asked, "And what does everyone else do?"

They answered, "A person who needs to support himself takes any work that he can find."

Marcus was insulted by this advice and thought to himself, "These clerks don't know me and don't know how important and respected I was in Pihokovah, or they would never speak to me like this." At first he was about to tell them who he was and what he had done in Pihokovah. Then he decided not to say anything. It was beneath his dignity. He had heard that others in the same position banged their fists on the clerks' desks, and if necessary even lifted a chair and threw it at the clerk's head, but he would not do such a thing. It was beneath his dignity. Marcus, his heart bitter, left the clerks and knew not where to turn.

We have no idea how the missionaries discovered that Marcus was so bitter, but it makes no difference. They found out and they sent an agent to him.

One day, someone knocked on Marcus's door. Marcus was sitting at home, pondering his sad plight. He called out in a loud voice, "*Ken*," one of the few Hebrew words he had learned from his daughters. The door opened and a tall thin man entered. Marcus looked at him and saw that he was not one of the neighbors. He knew them all already. Seeing that he was a stranger, Marcus motioned to a chair and invited his guest to sit down. The man thanked him and began to speak in a weak, thin, voice, counting his words as though they were pearls. Marcus strung the words together and gathered that the guest was asking if he, Marcus, would agree to accept help in his plight.

Marcus was insulted. To take help from others? Was he a beggar, Heaven forbid, to take help from others? Nevertheless, he showed no signs of being insulted nor did he insult his guest. He was depressed after his conversation with the clerks, and he restrained himself. First he would hear what the man had to say.

Marcus asked, "What do you wish to do for me?"

The guest answered, "If you are interested in emigrating to another country, we will help you."

When Marcus heard that, he felt differently. This was a very dignified offer. After all, even rich people who want to emigrate need help. Marcus asked, "Which country can you help me reach?"

The guest answered, "We can bring you to many countries."

Marcus asked, "For instance?"

The guest answered, "For instance, Brazil."

When Marcus heard that, he was ready to jump for joy, but he restrained himself. It was beneath his dignity. Just then, Marcus recalled that he had not asked his guest's name or whom he represented. Marcus said, "Excuse me, sir. Please tell me who you are, and what your name is."

The guest answered, "My name is Peter." Marcus looked at him, surprised. The man spoke Yiddish as well as any Jew, but he had never heard of any Jew with a name like Peter. Peter saw his surprise and said, "My name used to be Shimon, but after I came to the truth, I changed my name to Peter."

Marcus asked, "What truth do you mean?"

Peter answered, "I mean the truth of Christianity." Marcus began to ponder his words and didn't know what to say further. Peter said, "All that we ask of you is to accept our help. Jesus commanded us to help others, and we are fulfilling his command. We don't ask anything from you but to believe in Jesus. That belief is sufficient for us."

Marcus sat there, not knowing what to answer. On the one hand, the offer was incredible — to send him to Brazil. On the other hand, he was a Jew and didn't believe in Jesus. Although he was not strictly observant, he did believe in God. When Peter saw his bewilderment, he said, "You don't have to believe in Jesus wholeheartedly. You merely need a document stating that you have been baptized a Catholic. That's all you have to do."

After pondering this for a while, Marcus said, "I need time to think about this. Please come back in three days' time."

Peter rose, offered his hand to Marcus, smiled and said "Shalom." Marcus shook his hand weakly and Peter left. It must be noted that Marcus was not inclined to follow Peter, but he didn't have the courage to refuse his help.

When Rosa returned home shortly after, Marcus told her all that had happened. Rosa didn't think twice. "Thank God!" she said.

Marcus asked, "Why are you thanking God?"

Rosa replied, "I thank God for sending us an angel of mercy. I owe so much money to the grocer that I have no idea how to pay the debt." Marcus, seeing that his wife was in favor of accepting Peter's help, began to doubt himself. Perhaps Rosa was right?

That very evening Peter came by with a large package of food and clothing. Had he brought the package in the morning, Marcus would have thrown him out of the house. He was not a beggar. But now that they were discussing the possibility of emigration to Brazil, the matter of the package

186 / *The Twins*

was of secondary importance. Peter would not sit down, as he was in a hurry. He didn't want to influence Marcus in any way. In matters like this one must be guided by one's own conscience.

Sabina and Coralla were home when Peter came. They saw the man and the package and heard what he said. They knew something had happened at home that they were unaware of, and their curiosity was aroused. Listening in on their parents' conversation after the man had gone, they realized that their parents were thinking of leaving Israel. This possibility saddened them. They had good teachers and close friends from whom they didn't want to part.

For three days and three nights doubt gnawed at Marcus's heart unmercifully, until it seemed to him that it would eat away a hole. Rosa's heart remained untouched. She tried to convince Marcus that what Peter was asking was not such a terrible thing. What difference did a piece of paper make? In his heart, he could remain the same as he had always been. Rosa's tongue was as soft as butter as she tried to help both her husband and Peter.

Nevertheless, when Peter returned three days later, Marcus answered neither yes or no. The three days had not been sufficient for him to reach a decision. Rosa, who had made sure she would be home then, began to answer yes. Marcus gave her a sharp look, and she refrained. She both respected and feared her husband, and he didn't allow her to dominate him.

This time, also, Peter had not come empty-handed. The package he brought only served to increase Marcus's agitation. Nevertheless, he could not bring himself to say yes.

When Peter saw that Marcus was not so easily convinced, he changed his tactics and said, "If you are not willing to accept the offer we made to you, perhaps we can help you in a different manner." When Marcus heard that his eyes lit up. What a relief that Peter had dropped the idea of baptism. Had he kept on discussing it, Marcus might have given in. Now he listened carefully to Peter's new proposal. Peter said, "We will accept your daughters in our school, tuition free. They will also eat there and receive proper clothing for free."

When Marcus heard this proposal, a great stone was lifted from his heart. He saw nothing wrong with this idea, and he could not refuse the good-hearted Peter another time.

Marcus quickly answered yes like one who is afraid of missing his chance. Rosa nodded her agreement and Peter smiled with satisfaction.

Marcus accompanied his daughters to their new school in Jerusalem. After Peter had gone that evening, he realized that he had acted hastily in agreeing so quickly but to change his mind now would be beneath his dignity. He could not hesitate and waver all the time. Nevertheless he wanted to see with his own eyes what the place was like.

They reached Jerusalem towards evening, as Peter had advised him. When they reached the Convent of St. Paul it was already dark outside. Marcus's heart was filled with impressions of his trip. This was the first time he had traveled to Jerusalem, and he was greatly affected by the Judean hills. They did not look like any other place that he had seen before in Eretz Yisrael. The other scenery in Eretz Yisrael resembled similar views all over the world, but these hills seemed to be shrouded in mystery. Wherever there is mystery, there is sanctity. As he rode in the bus, he looked out the window with awe.

At that time he thanked God that he had not succumbed to Peter's enticements and had not agreed to detach himself from the Jewish people. This sanctity of the Judean hills belonged to the Jewish people and to himself.

One who cut himself off from the Jews would have no part in the sanctity of these hills. Jewish heroes such as the Maccabees had fought for these hills. The *Beith haMikdash* had been in Jerusalem. As long as he remained Jewish he would always have a share in this. How stupid Peter was to have broken away from all of this. Marcus lost his respect for Peter and regretted that he had not refused the offer of the school, too. But now it was too late. He was already in Jerusalem and was obliged to enter the school and see for himself what kind of people would be educating his daughters. Now and then Marcus gazed at his daughters' eyes and saw their dejection. Probably they were depressed that he had taken them out of the Shivath Tzion school. Were they right? Was a Catholic mission school the proper place for Jewish girls?

Lost in his thoughts, Marcus found himself standing before the narrow gate of a large courtyard, his two daughters beside him. At this time of day, the gate was not locked so he opened it, and they entered. Deep inside stood a building. They approached it and stood before a heavy, locked door. Marcus rang the doorbell. The tall young man who opened the door asked whom they wished to see. Marcus quietly answered that Peter had told him to bring his two daughters here. When the man heard Peter's name he smiled thinly and invited them inside. Then he closed the door and led them along a long, dark hallway. When he knocked, someone inside answered, "Yes." The young man opened the door, showed Marcus and the girls inside, and closed the door after them.

Sitting at a massive desk inside the room was a middle-aged man, a huge cross hanging on his chest. When Marcus saw the cross he had an urge to run away, but felt it was beneath his dignity. The girls looked at each other in amazement.

Lucas, the head of the convent, offered Marcus a chair. Marcus hesitantly approached and sat down. The girls remained standing. Lucas asked, "What do you wish, good sir?"

Marcus answered, "Peter sent me here."

Lucas said, "Then you want to enroll your daughters in our school." Marcus nodded his head in agreement but did not say a word. Lucas pressed a button on the table, and in a few seconds the door opened and a dark haired girl of about twenty appeared at the door. Lucas gestured to her and she entered. Lucas, looking at the girl and pointing to Marcus, said, "This good man has brought you two new pupils." Barbara looked at the girls and smiled.

"Sit down, Barbara," said Lucas. Barbara took a seat opposite Marcus and gestured to the girls to sit down on the chairs along the wall.

Suddenly Barbara turned to Marcus and asked him in Yiddish what his name was. Marcus lost his wits. So far the conversation had been in Polish. That was understandable. These people were apparently Catholics from Poland. But what connection did Catholics have with Yiddish? The girls also looked at Barbara in astonishment. Marcus didn't answer her question. He was so taken aback by her Yiddish that he completely forgot that he had been asked a question. Barbara smiled warmly and repeated her query, which he now answered. She then asked, "Are you Jewish?"

This time Marcus nodded his head in affirmation. Barbara said, "I, too, am Jewish."

At this, Marcus breathed deeply and said "Yes?" in a questioning tone.

Barbara laughed and said, "What is so surprising? The first Christians were all Jewish. Even Jesus Christ was Jewish."

Actually, Barbara had not told him anything new, and he wondered that he had never before been aware of the close relationship between Jews and Christians until Barbara had spelled it out. They had always seemed to him to be worlds apart. Now Barbara had come and broken down the barrier separating them.

Then Barbara turned to the girls and asked them in Hebrew for their names, ages and grades in school. The girls answered the questions with no hesitation. Barbara's Hebrew attracted them to her very much. Sabina said that she was twelve and in sixth grade. Coralla said that she was ten and in fourth grade. Marcus wondered to himself whether they really spoke Hebrew in the convent. Barbara said, "If you agree to entrust me with the education of these lovely girls, I shall be delighted. And we will also teach them Hebrew."

Marcus was deeply touched by and appreciative of this lovely girl who was so anxious to teach his two daughters, tuition free. He could not speak, and his eyes filled with tears — not tears of sorrow, but tears of gratitude. Barbara said, "I see that you agree to entrust me with the girls and I am very happy. You can go home with a quiet heart. Your girls are in good hands."

Marcus arose, went over to the girls and kissed them, and then nodded to the man with the cross, thanking him in Polish. Finally he bowed to Barbara and thanked her in Yiddish, choosing this language to emphasize his warm feelings towards her and the confidence she had inspired in him. Barbara smiled at Marcus as if to say, "I understand you." She escorted him to the door, and he left the building.

All the way home from Jerusalem, Marcus was very happy. Barbara's image stood before him the whole way, never leaving him. "Such a fine young Jewish woman! There are few like her," thought Marcus. "There can be no danger in entrusting the education of my daughters to a girl like that." He was so deeply absorbed by these thoughts that he forgot to look out the window at the Judean hills. Soon the trip was over and he was home.

But Marcus did not sleep peacefully that night. As a matter of fact, he hardly slept at all. After he told Rosa all that had happened to him in Jerusalem, repeating everything that he had seen and heard there, the scenes repeated themselves in his dreams and disturbed his sleep. Rosa, on the other hand, was extremely happy and accused her husband of not having trusted Peter. She had had faith in him from the very beginning. The plan to go to Brazil was also a very good one. Marcus answered, "Even if Brazil was a good idea, I have no intention of taking the girls out of their new school, so there is no point in discussing any trip now."

Sabina and Coralla received clean beds for the night and fine new clothes for the day, and they were happy. Nevertheless, they also had a few unpleasant surprises. There were forty girls in the school, thirty of them Jewish. Before bedtime, all the girls knelt down before an icon of the mother and child in the corner of the room and recited prayers. Sabina and Coralla were angry and upset. They knew that Jews do not kneel during prayers nor do they stand in front of any picture while praying. In the Shivath Tzion school they had studied the Torah which commands, "You shall not make for yourself any statue or picture." In their bewilderment they looked to Barbara who herself was kneeling with the other girls. They saw that she was smiling at them, and they were reassured. If Barbara agreed to such practice, perhaps there was no harm in it.

On Shabbath there were no special prayers. It was just like every other day of the week. On Sunday a festive prayer service was held. The girls all kneeled for a long time, singing hymns. Whenever Sabina and Coralla saw strange things in their new school and were not sure how to behave, they turned to Barbara. She was Jewish so she would tell them if it was right for them or not. They did not ask her with words, but with their eyes. She answered them in the same way, not with her mouth, but with her eyes. Barbara's warm smile sanctioned the practices of the convent, and her approval allayed their anxiety. The girls trusted her completely because she was Jewish. She knew better than they did what actions befitted Jewish girls.

Of course Sabina and Coralla were homesick for their parents and their friends from the Shivath Tzion school. Once, they appealed to Barbara, and she promised to allow them to go home for a visit when the time came. The girls didn't know when this would be, but they rejoiced in the promise. They saw that none of the other girls went home and realized that that was the rule of this school. The fact that they were no exception comforted them.

Marussa and Yanka were planning to immigrate to Israel, to be with Yank. Marussa was in a great hurry. She had to leave the house before Stashek returned home. She had no doubt that if Stashek were home he would do everything in his power to prevent her from going to Israel. She didn't hold it against him. She could actually even sympathize with him. This move would stain their family name with a stain which could never be erased. It was no small thing for a Polish Catholic woman to be the wife of a Jew and live in a Jewish state. Nevertheless she was not willing to abandon Yank. She knew that this was also the best thing for her daughter, Yanka. More than once Yanka had been insulted by her Polish schoolmates, who called her "Jidovka"—dirty Jew.

Even in post-war Poland, under a pro-Russian regime, Jews were not loved. Marussa didn't know whose fault this was, but she knew it was a fact. She had been told that even in Russia itself there was anti-Semitism. This was a bit hard for her to believe. She had always heard the Poles accusing the Jews of being Communists. If so, the Communists should like the Jews. But she was no expert in politics, and all the explanations that she had heard about anti-Semitism made no sense to her.

In actuality, it made no difference to her whether the anti-Semites were right or not. All that mattered to her was that the Jews were hated everywhere, and that her daughter was considered a Jew. She was not willing for Yanka to be at the mercy of other people's hate. Until now she had been powerless to help Yanka and had tried to ignore her troubles, but now that Yank was alive and living in the Jewish state, she must take Yanka there as well. Then she would never again have to hear anyone call her "Jidovka."

Yank's latest letter inspired Marussa to work even harder to leave Poland. He described the country as being very beautiful. He wrote of the tall buildings being erected, the public parks and lovely wide boulevards in the larger towns; the *kibbutzim* and *moshavim* whose members worked with great enthusiasm.

Marussa assumed that Yank had exaggerated greatly. She wasn't foolish enough to believe every word of the letter. After all, no one can change his skin, and she had known Jews for a long time. She couldn't believe that Jews could build houses with their own hands. She had never even seen a Jew on a scaffold. The business about Jews on *kibbutzim* and *moshavim* was also not clear to her. A Jew working in the field? A Jew milking a cow? A Jew raising chickens? None of these was work for a Jew. Least of all could she believe in the parks. She laughed at the picture of a Jew holding a flower. Yank had just written these things to heighten her desire to join him. Nevertheless, he couldn't be making it all up. He was certainly exaggerating, but there must be a grain of truth in it. Even one grain of truth made her very curious to see it all with her own eyes.

Yanka also encouraged her mother to act. In her first letter she had promised her father that she would do so, and she kept her promise. She, too, could not ignore the name "Jidovka" which she was called from time to time. True, it did not affect her as strongly as it did her mother. She told herself that it was true and nothing to be ashamed of. Nevertheless, she was hurt because she knew that those who called her names intended to insult her.

When Marussa reached Yank's question about Brachah at the end of his letter, she was disconcerted. Was it her duty to write that Barbara had gone to the Holy Land in the service of the mission, and not with the Jews? After all, she herself was a Catholic. How could she reveal matters which the Church wanted kept secret? At first she thought that she would simply ignore the question. It would look as if she had just forgotten to answer one part of the letter. Later she decided to give an unclear answer. She would write that since she was to immigrate to Israel as quickly as possible, there was no need to answer this question in writing. She would tell him everything she knew about Barbara Sokolsky once she arrived in Israel. Whoever was waiting for Barbara had already waited a long time and could wait a little bit longer. Once she had seen Yank in person she would decide whether she should tell him the whole story or withhold part of it. She would know then who was waiting for Barbara and whether there was any danger to Barbara in revealing all that she, Marussa, knew about her. For now, she would keep her secret.

Marussa had already visited the capital several times in order to speed up the arrangements for her journey. Each time she made the trip she did so secretly because she was afraid that if her neighbors ever found out, they would not hesitate to ridicule and scorn her. To them, immigration to the Jewish state was equivalent to becoming Jewish. They would consider her a heretic. She also feared that if her travel plans became known, Stashek would find out and return home to prevent her passage. No one must find out until she had left Nachrovah.

Unfortunately, all her precautions were to no avail. It can only be guessed how her secret was exposed. One possibility is that the postman suspected something. Marussa — like many other people — received letters from abroad from time to time. As long as the letters came infrequently, they aroused no curiosity; but when they began to arrive regularly, the postman began to wonder. What connection did Marussa, whose parents and grandparents had been born in Nachrovah, have abroad? The postman searched for a return address on the envelope, but found none. This seemed quite strange to him, for it was customary to write the name and address of the sender on the back of the envelope so that in case the letter could not be delivered, it could be returned.

Next, the postman examined the writing on the stamp but did not recognize its large strange letters. He looked more closely and found small print in Latin letters below the stamp. These letters formed the word Israel. The postman knew that Israel was the Jewish state, and he wondered what connection Polish Marussa had with Jewish Israel.

When he returned home from work, he discussed this with his neighbors, and they discussed it with their friends until all Nachrovah assumed that Marussa was about to go to

Israel. Whom could she have in Israel? That they didn't know. As far as they knew, Yank Shmendrikovitz had been murdered together with all the other Jews of the ghetto. It must be one of Yank's relatives who was writing to her. Although no one knew what was written in the letters, they guessed that she wanted to go to Israel. Had she been a good Catholic, she would never have corresponded with a Jew. If she was writing to them, her heart must be with them. Yank had poisoned her heart, and she couldn't free herself from Jewish sorcery. True, she had brought Barbara to the convent and had been present at her baptism, but that was only for the sake of keeping up appearances. In her heart she was Jewish, and as such, she was a traitor.

No one approached Marussa, but she read in their eyes their knowledge of her secret. She read both scorn and hatred, and she knew she must leave Nachrovah as quickly as possible. Every additional day that she remained endangered her journey. It was even possible that someone had already notified Stashek, or had set some other pitfall for her. The sooner she left, the better.

Marussa traveled to the capital once more. From there she sent her last letter to Yank, asking him not to write any more to Nachrovah, for her secret had been exposed and his letters might even be opened. If it were known who was writing and exactly what her plans were, it could harm her. Aside from that, there was no need for him to write any more, for the passport agency had promised that she could leave Poland in two months on a plane to Rome, and from there she would make her way to Israel.

Marussa returned to Nachrovah with mixed feelings of

happiness and fear—happiness that she now knew the date of her departure and fear that something would happen at the last minute—or that Stashek would return just before she had left.

Marussa was not in an enviable position in those days. The number of days seemed endless. Each one was fifty years long. The nights were no better. Various strange dreams—both good and bad—disturbed her sleep, and from time to time she would wake up, excited, her heart beating fast.

Sometimes, in her dreams, she would see herself walking down the sun-drenched streets of Israel, Yank on one side of her, Yanka on the other. Yank would be telling her all he had gone through during the years they had been separated and she would be listening and sighing. She would be sighing, not from grief, but from relief that it was all over and had ended happily.

In another dream, she saw Stashek, his face ablaze, run to the kitchen and grab a long knife to murder her for wanting to go to the Jewish state. Suddenly Yank was standing beside her, and she was afraid that Stashek would murder Yank. In her terror she began to scream. At that moment she felt a caress. A soft hand touched her gently. When Marussa opened her eyes she saw her daughter's hand, as Yanka said, "Mother, you must have had a bad dream."

When the day of departure arrived, there was no one happier than Marussa. Had the wait been any longer, she might not have endured.

Sabina and Coralla had not returned home for over two months, although the girls had written several times that they would come, and Rosa missed them. Rosa began to be angry with the convent staff for not permitting her daughters even a short visit home. "Don't they understand a mother's heart?" she asked herself. Nevertheless, she didn't discuss her feelings with Marcus. She didn't want to give him any reason to find fault with Peter, as she had not yet given up her hope that he would sent them to Brazil. Although she would not allow herself to express her anger at the mission staff, she still could tell Marcus how much she missed her daughters. One day, Rosa suggested, "Shouldn't we go to Jerusalem to visit our girls?"

"Yes," Marcus answered, "Let's go."

"When?" asked Rosa.

"Tomorrow," answered Marcus. "I have no work today and will have none tomorrow. At least I have plenty of time to travel."

Rosa comforted him, "Don't be discouraged, Marcus. You will have work yet. Peter is a good man and he won't forget us."

The next day Marcus and Rosa set out for Jerusalem. They left early in the morning in order to return home that same day. Last time Marcus had returned home late at night and had just managed to catch the last bus from Jerusalem to Tel Aviv; had he been any later he would have had to stay in Jerusalem overnight. This time they would have to be more careful. They didn't know anyone in Jerusalem, and they surely couldn't afford a hotel.

The sun climbed over the Judean hills, playing a game of light and shade. Rosa looked at the hills but saw nothing special. Marcus, also looking at the scenery, wondered why these hills made no impression on him now, when the first time he had not been able to take his eyes off them. Was it because he had already seen them once before? Perhaps. But it seemed to him that it also had to do with the convent. Since he had enrolled his daughters in the mission, these hills had lost their beauty for him. Now he recalled that he hadn't noticed the scenery on his way home from the convent either even though he had been sitting by the window the whole time. If one is not interested, he can look at something a million times, but not really see it even once.

Marcus and Rosa arrived in Jerusalem and transferred from the Egged bus to a Hamekasher bus which brought them to Inquisition Street. St. Paul's Convent was No. 6. As they approached the courtyard gate, the guard recognized Marcus and let them in. Sabina and Coralla were playing with the other girls. They were so absorbed in their game that they didn't notice their parents' entry.

Two young women came up to Marcus and Rosa and welcomed them. Marcus immediately recognized Barbara, the Jewess, and gave her a friendly smile. Barbara introduced them to Paulina, who was Sabina and Coralla's teacher. Paulina said, in a German that was similar to Yiddish, "You have lovely daughters."

Barbara added, "I also like them," and she smiled.

Rosa blushed, saying, "Lovely girls have lovely teachers."

Just then, Sabina and Coralla came running up and fell into their parents' arms with cries of joy. When they finally let go of their parents, Barbara told them something and they answered her gracefully. Marcus and Rosa listened, amazed. They knew that their daughters spoke Polish, Yiddish and Hebrew. Now they had spoken another language. When Rosa inquired, Barbara informed her that they were speaking French.

Marcus and Rosa asked simultaneously, an amazed expression on their faces, "French?"

Barbara said, "The girls have begun to learn French. We also teach foreign languages here." That was enough to make Rosa forgive the mission people for not letting the girls come home for a visit. Marcus licked his lips with his tongue and repeated the magic word, "French," in a whisper. Barbara didn't forget to add a few words in Yiddish. Although Rosa had already heard from her husband that there was a Jewish teacher in the convent who spoke Yiddish just like a Jew, now that she had heard her with her own ears, she could not help but be impressed. Barbara saw the impression she had made on Rosa with her Yiddish and realized her great power.

Barbara invited the guests into the house so that they

could rest up a bit from their trip and spend some time with their daughters. As they walked down the corridor, Lucas — a large gold cross on his chest — passed by and greeted them. Marcus returned his greeting with his head bowed, but Rosa did not answer him. Although she had known that this was a Jesuit convent, the actual sight of the cross confused and overwhelmed her. After Lucas had passed them, she regained control of herself and was ashamed of her behavior.

Marcus and Rosa spent two pleasant hours in the convent, their hearts happy and relieved. Everything was clean and neat. Everything here was respectable. People were generous and polite, wanting only to help them. The cross that Lucas, the chief clergyman, wore was a bit repugnant, but on the other hand, Barbara was Jewish and even spoke Yiddish. Before Marcus and Rosa left the convent, they went over to Barbara and asked her to allow the girls to come home for a visit once in a while. Barbara listened to their request and said, in Yiddish, "I have already promised them this more than once. Had you not come today, they would have gone to visit you tomorrow." Had anyone else said that to them, they probably would not have believed him, but because Barbara was a Jewish girl who only wanted to help them they believed her.

Sabina and Coralla walked with their parents to the courtyard gate and stopped there. Rosa tried to persuade them to accompany her and their father to the bus stop, but the girls shook their heads. When Marcus asked them why not, the girls said that they had already requested permission but Barbara would not allow it. Rosa was a bit surprised at this refusal, but she did not want to doubt Barbara's intentions. Perhaps it was not under Barbara's control. Rosa and Marcus took leave of their daughters with warm kisses and promises to come again to visit.

Marcus and Rosa had to stand in line to wait for the bus home. As the line got longer and longer, and the bus still didn't come, Marcus impatiently turned around to check the length of the line and express his bitterness over the bus's delay. His glance fell on a young man who happened to be standing just behind him in the line. Marcus was astounded. The young man was Chaim. Had it been a girl, Marcus would have cried, "Barbara!" but it was a boy who stood next to him, not a girl. It is not polite to stare at strangers, so Marcus looked away from Chaim. But he couldn't contain himself for long and he soon turned his head to glance at Chaim again. He tried to appear preoccupied so that the boy wouldn't notice his staring. His amazement grew greater and greater. Never in his life had he seen two people who resembled each other so much.

Marcus whispered to Rosa who was standing in front of him. A few seconds later, Rosa turned her head and looked, as if unintentionally, at the boy standing behind her husband. Marcus had used all his will power to keep himself from staring at the boy, but Rosa could not contain herself. Her curiosity was much too strong, and she turned her head a second time and stared at the boy until he was embarrassed.

Chaim realized that the couple in front of him were staring at him with great interest, and he wondered what they saw in him to make them stare so. He looked just like thousands of other young men his age. The bus finally arrived, and the people in front of Marcus and Rosa began to push forward. Marcus and Rosa, absorbed in looking at Chaim, didn't even notice the bus. They just moved forward automatically. As they drew nearer to the door of the bus, they began to turn their heads back and forth. They wanted to see when it was their turn to get on the bus, but they also wanted to look at Chaim as long as they could. Perhaps the boy would not be able to get on the bus.

Chaim wanted to ask them why they kept staring at him, but he was too shy. But finally he gathered up his courage and asked them what they were staring at. Marcus was taken aback by the question and didn't answer immediately. He hesitated and then said, "Today we saw a girl who looks just like you. You are as alike as two drops of water."

Chaim caught his breath and asked, his voice shaking, "Where did you see her?"

Marcus answered, "We saw her on Inquisition Street."

Chaim asked, "What's her name?"

Just then Rosa and Marcus reached the door of the bus and got on. Chaim also tried to get on, but the driver closed the door and he was left standing on the platform. His disappointment was unbearable. His heart cried out within him, and he began to pound the door of the bus, hoping the driver would open it and allow him to get on. But the bus began to move away.

In a little while, another bus arrived and Chaim got on. When he had calmed down a bit he recalled that the man had said that he had seen the girl on Inquisition Street. In his mind's eye, Chaim reviewed all the houses on that street until he reached the Jesuit convent. By this time, he already knew all of Jerusalem—all its streets, and all its houses. "Yes, on that street there is a convent." His heart began to beat fast. A convent. Who knows. Could it be Brachah? Could Brachah be in a convent? He became very excited. All the way to Tel Aviv he could not relax.

When he arrived at Peretz's house, Peretz came out to meet him sorrowfully. Peretz said, "A letter came from Marussa saying that she will arrive in Israel soon and then she will tell Yank all she knows about Barbara Sokolsky." Chaim told Peretz about the incident in the bus station in Jerusalem, and Peretz was infected by his excitement. "We must search for Brachah in Jerusalem," he said.

Eretz Yisrael was in an uproar. The mission had succeeded in infiltrating into many Jewish homes. The daily newspapers were full of accounts of the deeds of Peter and his friends. Many Jews had already left the country with their help, and many Jewish children had been lured into mission schools, where they were converted to Christianity and taught to hate those Jews who did not believe in Jesus. The newspapers asked, "Would Jews in a Gentile country dare to open missions and proselytize among the Gentiles?"

Both religious and non-religious Jews shared in the widespread sentiment of anger at the missionary activity. What was particularly disconcerting was the fact that the missionaries' methods were so deceitful and unscrupulous. They did not try to prove the truth of their beliefs in open discussion, but rather took advantage of the distress of the weak and poverty-stricken. A man who is starving for a loaf of bread and sees a package of food cannot judge impartially between truth and falsehood. A man who has found no gold in Eretz Yisrael may be blinded by the promise of gold abroad and he may not realize that he is being deceived.

The furor in the *yeshivoth* was even greater. These boys,

who were devoting all their time and strength to the study of Torah, could not forget that they had accepted upon themselves at Mount Sinai that dictum that, "All Jews are responsible for one another." They were not interested in proselytizing among the Gentiles, for whom observance of the seven *mitzvoth* of *bnei Noach* was sufficient, but they felt deeply the loss of each and every Jewish soul. Here there could be no compromise. The *yeshivah* boys couldn't hide their anger at the government which took no legal action to restrain the missionaries.

The students of Yeshivath haMathmidim were among the best in the country. They were also the leaders and the most active in the campaign to return Jews to their heritage. The students of this *yeshivah* were not content to simply express feelings of anger at the missions and at the inactivity of the government. One evening, they called a mass assembly of *yeshivah* students from all over the country to discuss missionary activity. They intended to develop a campaign to fight the missionaries, whose honey-coated tongues dripped lies and deceit.

Chaim came to the assembly. Each time he heard the word "mission," he felt as though someone had stabbed his flesh with a dagger. After the incident the day before in the bus station, Brachah had not left his thoughts. He pictured her with a cross hanging about her neck. As he put together all the details he had gathered about her, his conviction that Brachah was caught in the net of the mission became stronger and stronger. She had been in non-Jewish hands in Nachrovah. Her name had been changed to a Polish name, Barbara Sokolsky. She had immigrated to Eretz Yisrael, but not through the Jewish Agency. The man whom he had met at the bus station had seen her on Inquisition Street, where there was a Jesuit convent. Didn't all these details speak for themselves?

Those present at the assembly made many suggestions. Some said that Jews must be warned not to fall into the trap that the mission people had set for them. Some said that those unfortunate people must be helped, so that they would need no help from the mission. Some said that the government should be pressured to enact laws prohibiting devious missionary activity.

When it was Chaim's turn to speak, he rose and said, "Everything that you have suggested is helpful. All these things must be done. Jews must be warned of the danger of the missions. Unfortunate people must be helped before they fall into the hands of our enemies. Laws must be enacted prohibiting missionary activity. But all these things will take time. Meanwhile the danger is very grave. Every day more Jewish souls are lost. Something must be done immediately."

All eyes were glued to Chaim as he talked, all ears bent to catch his words. Chaim was held in great esteem. He was one of the outstanding students of the *yeshivah*, and his opinions were well thought out. When he paused for a minute, his friend David asked, "What do you suggest we do?"

Chaim answered, "We must make our way into the convents which have been barred to us and try to rescue the Jewish children who have been lured inside. Even if we don't succeed in getting them out—even if the mission staff and the police are able to prevent this—the publicity that this act will draw will awaken people to the danger and bring others to our side. It will also frighten the missionaries and cause them to limit their activities."

The words flowed from Chaim's mouth as if they had a will of their own. They expressed his determination and desperation to save his sister. Chaim had no time to wait for laws to be passed forbidding missionary activity. Brachah was in need of help now. She was in greater danger every day and must be saved as quickly as possible. When Chaim was asked which convent to enter, since it was impossible to enter them all, he answered, "We must begin with the convent on Inquisition Street in the holy city of Jerusalem." None of his friends questioned his choice, as any convent could have been chosen. So they agreed both to his proposal to hold an anti-missionary demonstration inside a convent, and to his choice of the Convent of St. Paul, on Inquisition Street.

The time for the demonstration was set for three o'clock the following afternoon. At that time, about a hundred eighteen- to twenty-year-old boys came to Inquisition Street. They came in small groups, each one from a different direction, in order not to arouse suspicion. When they were all on Inquisition Street, two boys went up to the gate and knocked. The guard came to the gate, peered through the peephole, and opened the gate a crack. When he asked what they wanted, they answered something or other, trying to engage him in a conversation. The guard was not happy with this conversation and tried to close the gate, but one of the boys put his foot in the opening. Just then, the second boy gestured to the others, and all the boys, who had been standing along the wall separating the convent yard from the street, hurriedly pushed through the gate and into the courtyard. The guard was pushed aside, dumbfounded.

The noise of all the footsteps and shouts of the demonstrators brought all the priests and nuns out of the convent, rushing outside to see what had happened. The pupils of the mission school ran after their teachers. The teachers, overwhelmed by all the excitement, completely forgot to send their pupils back inside. When the demonstrators saw the mission staff, they began to shout slogans such as: "Remove your hands from Jewish children!"; "No more selling of souls"; and "Where were Christian charity and mercy in the days of the gas chambers?" The mission staff was struck dumb and made no attempt to chase the demonstrators from their premises. They knew that the demonstrators outnumbered them by far and that they were no match for them. Lucas rushed inside to call the police.

Chaim feverishly searched among the nuns who had come out to the yard. Then his eyes fell upon Brachah, and he shouted with all his strength, "Brachah!" Chaim's friends couldn't hear what he was shouting, because they were busy shouting themselves, but Brachah heard Chaim's cry. When she heard her Jewish name pronounced by one of the demonstrators, her whole body shook. She turned towards the voice and when her eyes met Chaim's, she fainted.

A tumult arose among the convent staff. From all sides, the word resounded, "Water, water, water." Chaim tried to push his way through to the place where Brachah had been standing a minute before, but he was unsuccessful. The mission staff surrounded Brachah, who lay on the ground, trying to revive her. Just then the police arrived and began to forcibly remove the demonstrators. This was no easy task. The boys held out as long as they could and refused to leave. Meanwhile, the priests brought the children and Barbara into the convent. When Chaim saw that the yard was empty, he stopped resisting the police efforts to drag him away. The tense encounter had left him thoroughly exhausted.

A few of the demonstrators, including Chaim, were held for questioning by the police. On the way to the police station, Chaim debated as to whether he should reveal his secret to the police or not. At last he decided not to say anything. It would be better if this did not get into the newspapers. If it were printed, the mission staff would find out also. They would certainly hide Brachah or send her away, and he would lose her. If they had no knowledge of his secret, he would find a way to meet Brachah and get her out. And his reasoning was indeed correct.

The next day, the papers printed that the demonstrators had hit one of the nuns and knocked her to the ground. This enraged many people. "Jews don't behave like that," they said. The priests had misled the newspapers. This was the story that they had told the investigators. The demonstrators denied it completely, but not everyone believed them. "There must be some truth to the story," said many. "If she wasn't beaten, why did she fall to the ground in a faint?" Chaim, his eyes burning, devoured every word that was printed about Brachah to find out if she was well. When he read in the papers that there was no cause for concern, he was relieved and began to plan his next step.

Two days later, Chaim took a walk by himself down Inquisition Street. He walked back and forth in front of building No. 6. He knew that Brachah had fainted because she had seen him, and now that she had seen him, she would realize that he would come back to meet her again. He was not mistaken. In a short time Chaim caught sight of her at the convent gate, signaling to him to lead her in the direction he wanted her to take. Chaim turned and began to walk towards Yaffo Road. Brachah left the convent yard, following a few paces behind, and holding a small package in her hand. Since they were so careful, we didn't want to disturb them, and we did not follow them any further than our eyes could reach. They soon disappeared from sight.

Barbara Sokolsky's disappearance from the convent worried the mission staff considerably. Either she had been kidnapped or she had run away. They knew that the demonstrators had not hit her. She had fainted, apparently from excitement. Being Jewish, perhaps she regretted the missionary work she had performed. If she had run away, it would not be in the best interests of the mission to publicize it. So after much debate, they decided not to inform the police of Barbara's disappearance.

It was a beautiful summer morning. The sun was high in the sky, and the streets of Tel Aviv were drenched in sunlight. Three women walked slowly down Sanhedrin Street, one young woman on either side of an older woman. The woman in the middle had her head covered, while the girls were bare-headed. As they passed us, we recognized them immediately. They were Marussa, Yanka, and Brachah.

This was the day when Marussa and Yanka had been summoned to the rabbinic court, to convert. For a year they had been trying to join the Jewish people through conversion, but the court was in no hurry to grant their request. They were told that it was not easy to be Jewish. A Jew is obligated to fulfill 613 *mitzvoth* plus all the rabbinic edicts protecting these *mitzvoth*. But they did not give in. If women who were born Jewish could bear this heavy responsibility, so could they, they told the court. Meanwhile, a year had passed until their case finally came before the court and was decided in their favor. During that whole year Marussa and Yanka had studied Jewish law and prepared themselves for the conversion.

The conversion ceremony was to take place today, and

Brachah accompanied them. After the conversion, Marussa's new name would be Ruth, and Yanka would be called Na'amah.

When they entered the rabbinic court, we retraced our footsteps and went to visit Ya'akov Shimeonovitz. His house wore a holiday atmosphere. On a table in the center of the room was a gleaming white tablecloth covered with cakes and liquor. Around the table sat Ya'akov, the head of the house; Peretz and Yonah; Chaim and David; and Leah, Yonah's wife. They had taken a day off from work to be with Ya'akov Shimeonovitz on this, his day of rejoicing. They spoke not about current events but about things that had happened ten years earlier. They revived old memories. Those who were sitting here today lived more in the past than in the present. It was not the first time that they were telling these stories; nevertheless each time the stories seemed new to them.

Time flew by, and before they finished retelling one-thousandth of their tales, the door opened. Ruth, Na'amah, and Brachah entered. Those in the room stood up in their honor. There was a minute of deep silence. All the faces were serious, and all eyes were blurred.

Some tears were of happiness and some of grief. David's tears were of grief. From the moment that Brachah had returned to her brother, Chaim, he could not forget his sister, Sarah, who had been together with Brachah in the convent in Poland. But Sarah had remained in Poland. Brachah and Marussa told him that she had also been baptized, and no one knew where she was today. Even if she had immigrated to Eretz Yisrael with the mission, as Brachah had done, he didn't know how to find her. Sarah didn't resemble him as Brachah resembled Chaim, so he could not recognize her at first sight. It was a miracle that Chaim and Brachah were as alike as two drops of water. The tears of joy soon disappeared, but it took all of David's strength to hold his tears back. He didn't want to spoil the happiness of those assembled in the house today.

After a minute of silence, calls of "*mazal tov*" were heard from all sides. Everyone sat down, except for Ya'akov who poured liquor for everyone. Then he also sat down. Everyone took a sip and good wishes began to fly like angels around the room. Ruth and Na'amah were the most excited, for they had cut themselves off from one world and entered another. It was as if they had been born anew. To be reborn at the age of forty, or even at the age of twenty, is no light matter. But it had been impossible to live in two worlds at once—two worlds that could not coexist. And so they were relieved and joyful at having chosen to become Jews.

The guests spoke about everything except Brachah's escape from the mission in Jerusalem and Marussa and Yanka's conversion in Tel Aviv. They were all familiar with the Talmudic adage which prohibits a Jew from making derogatory remarks about Gentiles in front of a convert or his descendants unto the tenth generation. Therefore they avoided any subject which might bring them to disparage the Christians.

David sat absorbed in his own thoughts. Everyone knew what he was thinking. Ruth said, "Don't despair, David. Your fiancée, Brachah, and I are trying to find your sister. We have already begun our search and we are waiting for results." David thanked Ruth, but in his heart he believed that her words had no substance. Ruth had cut herself off from all her family in Nachrovah. She could never succeed in renewing her contacts with the Catholics of Nachrovah to the point that they would be ready to help her search for Silvana. Brachah would not succeed either. The newspapers in Israel had printed the story of Chaim and Brachah, and the story had undoubtedly reached Poland.

David was partially comforted by the fact that he was not alone in his troubles. As our Sages have said, *"Tzarath rabim chatzi nechamah"* — when trouble is shared by many, that in itself provides partial comfort. His sister, Sarah, was not the only lost Jewish soul. Rivkah, Rachel, Leah and Chavah had remained in Poland as Catholics. They were the ones he had heard about, but it was common knowledge that thousands whose names were not even known had assimilated, and they shared the plight of his sister.

After a while, the guests rose and took leave of their hosts. They all wished Ya'akov, his wife, Ruth, and their daughter, Na'amah, a long, happy life together. The hosts accompanied their guests to the gate, wishing them all the best and thanking them for rejoicing with them. On the street, the group split into couples: Peretz and his wife, Leah; Yonah and Chaim; David and Brachah.

When David and Brachah were alone, Brachah said, "What Marussa said about an attempt to locate Sarah is the truth. I also think that there is no cause for despair." David realized from Brachah's tone of voice that she was not saying this just to make him feel better. She spoke honestly and openly, with real hope and not just from wishful thinking.

Perhaps Brachah had some plan. After all, she was now personally involved. Sarah would soon be her sister-in-law. Nevertheless, David didn't ask Brachah exactly what she was planning to do to save Sarah. If she hadn't volunteered this information, he didn't want to cross-examine her or force her to reveal her plans. But a glimmer of hope was kindled in David's heart. He had heard tales of the deeds of Brachah's father and her mother, and he knew that they had been people of exceptional dedication. Brachah was their daughter. She might very well be like her parents. And with dedication, even the impossible can be accomplished.

We also share David's estimation of Brachah. She put her heart and soul into all that she did. When she was put into the convent in Nachrovah, she fought with all her heart and soul to preserve her Jewishness. Finally, when she was caught in the snares of the mission, she worked for them with great dedication. Now that she had been rescued and had returned to her people, she would certainly do everything in her power to save others. We believe that she will be able to accomplish the impossible. And if she is successful in her plan to rescue Sarah, we will spare neither time nor trouble to tell you that story too.

GLOSSARY

BAR MITZVA: a Jewish boy at age 13, when he reaches the age of religious responsibility

BERACHAH, BERACHOTH: blessing(s) said over food, new clothes, etc.

BEITH HAMIKDASH: the Holy Temple

BNEI NOACH: (literally, the sons of Noah) gentiles

BRITH MILAH: circumcision

CHASSID, CHASSIDIM: follower(s) of the chassiduth movement

CHASSIDUTH: a movement founded by the Baal Shem Tov in the sixteenth century, based on mysticism and devout observance

CHEDER: school of Torah learning for young boys

ERETZ YISRAEL: the Land of Israel

GEMARA: the commentary on the Mishnah forming the second part of the Talmud

GOYIM: gentiles

HAMASKIL: the "enlightened" — a member of the Haskalah movement, an eighteenth century movement which attempted to spread "modern" secular culture among Jews

KADDISH: the prayer recited in memory of the dead, sanctifying God's name

KEN: yes

KIBBUTZ, KIBBUTZIM: communal settlement(s)

KIDDUSH HASHEM: martyrdom

KOTHEL HAMA'ARAVI: the Western Wall

LANDSLEIT: people who come from the same home town

MASHIACH: the Messiah

MAZAL TOV: congratulations

MITZVOTH: commandments

MOSHAV, MOSHAVIM: communal farm(s)

OL MALCHUTH SHAMAYIM: the obligation to serve God

PEYOTH: ritual sidelocks of hair

REBBE: head of a chassidic group

SHABBATH: the Sabbath

SHEMA YISRAEL: the declaration of belief in one God, said twice daily and before going to sleep at night

SHEMONEH ESREH: the "Eighteen Benedictions" — the main section of the daily prayers

TALLITH: prayer shawl

TALMID CHACHAM: a scholar

TEFILLIN: two small, square, leather boxes containing parchments inscribed with passages from the Torah which are worn on the left arm and forehead of Jewish males during morning workday prayers

VIDUY: confession

YESHIVA, YESHIVOTH: talmudical school(s)

Rabbi Benzion Firer

THE LONG JOURNEY HOME

FELDHEIM PUBLISHERS
JERUSALEM   NEW YORK

contents

Eighteen-year-old Shlomo was the apple of his parents' eye and the pride and joy of the Jewish community of Chedalonova. Everyone in the small Polish town had watched this child prodigy grow into a budding young genius, the star pupil of Chedalonova's beloved *Rav*. Although students from all over Poland came to learn Torah with the *Rav* of Chedalonova, Shlomo remained his favorite pupil. The *Rav* had invested much effort in teaching Shlomo, and Shlomo had absorbed almost everything he was taught.

Whenever the *Rav* raised a difficult question for the class and asked for their suggestions before presenting his own solution, Shlomo would be the first to answer. Usually, he was also the last, for his answers generally made any further comments unnecessary. Even when Shlomo's ideas differed from the *Rav*'s, the *Rav* would often defer to him, withholding his own opinion.

Shlomo's father, Reb Kolonymos, was a well-to-do wholesale grain dealer and an honored member of the local Jewish community. His mother, Bathsheva, was well known and respected as a diligent housewife who also found time to devote herself to acts of kindness and charity. Shlomo had a brother David, who was ten years younger than he was, and a sister Sarah, who was two years younger than David.

Most of Shlomo's day was spent in the *Beith Midrash*. He would occupy himself with reviewing yesterday's lesson and preparing for tomorrow's. Shlomo was the envy, not only of his friends in the *Beith Midrash*, but also of their parents. It is natural for someone so gifted to arouse some jealousy, but this was a positive kind of envy, since it was "for the sake of the Torah." Shlomo's friends tried to imitate him and devoted themselves to studying, each according to his own abilities. Even their parents held Shlomo up as an example.

Looking at Shlomo as he sat in the *Beith Midrash*, you would not have guessed his thoughts. You could see his eyes moving across the small print in the open book before him, but you could not see his heart, and sometimes, his heart was elsewhere. Sometimes even his eyes, though glued to his *gemara*, were in reality seeing things that were far away. For Shlomo had seen things in the world around him that had turned his thoughts away from the *Beith Midrash*.

He was not really to blame, for he was born in the stormy era immediately after World War I. Large numbers of soldiers never returned home from that war, and many families had been utterly wiped out. The spiritual damage, brought by the new winds to towns even as small as Chedalonova, was even more devastating. New, "modern" philosophies began to compete with the *gemara*. It was not unusual for a young man to close his *gemara* for good and to leave the *Beith Midrash* without even kissing the *mezuzah*. And of those who remained, many remained in body only.

These new philosophies had one thing in common. They all attempted to right some wrong. Some came to reform the entire world, and others merely attempted to reform the Jewish people. Some emphasized the equality of all men in the world, while others emphasized the equality of Jews and non-Jews. One aimed to provide every human being with food and clothing, while another wished to win freedom and equality for Jews among the nations. And one demanded a homeland for the Jews, just like that of all the other nations.

Each of these factions opened its own clubhouse in Chedalonova. Those who strove for equality among all human beings opened a club for Jews and non-Jews together, while those who worried primarily about the Jews opened clubs for Jews only.

The group that strove for a Jewish homeland was called Hechalutz. Hechalutz did not believe, as their friends in the Bund did, that Jews could ever achieve equality in the Diaspora. But they did believe that if the Jews had their own homeland, they would gain the honor and respect of the non-Jewish world. They believed that anti-Semitism was the natural result of the fact that Jews had been "uninvited guests" in other peoples' countries. This understandable hatred of Jews had been fanned by the fact that Jews had traditionally turned to commerce instead of to constructive professions such as farming. Lending money was unjust; it was neither a necessary nor an honorable profession. Were Jews to work their own land, anti-Semitism would soon disappear.

The Bund also disapproved of commercial professions, but they believed that the country in which each person, Jew or non-Jew, was born, was his rightful homeland. Although most of the Gentile world still opposed the idea of equal rights for Jews, the Jews would nonetheless be able to achieve equality if only they cooperated with those few Gentiles who did seek justice in the world.

The Bund had two flags, neither of which was exclusively their own. One was red and white—the Polish national flag—and one was all red—the international laborer's flag. Hechalutz had its own special flag—blue and white—alongside the red, proletariat flag. Although none of the *chalutzim* lived by the sweat of his brow as yet, they saw themselves as workers of the future. They were still being supported by their parents, but soon they would be farmers in Eretz Yisrael. Hechalutz members also had their own uniform—blue pants and white shirt. Every year on the first of May they would march together with members of the Bund and non-Jewish idealists, waving the red flag and singing Polish songs. But on the twentieth of *Tammuz* they would march down the street in their blue and white uniforms, waving their own blue and white flag and singing Hebrew songs.

The boys who sat and learned in the *Beith Midrash* had nothing to do with either group. Nevertheless, on the twentieth of *Tammuz* a few boys could be seen leaving their *gemaroth* for a minute and going to the doorstep of the *Beith Midrash* to watch Hechalutz's parade go by and to listen to their songs, even though the Hebrew of the *chalutzim* sounded different from the Hebrew of the *Beith Midrash* and they could not always understand it. One of those who got up to watch the parade was Shlomo.

Why would someone like Shlomo, who was so engrossed in learning Torah, turn to these idle pursuits?
Heaven forbid that he be caught in the net of such a godless
group. When the *Rav* was told that Shlomo had left his
gemara to watch the parade, he sighed and said, "The Torah
grants protection. It will save him from sin." Nevertheless, it
was clear that the *Rav* was deeply disturbed.

The *chalutzim* had to train themselves to do manual labor. In Eretz Yisrael they would be farmers and raise their own crops, so it was essential for them to learn how to work. Their main interest was in farming, but unfortunately, there was no Jewish land in Chedalonova for them to farm. The Jewish houses were all built around the marketplace, one on top of the other, with the main street in front of them and the market behind. There was not enough room to stick a needle between one house and the next. Every inch of land was covered with buildings.

Only one of the *chalutzim* had the good fortune to live a bit farther away from the marketplace. He had a small yard where he planted green onions and garlic and radishes. He watered and weeded them faithfully, training himself to be a farmer.

The *chalutzim* who had no opportunity to do farming did any sort of manual labor they could find, but in the summertime there was hardly any work. Once in a great while Reb Kolonymos would give them a few sacks of grain to carry. All summer they waited for the fall, their best season of the year, for in the fall each household was busy storing up woodpiles to fuel the furnaces in the winter. The villagers would bring sawed-off tree branches from the forest. These had to be split into pieces that would fit into the furnaces. This was a job for strong men and sharp hatchets. Reb Kolonymos, who had a large house and many rooms to heat, provided them with employment for many days.

Sometimes uncut branches several feet long would be brought to the market. Then two *chalutzim* would stand opposite each other, the branch on a plank between them, until they managed to saw it in half. After they had split the branch into logs, they would split the logs into thin planks of the required size. Some of the *chalutzim* were the sons of well-to-do families who could afford to hire workers to split logs. In that case each *chalutz* would work for his friend's father. Splitting logs for your own father was not considered working.

A few of Chedalonova's Jews made a point of employing only non-Jews, thereby conveying their opposition to the *chalutzim*. But on the whole, the *chalutzim* were not taken very seriously. Few people believed that youths from good families would exchange the comforts of home for a farmer's life in Eretz Yisrael. Perhaps young people from poor families would do so, but not those from wealthy homes. One such youth had already gone to Eretz Yisrael and come back home to his family in Chedalonova. He claimed that the doctors there had sent him home, but no one believed that that was the whole truth.

The sight of *chalutzim* splitting wood was no longer a novelty in Chedalonova, and it drew no special attention.

People were too involved in their own affairs to stand around watching them. Each shop owner was busy waiting for customers to buy his food, clothing, or dry goods, and those shop owners who had competitors nearby were doubly busy, as they also had to keep track of how much business, if any, the competing stores were doing.

But not only the rich needed logs for heating their houses in the winter. If anything, the poor needed them more, for the rich had money to warm their hearts, as well as sufficient food and clothing. With a full stomach and warm clothing one is not so cold. Wood in the winter was much more important to the poor, who had no money and little food and clothing. They could not buy enough wood in the fall for the entire winter; a few weeks' worth of wood was the most they could afford. After that, they would look to charity, a quality never lacking among Jews. A few members of the community had accepted the responsibility for this *mitzvah*. They would make the rounds of the stores and collect money to buy wood for the poor. Among those who made the rounds was Shlomo's mother, Bathsheva.

The *chalutzim* also had a share in this *mitzvah*. They gave not money, but time. They would split cheap, uncut branches into logs, and then chop them into pieces. For this work they accepted no remuneration. First of all, they were not really in need of money — the purpose of their work was to acquire expertise and experience. Yankel the Miser had once jokingly remarked that he would hire the *chalutzim* only if *they* paid *him*, as it was he who was doing them a favor. If the *chalutzim* took money from the rich, it was only to show their disapproval of the wealthy and to make them a few pennies poorer. On the other hand, the *chalutzim* felt a special sympathy for the poor and wanted to help them.

Early one cold winter morning, the shopkeepers were standing in their empty stores. They hopped from one foot to the other to keep from freezing, as they warmed their hands around small cooking pots on the stoves. The marketplace was empty. It had snowed all night long and the thick layer of snow made walking difficult.

Two young men appeared and began splitting logs in front of the basement apartment of Senderil the Shoemaker. One of them was Shlomo Sharfson. At first, the shopkeepers who noticed him were so surprised that no one moved, but in a few minutes people started to appear from all directions. Men, women and children came to see Shlomo Sharfson, out of the *Beith Midrash*, chopping wood. As the news spread, boys even ran out of *cheder* to watch him. Shlomo, for his part, continued chopping wood in the center of the ever growing circle of onlookers. To some, this was a funny sight — to others, a sad one. Shlomo stood there splitting logs in his long black coat without even lowering his eyes, showing no visible signs of embarrassment or shame at all the attention. He looked straight into the eyes of all those surrounding him, smiling his usual good-natured smile.

But no one could stand the fierce cold for long. Little by little, the bystanders left, leaving Shlomo and his friend to their work.

Like people the world over, some of the Jews of Chedalonova were good-hearted and shared their friends' distress, while others took pleasure in their neighbors' downfall. Here, too, there were those who rejoiced at Reb

Kolonymos' misfortune, and wished to have a closer look. Reb Kolonymos' shop, with its transparent glass doors, was in the center of the market. Some evil-hearted Jews "happened" to pass by and look inside. When they saw that the store was empty and locked, they exchanged knowing grins as if to say, "We know why!"

Those who sympathized with Reb Kolonymos went to consult the *Rav*. One of them said to him, "Those branches that Shlomo was sawing for Senderil were bought from charity money collected that very morning by Shlomo's own mother. Rabbi Chanina ben Dosa already asked, 'Is it possible for the deeds of a righteous person to cause his descendants to falter and stumble?' "

The *Rav* looked straight at his questioners and answered, "Shlomo has not faltered. On the contrary, he is bringing his mother's act of charity to completion."

"But," objected the questioner, "Shlomo's actions have brought him into the company of freethinkers. They will eventually cause him to stop observing the Torah and the *mitzvoth*."

"The Torah will protect him," countered the *Rav*. "The Torah that Shlomo is learning will save him from sin."

"Excuse me," objected the questioner again, "the *Rav* said 'the Torah that Shlomo is learning'. Perhaps it would be more correct to say 'the Torah that Shlomo has learned until now.' The freethinking *chalutzim* do not usually learn Torah." The *Rav* did not answer.

When the men left the *Rav's* apartment they said to each other, "Love is blind. The *Rav* cannot accept the truth about his beloved pupil Shlomo."

Reb Kolonymos entered the *Rav*'s house as they were. leaving. Perhaps the *Rav* changed his mind somewhat about Shlomo after hearing what Reb Kolonymos had to say, but since there were no witnesses to the conversation, the outcome is a matter of pure speculation.

✳ 3 ✳ *Shlomo in Public and in Private*

From the very day Shlomo joined the Moadon He-chalutz — the pioneer's meeting house — his attitude toward certain *mitzvoth* underwent a subtle change. He no longer kept a basin and a cup of water near his bed to wash his hands each morning upon arising. He no longer got up so early in the morning, and more than once, he was late for prayers. Nor did he attend the *Rav*'s Talmud lessons any more. He missed going to the class very much, but he did not want to compromise his teacher. He was afraid of the gossip, of the people who might accuse the *Rav* of not following the Talmudic dictum, "One who teaches an unworthy pupil may be compared to an idol worshiper" (*Chulin* 133). Shlomo knew that he had been branded an errant son. Public opinion was against him, and if the *Rav* did not drive him away, people would speak evil of the *Rav*. Shlomo did not want to cause any injury whatsoever to his teacher, so he sat at home and no longer frequented the *Beith Midrash*.

His evenings were spent at the Moadon. There too, he was considered an alien, even though no one knew that he still prayed three times a day, put on *tefillin* daily, and kept Shabbath. These were things he did privately, at home. But

Shlomo betrayed himself whenever a discussion took place in the Moadon.

Everyone agreed that each nation must have its own country, but how the country should function was still a matter for debate. However, they all disapproved of the Jews of Chedalonova. They were sure that an independent Jewish people in its own homeland would be different from these Jews. The new generation in Eretz Yisrael would be Jews without Shabbath, without synagogues, without *tallith* and *tefillin* and the laws of *kashruth*; in short, without anything connecting them to the Jewish religion.

But Shlomo had other ideas. He didn't accept what everyone else seemed to think was perfectly clear. Once, in the heat of a spirited argument between Shlomo and his friends, Peretz jumped up and exclaimed, "Shlomo, how long are you going to straddle both sides of the fence? You must take your choice: either Torah or Eretz Yisrael!"

"No," answered Shlomo. "The two are indivisible. The Torah has commanded every Jewish person to live in Eretz Yisrael, not in Chedalonova. Therefore, *chalutzim* must not divorce themselves from the Torah. It supports and helps them."

But Peretz would not give in. "Someone with so many *mitzvoth* on his mind cannot concentrate on the *mitzvah* of Eretz Yisrael. Give up worrying about the other *mitzvoth* so you can concentrate on settling Eretz Yisrael!"

"You needn't worry," replied Shlomo, "Eretz Yisrael is not just one of the *mitzvoth*. It is a central *mitzvah*, and the *Geulah*, the Redemption, is a vital part of our prayers. It cannot be pushed aside or forgotten."

"Then why do your friends in the *Beith Midrash* oppose us? Why don't they also join the Moadon and strive to go to Eretz Yisrael? Apparently they don't agree with you either. No one seems to agree with you — neither they nor we. You must make your choice," concluded Peretz.

"I don't know why the other students in the *Beith Midrash* don't participate in the efforts to build up Eretz Yisrael, but I do know that my opinion is not my own invention. It is the opinion of the Torah. Any Jew who goes to Eretz Yisrael is fulfilling a commandment," declared Shlomo.

The *chalutzim* could not judge whether Shlomo's opinions were valid or not. They only knew that they could not accept them. Shlomo bothered them. They could not win an argument with him as he always had an answer to their questions and a question for their answers. And he always won. "It's no wonder," they explained to themselves, "after all those years he spent in the *Beith Midrash* sharpening his mind."

There were several girls in the Moadon. These *chalutzoth*, however, had no opportunity to gain any practical experience in pioneering work in Chedalonova. Woodchopping was not for them. Of course, all members of the Moadon opposed discrimination based upon sex. Men and women should be completely equal in their rights and duties, including work opportunities. This was fine in theory, but in practice, it was very difficult for the girls to saw logs or chop wood. Instead, they decorated the Moadon. They stretched strips of blue and white ribbon across the ceiling and hung pictures of labor Zionist leaders on the walls.

One of the *chalutzoth*, Zissel Blitz, was a graduate of the Polish gymnasium in Cracow. Zissel had noticed Shlomo from the very first day he appeared in the Moadon, although he had not so much as glanced her way. Shlomo was not used to being in mixed company, and did not pay any attention to the girls. Zissel had listened to the argument between Shlomo and Peretz and had been deeply impressed. Not that she always agreed with Shlomo, but she admired him and the confident, polished presentation of his ideas.

While she herself did not debate with Shlomo, Zissel often tried to draw her friends into an argument with him. She herself lacked the ideological background to become involved in these discussions, but she was content to sit back and listen to Shlomo argue with the others. Only once had Zissel asked for permission to speak in the Moadon. At that time she had turned to Shlomo and asked, "Shlomo, as a representative of the *Beith Midrash*, how do you justify the traditional discrimination against women?"

While Zissel was speaking, Shlomo had looked intently at his shoes. Now that she had finished, he continued to look down, but he smiled as he answered, "According to the Torah, men and women are equally liable to punishment for all infractions of the Torah."

Zissel laughed and said, "Very nice. Women deserve equal punishment but not equal rights."

Shlomo stopped smiling and became serious.

"In a household where two opinions are of equal weight, there can be no unity. A Jewish home must be unified, not divided. The man represents the head of the house and the woman represents the heart. It is proper to accord the head priority over the heart, for only the brain is capable of evaluating and controlling a person's actions. Emotions are unstable and can change constantly. They should be controlled by the brain; not vice versa."

It was hard to tell whether Shlomo's answer satisfied or convinced Zissel; all one could say was that she listened to him intently. But perhaps she was more interested in the way Shlomo spoke than in the actual content of his words.

It is impossible to guess what the outcome of these debates would have been, or how long they would have gone on, had not fate removed Shlomo from the Moadon. No, he did not return to the *Beith Midrash*; he left Chedalonova completely. At that time, Eretz Yisrael was under the rule of the British Mandate. In order to prevent the growth of the Jewish population in the country, the British severely limited immigration. Only those lucky enough to hold a British certificate were allowed to enter. These certificates were immigration permits, issued by the British mandatory government and distributed by the Jewish Agency to Jewish communities throughout the world, according to the size of the local Jewish population.

That year, Chedalonova was awarded only two certificates. The members of the Moadon were called upon to decide who would be given the opportunity to settle in Eretz Yisrael. Peretz suggested that one certificate be given to Shlomo, but he met much opposition. Shlomo was only a newcomer; there were veteran *chalutzim* who had been waiting for a certificate for a long time.

"Nevertheless," declared Peretz, "we must send Shlomo to Eretz Yisrael as quickly as possible. He is not really one of us, and as long as he remains in Chedalonova, there is a chance that he may return to the *Beith Midrash*. Once he is in Eretz Yisrael, he will go to a *kibbutz*. There he will forget the *Beith Midrash* of Chedalonova and become a true *chalutz*.

"We must also consider the example Shlomo will set for his friends in the *Beith Midrash*. He will be the first to leave, and many others are likely to follow in his footsteps. Not all of them are as stubborn as he, nor have they learned as much Torah. With Shlomo in Eretz Yisrael, it will be easier for us to influence them." Peretz's speech was highly convincing, and his friends agreed to grant Shlomo one of the certificates.

In keeping with the rule that the sexes be treated equally, the second certificate was to be allotted to a girl. Here, too, Peretz spoke up. "The second certificate must go to Zissel Blitz. The trip to Eretz Yisrael is long. It takes weeks, or even months. It will give Shlomo an opportunity to influence his traveling companion in ways we might not approve of. Zissel is the only girl who would not be susceptible to Shlomo's influence because of her utter lack of any Jewish background. Her father is an assimilated Polish lawyer and she received a strictly Polish education. Shlomo cannot influence her, as she has no Jewish memories for him to awaken. No other girl in Chedalonova comes from such an assimilated family."

Once again, Peretz made his point, and Zissel received the second certificate.

Truth to tell, Shlomo's religious beliefs had weakened recently, along with his practical adherence to the *mitzvoth*. A few days before, he had forgotten to put on his *tefillin* in the morning, and the previous Shabbath he had absent-mindedly walked outside with a handkerchief in his pocket.

Nevertheless, he would not allow himself to be bested in the debates in the Moadon.

Man is a perverse animal. Shlomo had devoted many years of his life to studying Torah, and this Torah had become his own personal possession. Shlomo would not allow Peretz, who had never studied the Torah, to ridicule it or take it away from him. On the other hand, Shlomo felt that he himself could afford to neglect the Torah a bit, since it was his own "property." But he would protect it from any damage by others.

Perhaps, had Peretz accepted part of Shlomo's opinions on the centrality of the Torah to Eretz Yisrael, Shlomo might also have accepted part of Peretz's views about rebuilding a new and different Jewish people. However, since Peretz, not having studied psychology, said exactly what he thought, Shlomo felt called upon to defend his stand vigorously and at all costs.

In short, none of the girls of Chedalonova were in danger of being lured back to the Torah by Shlomo, since he himself was no longer as devout as he had once been. But because Peretz was ignorant of this fact, Zissel received the second certificate.

✴ 4 ✴ *On the Way to Eretz Yisrael*

The following evening, when Shlomo walked into the Moadon, he was greeted with cries of *"Mazal tov!"* He looked around uncomprehendingly. Peretz walked over to him and held out a folded piece of paper.

"You're a lucky fellow!" he said. "Here it is!"

"Here is what?" asked Shlomo.

"You have been awarded a certificate!" answered Peretz, opening the paper and displaying it for all to see.

Shlomo was stunned. He didn't know whether to rejoice or to refuse the honor. He covered his confusion with a smile and simply said, "Thank you."

Later, when his friends had turned their attention to other matters, Shlomo began to examine his own feelings.

Evidently the townspeople were right. These spoiled children did not readily exchange their comfortable homes for a life of hard labor in Eretz Yisrael and so they gave the prized certificates away to newcomers like himself. Words were cheap, but Shlomo would prove to them that he, at least, practiced what he preached. But he could not rejoice in his decision. The *Beith Midrash* in Chedalonova was still the center of his world and leaving it would be painful.

After a while, he went home to break the news to his parents. His father let out a deep sigh. Until now, he had been hoping that the Moadon was a passing fancy. He had hoped that one day Shlomo would sober up and return to the *Beith Midrash*. If Shlomo joined the *chalutzim* in Eretz Yisrael he might never set foot in a *Beith Midrash* again.

"What will you do?" Kolonymos asked his son.

"If I have been awarded a certificate, then I must go to Eretz Yisrael," answered Shlomo.

"Can't you thank them for their goodwill and return the certificate? There are many others who would be only too happy to take your place."

"I don't want people to say that an observant Jew does not practice what he preaches. That would be a disgrace—a *chillul haShem*," countered Shlomo.

"Perhaps there is still hope for him," thought Kolonymos. "He still considers himself a *ben Torah* who doesn't want to cause any *chillul haShem*!"

Kolonymos was silent. The *Rav* had advised him not to scold Shlomo or argue with him as Shlomo was stubborn and would not give in easily. Harsh words might drive him away from them forever. But now, when it seemed that Shlomo was leaving them anyway, perhaps the time had come to speak frankly and to tell him how much sorrow and shame he was causing his family by joining a group of nonbelieving, non-observant Jews.

But on second thought, Kolonymos decided no, the *Rav*'s advice still held. The spirit of folly that had entered Shlomo in Chedalonova might leave him in Eretz Yisrael.

Bathsheva, seeing that her husband had given Shlomo his

tacit assent, began to grieve. "Shlomoleh, my son, what will we do without you? The house will be empty. How can you do such a cruel thing to your father and mother?"

Shlomo answered haltingly, "I cannot put the *Beith Midrash* to shame. People will say, 'Look at him — the *ben Torah*! He talked a lot about the importance of *aliyah* to Eretz Yisrael, but when he was given the chance, he refused. All talk and no action, that's what they are in the *Beith Midrash*!' There could be no *chillul haShem* greater than that." Hearing Shlomo mention *chillul haShem* again, Bathsheva grew silent. She understood and accepted his words.

When Zissel received her certificate, the news came as a shock to her, too. At first she refused the honor, claiming that she was a new member of Hechalutz, and she had much to learn before she could become a pioneer in Eretz Yisrael. Peretz waited for Zissel to finish speaking, and then he smiled and said, "Shlomo Sharfson was also awarded a certificate." Zissel blushed, and lowering her eyes, she examined the certificate again.

At home, Zissel's announcement was met with a flat refusal. Her father, Edmond Blitz, claimed that Poland was their homeland. It was true that some Poles were anti-Semitic and even dared to use physical violence against Jews. As a lawyer he had recently brought two such Poles to trial. But the Jews were at fault. They angered the Poles by claiming that Palestine rather than Poland was their homeland. The Poles would not hate Jews who were loyal Polish patriots. Mr. Blitz had opposed Zissel's membership in the Moadon from the very beginning. He had permitted her to go because she had no other friends in Chedalonova. Very few Polish girls attended the gymnasium, and the girls from the Jewish gymnasium all belonged to the Moadon. But *aliyah* to Israel was an altogether different matter. It was absolutely unthinkable.

In his consternation, poor Edmond completely forgot to ask who else had received certificates. It was Rozeshka, Zissel's mother, who heard in the market that Reb Kolonymos Sharfson's son had received the second certificate. "What a disgrace — to go with a Talmudist from the *Beith Midrash*!" wailed Rozeshka.

"A Talmudist? What Talmudist?" asked Edmond.

"The boy with the long black coat who split logs for Senderil the Shoemaker — that's who she's going with!" cried Rozeshka.

That was the last straw. Calling her by her Polish name as befit a member of their family, Zissel's father decreed, "Zushka, I absolutely forbid you to take part in this!"

Now Zissel was an only child who knew her own power. There was nothing she could not get if she was only stubborn enough. She let her parents vent all their frustration and anger, knowing full well that, in the end, she would get her own way. And she was right.

You may indeed ask how Zissel's parents — with no ties to their fellow Jews or to Eretz Yisrael — could give in. How could they allow their only daughter to forsake them and leave Poland to live in a foreign land? Their reasoning was that when Zissel had experienced hunger and hard life in the new country, she would quickly return. Her own experience would prove to her that her place was in Poland.

The date was set for Shlomo and Zissel's departure. The

route was well known: a train would take them from Chedalonova to Cracow, the meeting place for *olim* from Galicia. From Cracow they would take another train to Vienna, then on to Trieste, and from there they would set sail for Haifa.

The *chalutzim* celebrated the day of their departure as if it were a holiday. Dressed in blue and white, they accompanied Shlomo and Zissel from the Moadon to the train station, singing all the way. Edmond and Rozeshka Blitz had come by themselves and were already waiting at the station. They had not wanted to accompany the *chalutzim*, who were much too Jewish for them. They had never dreamed that such a tragedy would befall their family. When Zissel finally arrived at the station and caught sight of her parents, her heart sank. Their anguish was so great that she wondered if she was doing the right thing. Her friends acted as though she were a bride being led to the wedding canopy, but her parents looked as though they were at her funeral. Zissel ran over to her parents, kissed them hard and whispered something that was lost in all the noise. Perhaps she asked their forgiveness and promised to write. Their eyes were full of tears. They prayed that none of their Polish friends were present to witness their disgrace.

Reb Kolonymos and Bathsheva, together with Sarah and David, stood at the other end of the station, searching for their son Shlomo among the crowd. They had already taken their leave of him at home before he left for the Moadon. Good-byes such as these were not public affairs. Shlomo left his friends for a minute and went over to his family. They said a simple good-bye once again, nodding their heads to one another. The adults in Reb Kolonymos' family did not kiss in public. When the engine began to shriek, Shlomo shook his father's hand, nodded to his mother, and said "*Shalom.*" He kissed little Sarah and David again and reminded them to be good. Then he quickly returned to his friends. Zissel left her parents and ran toward the group from the opposite direction. People jostled each other as they got off and on the train. Shlomo and Zissel were lost in the crowd as they, too, pushed their way toward the train. Only the group of *chalutzim* stood out, singing their Hebrew songs, causing Poles to spit and curse, "Let the damn Jews go to Palestine."

Once aboard the train, Shlomo and Zissel hurried to the window for a last glimpse of their friends and families. The locomotive let out a shriek and the train started on its way. Everyone waved his handkerchief and shouted "*Shalom*" until the train pulled out of the station.

Shlomo and Zissel left the window and turned toward the train's passengers. Just then several young people approached them, and welcomed them aboard. Shlomo and Zissel returned the greeting with a blank stare until the youths explained that they, too, were on their way to Eretz Yisrael. Shmuel and Sheindel were from Nachrovah and Aharon and Elka were from Temyonovah. They were members of Hashomer Hatzair, not of Hechalutz. Shlomo had never before heard of Hashomer Hatzair. As a newcomer to the Moadon — straight from the *Beith Midrash* — he had thought that everyone who wanted to live in Eretz Yisrael was a *chalutz* and that there were no differences of opinion among *chalutzim*.

The six boys and girls sat down in one corner of the coach and began to talk.

"Could you explain exactly what Hashomer Hatzair is?" asked Shlomo.

"Hashomer Hatzair emphasizes self-improvement and social reform," answered Aharon. "If every individual relinquishes his privacy and his personal property in order to share a communal life in which no one owns anything of his own and all are equal, then we will have cured all of the world's ills."

"But you could do that in Poland," said Shlomo. "Why are you going to Eretz Yisrael?"

"Because we are also Zionists," replied Shmuel, "but we emphasize social equality. We are going to Eretz Yisrael to establish a communal life. For us, Eretz Yisrael without social reform has no value. We want to realize in Eretz Yisrael what other idealistic nations will realize in their own homelands. Actually, we feel much closer to fellow idealists who are not Jewish, than to Jews who go to Eretz Yisrael simply out of fear of the gentiles. For us, Eretz Yisrael is the means to an end, not the end itself. Our real goal is social reform, and if we had to choose, we would prefer social reform in the diaspora over life in Eretz Yisrael without reform."

Shmuel's speech shocked Shlomo. He had always thought that those who waved the blue and white flag were unconditionally committed to Eretz Yisrael. Now he had learned that for at least one sector, social reform rather than Eretz Yisrael was the primary goal. But Shlomo had never been an easy person to convince, and he stuck to his own opinion now, too.

"Why go to all the trouble of settling in Eretz Yisrael if social reform is possible in Poland? Eretz Yisrael itself is my ideal, and fellow Jews who share this feeling are closer to me than any non-Jew, idealistic as he may be."

"What about religion?" asked Elka. "Whom do you prefer — a 'synagogue Jew' or an enlightened, tolerant non-Jew?"

"From my experience," insisted Shlomo, "the synagogue Jews are devoted heart and soul to Eretz Yisrael, even if they do oppose the *chalutzim*. On the other hand, I do not trust non-Jews, enlightened or tolerant though they may be. Their tolerance is just a mask, and their equality a ruse."

After a short pause, Shlomo added, "I, too, could be called a synagogue Jew. I have learned much Torah in the *Beith Midrash*, including the saying of our sages, 'It is an incontrovertible law that Esau hates Jacob.' "

"I'm surprised that you are a member of Hechalutz," Sheindel replied. "You would fit in much better in Betar."

Shlomo knew that Sheindel was right, but there had been no branch of Betar in Chedalonova. Now that he was going to Eretz Yisrael as a representative of Hechalutz, he had to rationalize his choice somehow. To Sheindel he replied, "I belong in Hechalutz because I believe in pioneering action."

Zissel had not taken part in the debate as she was not certain of her own opinions. Nevertheless, she had followed the argument closely and she knew that she agreed with Shlomo only partially. She was pleased that equality was not his ideal in life. She, too, did not think that the prime goal of society was to achieve equality between Senderil the Shoemaker and her father, the lawyer. On the other hand, she disliked Shlomo's hatred of non-Jews.

For the *chalutzim* who were engrossed in the discussion, time flew by, but for Zissel, the hours seemed to crawl. While studying in the gymnasium she had often taken the train to Cracow and she knew the route well. Zissel got up and walked over to the window to watch the farmers working in their fields. It was a beautiful summer day and the landscape unfolded before her eyes like a patchwork quilt — large squares of grain and smaller squares of vegetables — each a different color. As Zissel gazed at the beautiful scenery, she began to doubt herself. No matter how she tried, she was not really at ease with these Jewish youths who felt themselves so foreign to Poland, and who thought only of Eretz Yisrael. They felt that their having been born in Poland was pure chance and had no meaning. Perhaps her father was right. Perhaps she really belonged back with her friends from the Polish gymnasium.

Not perhaps. Certainly. She knew that the real reason for her acceptance of the certificate was her attraction to Shlomo, but Shlomo hardly paid any attention to her. She wondered how he would have behaved had they been traveling without the group. Would he have bothered to talk to her at all? She could not forget how he had avoided looking at her when she had turned to him in the Moadon and asked him about discrimination against women.

Just then Zissel heard her name. She turned around and saw that the group was eating. Shlomo, a small suitcase on his lap and a piece of cake in his hand, said to her, " 'Without bread, there can be no Torah.' "

Zissel's doubts suddenly vanished and she beamed at Shlomo, "Thank you." Returning to her place in the circle, she took her share of the cake and said, "I, too, have a cake in my suitcase. Next time we will eat my mother's cake."

"We are already a commune," said Aharon, "sharing whatever we have."

"We're only six members now," added Shmuel, "but in another three hours the commune will grow larger and richer. In Cracow we will join a large group. The food we all own should last us for a few days."

But even as they spoke of communes and shared their food, there was a certain feeling of estrangement from Shlomo. They tried to ignore it or drive it away, but it persisted. When they finished eating, they all became quiet and withdrawn. The stormy debate had tired them out. One leaned against the wall and tried to take a nap. Another was engrossed in his own private world. A third went to look out the window and a fourth sat there, just plain bored.

Zissel, however, felt better. Her former doubts melted away. She had the feeling that, somehow, her future would be tied to Shlomo's.

A deafening whistle announced that they were rapidly approaching the familiar glass-roofed platforms of the Cracow train station. Straightening her dress, Zissel turned around and saw her friends taking their suitcases and knapsacks and preparing to get off the train. Suitcase in hand, she took her place among the group.

✳ 6 ✳ *Cracow*

In Cracow, the six youths found the Jewish Agency hostel a teeming beehive. Its large hall was lined with tables and benches. Piles of suitcases and knapsacks of all shapes and sizes were stuffed between the walls and the benches. In the center of the room were groups of young people. Some were idling the time away with gossip, others with jokes. Here and there someone was reading a newspaper or writing in a notebook. Some had already met on the train and were continuing the conversations they had begun during the trip. Although the first groups had arrived two or three days earlier, they had not yet all met. When all the certificate holders arrived, the Jewish Agency would send them all to Vienna.

The arrival of the six newcomers caused everyone to stop and see if these were familiar faces. Seeing that they were strangers, they all returned to their conversations. The newcomers found space for their suitcases and looked around the room. They, too, searched for familiar faces, but not finding any, they remained silent, seating themselves on benches to rest from the trip.

The time was late afternoon. The sun emblazened the sky with brilliant colors. It was the kind of sunset that inspires poets. Shlomo was no poet, but as he looked at the sunset, a verse from Psalms burst from his lips: " 'The heavens declare the glory of God and His works are told of by the firmament.' "

"What did you say?" asked Zissel.

"I said, 'Lift up your eyes to the heavens and see Who has created all these,' " answered Shlomo, indicating the sunset while he quoted from Isaiah.

"Whom were you talking to?" asked Zissel.

"To everyone here."

"But no one was listening."

"Even if they had heard me they would not have understood."

"If so, then whom were you talking to?" persisted Zissel.

"I suppose I was talking to myself," muttered Shlomo.

"You were talking to me, too. I understood what you said," Zissel tried to comfort him.

Shlomo laughed. "You will end up a *rebbetzin* yet and you will cause your father much suffering."

"There could be worse tragedies," laughed Zissel.

After a while, some of the *chalutzim* began to set the tables with trays of bread and butter, cheese and radishes. Others brought cups of steaming coffee, and everyone was called to supper. The invitation met with an immediate response by the hungry pioneers. When they finished eating and ended the discussions begun before supper, it was time to go to sleep. The young men remained in the dining hall. They covered the floor with straw mattresses and each traveler received two sheets — one to cover the mattress and one to cover himself. The young women slept in another room, but they, too, were pioneers and were treated accordingly. They, too, slept on sheets and straw mattresses.

Shlomo was tired. The second he put his head down on the mattress he fell asleep. But after an hour or two he awoke. He suddenly recalled that he had neither recited the afternoon *mincha* and evening *maariv* prayers, nor had he said the *Shema* before retiring. This reminded him that he had not recited the Grace after Meals either, nor had he washed his hands or recited the blessing before eating. The blessings over food were lost forever, but he could still make up the evening prayers that he had forgotten. He could get up now and pray. And he could recite the *Shema* all night long. Nevertheless, he did not get up. He didn't know the reason why, but he did know that he remained lying in his straw bed.

Shlomo thought to himself, "There must be two Shlomos inside of me: one who scolds for not getting up to pray, and the other who holds me back from praying. I know the Shlomo who is scolding me, but where did the other Shlomo come from?"

The "other Shlomo" was, of course, from the Moadon. When Shlomo left the *Beith Midrash* and entered the world of the Moadon, the other Shlomo made his appearance. Now both halves of Shlomo were fighting, not letting him sleep. One urged him to get up—the other to lie down. Between the two, he lost a good night's sleep. When the Angel of Sleep saw Shlomo's suffering he took pity on him and made him drowsy. Nevertheless, Shlomo remained half asleep and half awake. Not even the good angel could help him sleep peacefully that night.

The next morning Shlomo was very tired. The boys collected the mattresses and stacked them outside so the room could serve as a dining hall again. Everyone washed up, polished his shoes or sewed a button on a shirt, and soon all were ready for breakfast.

As Zissel walked into the dining hall, she searched for Shlomo, and when she found him, she came over.

"Good morning," he said.

"Good morning to you," said Zissel. "How did you sleep?"

"I would not be so tired now if I had slept at night," grumbled Shlomo.

"And why didn't you sleep?"

"It's hard to sleep in a new place."

"I slept very well."

"Well, not everyone is so lucky. Enjoy your good fortune."

Seeing that Shlomo was in a bad mood, Zissel changed the subject. "After breakfast, let's go for a walk. Cracow is a beautiful city and I can show you some things that will help you forget your fatigue."

The *chalutzim* had not expected the Jewish Agency to feed them royally and the simple breakfast was identical with their supper. It did not take long to finish eating and leave the table.

Shlomo did not eat at all. He was still disturbed by the night's struggle. Zissel noticed his lack of appetite and began to think that perhaps he was ill. As they left the table, she again invited him to go for a walk.

"Where shall we go?" he asked.

"Let's go out of the Jewish ghetto and walk south toward Vavel," suggested Zissel.

"What can we see there?"

"The graves of Polish royalty."

"I am not interested in Polish royalty," said Shlomo, "Poland is not my homeland. The Poles hate us."

But Zissel persisted, "The famous poet Adam Mitchkevitz is also buried there. I will recite some of his poetry to you. Some say that he was of Jewish descent and was a friend of the Jews."

"What good will it do to hear Polish poetry? I don't speak Polish. You are right, though; he was of Jewish descent. One of his ancestors was a Frankist who converted to Christianity."

"Who were the Frankists?" Zissel asked.

"Let's walk. I'll tell you about them on the way. I can't stand still any longer."

As they walked from street to street, Shlomo told Zissel about Shabtai Tzvi and Yaakov Frank, the false messiahs who eventually converted — the former to Islam and the latter to Christianity — after sewing the seeds of destruction in a multitude of Jewish communities.

"Jews either believed in them adamantly or violently opposed them," explained Shlomo. "The Jews of the Diaspora were drowning in a sea of never-ending troubles, and they clutched at any straw that might save them. They were easily taken in by these false messiahs. Today those episodes are all but forgotten, but at the time they threatened to destroy many Jewish communities. Husbands and wives, fathers and sons found themselves split over the controversy. Countless families were ruined."

Zissel, who had never studied any Jewish history, was all ears. Shlomo spoke only Yiddish, but she was able to speak with him thanks to her grandparents who had spoken to her in Yiddish as long as they were alive. Now she was especially grateful for this heritage. If not for them, she would not have been able to communicate with Shlomo at all.

As long as he was involved in his story, Shlomo had paid no attention to his surroundings. When he was finished, he suddenly noticed where they were and an expression of awe and surprise crossed his face. Zissel asked why.

"This is exactly the place I wanted to see. As Hillel said, 'My feet bring me to the place that I love,' " said Shlomo, quoting Tractate *Sukkah*.

"What's so special about this building?" asked Zissel.

"This is the synagogue of the Rama," he answered.

"Is there any lack of synagogues in Cracow? We must have passed at least half a dozen as we walked."

"This is not just any synagogue. This one is special."

"Why?" she asked.

Shlomo began to tell Zissel about the Rama, "The day-to-day life of every Polish Jew and of many other Jews as well, is dictated by the works of Rabbi Moshe Isserles of Cracow. He condensed the whole Torah into his books and lit the way for observant Jews all over Europe." Shlomo paused and added, "I want to go into the synagogue and put on *tefillin*."

"Why didn't you put on your *tefillin* in the morning?" asked Zissel. "It's almost noon. What happened to you?"

"I guess I forgot," mumbled Shlomo.

"What? How could you forget something you've been doing for so many years?"

"Well, when I used to sit in the *Beith Midrash* in Chedalonova, more than once it happened that I became so absorbed in the *gemara* that I forgot to eat. I suppose one can forget spiritual needs as well as he can physical ones."

Zissel laughed. "You have an answer for everything."

In his heart Shlomo knew that she was right. The true reason for his forgetfulness was that Shlomo of the Moadon had not wanted to put on *tefillin*. But facing the Rama Synagogue, Shlomo of the *Beith Midrash* once again had the upper hand.

"Wait here for me," he said to Zissel, "while I go into the synagogue for a few minutes."

Shlomo entered the synagogue, inspired by the holiness of the site. He turned to the caretaker and asked if he could borrow a pair of *tefillin*. The *shammash* eyed him suspiciously, but finally gave him the *tefillin*. Shlomo put them on and recited the *Shema* and *Shemoneh Esrey* prayers. Then he left.

"Let's go back to the hostel," he said. "We have to continue our journey this afternoon."

Zissel studied Shlomo's face and saw that some change had taken place in him. In the morning he had been restless and distracted. Even while he was telling her about the false messiahs, he had been preoccupied. He was in one place while his thoughts were in another. Something had been bothering him. Now he was different. His peace of mind was mirrored in the expression on his face.

Shlomo and Zissel returned to the hostel, and after dinner and a short rest, the *chalutzim* continued their trip.

On the train, the *chalutzim* had time to become better acquainted. In Cracow they had split up into small groups to go sight-seeing, spending only mealtimes together. Now, as some sixty-odd *chalutzim* were crowded together into three railway coaches, they began to form friendships.

In Trieste, they joined the hundreds of others already housed in the Jewish Agency transit camp, all awaiting their turn to set sail for Eretz Yisrael. A ship left every two weeks. Some *chalutzim* were lucky and received a place on board after only a few days' wait; others had to wait weeks. This was a typical youth camp. Each morning began with exercises. Between breakfast and lunch, the *chalutzim* either participated in various sports or went sight-seeing in town. Those who were tired of both activities would spend the morning at the port, watching the ships and marveling at the sea. For most of them, this was their first encounter with the sea. Some had not even lived in the vicinity of a small river. Thus the sea was a novel experience, and they did not want to be afraid of it when they began the long boat voyage to Eretz Yisrael.

Between lunch and supper, the program was the same as

it had been in the morning. The food, too, was the same, just as it had been in Cracow. Occasionally, a bit of meat was served at lunch. When they had nothing left to do but await their turn to set sail, the *chalutzim* would sit around the camp and engage in interminable discussions on one subject only—ideology. These ideological discussions invariably turned into debates, as there were almost as many ideological positions as there were *chalutzim*. Shlomo had thought that they were all united under one flag. Now he learned that for some *chalutzim* the blue in their flag was a strong, deep blue like the sky in Eretz Yisrael. For others it was a pale blue like the sky in the diaspora. Shlomo found out that there were even some *chalutzim* who did not accept Hebrew as their national tongue. They thought that Yiddish should be the Jewish national language. This he could not understand. He learned that these *chalutzim*, the Poalei Zion, had initially been opposed to Zion. After a while Shlomo gave up trying to figure out such an impossible puzzle.

For some of the *chalutzim* the return to Zion was their main goal; for others it was subordinate to the cause of social justice. For still others it was not even of secondary importance, as they were totally devoted to the ideal of equality among mankind.

When Shlomo asked one of them why in the world he wanted to go to Palestine when he could find all the equality one could desire in the Soviet Union, he was told, "You are right. But instead of my going to Soviet Russia, I intend to bring Soviet Russia to Eretz Yisrael. The revolution of the masses must encompass the whole world."

Shlomo could not accept such an answer. One did not

have to go all the way to Eretz Yisrael to promote the Soviet Revolution. This could be done in Poland, too. Shlomo thought to himself, "The blue in his flag is so washed out that it looks more like the white of surrender than the blue and white flag of rebirth."

Since Zissel had found many Polish-speaking friends in the camp she no longer spent so much time with Shlomo. It was much easier for her to express herself in Polish than in Yiddish, especially now that Shlomo had even begun trying to speak in Hebrew. When the *chalutzim* first heard Shlomo's Hebrew they burst out laughing at his Ashkenazic accent. Embarrassed, Shlomo retorted, "Were it not for the Holy Tongue heard in the *Beith Midrash* and synagogue, there would *be* no Hebrew language for you to speak!"

Lately, Shlomo had begun to walk around bareheaded. Nevertheless, when he heard any of the *chalutzim* mocking the *yeshivah* world he would fiercely come to its defense. He spent many hours in introspection, torn between two extremes. Sometimes he had an overwhelming desire to go back to the *yeshivah*, and other times he felt compelled to flee as far as possible from it. Distressed and worn out by the terrible struggle within himself and realizing that he could not just return to his old place in the *Beith Midrash* as if nothing had happened, he decided that he must cut off all his ties with his past. He must remove himself completely from anything that might remind him of the *Beith Midrash*. In one corner of his suitcase were a pair of *tzitzith* and the precious set of *tefillin* his father had bought him for his *bar mitzvah*. When he left Chedalonova it would never have occurred to him that he could do without them, but now he began to consider the possibility. When he tried to take them out of his suitcase, however, his hand refused to obey him. He could not bear to touch the *tefillin*. With a sigh, Shlomo said to himself, "I am destined to struggle with myself. My suffering is not yet over."

One day, the names were announced of those who were to set sail for Eretz Yisrael on the morrow. Zissel heard her name called. Afraid that she would have to travel alone, she listened nervously to the rest of the list until finally, Shlomo's name was also called, and she let out a sigh of relief. That day was a holiday for all those would be on the boat. After packing their meager belongings and eating supper, they gathered together in the camp yard and sang and danced late into the night.

In the morning all the *chalutzim* accompanied them to the boat. The new passengers boarded the ship and immediately went to the rails to catch a last glimpse of their friends in the port. When the gangplank was removed, they started to sing *Hatikvah*. But some, such as the Poalei Zion, sang with no enthusiasm, barely opening their mouths. As the boat began to move away from the port, everyone waved.

Even when the boat was far away and they could no longer see their friends, the *chalutzim* remained on deck, staring at the sea and contemplating the future. Their homes, their family and friends, the country where they had been born and had grown up—all this was behind them. They were now beginning a new life. Would they ever come back here?

Finally, they went below deck to examine their new living quarters. There were several large cabins, each holding a few dozen passengers. There were also smaller first-class cabins for the tourists and merchants who were used to living in comfort wherever they went.

Some of the ship's passengers were elderly men and women. For years they had been planning to go to Eretz Yisrael, and now, with their last ounce of strength, they were realizing their dream. They were familiar with our sages' dictum "Whoever is buried in Eretz Yisrael is considered as if he were buried under the Temple Altar (*Kethuboth* 111)." What better resting-place could there be for their weary bones than under the Temple Altar, in the very ground from which Adam had been created. Rambam wrote, "Man was created from the selfsame place from which he receives atonement" (*Mishneh Torah*, Laws of the Temple, ch. II).

Rabbi Meshullam Charif of Pogromova was one of the elderly people on board, although he was not old enough to be sailing toward death. But he had despaired of Poland and was fleeing to Eretz Yisrael after several Jews from his town were murdered by the Poles. He intended to settle in the holy city of Jerusalem and establish a *yeshivah* in memory of the Jews of Pogromova. He would devote himself to teaching Torah until God in His Grace would gather in all the exiles and redeem His land and His people.

Rabbi Meshullam didn't wait to arrive in Jerusalem in order to begin teaching Torah. The first day on board he had gathered together all the old men and formed a *shiur*. His group also prayed together, morning and evening, in one corner of the deck. Since they were only nine men they had to recruit a tenth from among the non-observant passengers, but the *chalutzim* would not agree to join the *minyan*. They were opposed to prayer on principle, and always went bareheaded. It was no coincidence that Shlomo was never on deck at prayer time. He knew very well that they needed a tenth man for a *minyan*. Were they to approach him he would have to decide one way or the other. He knew that he would not be able to refuse, so he chose to stay below deck.

Once, Shlomo put on his cap and joined the *gemara* lesson. He had heard of Rabbi Meshullam Charif years ago in Chedalonova and was eager to hear him in person. The passage they were learning was familiar to Shlomo and he could not restrain himself from asking the *Rav* a question. The *Rav* paused, surprised, and exclaimed, "You have asked well, my son!"

Even before the *Rav* could word his answer, Shlomo countered with an answer of his own. Now the *Rav* was really amazed. Whether or not this was the answer that he himself had intended to give, he now added nothing. Instead he said, "I can see that you are a *talmid chacham*. Why don't you join our *minyan*?"

Shlomo hesitated, and then replied, "Our sages of blessed memory stated in *Pesachim*, 'One who has studied and then deserted the Torah is worse than all others.' "

Hearing such a cynical answer, the *Rav* looked closely at Shlomo. What he saw was suffering and sadness, not mockery.

"If you know the teachings of our Rabbis, then why don't you return to our Torah?" asked the *Rav*.

Shlomo answered slowly. "A man's soul is very complex. Some things are within man's control, yet they are not. Life is not simple."

"Explain yourself," urged the *Rav*.

But Shlomo would not. Instead, he left the group.

On the seventh day, those on deck saw the first houses of Haifa on the horizon. They ran to spread the news that the end of their trip was near. All rushed on deck to catch their first glimpse of Eretz Yisrael. The port seemed to be approaching them rapidly. Shlomo, very excited, stood beside the rail, absorbed in himself. His head was filled with so many different, contradictory thoughts that he was overwhelmed. He couldn't even tell which thoughts were his own and which were foreign to him. So absorbed in himself was he that he didn't even notice Zissel at his side until she asked, "What strange thoughts are you thinking, Shlomo?"

"What?" asked Shlomo, startled.

"Now that we've arrived at our destination, we should rejoice and prepare ourselves for practical deeds. Put your disturbing thoughts aside," said Zissel gently.

Shlomo sighed. "You are right, of course. The first thing we must do when we get off the ship is write to our parents. When we wrote last week from Trieste, we had no return address to send them. I am very anxious to hear how things are at home. These are troubled times for the Jews in Poland, and I am worried about the people of Chedalonova."

"Yes," said Zissel, "I will write home first thing. I miss my parents very much. We left home only a short time ago, but it seems like years have passed."

The ship cast anchor, the gangplank was lowered and passengers began to alight. The first of the *chalutzim* were already standing on the soil of Eretz Yisrael.

The situation in Poland was bad. Since Hitler's ascent to power in Germany, conditions in Poland had worsened from day to day. Anti-Semitism had ancient roots in Poland and appeared in many guises. In times of trouble, when the Polish eagle was preyed upon by her ever-hungry neighbors and Poland was in danger of being torn to bits, the Poles would bury their hatred for the Jews and share their troubles as if they were brothers. At such times the Polish national poets even spoke of the redemption of Poland and of Israel in one breath. But the hatred remained hidden deep in their hearts, silent, waiting. When the day came that Poland gained the upper hand and was free again, the old hatred for the Jews would ooze out of the hidden places in Polish hearts until it overflowed. Now, ever since Hitler had legitimized the spilling of Jewish blood, Poland was eager to follow the German example. True, the Poles had always hated the Germans, who were constantly trying to cut Poland into pieces. They had successfully done so three times in the last two hundred years. Now again, for a fourth time, the Germans were threatening Polish sovereignty. Nevertheless, as far as the "Jewish problem" was concerned, the Poles were in complete agreement with the Germans. They were quite willing to drive the Jews out of Poland, just as the Germans were doing in Germany.

The trouble was that the situation in the two countries was not the same. The Germans could claim that many of the Jews were not true German citizens and therefore had no right to remain in Germany. Either they themselves, or their fathers or grandfathers before them, were foreigners who had emigrated from Poland and settled illegally in Germany. Therefore they could be sent back where they came from. The Jews of Poland, however, had lived in the country for over a thousand years.

Nevertheless, the Poles did not give up. If they couldn't actually expel the Jews, they could at least make them feel highly unwelcome. For instance, two strong young Poles would stand outside every Jewish store, bearing a large placard. It was illegal discrimination to prohibit customers from shopping in Jewish stores — and it would also paint a poor public image of Poland internationally — but there was no law against putting up a sign stating that a certain store was owned by a Jew. The point was obvious. If, despite the placard, some good-hearted Pole would attempt to patronize the store, the sign holders would take a few steps forward and block the entrance, managing not to notice that someone was trying to get inside. No one could be arrested for misunderstanding another person's intentions. Hearts do not stand trial.

Thus, the Jewish stores stood empty all day long. Merchandise lay untouched on the shelves, as worthless as an unturned stone. When the shop owners' bills were due, they found themselves penniless. One might ask why they didn't make a living from one another. After all, *Jews* could not be prevented from entering Jewish stores. Three thousand years ago, when the sages had come to King David with a similar problem, he had advised them to make a living from one another. Even then they had objected to this piece of advice, stating: "A handful cannot satisfy a lion" (*Berachoth* 3).

The situation degenerated so, that some Jews began to think of emigrating to a friendlier country. The vast majority, however, were unable to do so. They remained in their own places and accepted their misfortune.

The hatred of the Poles, when they saw that they had not succeeded in driving the Jews out of Poland, knew no bounds. What *chutzpah* these Jews had — opening their stores in the morning and closing them in the evening as if everything were 'business as usual'. It was as if keeping their stores open was more important to them than the business itself. This was an open provocation, as if the Jews were proclaiming to the Poles: You want us to run away, but we will not budge, for Poland belongs to us!

Could there be any greater *chutzpah* than that of a Jew who claims that Poland belongs to *him* and not to the Poles? A money-hungry Jew — a Shylock — might possibly be forgiven, but not a Jew so stubborn as to keep his store open in the face of Polish objection.

The Poles' anger grew to murderous proportions. They set aside their placards and took up clubs instead. Some of these clubs were used on the heads of the Jews of Chedalonova.

One incident involved Zissel's father, the lawyer Edmond

Blitz. Two members of the Jewish Bund approached two Poles who were blocking the entrance to Moscovitz's store. "You are breaking the law," said the Bundists. "It is prohibited to boycott a store."

"We are not boycotting the store," retorted the Poles. "We are simply proclaiming that this store is owned by a Jew."

"It is forbidden to boycott indirectly," said the Bundists.

"Who are you to teach us what Polish law forbids?"

"We are citizens of Poland," answered the Jews, "just like you. And we wish to cure the social ills of our country."

At that, the Poles' blood began to boil. They were speechless. But actions speak louder than words, and without wasting words, they took justice into their own hands. The two poor Bundists were badly beaten and only managed to escape thanks to a few Jewish bystanders who came to their aid.

The Bundists spent several days in bed. When they were back on their feet, they approached Edmond Blitz and retained him as their lawyer in a suit against the Poles who had beaten them.

The trial took place a few days later in a courtroom packed with Poles, a few Jews interspersed among them. Edmond Blitz represented Aryeh and Ze'ev, the Bundists. The lawyer Polinski represented Stashek and Yantek. One of the Bundists was called to the witness stand to tell his story. Then the lawyer began to cross-examine him.

"Your words were an open provocation, purposely intended to incite these two upright Polish citizens to violence. You were just asking for a fight," accused Polinski.

"What kind of provocation are you talking about?" asked Ze'ev.

"That statement of yours 'We are Polish citizens just like you are,'" answered Polinski.

"Yes," said Ze'ev, "that's what I said. But that's no provocation. That's the truth."

"No," said Polinski. "That is not the truth. Poland belongs to the Poles — not to the Jews. Even if you are legally Polish citizens, you are still merely guests in Poland. The comparison that you drew was insulting, and one which the Polish people cannot forgive."

"I am no guest in Poland. I was born here and have never lived anywhere else," protested Ze'ev.

"You only happened to be born in Poland because your father happened by chance to be in Poland at the time of your birth. And your father only happened to be born in Poland because his father chanced to be staying in Poland when *he* was born. Even if your family happened to have lived in Poland for a thousand years, you would nevertheless remain guests, not true Poles."

Edmond Blitz tried to correct Polinski. "Assimilation is a perfectly natural phenomenon. People whose fathers and grandfathers were born in Poland — people who speak Polish, are educated in Polish schools, and are at home in the Polish culture — are Poles in every respect. No discrimination should be made between them and between Poles of Slavic origin."

At these words a murmur ran through the crowd. Edmond Blitz's comments had made their ears ring. That Ze'ev the Bundist could speak of equal rights and Polish citizenship for both Poles and Jews — that might be understandable. But to speak of Poles of Jewish origin and Poles of Slavic origin — as though the Polish nation was a conglomerate of two races — that was absolutely too much. The audacity of this *"Jid"* who considered himself Polish infuriated them.

Then it was Stashek's turn at the witness stand. He told the following story.

"Yantek and I stood peacefully beside the store of the *Jid* Moscovitz. We held a placard stating that this was a Jewish store, so that people could decide for themselves whether they wanted to shop there or not. Along came these two Jews" (here he pointed at Ze'ev and Aryeh) "and provoked us until they made our blood boil! What happened afterwards we can't even remember."

The cross-examination began. Polinski asked, "How exactly did the Jews provoke you?"

Stashek answered, "They told us that they had come to correct the social injustices in Poland."

"Come where?" asked Polinski.

Stashek hesitated and then answered, "They said they had come to Poland to cure the social injustice here."

Here Edmond Blitz objected, "Did they say that they had come to Poland — or to the boycotted store — to cure the social injustice there?"

"They were obviously saying they had come to Poland to correct the social injustice here," replied Stashek.

This answer aroused the audience to a state of agitation. The Poles were furious at the Jews' insulting comment that they had come to Poland to cure its social injustices. The verdict was to be pronounced in two days' time. Nevertheless, it was already perfectly clear what the verdict would be. Whenever Polinski took the stand, the judge would look directly at him, nodding his head in agreement as he listened. Whenever Edmond Blitz spoke, the judge turned his cold eyes on the empty space in the middle of the hall, his face a wax mask.

Two days later, the townspeople of Chedalonova assembled in the Court Hall to hear the verdict. No Jews were present. They had already read the verdict in the judge's eyes during the cross-examination. While waiting for the judge, the Poles in the courtroom repeated Stashek's testimony, egging each other on with comments about the insolence of the *"Jids."* Polinski and Blitz sat, each one in his own seat, as if the other did not exist. Ze'ev and Aryeh sat in their chairs, their eyes betraying their fear of the future. Stashek and Yantek sat looking as though they were at a wedding, their faces beaming with joy.

When the judge entered the courtroom, a tension-filled silence spread through the room. He took out a document and began to read:

"The accused Stashek and Yantek are found innocent of the charges pressed against them on the following grounds: Stashek's testimony rings true. It is not honorable for a Pole to lose control of himself to such an extent that he cannot even recall what he did. Yet even if we do accept the testimony of the prosecution that Stashek and Yantek actually did perform the acts of which they are accused, they cannot be blamed. It is well known that the Polish people defend their country's honor with all their might. Anyone who insults Poland must know that he will elicit a very strong reaction from the Poles—a reaction so strong that a Pole might not even recall what he did. The prosecution must apologize to the Polish people for their arrogance in claiming that they came to Poland to correct its social injustices. Poland has no need of strangers to help correct its social ills."

When the judge finished, a furor arose among the crowd in the courtroom. A hearty round of applause for his speech was mixed with cries of *"Jids* to Palestine!"

Who knows what might have befallen Edmond Blitz and the Bundists Ze'ev and Aryeh had not two policemen escorted them out of the courtroom and sent them home.

Edmond Blitz was heart-broken. That day, his entire world collapsed. For years he had tried to be a Pole in every possible way, and now the judge had ruled that he was only a stranger in Poland, not a real Pole at all.

For two days Edmond stayed away from his office. In no condition to work, he was completely disoriented and incapable of concentrating. Finally, on the third day, making a tremendous effort to pull himself together, he forced himself to go to work.

When he didn't return home on time, Rozeshka went to the office to find him. Upon entering his room, she found her husband slumped in his chair, his head leaning against the backrest, as if he were asleep. When she came up to him and gently tapped his shoulder to wake him up, he fell out of the chair. Hearing Rozeshka's screams, the neighbors came running in. Someone ran to call the Jewish doctor, Raphael Gutheartz. One look at Edmond was sufficient for the doctor to pronounce him dead. After examining the body thoroughly, he saw the small round hole in Edmond's skull. But no weapon could be found.

"Blitz did not die," the doctor announced. "He was murdered."

The entire Jewish community of Chedalonova attended the funeral. If during his lifetime Edmond Blitz had cut himself off from his people, he returned to them upon his death. A Jew who dies a martyr's death is forgiven all his sins and is called a *chassid*, a righteous person (*Sanhedrin* 47). And any Jew murdered by Gentiles simply because he was Jewish, has died a holy death. Jewish law states that he who dies *al kiddush haShem*, to sanctify God's name in this world, is a part of the Jewish community. Even those who had no contact with the deceased during his lifetime must now tear their clothing and mourn for him. And he must be eulogized in the synagogue and *Beith Midrash*.

The Jews of Chedalonova treated Edmond accordingly. At his funeral oration in the *Beith Midrash*, mention was made of the increasingly troubled times for the Jewish community. There were new signs every day. The Jews of Chedalonova were urged to strengthen their spirits and not, God forbid, fall into despair.

Rozeshka Blitz was left all alone. Zushka had left home for Eretz Yisrael, and she had no one to comfort her in her heartbreak. She had no friends among the Jewish women of Chedalonova, having purposely cut herself off from the Jewish community, just as her husband had done. All of her friends were Polish. But now the Polish women wouldn't even look at her. Since the trial she was no longer a Pole but a Jewess—no better than any of the others. She had no family in Chedalonova either. There was no way out. Zushka must come home. Rozeshka was sure her daughter would come when she heard what had happened. She must notify Zushka of the tragedy, but how could she, when she hadn't yet received any mail and didn't know her daughter's address?

Rozeshka went to visit Mrs. Sharfson to ask if she had received a letter from Shlomo, but her answer, too, was negative. She even went to the Moadon Hechalutz to ask how to address her letter, but they also told her that it was too early to write to Zushka in Eretz Yisrael. She might even still be on the boat. There was nothing to do but to wait patiently for Zushka's first letter with a return address. Rozeshka had no strength to wait patiently. She could do nothing but sit forlornly alone, yearning impatiently for the first letter from her beloved daughter.

Not all of the *chalutzim* had the same destination. There were those who turned to the *kibbutzim* and *moshavim* to work the land, and there were others who went to the villages or to the city to do manual labor — each according to his training and experience. Shlomo and Zissel went to Kibbutz Dath Ha'avodah. Zissel worked in the children's house while Shlomo, who had not yet mastered any particular skill, worked at a different job every day.

The *kibbutz* was large, with room for a wide spectrum of opinions. Everyone agreed that work was their "religion," but some were more "religious" than others. Those who believed devoutly worked even on Shabbath, and with religious fervor. Those who were less devout also worked on Shabbath, but only because they could not distinguish between the holy and the profane.

There were other differences of opinion among the members of the *kibbutz*, such as their attitude toward the Arabs. The *chalutzim* whose only religion was work, could not forgive the Arabs for letting the country lie desolate for so many centuries. Even now, the work of the Arabs brought no blessing to the land. Content to continue in their traditional ways, the Arabs would never build up the country or make the wilderness flower. Therefore, these *chalutzim* did not value the Arabs, their work or their opinions. They considered Eretz Yisrael their own, and they felt free to build it as they wished.

On the other hand, there were *chalutzim* who believed fervently that equality was also a supreme value, and they were troubled by the knowledge that their lives were more comfortable than those of the Arab villagers. Furthermore, now that they were in Eretz Yisrael, they saw things differently than they had in Chedalonova, Nachrovah and Temyonovah. There, they could only imagine what Eretz Yisrael was like; here, they were confronted with reality, and there is a tremendous difference between imagination and reality. What can be built by one's imagination in an hour may take a thousand years to build in reality. In their imagination, life in Eretz Yisrael had appeared idyllic, but in reality nothing is ideal. Before arriving in Palestine, they had imagined that *chalutzim* worked all day long, singing and dancing in their free time. Now that they were actually living in Eretz Yisrael, they were confronted with the truth — not everyone was a worker. There were small businessmen and rich merchants. One could even eke out a living at unproductive labor such as selling cold drinks.

And there was unemployment. While some people were indeed singing and dancing, others were sighing because they had looked for work but couldn't find any. In short, there was no equality in life, a fact which disturbed the peace of mind of the *kibbutzniks*. The *kibbutzim* had equality, but how could they come to terms with the world outside the *kibbutz*?

Shlomo also could find no peace of mind. He was not disturbed by the conflict between the religions of work and equality, but by the conflict between the *kibbutz* and the *Beith Midrash*. He was still torn between two worlds and neither would relinquish its hold on him.

One day the news spread in the *kibbutz* that riots had broken out in several areas in Eretz Yisrael. Arabs had murdered a number of Jews, and the Jews had retaliated vigorously.

Tempers rose on the *kibbutz*. A small minority defended the Arabs, saying that they were not to blame for their violence. They felt that they were being driven off their land. They should not be held responsible if their discontent caused them to overreact and to take revenge.

But this was a small minority. The vast majority of the *kibbutz* members joined the Haganah to defend the Jewish homeland in Eretz Yisrael. Those who had defended the Arabs began to feel uncomfortable on the *kibbutz*; they were like outcasts. Their friends avoided them and considered them traitors to the Jewish cause. Gradually they realized that they would have to leave the community, but there was nowhere for them to go. They knew that there was no point in going to a different *kibbutz*, for the situation would be the same wherever they went. Neither did they wish to move to the city. After all, they were *chalutzim*, and their place was in the fields. But the more the riots spread, and the more Jewish blood was spilt,. the worse their position in the *kibbutz* became.

Finally, the minority group called a meeting to decide what to do. One of the group, Elka of Temyonovah, said,

"Apparently we were mistaken. The only place in the world that will ever be a true home for us is the Soviet Union. There, honesty and justice, equality and freedom, rule supreme. That is the only place for true lovers of peace. If we really want to live a good life we must leave Palestine and go to Russia."

Elka's words struck her listeners like thunder. They shocked, but in some hearts, they rang true. And eventually, they convinced. There did not seem to be any other alternative. It had obviously been a mistake for these *chalutzim* to come to Palestine. They should have immigrated to the U.S.S.R. and taken part in the Workers' Revolution. Then, after the revolution, they could have come to Eretz Yisrael. What kind of life could one live in Eretz Yisrael without the Socialist Revolution? No, they were not giving the Jewish homeland up, but first they must bring the Socialist Revolution to the Jews. Then they would establish a binational Jewish-Arab state. They would even have two national languages: Yiddish and Arabic.

After a prolonged discussion in which everyone repeated and rephrased the same views, they agreed to Elka's proposal. It could not, however, be carried out immediately. They must prepare themselves.

Zissel was not disturbed by the state of affairs in Eretz Yisrael. She had not come searching for equality; she had come because of Shlomo. If nothing disturbed Shlomo, then nothing disturbed her either. She had already written a second letter to her parents and was awaiting their reply. Despite her intense homesickness, Zissel had no intentions of returning to Chedalonova. A letter from her parents would suffice to make her feel better.

Every day after work the daily mail was distributed. Zissel would stand, all ears, listening to the names of those lucky people who had received mail. When the whole list had been read and her name had not been called, she would sigh with disappointment.

One day, Zissel's name was called and she was given an envelope. She caressed the letter, but did not open it in public. Everything was common property on the *kibbutz* except one's emotions. This was her own private affair and she didn't intend to share it with anyone. Zissel went back to her room, where she could open the envelope in privacy. Before beginning to read it, she noticed spots on the paper, as though drops of water had fallen on it.

As Zissel read, her heart fell. The letter raised many more questions than it answered. Her mother was begging her to come home as soon as possible. Something had happened that her mother didn't want to write about, but Zissel would find out when she came. Zissel had also expected to receive a few lines from her father, but there were none. Could it be that he had not yet forgiven her for leaving home? Her father was a Polish patriot and he had considered her act a betrayal of the Polish homeland. Zissel smiled to herself at the thought. Her father had absolutely no idea of what a national Jewish homeland meant. The agitation in the Jewish world over the idea of a Jewish state had not touched him. To him, there was no Jewish problem. He didn't believe that there was any reason for the Jewish nation to continue to exist. Instead, all the Jews of Poland should become Poles; all the Jews of France, Frenchmen; the Jews of England,

Englishmen; and so on all over the world.

Very well. Her father was angry at the moment. Eventually, he would come to terms with his daughter and her "betrayal." She needn't take it too seriously. He would probably write a few lines in the next letter.

But what could have happened in Chedalonova? Why hadn't her mother explained in her letter? Perhaps it was only a trick to get her to come home. Her mother knew that if she wrote the whole story, it probably wouldn't be important enough to make Zissel return, so she only hinted dramatically at some imaginary catastrophe in her letter. Poor Mother. She must miss Zissel terribly. Zissel missed her too, but she still couldn't see herself going back to Poland.

Zissel sat in her room, weighing the pros and cons of the matter, unable to reach a decision. Finally, she had an idea. If she had received a letter from home, Shlomo might also have received mail. If something had really happened in Chedalonova, his parents would have written, and he would be able to tell her. When her letter had come, she had rushed immediately to her room, not waiting for all the mail to be distributed. She wasn't sure that Shlomo had received mail, but it was logical to assume so. Both their parents probably answered their letters the same day they received them.

Zissel ran to find Shlomo.

"What news did you get from home?" she asked.

"I haven't even received one letter yet," Shlomo replied. "Why do you ask?"

Disappointed, Zissel pulled her letter from her pocket and handed it to Shlomo.

Shlomo opened the letter, read it once, and then reread

it. At the second reading he understood that something of real import must have happened in Zissel's family. He noticed the spots on the paper and recognized them for what they were — dried tears. Returning the letter to Zissel, he said, "Perhaps I will get a letter tomorrow or the next day and then we'll know what happened." Disappointedly, Zissel pocketed the letter. Who knew when Shlomo would get mail? It might take more than just a day or two.

When he was alone, Shlomo began to think. He must prepare Zissel for bad news. If necessary, he could conceal whatever news he received from home. His mother wrote in Yiddish, and his father in Yiddish interspersed with phrases from the Holy Tongue. Zissel was just beginning to speak Hebrew and could read neither Hebrew nor Yiddish. She would certainly not be able to decipher his father's fancy rabbinic handwriting.

Nevertheless, he decided that it would be best to tell Zissel the whole truth when he found out what had happened so that she would fulfill her mother's request. Otherwise Zissel would never agree to go home. He himself didn't yet know exactly what had transpired, but Shlomo was sharp, and he realized that it was no mere caprice that had prevented Edmond Blitz from adding a few lines. Obviously, he had not written because he could not. A person who is even half alive can write at least a line or two. Therefore, reasoned Shlomo, Edmond Blitz was either dead or close to it.

The truth was that Shlomo really didn't want Zissel to go home. He knew that she cared for him and he had grown to care for her as well. More than once he had thought of asking her to marry him. Nevertheless, he did not want to be the cause of her refusing her mother's request. He couldn't place his own personal wishes above her poor mother's welfare.

All that evening Shlomo discussed the dangers facing Polish Jewry with Zissel. Esau was giving free reign to his murderous hands and the voice of Jacob could not silence them. The lives of Polish Jews were cheap. Every day there was a new incident in one place or another.

It took another week until Shlomo received a letter from home with the news of the trial and Edmond Blitz's death. During that week Shlomo had also begun to worry. If Zissel had already received mail and he had not, perhaps something really terrible had happened in Chedalonova. Now that he knew the whole story, he was filled with sorrow over the tragedy that had befallen Zissel's family.

He made a great effort and managed to tell Zissel the news. For days, she was in tears. She cried over the death of her father, but she was also unhappy because now she would have to return to Poland and to part from Shlomo. Shlomo tried to comfort her.

He also promised Zissel, "We are not parting permanently — only for a while. Go back home to your mother and convince her to come back to Eretz Yisrael with you. When you come back you will find me waiting." Forcing a smile, he added, "I'm sure no other girl will carry me off in the meantime!"

Even Zissel smiled through her tears.

Zissel had little to do to prepare for her trip. Shlomo took care of her tickets. She had no idea where the money even came from. He was not one to discuss his actions when it came to matters of charity. A few days later several members of the *kibbutz* accompanied Zissel to the port. When she reached the gangplank just before boarding the ship, Zissel and Shlomo looked into each other's eyes for a long time. One pair of eyes said, "Promise!" The other answered, "I promise."

Zissel boarded the ship, and on the verge of tears, she waved to Shlomo from the deck. He waved back, for from that distance, it was no longer possible to look into each other's eyes.

When the news spread throughout the *kibbutz* that Elka and her group had decided to emigrate to Soviet Russia, the *kibbutz* members reacted very strongly. Some were so furious over this betrayal that their anger knew no bounds. Others were quite happy to be rid of Elka and her followers. They wanted to see the country purified from those rebellious sons whose hearts belonged to foreign masters. If they did not rejoice in the rebuilding of Eretz Yisrael, let them go. Let only those who were absolutely faithful to the Jewish homeland remain.

When it became known, however, that Shlomo was part of the group, many eyebrows were raised. This young man who still had the *Beith Midrash* deep in his heart, what in the world could he find in Bolshevik Russia where it was forbidden to even mention the word *Beith Midrash*? Some refused to believe that Shlomo was really leaving, while others simply said, "Poor fellow! So much learning has confused him completely; he cannot tell his left hand from his right."

The members of the *kibbutz* had often asked Shlomo whether he had been to Jerusalem yet. When he would answer in the negative, they would look at him quizzically and ask, "Not even once?"

"Haven't you even gone to the Western Wall once?" asked Shmuel of Nachrovah. "How do you explain that? Every observant Jew the world over would give fortunes to see the Wall or touch its stones. They cannot, because they are so far away, but you — you who live in Eretz Yisrael — why haven't you ever gone to the Wall?"

The longer Shmuel went on with his teasing, the harder Shlomo tried to compose a convincing answer. Finally, he said, "The Wall doesn't have the same significance for you that it does for me. To you it is a historical site as interesting as any other site described in your history books. But to me, the Wall is not merely a historical site; it is a Holy Place. The Divine Presence has never left there. One must prepare himself before he approaches such a place. One cannot take his knapsack and walking stick and hike over to a place like the Temple Mount. The profane and the holy do not mix. But one day, when I am ready, I will go up to Jerusalem and kiss the stones of the Wall." As he spoke, Shlomo himself became convinced by his enthusiastic speech.

When he was all alone, Shlomo admitted to himself that this was not the real reason for his hesitation. In truth, he had not even begun to prepare himself to go up to Jerusalem. His real reason for postponing the visit was his fear that the stones of the Wall would not allow him to return to the *kibbutz*, and that he would not be strong enough to resist their pull. The Wall must be a much stronger spiritual force than the *Beith Midrash*. If he was still fighting to escape the influence of the *Beith Midrash*, how would he be able to resist the Wall?

But, after his inspiring speech to Shmuel, he had no

choice but to go up to Jerusalem at least once. There must be an end to his preparations.

One day, Shlomo made his trip. He left early in the morning so as to be back home by dark. One bus took him to the crossroads and another brought him to Jerusalem.

Once in the city, Shlomo did not go straight to the Wall. He postponed the confrontation as long as possible. First he headed for the Jewish Quarter of the Old City, walking through the crowded narrow alleyways and examining the houses, stores and workshops from the outside. What surprised him most was the large number of synagogues, *Batei Midrash* and *yeshivoth*. He would never have guessed that there could be so many synagogues and houses of learning in such a small area. Back in Chedalonova, he had heard of some of the more famous ones, such as the Churvah of Rabbi Yehuda *heChassid*. But here he found many synagogues and *yeshivoth* he had never heard of. Shlomo walked around, trying to see everything. Everywhere, he found people learning. Some were younger and some older, some were reciting *Tehillim* and others learning *mishnah*; some were learning *gemara* while others discussed the commentaries of Tosaphoth and Maharsha. It was such a warm, familiar atmosphere — an entire self-contained world, free of problems and doubts — not wrestling with itself, not struggling or searching for solutions to the riddle of Man and his world. This was a straight, paved road that one could safely follow.

Shlomo peered inside many buildings, but he didn't stop. Finally, he said, "I must go to the Wall. It's already late. By the time I get home it will be dark."

Passing one house with open windows, Shlomo heard a familiar voice. He paused for a minute to listen, trying to identify the speaker. Then, unable to resist, he entered the building, suddenly realizing it was a *Beith Midrash*. A few fifteen- and sixteen-year-old boys were sitting on benches around a medium sized table, their *gemaroth* open before them. At the head of the table sat Rabbi Meshullam Charif, explaining a passage to his students. They were so absorbed in their learning that they didn't even notice Shlomo, who took a seat on the end of one of the benches. The boy next to him gave him a passing glance and quickly turned back to his *gemara*.

Shlomo sat and listened. Rav Meshullam's voice was pleasant, and the eternal tune of the *gemara* sounded very sweet. Shlomo thought of the *Beith Midrash* in Chedalonova. He remembered his revered Rav with his long beard, surrounded by young boys, one of whom was Shlomo. He was filled with longing for those days, the best years of his life.

"Why did I ever leave? What have I found to replace that world?" he asked, unable to answer his own questions. The voices of the *Rav* of Chedalonova and Rav Meshullam merged as Shlomo was in both places at once. How good he felt. He had come home. Everything that had passed over him since he left the *Beith Midrash* in Chedalonova until now had been a nightmare. No, he had never really left, and therefore there was no need to return. Suddenly, the *Rav* was silent.

Just as Shlomo began to wonder why the tune had been interrupted, he felt a hand on his shoulder. He pulled himself out of his revery, focused his eyes, and saw Rav Meshullam before him. The *Rav* had looked up from his *gemara* to explain a difficult point and had seen Shlomo. Recognizing him immediately, he stopped the lesson, stood up and came over to him. For a few seconds, Shlomo was confused and disoriented; but he quickly pulled himself together, and stood up in deference to the Rav.

"How good that you have come to us," said the *Rav*. "You belong here. There are many young people who are beset by doubts and must struggle with themselves, but if they have learned Torah, the Torah comes to their aid and brings them back to themselves."

All the students were staring at Shlomo. He was not dressed like a *yeshivah* student. Where had the *Rav* made his acquaintance? What did he mean by "young people beset by doubts"? What kind of doubts? If the doubts revolved around Jewish law, why did he specify *young* people beset by doubts? Even *talmidei chachamim* and heads of *yeshivoth* had to wrestle with difficult questions. These youngsters were not aware of any other kind of doubts. They knew that there were religious and nonreligious Jews, but neither of these was in doubt. Each believed firmly in his own way.

Before returning to his seat at the head of the table, the *Rav* spoke to Shlomo again. "You will stay with us?"

"I am on my way to the *Kothel*," answered Shlomo. "That is why I came to Jerusalem."

"Then after you visit the Wall," said the Rav, "come back to us. We will find you a place among us. This is the younger group, but there are older students here for you to learn with. You need not worry about money. Our students receive free board and lodging."

Shlomo listened but did not answer. Then he said "*Shalom*" and left the *Beith Midrash*. Suddenly he realized how hungry he was. He had not eaten since early morning. He took out a few slices of bread and some olives he had brought with him from the *kibbutz* and found himself a place to sit on some stairs in an alleyway near the Dung Gate. When he finished eating, he got up to go to the Wall.

As he approached the *Kothel*, Shlomo saw a few old men standing on one side and a few old women on the other. "Why don't they put up a *mechitzah* between the men and women here, just as there is in a synagogue?" he wondered.

He noticed that some of the men were sitting on the ground. "They must be too old and tired to stand for long," he thought. "But why don't the Rabbis of Jerusalem set up a few benches for these old people who must be regular visitors here?"

Gazing at the Wall itself, Shlomo lifted his head up to count the rows of huge stones. Above and behind the top rows, he saw a shining golden dome. Moving back a bit to get a better view, he caught sight of a second, smaller dome of silver. Shlomo wanted to see these domed buildings. He went through one of the narrow passageways to the left of the Wall leading to the Temple Mount. At the entrance, an Arab asked him what he was looking for. Shlomo, who didn't understand Arabic, kept on walking. The Arab pushed him backwards hard, causing Shlomo to trip and fall.

Picking himself up, Shlomo returned to the Wall, and looked for an Ashkenazic Jew who spoke Yiddish and could explain what was happening. The Ashkenazim and the Sephardim dressed differently, so he had no trouble singling out two Ashkenazic Jews. But one was leaning against the Wall, lost in meditation, and the other was deep in prayer. Shlomo stood there, waiting. Finally the man who was praying took three steps backwards, bowed to his left, to his right, to the front and took three steps forward. He had completed the *Shemoneh Esrey*. Then he recited the concluding prayer, *Aleinu*.

When he finished, Shlomo came up and asked his questions. The old man looked at Shlomo closely and said, "I see from your questions that you are new to this country. This may even be your first visit to the Wall."

"That is true," answered Shlomo.

"You see, my son, we are in exile, even in Eretz Yisrael. The Wall is still in exile, too, for the Arabs have proclaimed the Wall a holy Moslem site, and the British mandatory government supports them. They believe it is quite generous of the Arabs to allow us to pray here for a few hours every day. However, we are not allowed to bring so much as a stool, not to speak of chairs or benches, or a partition or curtain to separate the men from the women.

"Up there on the Temple Mount are two Arab mosques. They stand on the site where our *Beith haMikdash* once stood, before its destruction. Jewish law forbids us to enter the Temple Mount, and the Arabs make sure that this law is kept, even by those Jews who do not observe other laws of the Torah." These last words were accompanied by a bitter smile.

Listening to the old man, Shlomo felt his spirit darken within him. This was not the Wall he had dreamed of. In Chedalonova, he had pictured the Wall as the prize possession of the Jewish people, who guarded it with all their might and did not allow any strangers to defile it.

"The Temple Mount is ours alone! This is where Avraham brought Yitzchak as a sacrifice. This is where Shlomo *haMelech* built the First Temple and Zerubavel ben Shealtiel the Second Temple. What could this old Jew mean when he says that the Wall belongs to the Arabs? How had it fallen into their hands? Why was a Jew forbidden to even sit on a chair in front of the Wall?"

No, this wall did not uplift his spirit. Who could have dreamed that there could be places in Eretz Yisrael itself, where Jews were forbidden to trespass? This was something he had not imagined in his wildest dreams and which he could not fathom.

Even in Poland, in that wicked land where gentiles were free to murder Jews, there was no place officially forbidden to Jews.

The mandatory edict forbidding Jews to bring chairs to the Wall or to enter the Temple Mount sent Shlomo into a deep depression. He had fled Poland and come to Eretz Yisrael to become a free man—one who could not be brutalized by the strong hand of the Gentiles. Now, suddenly, he had discovered that the strong hand of the Gentiles reached even to Eretz Yisrael.

Shlomo had intended to recite a prayer beside the Wall. True, he was no longer in the habit of praying, but he thought that here he would feel differently. But now his desire to pray disappeared. His spirit rebelled, pulling him away from this place. The decision was growing within him to flee from all the Gentiles who were denying him his freedom. Where could he go? He would go to those who had completely thrown off *all* religion, and who did not discriminate between Jew and non-Jew; to a place where he would be able to live in a truly free society with no barriers between one man and the next. He would join Elka's group. In Soviet Russia he would at last find peace of mind.

There was, however, one thing that bothered him. He had promised Zissel he would wait for her. After a prolonged debate with himself, he decided that he had not made any *explicit* promise. True, his eyes had promised, but he had learned in the *gemara* that one's unspoken thoughts are not legally binding.

Shlomo himself was not really satisfied with this reasoning, until one day he received a letter from Zissel, a letter full of despair. Her mother wouldn't even consider coming to Palestine. She was totally committed to Poland and would not leave her homeland. "Although there are wicked Poles, there are also good Poles," her mother had said. "Everywhere in the world there are both good and bad people."

Zissel's letter cried despair from every line. All hope of returning was gone. There was nothing she could do.

When Shlomo finished reading, he thought, "Now that Zissel is not coming back, I won't be betraying her. She is the one who has left me; it is not I who am forsaking her." He felt very sorry for Zissel, but he was also relieved that his own dilemma had been resolved.

A few days later Elka's group left Palestine for the U.S.S.R. Shlomo went with them.

Following the pact between Hitler and Stalin, Poland was split between Russia and Germany, and Chedalonova fell under Hitler's jurisdiction. The Jews of Chedalonova suffered the same fate as those of all the other towns under Nazi dominion. Their lives were worth less each day. Finally the bitter day came when they were confined in a ghetto. Two streets were allotted to house the entire Jewish population of Chedalonova and were closed off with barbed wire. All Jews were ordered to move into the ghetto within twenty-four hours. Any Jew who had not moved by Sunday, the Christian Sabbath, would be punished "with all due severity." The Nazis knew that this was sufficient. The Jews were terrified enough of "light" punishment by the Nazis. Threat of "serious" punishment would certainly send them scurrying into the ghetto.

Nevertheless, the Germans did not take anything for granted. They knew that Jews simply could not be trusted. Some might try to postpone their move for a day or two in defiance of the law. Therefore the Germans marched from one Jewish house to the next, "helping" the Jews leave their homes and move into the ghetto on Sunday, as required by law. The Germans knew that Jews had sharp minds and might find all sorts of excuses to exclude themselves from this edict, and they also knew that they, speaking only German, would not be able to understand the Jews' claims; therefore they took a few Poles with them to serve as interpreters.

When the Nazis entered the Jewish homes, they found them deserted. Some of the houses had even been emptied of their furniture. Most people, however, realizing how overcrowded the ghetto would be, had left their furnishings behind, hoping to reclaim them upon their return. The apartments all had one thing in common: they were in a state of utter chaos. Closets and drawers were left open, clothes were strewn all over. There had been no time to arrange things. Or perhaps, now that their whole world had been turned upside down, the Jews had lacked the presence of mind to leave things in order. In either case, chaos reigned.

The German and the Pole assigned to the apartment of Rozeshka Blitz found the door unlocked. Inside, Rozeshka and Zissel were sitting opposite each other at the table, Rozeshka mending socks and Zissel reading a book. The German could not believe his eyes. The nerve of these two Jewesses was unbelievable. They had not even bothered to hide; they had simply ignored the edict as though it did not exist. The German transferred his gun from his shoulder to his hand, and waited for the Pole to investigate.

"Didn't you hear of the edict commanding all Jews to move to the ghetto?"

"Yes," answered Rozeshka, "we heard."

"Then why didn't you move? You don't look as if you have the slightest intention of moving."

"That's right; we have no intention of moving to the Jewish ghetto."

"Do you want to be punished?"

"No, we do not deserve any punishment. The edict does not apply to us."

"Why not?"

"I am a Polish woman."

At that, the Pole, who knew Rozeshka, grinned and said, "The Polish court has already ruled that you are not Polish. Your husband has already been punished for his presumptions, and now you, pigheaded Jewess, will be punished for yours!"

The German stood on the side waiting for the conversation to terminate. Finally he asked what was going on. Hearing the Pole's explanation in his broken German, the Nazi picked up his gun and focused it on Rozeshka. At that, Zissel jumped up from her chair, grabbed her mother by the arm and dragged her out of the house.

That morning, before the Nazis' visit to their house, Zissel and Rozeshka had thoroughly discussed the entire subject, and now, once again, on their hurried way to the ghetto, Zissel took her mother to task for not wanting to be what she was—a Jew; and for trying to be something which she wasn't—a Pole.

Rozeshka and Zissel arrived in the ghetto empty-handed. Zissel suggested to her mother that they look for Shlomo's family, the Sharfsons, and ask to stay with them. Upon Zissel's return to Chedalonova from Eretz Yisrael, she had visited the Sharfsons and given them Shlomo's regards. From that time on, Zissel had become friendly with them.

They knew nothing of Shlomo's promise to Zissel, or that Zissel had followed Shlomo to Eretz Yisrael, but the mere fact that Shlomo and Zissel had been together in Eretz Yisrael was enough to endear her to them.

Zissel made a special effort to become close to Shlomo's family. She considered them her own relatives. And now, the ghetto edict had instilled new hope in her. Since the Germans had forced her mother to "become" a Jewess, perhaps she would finally agree to immigrate to Eretz Yisrael when they got out of the ghetto.

Bathsheva received Zissel and her mother warmly. Zissel, who had not yet lost hope of returning to Shlomo, considered this a good sign. It was as if she were already almost a part of his family.

Life in the ghetto grew worse from day to day. People were starving. The crowded conditions and filth had led to epidemics, and everywhere people were sick and dying. Little by little, despair took hold. Rozeshka, however, was not about to give up. After all, she came from a stubborn nation. Although she was being forced to live in the ghetto together with all the other Jews, it was her dream to leave before the other Jews did. Even if the other Jews stayed, *she* would leave. She could depend on her Polish friends. They would get her out. Not all the Polish women had alienated themselves from her after the trial. There were still some who considered her one of their own. Nevertheless, each additional day spent in the ghetto eroded her confidence.

One day, the door opened and Mrs. Chasidov, a Polish friend who had been faithful even after the trial, stood in the doorway. Surprised and delighted, Rozeshka jumped up and ran to the door. The two friends hugged and kissed each other, tears flowing from their eyes.

"I knew you would come!" cried Rozeshka.

Zissel also stood up, approached Mrs. Chasidov and shook her hand. The Polish woman looked around the room and sighed. Then she turned back to Rozeshka and said, "At least you have a room of your own."

"You are mistaken," said Rozeshka. "We are not alone in this room. A family with two children lives here, too. Just now they are out."

Remembering that she had forgotten to ask Chasidova to sit down, Rozeshka apologized, took her hand, led her to the table and offered her a chair.

"I can only stay a few minutes," said Chasidova.

"Every minute that you spend with me lightens my suffering," answered Rozeshka. "I have no friends here. Physically, I am in the ghetto, but my heart is outside. I belong with those outside."

"I must leave as quickly as possible, for my own good and also for yours," continued Chasidova.

"But, why?" asked Rozeshka.

"Listen, and I will tell you how I got into the ghetto and what I have heard."

Chasidova told the following story: When she came to the ghetto gate she found a Polish guard on duty — one of the German collaborators. She told him she wanted to enter the ghetto.

"I know that those on the inside want to get out," he said, "but I wasn't aware that there was anyone outside who wanted to get in! Whom do you want to visit? There are no

Poles here—only the damn Jews. What business do you have with them?"

"There is a Jewess here who owes me money," she had answered, "and I want to collect my debt."

"You want to collect a debt from a Jew?" he asked. "The Jews don't repay debts. If you wish, I'll call one of the Germans and he will collect your debt for you."

"No, no," said Chasidova, "if you call one of the Germans, I'll never get my money back. He may succeed in getting the money from the Jewess, but the money will go to his wife—not to me. The Germans are not too fond of Poles either."

"I promise you the German will give you your money," said the guard.

"No," said Chasidova. "Let me first try to collect the money without the Germans. If I don't succeed, I can always ask for their help."

The guard hesitated, scratched his head, and wondered if he could let this woman enter the ghetto. Finally, he replied, "All right. Go on in and try your luck. You should know, though, that in two hours there will be a rounding up of ghetto children. If the Germans catch you in the ghetto, both you and I will be in a lot of trouble."

Chasidova promised not to stay for long. She walked inside and began to look for Mrs. Blitz's apartment. She asked a few people in the street, but no one knew her. Meanwhile, time was running out. She had promised to leave shortly, and so only a few minutes remained for her to visit.

When Chasidova had finished her story, Rozeshka said,

"That is very discouraging. I am not afraid of the Nazis, but I cannot remain in the ghetto. There is not even anyone here for me to talk to. They all speak Yiddish. I am all alone here."

Chasidova answered, "In my opinion, you need not set yourself apart from the Jews. I would have come to visit you even if you considered yourself Jewish instead of Polish. I am full of pity for the Jews, suffering so much from the Germans. And the Germans are also the enemies of Poland."

Rozeshka, embarrassed by Chasidova's rebuke, lowered her eyes. For a minute, no one spoke. Then Chasidova added, "If you find a way to get out of here, I am willing to hide you in my house. After all, the Germans will only occupy Poland until the war is over, and that cannot go on forever. Maybe I can even help you escape."

With those words, Chasidova rose and offered her hand to Rozeshka. Rozeshka shook her hand again and again, without a word. She was too upset and depressed to speak. Finally, she succeeded in saying "Thank you." Rozeshka was very upset. The happiness she had felt just a few moments ago had faded away. Who knew if it would ever return.

Chasidova offered her hand to Zushka and said, "I will make you the same offer I made your mother. I will try to find a hiding place for both of you."

"Thank you," answered Zissel. "If there are still Poles like you, Poland is not yet lost. But I have no intentions of leaving the ghetto. My place is here among my fellow Jews."

The Polish woman looked at Zushka benignly and said, "May you be blessed, my daughter. If there are still Jews like you, hope is not yet lost for the Jewish people. No man

should alienate himself from his people or his religion—
no matter what. No one should—or can—run away from
himself."

Rozeshka stood on the side listening, her heart weeping
within her. She cried because her own daughter, her own
flesh and blood, had betrayed her by identifying with the
Jewish people, and she cried because even her loyal Polish
friend considered her a Jewess and not a Pole. Never before
had Rozeshka felt so alone.

After Chasidova left, Zissel ran to look for Bathsheva to
warn her that there would be a search in the ghetto in less
than an hour. The children of the ghetto were in danger, and
a hiding place must be found for little Sarah. Zissel had not
left earlier so that she could hear everything Mrs. Chasidov
had to say to her mother. She was afraid her mother might
not repeat the conversation exactly as it had taken place.
Neither mother nor daughter had much faith in each other
when it came to matters of Jewish identity. All that time,
however, Zissel had been watching the door, hoping that
Mrs. Sharfson would come in. Now she lost no time, and ran
to look for the Sharfsons, who were visiting some neighbors
in the house.

Zissel called Bathsheva out of the room and, in a
trembling voice, told her the bad news. Bathsheva turned
white. She immediately called her husband and told him
what Zissel had said. Kolonymos was badly shaken. "The
first thing we must do," he said, "is to spread the news
throughout the ghetto."

Without losing a minute, he returned to the room he had
just left and whispered the news, telling his neighbors to pass

it on to all the inhabitants of the ghetto. When he came out of the room again, Bathsheva grabbed his arm and asked, "What shall we do?"

Kolonymos looked at his wife and answered, "What *can* we do?"

"We must find a hiding place for Sarah. Time is not standing still," cried his wife.

But Kolonymos stood still, helpless as the captain of a sinking ship at sea. "Where in the ghetto can there be a hiding place? Every hole is occupied by someone. There are no secret places."

"Maybe in the *Rav*'s house," suggested Zissel.

She wanted to say more, but Kolonymos was already gone. He ran into the room, grabbed Sarah's hand and ran with her to the *Rav*'s house. He had realized immediately that Zissel's suggestion held the key to Sarah's salvation.

The Jews of Chedalonova held their *Rav* in great esteem, and even in these troubled times had given him and his wife their own private room. The *Rav*'s children had grown up and moved away from Chedalonova, so that only he and his wife were left. Their room was very small, but it was enough for the two of them. In this same room, the *Rav* also taught Torah to his students. There were two beds, a table, one chair, and a small bench. It was so small that there was almost no room between the table near the door and the beds along the wall. Sarah could hide under the bed farthest from the door. Anyone entering the room and finding two old people there would probably not think of searching for children.

When Kolonymos hurriedly brought Sarah into the

Rav's room and told him the story, the *Rav* answered, "I will certainly do all I can to help save a Jewish soul." Then he sighed at the thought that he could not save more than one.

Little Sarah listened to the story her father told the *Rav*. She didn't understand everything, but what she did understand was enough to plant a deep fear in her heart, a fear reflected in her bright eyes. As soon as her father withdrew his hand from hers and told her that she must remain in the *Rav*'s house for a while, her tiny body began to quake. The *Rav* placed his hand on Sarah's small head and said, "Sarah'leh, God is with you. Don't be afraid. The *Rebbetzin* and I will take good care of you."

Sarah looked into the *Rav*'s generous eyes and saw his good-hearted smile and was calmed. Kolonymos said, "Sarah'leh, be a good girl and listen to everything the *Rav* and *Rebbetzin* tell you to do." Sarah nodded her head in assent and lowered her eyes.

When Kolonymos left, the *Rav* sat Sarah down on the bench beside him and said to her, "Soon it will be Purim. Come Sarah, tell us the story of Queen Esther. I'm sure you know it."

"Yes, I do," she answered, and proceeded to tell them all about Mordechai and Esther. When she had finished, the *Rav* said, "All those who hate the Jews will be punished, just as the wicked Haman was." He lifted Sarah's small head and looked into her eyes, his smile instilling confidence in her.

Then the *Rav* stood up, walked over to the window, and listened to the sounds from outside, sounds of alarm. People were not walking; they were running. Usually, people shut themselves up inside at night and did not walk outside in the ghetto streets. Tonight there was an unusual amount of movement.

"The news Kolonymos brought must be true, " thought the *Rav*. Taking Sarah's hand, he said, "Come, Sarah'leh, and I'll show you where you must hide for a little while. The *Rebbetzin* and I will sit here beside you and watch over you."

Sarah got up from the bench, walked over to the bed the Rav had indicated, and crawled underneath.

In a few minutes the ghetto was surrounded by Nazis and the hunt was on. Heartbroken cries of mothers whose children had been snatched away were mixed with the raucous cries of the Germans. Many children of the ghetto were taken away that night. Only a few were saved; Sarah was one of those few. As soon as the cries began, the *Rav* and the *Rebbetzin* sat down at the table facing each other like two old people with nothing to do. When the Nazis opened their door, they could only check the room from the doorway as the entrance was blocked by the table. Seeing a sleepy old couple, they slammed the door and left.

As soon as the hunt was over, Kolonymos ran back to the *Rav*'s house to see if all was well with Sarah. Catching sight of her father, little Sarah burst into tears. The *Rav* put his hand on her head and said, "Now, my daughter, you may cry."

At home, Bathsheva and Zissel waited impatiently. When Kolonymos arrived, he let Sarah walk into the room first. Bathsheva ran over to her, Zissel close behind, and little Sarah was overwhelmed with kisses from her mother, from Zissel, and even from Rozeshka. Sarah told them the story, happy that everyone was so pleased with her. After

Bathsheva had her fill of looking at the daughter who had miraculously been saved, she turned to Zissel and over-whelmed her with kisses as well, saying "Bless you, my daughter, for saving my daughter Sarah."

Zissel was especially pleased that Bathsheva had called her "my daughter." She began to think of Shlomo and tears filled her eyes.

"Sarah is an alert, intelligent child," said Zissel. "She passed the test. The whole time she was lying under the bed she didn't make a sound, even though she knew that her mother and father were nowhere nearby." Hearing herself praised so, Sarah was proud. She knew that from now on she must live up to Zissel's praise.

There had been no need to hide David as he was no longer a child. So far there had been no hunt for boys his age.

One more note must be added. When Chasidova came to the ghetto gate on her way out, the Polish guard recognized her and asked if she got her money. When she answered, "Yes, all of it," the guard looked at her suspiciously. He didn't believe it.

Like all the other Jewish ghettos, the ghetto of Chedalonova was surrounded by barbed wire, but this did not prevent it from becoming a gold mine for the local Polish population. Two people could carry on a conversation or pass small objects back and forth through the barbed wire, and the starving Jews of the ghetto were willing to pay high prices for anything that could be put into their mouths.

Among these starving Jews were some who had brought sizable sums of money and other valuables with them to the ghetto. Although they had lost their furniture and the merchandise in their stores, they did manage to salvage money, rings, watches, jewelry and precious gems. A brisk business developed between the Jews on one side of the barbed wire and the Poles on the other.

The Jews paid high prices for the loaves of bread and the potatoes smuggled in by the Poles. Those who had no money left could pay with a gold ring or some other piece of jewelry. Of course, a gold ring is worth far more than a loaf of bread, but the Jew knew he could not expect a Pole to have enough change to cover the difference between a loaf of bread and a gold ring. He was therefore left with the choice: He could exchange the ring for the bread or he could starve to death. If the Pole — who knew in advance what choice the Jew must make — was honest, he would give the Jew a few gold coins change, so that the Jew could buy another loaf of bread or a few more potatoes once again — but no more than once.

Although this trade was strictly forbidden and anyone caught was liable to severe punishment, both sides were willing to take the risk. Hunger for food made the Jew reckless, and hunger for gold made the Pole reckless. They learned to escape detection by the German patrols who stalked back and forth along the wire. It was possible to sneak up to the fence behind the guard's back and to cling so close to it that one could not be seen from afar.

Rozeshka had no money. She had fled from her house empty-handed and had not taken a single penny with her. Luckily for her, the generous Bathsheva did not let her starve, perhaps because of Zissel who had become almost a member of the Sharfson family. After Zissel saved Sarah, the ties between them became even stronger. Kolonymos had been one of the wealthiest men of the community, and he still had a little money left. Bathsheva "lent" some of this little to Rozeshka. Whenever she received a few gold coins from Bathsheva, Rozeshka would go over to the barbed wire fence and wait for a Pole to come selling food. The fence was only a few feet away from their house.

One day, as she approached the fence, Rozeshka let out a cry of joy. There was her friend Chasidova standing on the other side! In her joy Rozeshka forgot about the barbed wire and stretched out her hand to Chasidova. Striking the barbed wire, she cried out and withdrew her hand.

"I have been here every day for the past few days," said Chasidova, "but I could not find you."

"It's not every day that I have the money to buy food," replied Rozeshka. "We get along on very little. Each loaf of bread must last a few days."

Chasidova pushed a loaf of bread through the barbed wire, followed by a small package of butter and cheese, commenting, "This is not the most important thing. I came here to bring you something more important."

"What could be more important to a hungry person than a loaf of bread?" asked Rozeshka.

"There is something more important than bread," answered Chasidova, "there is freedom."

Hearing that, Rozeshka's eyes glittered. Chasidova had good news! A spirit of lightheartedness seized her and she asked, "How can you pass my freedom to me through the barbed wire? Once it is inside the ghetto, it will no longer be free!"

Chasidova was happy to see Rozeshka in a good mood, but she reminded her that this was not the time or place for unnecessary conversation. Looking carefully all around, she pushed a folded piece of paper through the barbed wire. "Take this. It is an identity certificate for Vanda Yagelska. With the aid of this certificate, you will be able to leave the ghetto."

"But how will I get out?" Rozeshka asked. "What can I say to the guard at the gate? What is a Polish woman doing in the ghetto?"

"You heard the story of how I got into the ghetto. You can get out the same way. There is a different guard at the gate now." Chasidova paused, then added, "I heard there was a search for the ghetto children, and many of them were snatched from their mothers' arms."

"It was horrible," answered Rozeshka. "My Zushka saved our neighbor's daughter."

"I visited the convent of Nachrovah and asked the sisters to take in a few children from the ghetto of Chedalonova in the name of Christian mercy. They told me I could bring no more than four or five girls to the convent. I don't know why they prefer girls to boys, but that's what they said. If there is anyone in the ghetto who is willing to accept this Christian charity, I will transfer the girls to safety in the convent."

Just then Chasidova looked around and saw that the German guard was approaching. Hastily she whispered, "I will come again in a week." Then she disappeared.

Rozeshka left the wire quickly, before the guard caught sight of her. Excited, she hurried home to tell Zushka all that had happened.

She could now save herself, but at a terrible price, for she would have to part from her only daughter. Heaven only knew what would be the fate of those remaining in the ghetto. Should she pay such a price to save herself?

Returning home, Rozeshka found only Bathsheva in the room. She showed her the bread and cheese and butter, and Bathsheva congratulated her on her good fortune. Rozeshka didn't know whether to tell Bathsheva about the certificate or to wait and tell her story to Zushka first. She decided not to say anything until she had heard Zushka's opinion. Rozeshka walked over to the window to see if her daughter was coming. The window overlooked Yevshova Street, but when Rozeshka looked outside, she conjured up a picture of Carolevska Street. Here, frightened, bent over Jews with burned out eyes were stumbling along the street, but on Carolevska carefree people were going about their business or strolling merrily. She was in the ghetto, but her eyes and heart were on Carolevska Street. So engrossed was Rozeshka in her daydreams that she didn't even notice Zushka walk into the house.

Zissel saw her mother standing at the window deep in thought. She walked up to her and gently put her arm on her mother's shoulder.

"Hello, mother."

Rozeshka turned around. "Oh, I didn't even see you come in. I was thinking."

"What about?" asked Zissel.

Rozeshka told her story in a whisper so low that not even Bathsheva could hear. Zissel listened and was sad. On the one hand, she wanted her mother to save herself by leaving the ghetto, for by now, it was clear that the Jews of the ghetto were all in danger of losing their lives. Who knew what the Nazis would do to them next? On the other hand, she would be left all alone, with neither father nor mother.

Zissel soon came to the conclusion that her mother must be saved, and her own personal feelings must not be allowed to interfere. Zissel herself wished to stay in the ghetto, and she had no right to hold her mother back.

"What do you think, my daughter?" asked Rozeshka.

"I think you should leave," said Zissel, "not so much because of the danger, but simply because you cannot get used to this environment. I will be fine here with the Sharfsons, and someday we will be reunited, perhaps even before the war is over."

Rozeshka sighed. "But how can I go without you? Come with me."

"No," said Zissel, "I already told Mrs. Chasidov what I think, and that is my final decision."

Mention of Chasidova reminded Rozeshka of the proposal to take girls into the convent. She told Zissel about it.

"That is very important," said Zissel. "We must tell it to the Sharfsons immediately."

Kolonymos soon came home with the children.

"This is not a story for the children to hear," decided Zissel. "We'll discuss it with the Sharfsons when we are alone."

That evening Zissel related the story while Rozeshka nodded her head in assent, for Rozeshka spoke only Polish although she understood simple Yiddish, whereas the Sharfsons spoke only Yiddish although they understood Polish. When she had finished the story, Zissel looked at the Sharfsons and asked, "What do you think of Mrs. Chasidov's proposals?"

Kolonymos began to speak, slowly and carefully. "Simple common sense dictates that anyone given the opportunity to leave the ghetto and save his own life should certainly do so. If Mrs. Blitz has the chance to get out she should go. If Zissel wants to leave, it is her right, too, but if she wants to stay behind and share the lot of the Jewish community here, she should not be prevented from this act of *kiddush haShem*. If she chooses to throw her lot in with her Jewish brethren, may she be blessed."

"What do you think of the proposal to send Sarah to the convent?" asked Bathsheva.

"That is another matter," he answered. "We must consult the *Rav* about that. It is no small thing to place a Jewish girl in Christian hands, and especially in a Catholic institution. Tomorrow I will speak with the *Rav*. This question does not only concern our Sarah'leh. It applies to all the children of the ghetto and also to those in other ghettos throughout the country."

A dismal feeling engulfed everyone in the room. Anticipation of the imminent parting made their hearts heavy. These loving souls might soon be forced to separate — perhaps forever. Their sadness was overwhelming.

The very next day, Rozeshka readied herself to leave the ghetto. "Wear one of my good dresses," offered Bathsheva. "It will take more than an identity card to fool the guard at the ghetto gate. You won't get very far in the rags worn by ghetto dwellers. If you want him to believe you are a Polish woman, you must dress properly."

Rozeshka thanked her for her generosity and "borrowed" a nice dress and an "almost new" purse. When at last Rozeshka was ready, she found that she could not leave. Her legs refused to walk through the door. Zissel stood beside her mother, unable to say a word, motioning her to go. Rozeshka, sensing her daughter's suffering, began to doubt whether she had chosen the right course of action. Finally, Bathsheva, watching the two of them, put one arm around Zissel and the other around Rozeshka and brought them close enough to embrace.

"*Nu*," she whispered, "now it is time to say good-bye.

There is no other way." Both mother and daughter began sobbing. The tears flowed from one set of eyes into the other. When they had no more strength left to cry, Zissel pulled herself up and said in a trembling voice, "Go, mother, and may God be with you."

Bathsheva kissed Rozeshka good-bye and wished her much success. Rozeshka walked over to the washbasin, washed her face again, straightened her clothing and then left the room without even glancing behind her. She was afraid that she would not have the strength to leave if she looked back at Zissel. One more glance and she would burst into tears again, and this would ruin her disguise. A Polish woman who had just collected a debt from a Jewish woman in the ghetto would not have been crying.

Secretly, Zissel followed her mother to the gate. She wanted to see with her own eyes that her mother had left the ghetto safely. Rozeshka reached the gate just after the guards had changed shifts. A new guard was standing at the gate. When Rozeshka approached him and asked for permission to leave, he looked at her in surprise and asked, "Who are you?"

Rozeshka pulled out her certificate and handed it to him. The guard looked at the certificate and asked, "What is a Polish woman doing in the Jewish ghetto?"

Rozeshka told her story about collecting a debt. The guard looked her over again, hesitating. Knowing that every second lost increased the danger, Rozeshka pretended to be insulted and began rebuking the guard.

"I am sure that neither your father nor your grandfather ever heard better Polish than mine. How can you even imagine that a ghetto Jewess could speak such Polish? Aren't you ashamed?"

Embarrassed that he himself had not thought of that, the guard bowed according to Polish custom and apologized as he opened the gate. Rozeshka walked out and headed straight for Chasidova's residence at Thirteen Milkudevska Street. Zissel returned home, her face awash with tears.

Kolonymos had left the house even before Rozeshka. He knew that she was planning to leave and he had already said good-bye and wished her much success. Then he went to speak to the *Rav*.

Listening closely as Kolonymos explained the problem, the *Rav* answered, "You are not the first person to bring up this question. For several days I have been searching for an answer." Pointing to the Rambam's *Mishneh Torah* open before him, the *Rav* continued, "I am studying the laws of *kiddush haShem* in the Rambam, but I have not yet found the answer. The girls are not being asked to convert, but placing them in a convent may lead to their eventual conversion. There is no clear-cut decision here as to whether the mere possibility of conversion overrules the *mitzvah* of saving lives. A Jew faced with forced conversion is commanded to die rather than worship false gods. The question is whether one must choose death over the *possibility* of later being forced to convert."

The *Rav* paused and then continued, "What will happen if, God forbid, we are fated to . . . , if no one remains to reclaim the children from the convent and they are simply swallowed into the Christian world? No, I cannot answer this question."

Looking at the *Rav*'s face, Kolonymos noticed how creased it had become. It was literally lined with sorrow. Kolonymos sighed and asked again, "Then what shall I do?"

The *Rav* looked down and did not answer. He *could* not answer the burning question of the hour. Kolonymos sensed his anguish and asked no more. Instead, he said, "We will take each new trouble as it comes. The child hunt is over now, and there is nothing to gain from any further discussion. Let us hope and pray that God answers our prayers and delivers us from further suffering."

"Amen," said the *Rav* as Kolonymos rose to leave.

At home, Bathsheva was waiting impatiently. There was no need for her to voice her question; it could be read in her eyes. "The *Rav* had no clear answer for us," replied Kolonymos. "Apparently this question never came up before and was not dealt with in any of the responsa."

"Then what shall we do?" asked Bathsheva.

"If there is no clear-cut prohibition involved, we must save the child," answered her husband.

Bathsheva heaved a sigh of relief. It was evident that this was what she had wished to hear.

They had one week to prepare Sarah for the parting. In one week Chasidova had promised to be at the fence again. Bathsheva enlisted Zissel's help. Sarah loved Zissel. It was she who had saved her the night of the child hunt and had told her how bright she was. Sarah was anxious for Zissel to praise her again, and she constantly tried to earn more praise. Every day, Sarah and Zissel would discuss the future. Zissel described to Sarah the good woman who would come to take her to a house in which there were other girls like herself from the ghetto, and there she would live happily for a time. Before long her father and mother would come to take her home.

Of course, continued Zissel, Sarah was still very young, but she was also very bright, and a bright girl doesn't cry even if she has to be away from her father and mother for a short time. Sarah listened to Zissel and tried to act grown up. She promised not to cry.

How would they smuggle Sarah out of the ghetto? Kolonymos checked the barbed wire fence and discovered that it was possible. The fence had been bent in one corner to enable small packages to be passed underneath it. The thin body of a ghetto child could also pass through such a space.

During those days, Shlomo's name was frequently mentioned. Shlomo had parted from them of his own free will and not through force of circumstance.

"It was God's mercy that Shlomo went to Eretz Yisrael to live there in peace, instead of remaining in Chedalonova," Kolonymos would say.

Bathsheva sighed and answered, "We haven't heard a word from him in such a long time."

"There is a war going on, and no mail comes to Germany or Poland from alien countries," replied Kolonymos.

"True," agreed Bathsheva, "but for an entire year before the war broke out we didn't receive a letter. Who knows what's happening to him?"

Zissel tried to reassure them. "People work very hard on the *kibbutz*. At night they are too tired to sit down and write letters. Once one gets in the habit of postponing letter writing from day to day, the letter never gets written."

To tell the truth, Zissel herself was quite worried by the fact that Shlomo had not written to his parents for such a long time, but she tried to reassure them—and herself—that all must be well with Shlomo.

The parting of Bathsheva and Kolonymos from their daughter Sarah was a painful one, especially for the parents, who knew that their promises of a swift reunion might only be wishful thinking. On the set date, they went to the fence. Kolonymos and Bathsheva stood back while Zissel approached the fence. A minute later she returned to say that Chasidova had arrived. Zissel and Bathsheva remained in the background while Kolonymos took Sarah's hand and walked with her to the opening. Sarah crawled on all fours through the hole. Her father helped push her through while Chasidova helped pull her out. Then, Chasidova and Sarah, their hands linked, left the site immediately. Kolonymos returned to Bathsheva and Zissel. Bathsheva was so overwhelmed with misery that she could not walk home without the help of Zissel and Kolonymos.

A few people passed them on the way, but even if there were any witnesses to Sarah's escape, there was no danger that anyone in the ghetto would report it.

No one sent Elkas's group off or wished them well as they left the Holy Land and their fellow Jews for Soviet Russia. No one knew or cared how they planned to go. Either they went by train from Damascus through Syria and Turkey, or they went by sea to Turkey and from there to Russia. In any case, they reached the small Jewish collective "Red Joy" in Birobidzhan. The few dozen families who were members of the collective gave them a warm welcome. They showed them the houses and barns and chicken coops and tried to make them comfortable.

Elka's group had seven members: Shmuel and Sheindel of Nachrovah, Aharon and Elka of Temyonovah, Shlomo of Chedalonova, Tzvi of Efesova, and Dov of Ovdanova. They had not gone to the city to become factory workers for they were all *chalutzim*, and their place was in the fields. Their first days in the collective were days of rejoicing. They were home at last. Everyone spoke Yiddish. Even the sign at the train station was in Yiddish, and of course, there was a local Yiddish newspaper, *Truth from Birobidzhan*.

Reading the newpaper for the first time, the *chalutzim* raised their eyebrows in surprise at the numerous spelling mistakes. No final letter forms were used at the end of a word. When they first noticed the funny spelling of Birobidzhan at the train station, they had shrugged their shoulders and joked, "The manager of the train station need not be a Yiddish scholar." But newspaper editors should know better. In addition, Yiddish words of Hebrew origin were spelled and pronounced strangely.

When Shlomo asked Aron, the editor of the paper, about this, he laughed and said, "It says in the *gemara* that the final letter forms were dictated by the prophets. What do we have to do with prophets? And we have divorced 'Hebrew' words from the Holy Tongue. We want nothing to do with the language of the clericals."

Shlomo understood from this that Aron, too, was a former *yeshivah* student. Little by little, the *chalutzim* got used to the strange spelling and learned to read the newspaper fluently.

There were different branches of work on the commune. Some members worked in the barns and some in the chicken coops. But most, including Elka's group, worked in the fields. Surprisingly, the field work was mechanized. Ploughing was done by a tractor, not by horses or bulls. The new members asked the veterans why their collective was luckier than all the others they had passed on the way. No one else had a tractor.

"This tractor is a present from the Jews of America," answered Borich, the head of the collective.

"What?" Shlomo was astounded. "You accepted a present from your enemies the capitalists? Why did the Jews of America donate a tractor to those who hate them?"

"We only know what we see with our own eyes," answered Borich. "Not every question can be answered, but this need not hinder our building a Socialist society."

Everyone in the collective worked from sunup to sundown, with an hour break at lunchtime. The field hands did not go home to eat. They ate their bowls of cereal in the fields, while sitting on piles of hay. The food was plentiful but the menu was monotonous. Every day they would make a small fire in a pit in the field and heat up a huge pot of cereal.

At sundown, everyone went home. "Home" for the new members was two rooms in a wooden hut where they ate supper together. Elka and Sheindel managed to cook a good meal from only a few dairy products and vegetables. The time was summer.

After long days of hard work, the new members became impatient for a day of rest. They had worked for two weeks without stopping. Tired and eager to have a day off, they were disappointed when no such day came. A month passed, and still no day off. On the *kibbutz* no one had observed Shabbath on the seventh day, but everyone was given at least one day of rest each month. Not all rested on the same day, but in the course of a month, everyone had at least one day off. Tzvi and Dov went to the director of the commune to ask for a day of rest.

"What do you want to do on that day?" asked Borich.

"Nothing," answered Tzvi and Dov. "We want one day off to do nothing. We only want to rest, to gather strength to work the next day."

"Well," answered Borich, "the Soviet constitution grants

workers one day of rest a week, and soon the workweek will be reduced to five days, unlike the capitalist countries, which take advantage of their workers six days a week. The workday will also be reduced from eight hours a day to seven, in contrast to that of capitalistic countries. However, the local party committee has requested that we volunteer to work a ten-hour workday seven days a week."

"Why?" asked Dov and Tzvi. "We are not at war and there is no state of emergency."

"I don't know why," answered Borich, "but if you like, you can ask the *politruk* when he comes on his next visit. He must surely know the answer. You can talk to him as if he were one of your group. Here in Russia, we are all friends. What could be easier or pleasanter than to talk to a friend? When he comes, I'll call you and you can ask him all the questions you asked me."

A few days later, Borich summoned Tzvi and Dov to his office. As they entered, a stranger stood up, shook their hands and greeted them warmly, "Welcome, my comrades."

Tzvi and Dov returned the greeting.

"This is our Comrade Itzik, the *politruk*," introduced Borich. "I have called you to ask Itzik everything you asked me. Please sit down."

Tzvi and Dov took their seats and repeated their questions before Itzik, adding a few new ones. Itzik sat and listened. The more they asked, the smaller his smile became until finally it disappeared altogether. It was replaced by a look of fury.

"Where do you come from?" asked Itzik when both Dov and Tzvi had finally finished.

"We come from Eretz Yisrael," they answered.

"The fascist Zionists poisoned your souls," said Itzik. "They accustomed you to unregulated criticism and planted doubts in your heads about the most obvious facts. The Socialist State cannot be built on a base of criticism, doubts and unlimited questions. Socialism is based upon discipline. Nevertheless, I will answer a few of your questions, just to prove that they can be answered.

"You asked why we accept presents from our enemies, the Jews of America. Personally, we may hate them, but we have nothing against their money. On the contrary, the money that they gained so unjustly is now being used to build the Socialist State and bring justice to the world.

"As to your question regarding volunteer work with no day of rest, this proves your misunderstanding of Socialism. We believe that man must sacrifice his own personal interests on behalf of Socialism. What value does one life have compared to the ideal of a Socialist world built on justice and integrity? There is nothing more praiseworthy than a man who volunteers to work with his last iota of strength.

"However, since not all Soviet citizens have the maturity to volunteer of their own free will, as bourgeois education has spoiled them and taught individuals to put their own needs before those of society, the Politburo and the Party have taken upon themselves to decide on our behalf how much each person must volunteer, and also to see that no one shirks his duty. This will be unnecessary once all Soviet citizens become sufficiently educated to volunteer of their own free will. The bread grown in the collectives is needed to feed the factory workers, who also work voluntarily to produce machinery for the State."

Tzvi and Dov listened but did not understand. They had always thought that Man was the supreme consideration in the U.S.S.R. All efforts were to be directed at improving the lot of the individual. Now, they had just been informed that Man must sacrifice himself, to his last ounce of strength, on behalf of the Socialist State.

But if each individual sacrificed himself, who would be left to enjoy the results? If they were all sacrifices, for whom were they sacrificing themselves? If it was all for the sake of the next generation, then each generation would have to sacrifice itself on behalf of the next until the end of all the generations — and the generation that realized that it was the last of all generations would certainly not be able to enjoy life.

Itzik looked at Tzvi and Dov and saw that his answers had not satisfied them. Angrily, he stood up and proclaimed, "We will not allow everyone to think as he pleases. We must all think alike!"

Dov dared to interrupt. "Well, then, let everyone else think just as I do, and then everyone will think alike! How can everyone tell what everyone else is thinking?"

This made Itzik's ears ring. He was a member of the Komsomol and never before in his entire life had he heard such heresy. He pounded on the table and shouted at the top of his voice, "You are counterrevolutionary! You came to the U.S.S.R. to spread fascist Zionist propaganda! Be careful, or you will get what you deserve! Now out of here!"

Borich stood in a corner, his body quaking. He feared that he would be blamed for accepting these people into the collective, knowing who they truly were. Tzvi and Dov left the room in a state of shock, unable to believe what had happened. It had all taken place so fast that they didn't yet grasp fully what had occurred. What had they said to make Itzik so angry? What was their sin? Why had he labeled them counterrevolutionary? Is anyone who asks a question because he wants to know the answer counterrevolutionary?

The news spread throughout the commune like wildfire. Everyone took Itzik's side against the new members. It was not only Borich who was afraid for his own skin. Every member of the collective was afraid that he would be punished for the sins of the new members. They knew that all over the U.S.S.R. counterrevolutionary forces were being eradicated. Anyone who had any contact with someone suspected of being disloyal to the government was in danger. Hundreds and thousands of people were disappearing nightly, and no one knew where they were. If the N.K.V.D. heard of the incident in Red Rejoicing, its members would all fall under suspicion. Even if they had not invited these new members to their commune, they should have notified the government at once of their treason. If they had not done so, they were party to the crime against the government.

One might ask how the members of Red Rejoicing could have notified the government before they themselves were aware of the treason. The answer is that in the U.S.S.R. anyone not proven innocent is assumed guilty. Even if we assume that the veterans of the commune did not report Elka's group because they were unaware of their opinions, the possibility remains that they themselves were subconsciously influenced by the foreigners. Counterrevolution is a contagious illness, and an ill or infected person does not always realize that he is sick. There was ample reason for the other members of the collective to be afraid.

From that day on, they refrained from any unnecessary contact with these newcomers who had so quickly brought ill fame to their collective. They were sure that Itzik would report his meeting to the government, and that the results would soon follow. No one spoke a word to the *chalutzim* except for their fellow workers in the fields, and then only concerning their work and only when absolutely necessary.

After Dov and Tzvi had reported their conversation with Itzik to the group, all sank into despair. In less than no time, the rosy future that they had envisioned was utterly destroyed. They had believed that here, in the Soviet Union, they would find a state that sacrificed itself for the sake of mankind. Now Itzik had informed them that it was they who must sacrifice themselves for the good of the State.

These *chalutzim* knew the Socialist dialectic inside out, and now they delved deeper and deeper, trying to find a dialectic rationale for Itzik's pronunciations, but in vain. His words had no logical basis whatsoever, and there was no satisfactory explanation for the discrepancies. Neither could the *chalutzim* make any sense of Itzik's declaration that the individual is prohibited from independent thought and must think what everyone else is thinking. How was such a thing possible?

Not only were the members of Elka's group disappointed and disillusioned with the Soviet ideology, they again found themselves at odds with society since the members of the collective ostracized them completely. They had fled from the *kibbutz* in Eretz Yisrael because they felt isolated and left out, but now they had met the same destiny in Soviet Russia.

Nevertheless, the *chalutzim* did not allow themselves to mope for long. In a few days the spirit of rebellion drove away their despair. They would show the other members of the collective that they were self-sufficient, that they had a world of their own. They began to speak Hebrew among themselves loud enough for the others to hear. As soon as a few Hebrew words were heard, all those around them would disappear, and the *chalutzim* would find themselves standing alone. No one even dared listen to them, for Hebrew was outlawed as a counterrevolutionary language. In their own cottage the group sang Hebrew songs and danced the *horah* just as they had on the *kibbutz*. It was a real state of rebellion.

No more than three days later, the members of Elka's group were summoned to the director's office. They were met by an officer of the N.K.V.D. — not a Jew this time, but a Russian. He did not shake their hands, nor did he even return their greeting. Wordlessly, he gestured to them to sit down. Borich was their translator, as they had not yet learned to speak Russian. The officer's first question was, "Who is your leader?"

"We have no leader," answered Aharon. "We are all equal."

"Well, then," asked the officer, "who brought you here?"

"We all agreed unanimously to come."

"There is always one person who speaks up first and whose ideas are adopted by the others," insisted the officer.

"I was the first to suggest that we immigrate to the U.S.S.R.," volunteered Elka.

The officer looked at her and pronounced, "If so, then you are their leader." Turning to Elka, he accused them all: "You are Zionists!"

"We *were* Zionists before we emigrated," Elka corrected him. "We came to Russia only after we ceased being Zionists."

"If so," asked the officer, "why do you continue to speak Hebrew?"

"That is the language of the Jews," answered Elka.

"No," disagreed the officer, "the Jewish language is Yiddish, as spoken here in Birobidzhan. It is not Hebrew!"

Elka had no answer. Shmuel tried to come to her defense. "It is just a question of habit. We were used to speaking Hebrew before, and we simply continue out of habit."

"It is a bad habit," cut in the officer. "It must be forcibly eradicated. You came to the U.S.S.R. to propagate Zionist propaganda and to incite other Jews to leave Birobidzhan and immigrate to Palestine. We know exactly who you are. You cannot fool us. We have no faith in Hebrews." (The word "Jew" had been outlawed in the U.S.S.R.).

Looking at Borich, he continued, "Except for a few, you are all traitors. You cause trouble throughout the entire world."

Shlomo, listening to Borich translate this conversation into Yiddish, wondered to himself, "How can a Jew listen tranquilly to such words? Doesn't he realize how he is being degraded?"

Looking into Borich's eyes, Shlomo suddenly realized that he was actually enjoying the conversation.

"This Borich has the soul of a slave," thought Shlomo. "Even while his ear is being pierced he continues to declare, 'I love my master and don't want to be free.' This Russian's comments would pierce the ears of any free Jew, but Borich is not even aware that he is being humiliated. He loves his master too much."

Shlomo could no longer remain silent. "I fled from the Gentiles who hate Jews to come here," he said, "because I thought that there was no anti-Semitism in Russia. Now I see that you, too, hate Jews."

The official coolly corrected him, "Here there is no anti-Semitism. You are simply traitors who must be reeducated. Those who cooperate with us in their reeducation may later become productive members of society and play a role in spreading Socialism throughout the world."

The minute of silence that followed seemed to last a thousand years. Then the officer continued, "You must confess the truth — that you came to the U.S.S.R. to disseminate Zionist propaganda and to incite Jews to emigrate from Birobidzhan to Palestine."

"That is not true," protested Shlomo. "We have nothing to confess."

"Only we know the truth," answered the official.

"No one can truly know what anyone is thinking but he himself," persisted Shlomo.

"There can be only one truth, not two," countered the official. "That you must admit."

"Yes," agreed Shlomo. "That I admit."

"Well, then," continued the official, "we are the sole possessors of that one single truth. If you disagree with us, then you cannot claim to be speaking the truth. Can there be any other truth? You Hebrews love to study the Talmud, and the Talmud teaches you all kinds of twisted logic, but you will not succeed in fooling us. We know you better than you know yourselves."

Shlomo was stung by this reference to the Talmud. He turned in his seat as though bitten by a snake. Fortunately he was able to control himself. He pressed his lips together, stifling his opinion of the Soviet government.

The officer continued, "You may now go home and begin packing. This afternoon you will be transported to your new places."

The seven rose and left the room without so much as a word of parting to the Russian. Why should they wish the official well if he would not respond in kind? On their way home they didn't meet a single member of the commune. It was as if no one else lived there any more. They had no idea where they were being taken, but they were reasonably sure that it would not be a paradise.

Two hours later a car came and transported Elka's group from the collective to the train station. For the last time they read the funny Yiddish spelling of Birobidzhan. They were loaded on freight trains, not passenger coaches, each individual in a separate car. Apparently the group was to be split up. Nevertheless, they were not alone. Each car was packed to capacity. Many people in the U.S.S.R. must be in need of reeducation, and the government had undertaken to supply it to all free of charge.

Elka did not board the train. Two N.K.V.D. officers escorted her somewhere on foot. Apparently the leader of the group was accorded special treatment.

After a long, tiring trip, part by train and part on foot, with only bread and water to sustain him, Shlomo arrived at his destination, a forced labor camp.

Elka's group was fortunate in that they were not first brought before a police investigator. Perhaps all the investigators were too busy that day to be able to devote any time to them. It was really just as well, for they would only have ended up in the same place after the investigation and the torture.

People were very surprised when Rozeshka left Zissel behind in the ghetto, but Zissel's strength of character was even more surprising. She was prepared to forgo her own salvation and to share the destiny of the other Jews of Chedalonova, an act worthy of a true spiritual leader. People of this caliber were desperately needed to provide guidance and support at such a troubled time. But what motivation could bring a young girl, in no public position of leadership, to disregard her own personal interest and share in the common misfortune?

Rozeshka's behavior, on the other hand, was considered appalling. What kind of a mother deserts her daughter to save her own skin? One can understand the opposite situation, such as Bathsheva helping her daughter Sarah leave the ghetto. But the sight of a mother leaving her own daughter behind while the mother herself leaves for safety was quite singular. It is an unusual mother who thinks only of herself and forsakes her daughter instead of sharing her fate, even if she is unable to help her in any way.

The truth was that both Zissel and Rozeshka had good reasons for what they did. Two things prevented Zissel from leaving the ghetto. First of all, she still felt that her fate was bound up with Shlomo, and she could not bring herself to forsake his parents. What would Shlomo say about such an act? A daughter would not desert her own father and mother, and Zissel, who felt as though Bathsheva and Kolonymos were her parents, could not leave them. A small child like Sarah could leave her parents behind, but not a young woman of twenty.

There was a second reason. Once the Jews realized that the forced deportations terminated in death, the ghetto youth had united and were organizing mass resistance to their German oppressors. They were not willing to let the Nazis take their lives without paying a high price. They would wait until it was clear that all hope was gone, but then they would revolt and oppose the Nazis with force. At least they would die honorably. They might not be able to save their own lives, but at least they could save their honor and the honor of the Jewish people.

Zissel, having lived in Eretz Yisrael, felt even more responsible for the honor of Israel. How could she, who had immigrated to Eretz Yisrael because of the abuse her people suffered in the diaspora, desert the youth now when they had all united to save Israel's honor? Were she now to leave the ghetto in the guise of a Pole, she would be a traitor, both in her own eyes and in those of her friends.

Rozeshka, on the other hand, had ample reason to leave, even though it meant leaving her daughter Zushka behind. She knew that Zissel would be loyal to the Sharfsons and to the other young people of the ghetto. Nevertheless she did not lose hope. She knew how worried the Sharfsons were about their daughter Sarah in the convent in Nachrovah. Their fear that she would forget her Judaism kept them awake at night. She would wait until their fear had become almost unbearable, and then she would suggest that they send Zushka out of the ghetto so that she could visit Sarah in the convent and remind her that she was Jewish. Had Rozeshka remained in the ghetto, Zushka would never have consented to leave her mother. But now that Rozeshka had left, perhaps Zushka too would consent to leave—not in order to save her own life, but to save Sarah, who was so deeply attached to her.

As mistaken as Rozeshka was in her desire to be a Pole and not a Jew, she was not in the least mistaken regarding the surest way to draw Zushka out of the ghetto. She herself was settled in Chasidova's home, but all her thoughts revolved around her daughter. Every day that Zushka remained in the ghetto seemed like a thousand years. Nevertheless, Rozeshka held herself back, waiting for the critical moment.

Before Chasidova had smuggled Sarah out through the fence, she had spoken with Zissel and promised to return to the fence once each week to bring Zissel regards from her mother. These meetings were quite dangerous and could not be held more often, but they would suffice to keep mother and daughter in touch with each other. Great care was needed that neither Germans nor Poles notice Chasidova at the fence. Most Poles, unlike Chasidova, were in the service of the Angel of Death. Zissel was fully aware of this and was very worried about her mother. The very sight of Chasidova on the other side of the barbed wire was sufficient to quiet her fears. She knew that if, God forbid, something happened to her mother, Chasidova would not come to the fence. Not only would she not come to bring her bad news about Rozeshka, she herself would be the subject of bad news. Any Gentile caught hiding a Jew was liable to the death penalty.

But Zissel was not satisfied with seeing Chasidova standing beside the fence. She wanted to hear in detail how her mother was faring. The messages exchanged across the fence were like telegrams — short and meaningful. There was no time for lengthy conversation.

"Your mother wants you to watch over Sarah in the convent and keep her from forgetting her Judaism," said Chasidova.

"How can I watch over her if I am in the ghetto and she is in the convent?" asked Sarah, wondering why her mother was suddenly so concerned for Sarah's Jewish identity.

"You must leave the ghetto and come to us," replied Chasidova, "so that you can watch over Sarah. She is very attached to you. And only you will be able to get her out of the convent when no one else is left."

It was clear what Chasidova meant. The lives of the Jews in the ghetto were in danger. Zissel realized that her mother's primary concern was not over Sarah, but for her.

Just then Chasidova noticed that the German guard had reached the end of the street and was about to turn around and start walking back toward them. She disappeared at once, leaving behind a stunned Zissel. Even if her mother's main concern was for her, she was right about Sarah. When the day came for her to leave the ghetto, there might be no one left to claim her.

Zissel went home to talk to Bathsheva. As she told her story, she looked into Bathsheva's eyes, trying to read her thoughts. Bathsheva's eyes lit up with joy as she listened to the proposal.

"A blessing on your mother and Chasidova!" she said. "There are still good people left in this world — people who are still faithful to each other."

Just then the door opened and Kolonymos stood in the doorway. Bathsheva didn't even wait for him to enter the room before blurting out, "Did you hear, Kolonymos, what Zissel said?"

"How could I hear what she said before I was home?" asked Kolonymos. Bathsheva quickly told him Zissel's story.

"That is worth hearing," said Kolonymos. "Zissel, you must accept this offer. You will be able to work for a Jewish cause outside the ghetto as well as inside. Since we sent Sarah away a week ago, I have not been able to sleep at night. I am afraid that she will forget who she is and will not return to her people. The *Rav* did not forbid me to send her to the convent, but neither did he tell me that it was permissible. Sarah is in grave danger. This offer has given me a ray of hope. No matter what happens to those of us here in the ghetto, there will be someone to claim Sarah from the convent when the day comes."

Listening to Kolonymos, Zissel thought to herself, "Although I didn't repeat Chasidova's dire warning, Kolonymos is thinking along exactly the same lines. I spoke only of watching over Sarah until her mother and father came to get her, but Kolonymos spoke of the possibility that no one else would be left."

This convinced Zissel that she would not be betraying the Sharfsons by leaving. On the contrary, she would be fulfilling their request. Neither would she be betraying her friends, as she was not running away to save herself, but rather going to protect a Jewish child.

When Kolonymos saw that Zissel had taken his words to heart, he added, "Sarah cannot be the only ghetto child in the convent. There must be other Jewish girls with her. You, Zissel, must watch over them all. You have been chosen to fulfill an important task. I pray that you will succeed."

Kolonymos spoke fervently, as though this were a prophesy for Zissel. But then Kolonymos became very thoughtful. "We have been talking as though Zissel can simply walk out of the ghetto. We've forgotten that she can't get out even if she wants to!"

"There is a way to get out," replied Zissel, "if I receive permission from my friends."

"Then by all means, consult with your friends," agreed Kolonymos. "You cannot just leave them, but explain to them that your mission is to preserve Jewish lives on behalf of the Jewish people."

Zissel's friends had organized a group to resist the Nazis with force and they were in desperate need of weapons. There was an organization called the Polish Riflemen composed of young, armed Poles who also opposed the Germans. The Jewish youth fully realized that most Poles hated Jews no less than the Germans did, but they hoped that the Riflemen would agree to supply them with weapons to fight their common enemy.

Searching for a way to contact the Polish Riflemen, the

Jewish youth had discovered an underground sewage system connecting Yevshova Street in the ghetto with Carolevska Street outside the ghetto. One had to walk underground, through the sewage pipes, for a few blocks to Carolevska Street. If one of the Riflemen was on guard there, he would remove the cover of the sewage pipe when the street was empty, and the messenger could climb out onto the street. Chasidova had relayed a message from the Jewish youth to the Riflemen, who had then sent a guard to Carolevska Street. Menachem, who looked just like a Pole, was the messenger. He was not usually too successful in his mission, but something is better than nothing. It took several "strolls" through the sewage pipes before he succeeded in acquiring a few pistols that could be concealed under his clothing. Zissel had heard of this passageway. If she received permission from the group, she would accompany Menachem on his next venture.

That very day, Zissel approached Mordechai, the leader of the group. Mordechai insisted that her request be put to a vote, and the following day at their general meeting, Mordechai told the group of Zissel's plan and asked for their opinions. Some were opposed on the grounds that Zissel could only save individuals, whereas the ghetto uprising would redeem the honor of the whole Jewish people and so should take precedence. Others said that it was better to save Jewish lives rather than Jewish honor. Once all hope was gone, they would try to save their honor, but so long as there was a possibility of saving even a small number of lives, this certainly took precedence. At the final vote, it was decided to allow Zissel to leave the ghetto.

When Zissel returned home and told the Sharfsons, they sighed with relief. "How will you get out?" Kolonymos asked.

"I can't tell you," answered Zissel, "but there is a way."

At Chasidova's next visit to the fence, Zissel told her of her decision to leave the ghetto. With great joy, Chasidova promised, "I will prepare a place for you to hide. It is not advisable for two Jewesses to live together. Also, you'll want to visit the convent in Nachrovah, so it's safer for you to live there. It will save unnecessary train trips. Even with a Polish identity card it is dangerous for you to walk outside too much. You can easily pass for a Pole, but nevertheless there are evil people nowadays who are on the lookout for Jews everywhere. I have already spoken to my brother-in-law in Nachrovah, and they have agreed to take you into their house, which is not very far from the convent. We will have an identity card prepared for you. When you get out of the ghetto, you will come to my house to see your mother, and then my husband will accompany you to his brother's house in Nachrovah." Before the guard reached the end of the street, the two women had ended their conversation and said good-bye.

A few days later Zissel, bearing an identity card with the name Zushka Yosefova, left the ghetto and moved into the Chasidov home in Nachrovah.

There were no children in the Chasidov family of Nachrovah, only a husband and wife. He was a postal clerk and she a housewife. They received Zissel warmly and a bit apologetically, as they were fully aware of Polish complicity in the solution to the Jewish problem. They had heard from their brother-in-law of the death of Zissel's father and they were ashamed of their Polish brethren. Mr. and Mrs. Chasidov tried to make up all these wrongs to Zissel and to lighten her loneliness as much as they could.

Their house consisted of three rooms plus a kitchen and washroom, each room leading to the next. The house itself stood a bit apart from the neighbors' and there were few visitors. Zissel stayed inside, not going out unless it was absolutely necessary. Her mother Rozeshka had no reason to leave the house at all, but Zissel had left the ghetto to visit Sarah.

The house was not far from the convent, but when Zissel counted the streets she would have to cross to reach the convent, her heart began to pound. She had a Polish identity certificate stating that she was Zushka Yosefova from Chedalonova, and she looked Polish. Still, she must be extremely careful. The Poles were suspicious of all new faces. They knew that the Jews could not be trusted and were likely to masquerade as Poles, and they had already caught a few doing it. The sly, devious Jews would use any means possible to deceive the government, and the Poles checked all suspects carefully.

Chasidova helped Zissel get ready to visit the convent. She said, "First and foremost, you must stand up straight, put a smile on your face and a bit of mischief in your eyes, and look all passerbys straight in the eye, without looking down. In short, you must walk lightheartedly and with self-confidence, as if to say, 'The whole world was created only for my sake.' "

As she listened to Chasidova's speech, Zissel became increasingly worried and nervous. When Chasidova saw her agitation, she asked, "Why are you so upset, my daughter? We are all alone now. There are no strangers in the house."

"After hearing your description of how I must appear, I am afraid that I will not succeed," said Zissel.

"Don't worry," Chasidova reassured her. "There is no more dangerous enemy than worry itself. Worry is the father of all fear and the mother of all misfortune."

Zissel sighed and said, "How can I drive worry away? Did worry ask permission to enter my heart? No, it broke in like a thief and cannot be driven out."

Chasidova, seeing how tired and depressed Zissel was, said, "Lie down and rest for a while, my daughter. You will wake up with renewed strength, and your self-confidence will return."

Zissel went back to her room, lay down on the sofa and

immediately fell asleep. When she woke up two hours later, she felt much better. Walking over to the mirror, she examined her appearance. She stood up straight, put a smile on her face, and tried to look confident and nonchalant. She was satisfied that she could indeed pass for a Pole. She walked back and forth in front of the mirror, watching her own bearing. It made her happy to see that she was quite successful. She looked like a young woman with a rosy future— the whole world open before her.

There was only one detail that interfered with the picture—her eyes. The long months in the ghetto had cast sadness in her eyes—day by day, hour by hour. Now this sadness could not be erased. If she tried to force her eyes to smile, her face looked so distorted that it made a mockery of her. To smile with your lips was simple, but to put joy in your eyes, there must be joy in your soul as well. There could be no greater enemy at a time like this than Zissel's eyes.

Zissel began to despair. After one more look in the mirror, she burst into tears. Hearing Zissel cry, Chasidova came to see what had happened. She looked at Zissel and was stunned. All the suffering of the whole world was mirrored in Zissel's eyes just then.

"Why, you need sunglasses," suggested Chasidova. "The sun outside is blinding, and sunglasses can be very helpful."

Zissel stopped crying, and a smile spread across her face. She hugged Chasidova and said, "If there are still women like you in this world, there is no cause for despair."

Chasidova stroked Zissel's head and answered, "A girl your age should not be talking about despair."

In the evening, when Mr. Chasidov came home, Zissel

asked him what news he had heard. Every day she asked the same question. She knew that if there was bad news, he would not tell her; nevertheless she had not given up hope of hearing good news. So far, his answer had always been that there was nothing really new, and his answer that evening was no different.

In truth, there had been very bad news that day, but Mr. Chasidov did not disclose it. He had heard in town that there had been another roundup of ghetto Jews in Chedalonova, but he could not bring himself to tell Zissel. At night, after she was asleep, Mrs. Chasidov told her husband of Zissel's session before the mirror. Her husband sighed and said, "Poor girl. The world has gone crazy. Millions of people have forgotten all their desires and have only one passion in life—to murder Jews." Then he told his wife what he had heard in town.

The next day, Zissel visited the convent, her certificate in her purse and sunglasses on her face. She walked upright, perhaps even a bit too upright. Her gait was gay, almost dancing, her feet barely touching the ground. In the convent she introduced herself as a friend of the Sharfson family who had come to visit Sarah at her parents' request. Maria, the head nun, was not too enthusiastic about the visit, but she did not turn her guest away.

"I will call Sarah and you may see her," said Maria.

"I want to speak to Sarah privately. The child will be too shy to talk about her parents in public," said Zissel.

Maria hesitated for a minute, then gave her consent. "Very well, you may wait in this room and I'll send Sarah in to you."

She motioned to a room on the left. Zissel thanked Maria and went into the room to wait.

When Sarah entered and first caught sight of Zissel, her eyes filled with tears. Had she not suddenly remembered that bright, intelligent girls don't cry, she would have burst out crying. Zissel kissed her warmly and began to speak of her parents.

"How is David? Were any more Jews taken away from the ghetto?" asked Sarah.

"No," answered Zissel. "There have been no more manhunts and there will be no more. David misses you as much as you miss him. But soon your mother and father will come to take you home and you and David will be together again.

"Now I must go," Zissel continued, "but I promise to come and visit you again soon."

Then she added, "If Maria asks you how you know me and what my name is, tell her that we were friends at home, not in the ghetto, and that my name is Zushka. You are a clever girl and I can depend on you to remember. After all, Zissel and Zushka sound very much alike, don't they?"

She nodded her head. She did not want to remain in the convent by herself, but Zissel had reminded her again that she was smart, and she knew that now was not the time to cry. With great effort she held back her tears.

Zissel held Sarah's hand as they left the room together. She managed to ask Sarah one more question: Were there other Jewish girls from the ghetto with her in the convent?

"Yes," answered Sarah, "there are five — Rivkah, Chavah, Rachel, Leah, and Brachah. They are also from the ghetto." Withdrawing her hand from Zissel's, she pointed toward the yard, saying, "Now they are playing outside. I was playing with them before Maria called me in."

Zissel bent over and kissed Sarah, and the two of them left the room together. "Go back to your games and your friends," said Zissel. "I will come again soon."

Maria was waiting for them in the hall. Zissel offered Maria her hand and said, "Good-bye. I am very happy to see that Sarah is very comfortable here."

Maria shook Zissel's hand, took a long look at her, and asked, "Do you live here in Nachrovah?"

"No," answered Zissel, "I'm from Chedalonova. I come to Nachrovah from time to time to visit my relatives here."

"It is not advisable to visit these ghetto children too often," said Maria. "We are taking great risks on their behalf and cannot be too careful."

"Of course, I understand," agreed Zissel. "I have no intention of coming often. I shall leave long intervals between my visits." She tried to speak calmly, nonchalantly.

During this conversation, Maria's eyes had remained fixed on Zissel. Now two other nuns, Tzorerkeh and Sinavkeh, entered the room, walked over to Maria and stood beside her. They stared silently at Zissel as she said good-bye to Maria.

Once outside the convent, Zissel began to review all that had taken place — Maria's conversation and the nuns' stares, and she realized that she had succeeded in fooling no one. Nevertheless, she was not afraid of being reported to the Germans. First of all, the nuns were not allowed to hide ghetto children either, and if they reported her, they themselves would be found out. Secondly, anyone who preached

Christian charity and was willing to save the lives of Jewish children would not knowingly cause the death of a Jewess by reporting her. True, the nuns were primarily interested in providing spiritual, not physical salvation, but they would not take responsibility for another's death. Zissel did not allow herself to worry over their reaction. She returned home, happy to have seen Sarah.

At first, Rozeshka was extremely cautious. Not only wouldn't she walk out of the house, she wouldn't even look out of the window. She had brought the fear she had acquired in the ghetto with her to Chasidova's house. Before, all her thoughts had been concentrated on the dangers involved in escaping from the ghetto. Perhaps she would fail to fool the guard at the gate; perhaps one of the passersby outside the ghetto would recognize her. After all, they had lived in Chedalonova for many years. Her husband had been a prominent lawyer and she, too, was well known. When Rozeshka first walked into Chasidova's house, Chasidova was shocked by her appearance. Rozeshka was pale as a sheet and her eyes glistened with fear.

"What happened?" Chasidova had asked.

"Nothing," Rozeshka had answered. "The fear alone is enough to kill me."

"Your fear is very healthy," Chasidova had remarked. "If it keeps you from becoming careless, it will keep you alive."

The Chasidov family of Chedalonova consisted of husband, wife and son. Both husband and wife were teachers, and their son was a member of the Polish Riflemen. As teachers were held in high esteem in Polish society, the neighbors did not enter their house freely. Educated people were regarded with awe and were not expected to mix freely with the lower classes. Days would pass without anyone coming to the house. When someone did call, he would not stay long. The Chasidov house was therefore an ideal place to hide. Had she not become careless, Rozeshka could have lived there for months without being noticed.

When Rozeshka heard that Zissel had reached Nachrovah safely and had even managed to visit the convent successfully, she began to regain her self-confidence. The desire grew within her to return to her old house and check that all was in order.

"The time has come for me to visit my own house," she announced one day.

"I was there already," said Chasidova. "The door is locked and you will not be able to get in. It is not at all advisable for you to go near there. You must be careful not to be seen."

"The locked door won't stop me," answered Rozeshka. "I have an extra key that I took with me when I left the house. As far as caution goes, I shall be as cautious as possible."

"There is nothing that you can do about the house," said Chasidova. "What good will it do you to visit there? No matter what condition the house is in, you will only be able to look around. Why endanger yourself just to satisfy your curiosity?"

"It is not mere idle curiosity," Rozeshka explained; "it is a very serious matter. My valuables are hidden in a secret hiding place in the house. Lately, many deserted houses have been broken into. If my house is broken into, all my late husband's and my own life savings may be stolen."

Chasidova continued to object. "How can you take precautions? All your old neighbors will recognize you."

"Clothes make the woman," answered Rozeshka. "I can change the way I walk and the way I look. After all, I only want to do this once. I have faith in my destiny. So far both Zissel and I have managed to escape safely from the ghetto. Apparently we are lucky. There is no need to be overly cautious. It would be a terrible shame if our savings were lost."

Chasidova realized that she could not dissuade Rozeshka. She did not want to be held responsible if Rozeshka were really to lose her money, and so she was silent, even though the venture could endanger her, too. If, God forbid, Rozeshka were caught, not only Chasidova, but also her husband and son, were liable to pay with their lives for having hidden her. Nevertheless, Chasidova allowed Rozeshka's material interests to take preference over her own safety.

"Many families live in that apartment building," Rozeshka assured her. "People are always coming and going. No one will even notice me."

"Well, if you have made up your mind to go, I can only pray that the Lord watch over you and keep you from all evil," said Chasidova.

"Amen," answered Rozeshka.

Chasidova helped Rozeshka prepare her disguise. Clever use of clothing and makeup can do wonders. Rozeshka managed to make herself appear much older than she had been when she left her house in Chedalonova. She walked slowly, stooped over, not in the least resembling the Rozeshka her neighbors had known. When they were finished, Chasidova looked her over and said, "For one visit, it's good enough."

Rozeshka walked over to the mirror, looked herself over, and smiled. She was pleased with her disguise.

As she left, Chasidova again wished her much success. Once outside, Rozeshka tried to attract as little attention as possible. She did not walk down the main streets, but through the alleyways. When she first caught sight of her old house, her heart began to pound. Soon she stood in the hallway, just outside the entrance to her old home. Her hands shaking, she touched the doorknob and saw that the door was locked. Rozeshka opened her purse and took out her key. She put it in the keyhole, but could not turn the lock. Over and over she tried, unsuccessfully, to open the door. Suddenly the door opened from the inside. A young man stood in the doorway.

Surprised, he looked at Rozeshka and asked, "Who are you?"

Rozeshka managed to keep her wits about her, and croaked feebly, "Have you a handout for an old lady?"

"Beggars wait for the door to be opened," answered Vlachek. "Someone who tries to open the door of a strange house himself is called a thief, not a beggar."

Rozeshka stood there, the key in her hand, not knowing what to say.

"Thieves must be brought to the police," continued Vlachek.

Frightened, Rozeshka protested, "I am no thief. This was once my own house."

"Why, this house used to belong to Jews. How can you claim that it was yours?" asked Vlachek.

At that, Rozeshka burst into tears.

Vlachek's parents came to the door. They didn't know what to make of the strange scene before them — an elderly woman standing in the hall and crying and an angry Vlachek blocking her entrance. When Vlachek told them what had happened, his mother walked over to Rozeshka, looked at her closely, and exclaimed, "Why, this is Mrs. Blitz!

"What are you doing outside of the ghetto?" she asked Rozeshka. "Aren't all the Jews in the ghetto?"

"We must turn her over to the authorities immediately," said Vlacheck. "According to the law, any Pole who does not report a Jew found outside the ghetto is liable to pay with his life."

Rozeshka cried and begged for mercy, promising to go away, and never come back.

"Well, we must think this over," said the Polish woman.

Vlacheck stood at the door, guarding Rozeshka, while his parents went inside to decide what to do with the Jewess on their doorstep.

"If we let her go now," said Vlachek's mother, "she may remain alive after the Jews in the ghetto have all been killed, and then she may come back here and claim the house. We cannot take such a chance. We will only be able to sleep in peace, confident that this house is truly ours, if we report her to the authorities."

Vlachek's father agreed. "You are right. We Poles cannot

afford to risk our property for the sake of a Jewess. They brought their troubles upon themselves. Since Jesus cursed them, they are not deserving of our mercy. This house is ours and we must make sure that Mrs. Blitz can never come here again."

It took only a few minutes for Vlachek's parents to reach their decision, but to Rozeshka it seemed like ages. Vlachek's mother returned to the door and said to her son, "You are right. We may not transgress the law."

Vlachek walked out of the house, took Rozeshka's arm, and set out for the ghetto. On the way, Rozeshka tried in her best Polish to win Vlachek over, but to no avail. To Vlachek one Jewess was just like any other. Her superb command of the Polish language made absolutely no impression on him.

As they approached the ghetto, they saw a chaotic scene before them. A bunch of bent over people were clustered before the gate, two German overseers in charge of them. Over and over, the overseers would question each member of the group and mark something down in their notebooks. Vlachek headed for the gate, Rozeshka still trying feebly to resist as he headed for the officer in charge. Just then one of the soldiers caught sight of Rozeshka, lifted the butt of his rifle and came down hard on her back, screaming at her, "It's all your fault that we are stuck here, unable to finish counting. Why did you run away?"

Vlachek turned to the soldier to tell him his story, but at that moment, the second soldier opened the gate to the ghetto and his comrade pushed everyone inside, making sure that Rozeshka received a few extra blows. The gate was closed, and Vlachek was left standing all by himself outside the ghetto. With no one there to listen to his story, he turned around and went home.

These unfortunate people were the last survivors of the ghetto of Ovdanova. So few people had remained alive that the Nazis decided it was not worthwhile to keep the ghetto there any longer. The few remaining Jews were transferred to Chedalonova, which had not yet been liquidated. On the way, one Jewess managed to escape. This caused much delay and confusion, as the German overseers could not hand over the full quota of Jews assigned to them. They counted over and over again, hoping that there had been some mistake and that the missing woman would turn up, but to no avail. They were one person short. Now that the missing Jewess had turned up, they were so grateful that they did not even vent their anger on her, contenting themselves with one good blow on her back and a few punches in the ribs as she joined the group being pushed into the ghetto.

When she saw Rozeshka standing once again in the doorway, Bathsheva was shocked beyond belief. She jumped up and cried in dismay, "Can my eyes be deceiving me? Can it really be you? Why did you come back to the ghetto?"

Rozeshka remained standing in the doorway, perfectly silent and motionless. Bathsheva was surprised that she made no response. Perhaps Mrs. Blitz was tired or ill.

"Come in and sit down, Mrs. Blitz. After a little rest you'll feel better," she offered.

But Rozeshka remained standing in the doorway, motionless. Kolonymos got up and walked over to her. He looked into Rozeshka's eyes and then said quietly to his wife, "Mrs. Blitz is no longer in this world. She doesn't even hear what you are saying to her."

Bathsheva, too, looked into Rozeshka's eyes and saw no sign of life in them. Her eyes looked as if they were made of glass. Kolonymos told his wife, "She is in shock. Something terrible must have happened to her. All we can do is put her to bed and pray that time will heal her wounds."

Bathsheva took Rozeshka by the hand and led her to her old bed, which had been empty since she had left the ghetto. She removed her coat and shoes and helped Rozeshka lie down. Rozeshka did not even blink her eyes in response. She let Bathsheva do whatever she wished.

"Poor woman," said Kolonymos, "she is completely cut off from the world around her and from her own self. She must have gone mad."

"She would never have returned to the ghetto if she were in her right mind," answered Bathsheva.

"Perhaps she was forcibly returned."

Bathsheva tried repeatedly to elicit some response from Rozeshka. She sat beside her on the bed, trying everything possible to comfort her and draw her out from the depths of her despair, but to no avail. Rozeshka did not move. Had she not continued to breathe, she might have been taken for dead. Discouraged, Bathsheva left her by herself.

That very evening the ghetto was surrounded by the S.S. Rumors flew that there would be another roundup. People began running to and fro, frantically but vainly searching for a place to hide. Soon deafening screams were heard. The raucous shouts of the S.S. mixed with the broken cries of the deportees and added to the trauma. Altogether, about one hundred men and women were deported.

The truth must be told. Under Mordechai's leadership, the Jewish youth did try to defend themselves and resist the roundup with force. Pistols in hand, they positioned themselves on the rooftop of one of the houses near the gate. Unfortunately, their pistols did not function. Only two of the youths managed to shoot one bullet apiece. Either the Polish Riflemen had purposely deceived the Jews and sent them defective weapons, or else they simply had nothing better to offer. The Nazis immediately surrounded the house and arrested the youths. Two of them were shot immediately in return for the two shots they fired, and the others were taken with the rest of the Jews to the trucks that would transport them to the trains and to Auschwitz.

When the Nazis entered the Sharfsons' room, they herded Bathsheva, Kolonymos and David to the truck, shouting at Rozeshka to get up and follow them. When she did not respond, one of the Nazi soldiers walked over to her, took a good look and saw that she was not sane. He pointed his rifle at her head and remarked, "This is a mercy killing!"

"I didn't know you were merciful to Jews!" remarked his friend.

"I am willing to do anything to kill a Jew — even to be merciful," he answered.

A shot was heard and the bullet penetrated Rozeshka's head. The Nazis herded the Sharfson family into the truck downstairs.

Bathsheva's eyes were blinded by tears. But Kolonymos pronounced the verse from Koheleth, "I praise the dead, who have already died..."

The Jews who had been rounded up in the ghetto were crammed into two freight cars. The Sharfsons found themselves in the same car as the *Rav*, while the youths who had tried to shoot the Germans were divided between the two cars.

The Jews were not simply crammed into the freight cars. It would be more correct to say that they were thrown — or even beaten — in. Those who did not move as fast as the sound of the Nazi orders were "helped" along with murderous blows.

Inside, the situation was intolerable. There was no air, and no room to sit down. There was barely enough space for each person to stand on his own two feet. People were so packed together that no one could know for sure which were his own hands and legs and which belonged to his neighbors. Yet even in such desperate conditions, the Jews did their best to lighten the suffering of their aged *Rav*. Each person squeezed himself a bit closer to his neighbor, one person almost inside the other, until they succeeded in clearing a small space for the *Rav*, whose legs could no longer hold him up, to sit down.

Touched by their efforts, the *Rav* said, "Do not bother, my children. It is not permitted for a rabbi to cause his congregation so much trouble. Once I was young, but now I am old. My long life is over. Now we must worry about the young and try to help them find a way to remain alive. We old people will sanctify God's name through our death. We will meet death standing upright, proud to be Jews. Our youth, however, must sanctify God's name by remaining alive and by doing everything in their power to defeat the forces of evil."

Not a sound, not a sigh was heard in the car. The passengers were comforted by the words of their *Rav*, by the fact that he considered them martyrs. No one, not even the Nazis, could deny them this. On the contrary, the greater their suffering, the more they earned the title.

Peretz the *chalutz* and Mordechai were in the car with the *Rav*. As Peretz listened to the *Rav*'s speech, an idea began pounding away in his mind. Why not try to escape? The *Rav* had just charged the youth with trying to frustrate the Nazis' evil designs. In normal times, Peretz had not been one of the *Rav*'s disciples. Nor had he been a student of the *Beith Midrash*. But now that he heard the *Rav* decree that the youth must sanctify God's name by remaining alive and defeating the forces of evil—just as he and his friends had tried to do—there was not really any basic difference of opinion between them.

"Did you hear what the *Rav* said?" whispered Peretz to Mordechai.

"I heard," answered Mordechai, "but what good are speeches now?"

"The *Rav* spoke about action, not speeches," said Peretz.
"What action?"
"We must try to stay alive!"
"Is that up to us?"
"Perhaps."
"How?"
"We must try to escape this train."
Mordechai looked hard at Peretz and then said, "It's worth a try. We have nothing to lose."
"We can push a plank out of the side of the car, and when the train slows down around a turn, we'll jump. We have at least a fifty-fifty chance to save our lives. If we don't jump, we have no chance whatsoever. No one escapes from Auschwitz."
"You can't pull out a plank with bare hands," said Mordechai.
Peretz searched the freight car with his eyes. Suddenly they lit up. "I found it!" he cried.
Everyone near him turned around in surprise, not understanding what he could have found to make him so happy on the way to Auschwitz.
"What did you find?" asked Mordechai.
Peretz pointed toward the door. A metal ring, connected to a long iron bar, was screwed into the wall next to the door. The function of this bar was obvious. In normal times this had been a freight car used to transport herds of cattle. As cows were expensive, great care was taken not to damage the herds in any way en route. The Jews on their way to Auschwitz could be transported in stuffy, airless cars; but not the cows. While transporting cows, the car door was

opened and the iron bar put across the doorway to keep the cattle from falling out. The cows could then stand safely beside the open door and breathe fresh air on their trip. Now that the Nazis had locked the door from the outside, the bar was useless and had been hung on a hook at the top of the wall. It reached down almost to the floor.

Peretz and Mordechai lost no time. They pushed themselves over to the bar and tried to free the hook from the wall. This was no easy job. It had been screwed to the wall years ago and was all rusty, but the combination of youth, muscles, and above all, the will to live, forced the hook to surrender. The bar was in their hands.

Now the work was just beginning. They would have to bang a hole in the wall, which would make a lot of noise. Nevertheless, there was no danger that the Nazis in the last car would hear them above the din made by the train itself. Peretz and Mordechai took turns and finally succeeded in breaking through the wall.

Now they had to widen the hole. This was easier. They pushed the bar through the hole and twisted it back and forth, up and down, enlarging the hole bit by bit. The trip from Chedalonova to Auschwitz generally took about six hours. Three hours had passed, and the job was not yet finished. Peretz and Mordechai rolled up their sleeves and worked twice as hard.

When the first blow of the iron bar on the wooden wall was heard, all eyes turned to Peretz and Mordechai. Watching them try to widen the hole, some people murmured disapprovingly. As the work progressed, the complaints became louder. Finally, when the job was finished and it was clear that a hole large enough to jump through had been made, strong protests were heard.

"If even one Jew is missing from this car, the Nazis will punish us all. There is no doubt what our end will be. The hole you made will infuriate them and we will all be held responsible!"

Peretz and Mordechai were dismayed at the sharp criticism. Should they try to save their own skins at the possible expense of their fellow Jews? Had they heard these accusations before, they would never have tried to make the hole, but in all the noise, they had not heard the murmuring. And only now were people protesting loudly.

Instinctively, Peretz and Mordechai turned to the *Rav*. The fateful decision would be up to him.

"It is the right of each individual," declared the *Rav*, "to do everything in his power to save his own life, even if the Nazis may punish others for his actions. In any case, your worries are groundless. Anyone sent to Auschwitz has already been sentenced to death, and no one can die more than once."

Kolonymos and Bathsheva were shaken. What should they do with David? Should they ask Peretz and Mordechai to take him? Bathsheva suggested that they ask the *Rav*, but this was difficult. He was all the way on the other side of the car. Everyone had crowded together to make room for him to sit, and now they could not possibly get across the car to him. Kolonymos, not wanting to shout his question out loud for all to hear, turned to his neighbor and asked him to pass the question on until it reached the *Rav*'s ears.

After a few moments, the *Rav* announced, "A young boy

is here in this car. Anyone who can help him escape from the train will be deserving of God's blessing."

Bathsheva and Kolonymos heard the *Rav*'s answer, but David, although he heard the *Rav*'s words, did not understand that they referred to him until Kolonymos asked if he wanted to escape together with Peretz and Mordechai. Frightened, David began to cry. He was afraid to leave without his parents and he was afraid to jump. Bathsheva stroked his head while Kolonymos spoke soothing words. He explained that if Peretz and Mordechai took him, he would not be in any danger. They would see to his safety.

As they spoke, the train began to slow down. It was coming to a turn. Kolonymos turned to Peretz and asked if he would take David. Peretz was glad to try to save Shlomo's younger brother. David, hearing his father speak to Peretz, realized that the decision had already been made for him.

"Mordechai and I will jump first," Peretz said. "When we are out, lift David up to the hole and direct him to jump far forward, in the direction the train is headed, and to roll over a few times when he hits the ground. Boys his age are agile, so don't worry about him. We'll pick him up afterwards and take him with us."

There was no more time to talk, for the train had already slowed down. Peretz stood beside the hole, Mordechai in front of him. Hup! Mordechai jumped. Hup! Peretz, too, was out. Kolonymos, his hands trembling, picked David up and in a voice choked with emotion, he whispered, "Jump!" Bathsheva hid her face in her hands. She couldn't watch. A minute later the train picked up speed and rushed on toward Auschwitz.

No sound of crying was heard in the car. Bathsheva's and Kolonymos' eyes were dry. These poor people had not lost all feelings of mercy; they simply could not cry. They had no more tears left. Their hearts were crying, but their eyes were dry. On the train to Auschwitz no one cries.

David jumped off the train, did a few somersaults on the ground and stood up on his feet. He even managed to catch a glimpse of the train as it disappeared around the bend. He stood there, watching his father and mother going further and further away from him. Even after the train had disappeared completely, David remained rooted to the spot, not remembering why he was there.

It took a few minutes until he finally recalled that Peretz and Mordechai were supposed to get him. He looked around to see if they had come. He waited a few more minutes, but no one was in sight. Then he began to worry. Perhaps they had forgotten about him? David began to run back along the train tracks. They had jumped first and were therefore behind him. After a few hundred yards, David caught sight of Peretz lying quietly on the ground.

"I'm coming, Peretz," he cried.

But Peretz did not answer. As he approached Peretz, David, short of breath from his run, called out once again.

"Peretz, I was afraid you had forgotten me!"

But again, there was no answer. David began to worry. Was Peretz perhaps ignoring him? Had he decided not to take him along? David reached the spot where Peretz was lying. He bent over and grabbed Peretz's hand, ready to beg to be taken along.

"Vey!" he cried. Peretz's hand was limp, and his eyes, though open, were sightless. He was dead.

Recalling that Mordechai had jumped first, David left Peretz and began to run on, looking for Mordechai. He caught sight of him, also lying on the ground. David stopped running and began to walk slowly. What would he do if Mordechai was dead too? As David approached him, he called out "Mordechai!", hoping that Mordechai would respond, but there was no answer.

David stood still. He did not want to find Mordechai dead. If Mordechai was dead, who would take him away from here? Perhaps Mordechai would get up and come over to him. He was standing so close that Mordechai could not help but notice him . . . if he were alive. But Mordechai did not get up. He, too, was dead. David knew this even before he went over to see for sure. Neither Peretz nor Mordechai had jumped well enough.

David was in a state of shock. He stood beside the dead Mordechai, not knowing where to go. He didn't cry. Peretz and Mordechai were both dead, and his parents were on the train, far away. What was the point of crying if there was no one to hear him? As David thought of his father and mother on the train together with all their fellow Jews, he felt jealous. At least they were together. He was all alone. He looked around him, wondering where to go.

Perhaps he would not go anywhere. There was no one he knew anywhere, so what did it matter where he went, or if he went? He would sit down right where he was. At least he was near Mordechai who had been his friend. He could possibly find people who were alive, but he would not know them and they would not be his friends.

David sat there for a long while, until the pains began. It had been hours since he had last eaten or drunk, and his last meal had not been very substantial. Hunger forced him to start walking. "What a pity," he thought. "If not for my hunger, I could have remained with Mordechai."

He had no idea where to go, nor did he care. He walked only because he was too hungry to sit still. It didn't matter where he went. There was no place for him anywhere in the world.

David followed his own feet, on and on, until he stopped, startled by a barking dog. In the direction of the barking, David saw a few straw-thatched rooftops and realized that he had come to a village. One of the peasants came out of his house and saw David. He chased the dog away and went up to the boy, examining him from head to toe.

"Come with me," he said gently.

Although not very fluent in Polish, David could understand the peasant's speech. He knew that all Poles were anti-Semites and liable to harm him, but he was not afraid of this man. His father and mother were far away, and Peretz and Mordechai were both dead. Nothing less than a miracle could save him now. Not expecting help from any human being, he had lost all fear.

Perhaps, too, being alone seemed so terrible, that David was happy to see anyone, even a Pole. A short while ago, he had felt as though no one but he was alive in the entire world. He belonged to no one and no one cared about him. Then this Pole appeared and took him in.

The Pole offered David a chair in the kitchen, where an elderly woman was busy at the stove. She looked at David, but didn't say a word. The peasant whispered something to his wife, who took out a whole loaf of bread and a bowl full of butter and set them on the table before David.

He stared at the food, unable to believe what his eyes were seeing. It was like the miraculous tales he had heard in *cheder* about the prophet Elijah, who appeared to righteous people and saved them from distress. David was sure that the peasant must be the prophet Elijah in disguise, and that the house and woman were none other than miraculous creations sent from Heaven to save him. The starving boy began to eat and drink with great appetite, fully expecting that the prophet Elijah would then bring him to his father and mother.

When he finished his meal, the peasant asked, "Who are you, child?"

David thought, "Elijah must certainly know all about me, but since he has taken on human form, he is behaving like any person of flesh and blood would behave."

When the peasant repeated his question, David told him the story of the train. The peasant nodded his head and said, "You can stay here as long as you like."

"Thank you, but I want to go back to my father and mother," David replied.

The peasant sighed and said, "I am sorry, my boy, but that is not in my power to fulfill."

David was surprised to hear that Elijah couldn't fly him through the sky to his parents in Auschwitz. Too polite to express his surprise out loud, he was silent.

The peasant went on speaking, "Since there are wicked people in this world, and they hate Jews, you must be very careful. Pretend that you are mute, so that people in the village don't try to speak to you and ask who you are and what you are doing here."

David nodded.

"You will help me in the barn and in the field," the peasant continued, "but whenever you are not working, stay in the house and don't go walking around outside."

"All right," answered David.

"It's not as right as you may think," replied the peasant, "but you're better off here than in Auschwitz."

David could not understand that. Why was it better for him to be here, all alone, than in Auschwitz together with his father and mother? But he did not ask.

David was sure that this peasant was Elijah, but in truth he was just a plain, simple peasant. Nevertheless, he *was* different from other peasants, for Jewish blood ran in his veins. His name was Ivan Ivanovich. His father, at the age of eight, had also been called Ivan. But before that, his name had been Ephraim.

As a child Ephraim had fallen victim to Czar Nikolai's decree to conscript young Jewish boys into the Russian army. Ephraim's father had died when he was very young, and his mother did not have enough money to bribe the authorities to exempt her son from service. So at the age of eight, he was conscripted and sent to a colony of Cantonists.

As time passed, he forgot his family and his religious practices, remembering only that he had once been a Jew. After serving in the army for over thirty years, Ivan was released. He married a Russian woman who bore him three sons.

Ivan, the second son, was now over sixty. He had moved to Poland when it was still under Russian domination, before the Bolshevik revolution. After the revolution, Poland regained its independence, and Galicia, once a part of Austria, was annexed to it. Ivan then moved to Galicia, where his mother's relatives had left him a small heritage of land in the village of Agadatke. Ivan's nephews still lived in Russia, in the Ukraine, and one had a mute son David's age. The villagers knew of him. Now that the border between Russian and Poland was open, Ivan's nephew could have sent one of his sons to help the childless old man on his farm. Ivan told his neighbors that David was his nephew's mute son.

As a child, Ivan had heard about the persecution of the Jews from his father. He told him how he had been forcibly conscripted into the army and turned into a Cantonist instead of what he himself had wanted to become. Ivan's father never forgot that he had wanted to remain a Jew, but the Czar had forced him to forget his Judaism. Jewish blood still flowed in Ivan's veins and a Jewish heart still beat in his chest. Therefore he kept David in his house, and David was confident that his salvation was at hand.

Shlomo had found a friend. Rav Yonathan of Rishakova was also in the labor camp in Russia. Ten years older than Shlomo, he had been a child during the Bolshevik revolution. His father, the *Rav* of Rishakova, had continued to teach him Torah even after all the *yeshivoth* and *chadorim* in Russia were closed. Although he was warned that it was against the law to teach Torah to Jewish children, his father had paid no heed to these warnings and had continued to teach his son Yonathan and a few other boys.

One night two militiamen knocked on his door. The Rabbi, who was teaching the boys just then, was perfectly aware who was knocking and who these uninvited guests must be. He signaled to the boys to hurry out the back door, but the militiamen, who were Jewish, knew all the tricks and had already set up an ambush at all the entrances to the house. The boys fell straight into their trap. The militiamen brought them back into the house, lined them up before the *Rav* and said, "Here are the witnesses that you have transgressed the law!"

"That law is invalid," answered the *Rav*.

"What makes you think that?"

"Because it is overruled by the promise we made at Mount Sinai to teach the Torah to the People of Israel," said the *Rav*.

The boys were sent home and the *Rav* was taken away. To this day, Yonathan knew nothing of his father's fate. All his requests for information on his father's whereabouts had been ignored by the N.K.V.D.

From that day on, Yonathan taught himself. When he grew up, the Jewish community of Rishakova elected him to succeed his father as their Rabbi. He followed in his father's footsteps, secretly teaching Torah to a small group of youngsters.

The picture of that night, when his father was arrested, never left him. Instead of deterring him, it strengthened him. Rav Yonathan had inherited his father's dedication to the cause and had no fear of the government. He continued to practice and teach the Torah, successfully evading the N.K.V.D. for some time, until finally he, too, was arrested and sentenced to ten years of hard labor in a work camp.

When Shlomo arrived, Rav Yonathan had already served three years. His mother, his wife and two young children were waiting for him at home.

Shlomo was deeply impressed by Rav Yonathan's courage. Even here in the camp, surrounded by anti-Semitic Gentiles who breathed fire whenever the word "Jew" was mentioned, Rav Yonathan was not intimidated — neither by the government nor by the populace. He even refused to work on Shabbath, claiming that he accomplished in six days what he had been assigned to do in seven.

This was no easy feat, as the work was backbreaking.

More shacks and buildings were being erected nearby, either as an enlargement of the present camp or as an additional settlement. Deep pits had to be dug for the foundations of the new buildings, and they were dug by hand. A man would stand inside a deep, narrow hole whose diameter was only slightly wider than his own body, wielding a short-handled spade. As he dug, he would have to throw the dirt high up out of the pit or else it would fall back down on his head. Every day a large number of workers were punished for not completing their quota, and they received a smaller ration of food than usual. The *Rav*, on the other hand, would do more than his daily quota each day.

What gave him such strength? It was neither hunger nor the desire to receive a full ration of bread. If that were sufficient motivation, everyone would accomplish this feat, as there was no one in the camp who was not constantly hungry. It was not his physical strength either, as some of the peasants in the camp were much stronger than the *Rav*.

What, then, gave him his extra strength? It was the fear that if he did not finish the seven day quota in six days, he would be forced to work on Shabbath.

Nevertheless, Rav Yonathan did not succeed in convincing the camp director and the N.K.V.D. officer. They simply claimed that if he could do more than the accepted daily quota, then his daily quota should be raised, in which case he had not yet completed his quota for the seventh day. Furthermore, they considered his very attempt to observe Shabbath as a crime. Although Soviet law allowed for freedom of religion, this referred to the private, not the public, sector. By publicly abstaining from work on Saturdays, the

Rav might influence other Jews in the camp to observe Shabbath, in which case he would be disseminating religious propaganda.

Rav Yonathan had already been sentenced to solitary confinement several times for this "crime." He was often thrown into a cell less than six feet square, where he could neither spread out comfortably nor walk around. For days at a time he would sit or stand or lie with his legs folded in this cramped space, his whole body bent together, subsisting on a small ration of bread, just enough to keep him from starving.

One might object that even in the labor camps the diet included more than bread. Soup was served every day—a thin watery potato or beet borsht containing a few crumbs of pork fat or meat. Unwilling to eat nonkosher food, the *Rav* subsisted on bread alone. According to Jewish law anyone whose life is in danger may eat forbidden foods. As a rabbi, Yonathan was certainly aware that this law applied to him, for he was getting weaker by the day and would not be able to go on much longer on bread alone. Nevertheless, he chose the hard way. He took upon himself even those restrictions from which he was exempt. He chose to do even more than the Torah required.

Shlomo was deeply impressed by Rav Yonathan's behavior. Nevertheless he made no attempt to imitate him. Only a man who was committed heart and soul could do what Rav Yonathan was doing, and Shlomo was still torn between two worlds. The "two Shlomos" were still at war within him. Since Birobidzhan, Shlomo of the *Beith Midrash* had gained the upper hand, but he had not yet succeeded in completely exorcizing the other Shlomo. This would take a long time.

Shlomo of the *Beith Midrash* was strongly attracted to Rav Yonathan. Every day after work he would seek out the *Rav*'s company. After a few conversations, the *Rav* realized that he was talking to two people.

"I can see from your conversation that you are a *talmid chacham*. What, then, made you do such a stupid thing and immigrate to Soviet Russia?" asked Rav Yonathan.

"From Chedalonova I immigrated to Eretz Yisrael," answered Shlomo, "but when I saw that even in Eretz Yisrael Jews were hemmed into a ghetto, I rebelled. I fled to Russia, believing that here at last, there would be no anti-Semitism."

At his mention of Eretz Yisrael, Shlomo saw a tremor run through Rav Yonathan's body.

"How I envy you! You were in Eretz Yisrael!" he exclaimed. "How I wish I could go! That was the greatest mistake you could have made — to leave Eretz Yisrael! Eretz Yisrael is every Jew's home. No man deserts his own home just because he has trouble with the neighbors. A man who has his own home can stand up to his enemies and defend his honor. People may hate him, but they won't deride him.

"Anti-Semitism respects no borders. It thrives wherever there are Jews, even in Eretz Yisrael. Esau's hatred of Jacob began in Eretz Yisrael, and from there it spread throughout the world. You made one mistake after another. How could you — a Jew — even *imagine* that there might be some place in the world free of anti-Semitism?

"From the day that we stood at Mount Sinai, the rest of

the world has hated us. Even a Jew who runs away from Mount Sinai, denying the religion of Moshe *Rabbeinu* and the Jewish people, cannot succeed in escaping this hatred. The fragrance of Sinai clings to every Jew, whether he is aware of it or not, and this fragrance arouses the hatred of the Gentile world."

Shlomo listened intently and then asked, "You have spoken from your heart, but if what you say is true, then what should we do about it?"

"Do about what?" asked the *Rav*.

"Do about anti-Semitism," replied Shlomo.

"That is not within my control, and therefore it is not a problem for me to solve. I make no attempt to stop the Gentiles from hating me; I simply try to develop within myself the power to withstand that hatred."

"What power is that?" asked Shlomo.

"A man who fully understands why he is suffering finds it much easier to suffer. It is hardest for a man to suffer when he has no idea why, or to what end, he is suffering. The stronger I become as a Jew, the easier it is for me to bear the hatred of the Gentile. Therefore I try to make myself the strongest Jew I can possibly be."

After that, the daily discussions between Shlomo and the *Rav* revolved around one main topic — the meaning of being a Jew.

Noticing the growing friendship between the two, the camp supervisor began to interrogate Shlomo, asking him, "What do you and Yonathan talk about all the time?"

"We have much in common," answered Shlomo.

"What is that?" insisted the supervisor.

"We are both Jewish," answered Shlomo.

"But there is no racial discrimination in the U.S.S.R.," protested the supervisor.

"Oh yes there is," replied Shlomo. "Jews are hated."

"They are not hated because they are Jewish, only because they are traitors to the Russian homeland. Throughout the whole world, Jews are known to be traitors to their homeland."

These were the very same words that Shlomo had heard from the N.K.V.D. agent in Birobidzhan. Now he realized that this was the *Russian* excuse for anti-Semitism, although the anti-Semitism itself was the same in all places. Each country found its own particular reason to voice the same hatred.

Little by little, Rav Yonathan's words made an inroad into Shlomo's heart, until one day he reached a decision: he must try to imitate Rav Yonathan. On Thursday and Friday he finished his quota for three days, and on Saturday Shlomo did not report for work. When the supervisor came by to find out what was wrong, Shlomo answered that he had already done his quota for that day. On that Shabbath both Shlomo and Rav Yonathan were thrown into solitary confinement — Shlomo for not going to work, and Rav Yonathan for disseminating religious propaganda and convincing Shlomo not to work. Shlomo, who was by nature stubborn and independent, declared war on the camp management and refused on principle to work any longer on Shabbath. Being locked up had no more influence on him than it had had on Rav Yonathan.

Hitler had violated his pact with Stalin and had invaded Soviet Russia. Stalin, forced to seek aid in repulsing the Nazis, tried to make Soviet Russia look more sympathetic in the eyes of the Western world. The first thing he did was to decrease the number of prisoners in the forced labor camps. Then he invited the Red Cross to visit the camps and see for themselves that these were merely work camps — not places of torture, as the rumors had told. A few crumbs of bread were added to each day's ration, and the work quota was lowered somewhat. Relations between the government and the laborers changed from a master-slave relationship to a worker-employer arrangement. Those prisoners who had never even been formally tried were the first to be released, before the Red Cross investigation committees could ask why they were being held. Next to be released were those prisoners whose "crimes" were not really crimes. Shlomo belonged to the first class of prisoners and Rav Yonathan to the second.

One day, Shlomo was summoned to headquarters by the N.K.V.D. officer. Not informed of the reason for this summons, Shlomo was naturally quite apprehensive. Perhaps it was on account of the trouble he had caused the camp management lately by refusing to work on the Sabbath. Shlomo prepared himself to stand up to the authorities with every ounce of his strength, and to oppose any compromise.

Walking into the building, he was greeted by the officer in charge, but Shlomo failed to recognize him. It was simply not the same man that Shlomo had known before. Never before had this man's face been friendly or worn a smile. Anger had always been stamped on it like a tattoo. Now, some miracle had taken place. There was not a trace of anger left. In its place was a grin! Shlomo stared at the officer in amazement, wondering what could have caused such a transformation.

"It must be a trick," he thought. "The anger that will strike after such a smile will be even more devastating."

The officer shook Shlomo's hand, greeting him as free men outside the camps do. Shlomo returned his greeting, still telling himself, "It must be a trick."

For the first time, the officer gestured to a chair and asked Shlomo to sit down. What was the point of such a show? Shlomo tried to anticipate all the possible tricks such a person might play on him, but he could not solve the riddle, so he sat down and waited.

"We have checked your file and have decided to release you," announced the officer. "This is the strength of Socialist justice. Sooner or later the truth must come out. The minute we discover that a given person is not guilty, we release him. It is unfortunate that circumstances sometimes prevent a man's innocence from being discovered in time, but of course no man may be released until proven innocent."

Shlomo sat and listened without reacting. He had no way of knowing whether the officer was speaking seriously or playing vicious games with him. The officer reached into his drawer, drew out a piece of paper, and handed it to Shlomo. It was an identity certificate like that held by all free Soviet citizens.

"With this certificate you may travel anywhere in Russia except for those places where the certificate is not valid. If you present it at the train station, you will be given a train ticket. All of Russia is open before you,, except for those areas which are closed."

Shlomo was stunned. He arose, mumbled a thank-you and left. Once outside, Shlomo examined the certificate and wondered whether or not to rejoice. On the one hand, there could be no better grounds for rejoicing than this totally unexpected, newly gained freedom. Who can fathom the joy of a slave who has been freed?

On the other hand, Shlomo had no use for his new-found freedom anymore. He had nowhere to go. The members of Elka's group had all been separated, and he had no idea where his friends could be. Furthermore, he no longer felt much in common with them. His soul had returned to the *Beith Midrash*, and his world was now different from theirs. Even if he succeeded in locating them, he would no longer be comfortable in their company. He felt uprooted. There was no place for him to take his new-found freedom. The only person he was now attached to was Rav Yonathan, from whom it would be very hard to part.

Shlomo went to look for the *Rav* and discuss his problem. He looked all over the camp, but couldn't locate him.

Afraid that the *Rav* had once again been thrown into confinement, Shlomo became depressed. He entered his cabin, lay down and pondered his new status.

His sudden freedom had become a heavy, almost unbearable burden. How could he begin life all over again as a free man? Perhaps he should not leave the camp. He could remain here and work as a citizen, not as a prisoner. Many prisoners who had been freed after ten years of hard labor had chosen to remain in the camp. They had nowhere else to go anymore.

On second thought, Shlomo decided that this might be a satisfactory solution for a Gentile, but not for himself. How could any Jew who wanted to retain his identity settle among the Gentiles? The longer he stayed here, the more he felt cut off from other Jews and from Eretz Yisrael.

"How mistaken it is to imagine that good news automatically brings happiness. That is simply not true. I, for example, have just received the best news possible, that I have been freed from slavery, and nevertheless I am suffering. Instead of rejoicing, I am miserable."

Suddenly, Shlomo heard his name whispered. He jumped up and saw Rav Yonathan, looking very sad, at his bedside. The *Rav* stood there, clearing his throat as if he had something very important to say, but didn't know quite how to begin. Just as Shlomo was about to tell the *Rav* his story, the *Rav* himself began to speak, measuring his words carefully, as if afraid to voice them out loud.

"I have just come from the N.K.V.D. headquarters," he announced, pausing to look at Shlomo. Noticing the suffering in his face, he continued apologetically, "I am both happy and sad at this moment. What I was told would ordinarily be considered very good news."

"Did we perhaps both receive the same news?" interrupted Shlomo joyously.

"I was told that I am now a free man," answered Shlomo.

The *Rav*'s face lit up and he sighed with relief. "Then why do you look so sad, Shlomo?" he asked. "There is no happier news than that!"

"You wonder about me? Look at your own face! If you received the same news, why did you look so forlorn?" Shlomo answered.

"I was sad for your sake," said the *Rav*, "but now that I know that you, too, are a free man, all my sadness has vanished. Only happiness remains!"

Shlomo's face fell. "How can I rejoice when I have nowhere to take my new-found freedom? And how can I leave you after I have become so attached to you?"

The *Rav* lifted his forefinger and sang his answer in the tune used to learn *gemara*. "I am surprised at you, Shlomo, for not being able to answer your own questions. In your youth you were a diligent student of the Torah. You should know that it is always easier to answer two questions than one. If there is only one question, one must search for an answer, and it is not always easy to find. But if there are *two* questions, they must answer each other.

"For instance, if you didn't know where to go, but were not attached to me, then you would have to search elsewhere for the answer. Or on the other hand, if you had somewhere to go, but found it too hard to part from your close friend, you would really have a difficult problem to solve. But now, if, as you say, you have nowhere to go and you are attached to me, then the two problems solve each other. You will come with me and that will solve both your problems!"

Tears welled up in Shlomo's eyes.

"There is nothing finer than tears of joy," Rav Yonathan consoled him.

The very next day, Rav Yonathan and Shlomo left the forced labor camp and started out for Rishakova. It took weeks for them to reach their destination. Because of the war, all the roads were out of commission. Trains did not follow any timetable and were so overcrowded that they could take no more passengers. People stood hanging on the stairs or on the tops of cars, holding onto anything imaginable in order to reach their destination. To men who had just gone from slavery to freedom and from darkness to light, such adventures were child's play. Their great joy lightened their difficult trip. Slowly, bit by bit, they came closer and closer to their destination — Rishakova.

When they finally arrived, the *Rav* decided to go to a friend's house first, afraid that if he simply walked into his own home, the shock would be too great for his family to bear. As the members of his friend's family recognized him, exclamations of surprise and joy flew through the air. His friend's wife ran to break the news to Yocheved, Rav Yonathan's wife, and to his son and daughter, and to prepare them for the reunion.

Meanwhile the *Rav* listened to all the news about his fellow Jews since he had left. The Germans had come quite close and had almost conquered their town, but at the last minute, thank God, they were repulsed by the Red Army, and the town was saved.

Through the window, the *Rav* caught sight of his wife and children on their way to the house. Full of excitement he rose and went to the door to meet them. Yocheved and the children came in, the children falling straight into their father's arms. Yocheved stood there, her face radiating happiness as she watched her husband and her children embrace. Two gigantic tears of joy glistened in her eyes.

"Now let me say hello to your mother," said the *Rav* to his children.

He and Yocheved stood there, exchanging looks of happiness mingled with sorrow. The *Rav* had wondered why his mother had not come to greet him, but when he looked into his wife's eyes, he understood that his mother would come no longer. Later, when they were alone, there would be time enough to discuss all of their personal affairs.

"I brought a young friend with me from the camp," he said, turning to Shlomo.

"Welcome," Yocheved smiled.

Shlomo nodded his head in greeting to the *Rebbetzin*.

"Let us go home," said the *Rav*, and the two men, Yocheved and the children left the house together. Within a few hours, the whole town knew that the *Rav* had returned from the camp. The stream of friends eager to welcome him and share his happiness began. For several days the door opened and closed continuously all day long and halfway through the night.

In Rishakova no one was exempt from work, not even the *Rav*. To the Soviet government, teaching Torah or serving as a rabbi was not an honorable profession. An adult must work at a recognized job, so the *Rav* and Shlomo both decided to join the bookbinders' cooperative. All kinds of books were brought to them to mend and bind, including *gemaroth* and other old, worn Jewish books. As the *Rav* and Shlomo sat and bound these books, they would browse through those that interested them, renewing their ties with the Torah's knowledge.

Shlomo did not intend to remain in Rishakova forever, but the *Rav* advised him to wait until the war was over and transportation was not so difficult. Then they would find a way to send him back to the place he came from.

Soon after Mrs. Blitz disappeared, Mrs. Chasidov of Nachrovah visited her sister in Chedalonova. Needless to say, she was extremely upset by the news of Rozeshka's disappearance. She usually brought back a letter for Zissel from Mrs. Blitz each time she went to Chedalonova. Now she would return empty-handed. What could she tell Zissel? Would Zissel decide to risk her own life by going to search for her missing mother? The two sisters-in-law spent hours discussing the matter and finally decided not to tell Zissel that her mother had disappeared.

Chasidova returned home and gave Zissel regards from her mother, but Zissel immediately asked for her letter.

"She didn't write this time. She only sent regards," said Chasidova. "Perhaps she had nothing special to say."

"That's impossible!" exclaimed Zissel, searching Chasidova's face. "My mother would never begrudge her only daughter a few lines on paper, if only to write and assure me that all was well."

"I don't know why she didn't write," Chasidova responded. "All I can tell you is that this time she sent you her regards."

"Then I will go to Chedalonova and see for myself," decided Zissel. "Perhaps all is not well with her."

"Oh, no, that is much too dangerous a trip," objected Chasidova. "Evil people on the streets search the eyes of any stranger and follow his footsteps."

"But I made several visits to the convent and nothing ever happened to me," protested Zissel.

Chasidova realized that she would not be able to prevent Zissel from traveling to Chedalonova unless she disclosed the whole truth.

"Do you really want to know the truth about your mother?" she asked.

"Of course I do!"

"Well, the truth is that I don't know either," answered Chasidova.

Shocked, her voice trembling with fear, Zissel ventured, "Why, how could that be? You have just come back from Chedalonova, from the very house where my mother is supposed to be hiding!"

Chasidova stood up and told Zissel the story of her mother's disappearance, of how she had simply walked out of the house and not returned.

Zissel threw herself down on her bed, weeping until her pillow was drenched with tears. Chasidova let her cry, making no effort to console her. She knew there was nothing she could possibly say to comfort Zissel. She also knew that Zissel must cry herself out. Only her tears could wash the pain from her heart.

For a long time Zissel lay in bed, filled with the calamity that had befallen her. Her mind was ablaze with grief and sorrow, and from this grief and pain came forth a decision: to return to the ghetto. Since she no longer had any relatives alive outside of the ghetto, she would return to Bathsheva, who was now her only mother. No daughter should forsake her mother in times of danger. So long as her own mother had been outside the ghetto and had wanted her nearby, Zissel had acceded to her request, especially since Bathsheva had also told her to follow her mother.

But now that her own mother was no longer alive, Zissel felt that Bathsheva's request no longer applied. Zissel felt that the responsibility of watching over Sarah had only been an excuse that Bathsheva used to convince Zissel to save herself.

Zissel had no hope that her mother was still alive. She was as aware as anyone else of the treatment accorded Jews caught outside the ghetto confines. There could be no more convincing proof that her mother's identity had been discovered, and that she had been handed over to the Germans, than the fact that she had not returned to Chasidova's house.

When her plans to return to the ghetto began to take on more detailed form, Zissel decided to discuss the matter with Chasidova. Seeing that she had calmed down and had stopped crying a bit, Chasidova invited Zissel to eat lunch.

"I'm not hungry," said Zissel. "All I want now is to return to the ghetto in Chedalonova."

"There is no one left there to return to, my daughter," said Chasidova quietly.

"What? What did you say?"

Her voice steeped in sorrow, Chasidova replied, "Many tragedies have befallen us in this world. It is not within our power to reverse them."

"Where are all the Jews who lived in the ghetto of Chedalonova?" cried Zissel.

"The Nazis did not make any public announcements when they took the Jews away, but I heard rumors that they were transported to Auschwitz," was her answer.

Zissel herself had guessed the answer to her own question, even before she had asked, but she could not face the truth until it was explicitly told to her. Zissel did not eat at all that day, nor did she close her eyes that night.

The days following were difficult ones for her. Slowly, bit by bit, she began to realize that Kolonymos and Bathsheva had indeed sent her to watch over Sarah. They knew what the future had in store for them. They had foreseen their fate and had wanted Zissel to live — both for her own sake and so that someone remained alive to watch over their daughter. Gradually, protecting Sarah became the main goal of Zissel's life. It was no incidental duty, it was her sole reason for living. She decided that she must visit Sarah more frequently and pay closer attention to the poor orphan entrusted to her care.

As soon as she had partially recovered from the shock of the bad news, Zissel decided to return to the convent. She had to work very hard to improve her appearance. The two tragedies that had befallen her family and loved ones had left their mark on her. All her grief was reflected in her eyes, and her young face was veiled in sorrow. She could never appear on the street looking like that. She must erase all signs of sadness and act as if she had no cares.

This was not easy. Zissel worked very hard at making herself look young and happy and carefree. Chasidova followed her progress and finally assured her that she looked perfectly fine and could safely leave the house.

Zissel walked to the convent just as she had so many times before, not expecting any surprises. This time, however, was different. The moment she met Maria she knew that something had changed. Zissel greeted Maria as if she were an old friend, but Maria barely returned the greeting. She did not look directly at Zissel, and she answered her while busying herself with something else.

"I have come to visit Sarah," announced Zissel.

"We do not allow strangers to visit the girls," stated Maria.

"I am no stranger," protested Zissel. "Her father and mother have sent me to visit her."

Maria raised her head and said, "You are lying. Sarah's parents did not send you."

"Why should I lie?" asked Zissel.

"If you really come from Chedalonova and know Sarah's family well, then you must certainly know that the Germans have liquidated the ghetto. Sarah's parents could not possibly have sent you here." Maria looked at Zissel with colorless eyes, a victorious note in her voice.

Zissel did not hesitate a moment. "Certainly I know of the tragedy that befell the Sharfson family, but the request to watch over Sarah was not put to me today or yesterday. It was a long time ago. This is certainly not the first time I have come here to visit her."

Maria, a look of open hatred on her face, replied, "Now that Sarah has neither father nor mother, we are her guardians. She was entrusted to our care, and we will watch over her. You need not bother yourself any longer. You can depend on us. The Church knows how to be merciful, so Sarah has no need of anyone else's mercy."

She paused, then added loudly, "Certainly not the mercy of Jews." Two knives shot out of Maria's eyes, straight into Zissel's heart.

As Maria shouted these last words, the door opened and Tzorerkeh and Sinavkeh came out of the adjoining room, followed by the six Jewish girls, including Sarah, who was the eldest. Seeing them, Maria glared angrily at the two nuns and motioned the girls back.

But it was too late. Sarah had already seen Zissel. She ran to her and refused to leave the room. Maria did not want to physically pull Sarah away, so she said, "Very well. This time I will allow you to speak to Sarah. But it is the last time."

Zissel needed all her strength to face Sarah. She asked Sarah how she felt and if all was well, but instead of answering, Sarah asked, "How are my mother and father?"

Zissel evaded the question.

"You are a bright girl, Sarah. You will always be able to take care of yourself."

Suddenly, Zissel bent over and covered Sarah with kisses, sobbing and holding her tightly. Frightened, Sarah also began to cry. Maria immediately came in, took Sarah's hand, and pulled her out of the room. Zissel stood rooted in her place and could only repeat, "Take care of yourself."

Zissel was left standing alone. She left the convent and walked quickly back to Chasidova's house. It was best to get back as fast as possible, before someone on the street could take note of her tear-drenched face.

As soon as Zissel walked through the door, Chasidova understood that something had happened at the convent, but she was wise enough not to question Zissel. Even if she had, Zissel would probably not have been able to answer her, for her heart was overflowing with despair.

As long as the war continued, there was no way for Shlomo to go back to Poland. Only after the war was over did he find a way to return. As a Soviet citizen, it was illegal to leave Soviet Russia without an official exit permit, and that of course was impossible to obtain. Luckily, Shlomo found a way to smuggle himself across the border.

As a result of the war, there were many Polish refugees in Russia — people who had fled from Nazi Poland to Russian Poland — and these Poles had been classed as aliens and exiled to Siberia. Now that the war was over and Poland had become a Soviet satellite, these refugees were being shipped back to Poland in special freight trains. These trains stopped to refuel near Rishakova and at other stations, and the passengers had a chance to buy food. At each stop, a few Jews would manage to sneak onto the train and cross the border back into Poland. On their way into Siberia the trains had been heavily guarded, for then the passengers were classified as enemy aliens. But now the guard on duty was lax and it was fairly easy to sneak on without being detected. Shlomo was one of many who crossed the border from Russia to Poland this way.

The first place Shlomo headed for was Chedalonova. He combed the town thoroughly, but was unable to locate a single Jewish soul until he reached the cemetery. There he found many Jews—all those who had died before he left for Eretz Yisrael and many who had died afterwards. Unfortunately, Shlomo could not identify any of the graves as the stones had been uprooted and were scattered all over. Nevertheless, he knew that the dead had not been uprooted; these were the Jews of Chedalonova.

Shlomo continued on to Temyonovah and Nachrovah. He found Jews everywhere, but not live ones.

Shlomo wandered from one cemetery to the next until he finally reached Cracow. There he found several hundred Jews who were still among the living. None were originally from Cracow; most came from small towns where only one or two Jews had survived. After the war they had drifted to Cracow, that renowned center of Jewish learning, to join their few surviving brothers.

These Jews had no place in Cracow, just as they had no place in the rest of Poland. All of Poland was one huge Jewish cemetery—not a fit place for any Jew to live. The refugees in Cracow were temporarily housed in government buildings while they waited to find a permanent place for themselves somewhere else in the world. Meanwhile, their primary concern was to locate their relatives and friends, those who might have survived the tidal wave of fire and blood that had wiped out the entire Jewish world of Poland.

Upon arrival, each refugee registered at the American Joint Rescue Committee office, and received food and clothing donated by American Jewry. Copies of these registration lists were posted daily on the walls of the Joint offices, and all those who had arrived in Cracow could search the lists for familiar names. Each new arrival would write his own name and then read through the names of all those who had registered previously.

Every day, the veterans would check the lists anew, searching for familiar names among the newcomers. Besides this continuous search for names and faces, there was nothing else for the Jewish refugees to do in Cracow.

Shlomo, too, signed up at the Vaad offices for his food and clothing, and read the lists of names like everyone else. The lists were in alphabetical order, and Shlomo always went straight to the letter *shin*. One day he let out a gasp. There on the list was "Sharfson, David of Chedalonova"! There could be no mistake. Only one David Sharfson had lived in Chedalonova.

Shlomo ran to the clerk and asked where he could find David. The clerk consulted his records and told him that David Sharfson was in the Youth Aliyah dormitory with the other young boys. They would soon be on their way to Eretz Yisrael. Receiving directions from the clerk, Shlomo ran breathlessly to look for David.

Several years had passed since they had parted, but the two brothers recognized each other immediately. Shlomo recognized David because he knew that David was in the dormitory, and David recognized Shlomo because Shlomo still looked the same. He had a beard now, but it was not yet full enough to hide his face.

One might have expected such a reunion to be a joyous event. One might have expected two brothers to cry and laugh and hug and kiss each other. But it was not so. As soon as Shlomo recognized David, he went over to him, put his arms around the thin lad and whispered, "David, do you recognize me?"

David looked up at him, and gasped, "Oh, Shlomo!"

Before he could say another word, Shlomo asked in a trembling voice, "Where are Mother and Father?"

David lowered his head and did not answer. Now Shlomo knew what he had already felt before, but then he had only guessed it in his heart; now he read it on David's face. Shlomo took David over to a corner of the room, sat down facing him and asked David to tell him all the things he did not yet know.

David recounted the entire story, beginning with their life in the ghetto together with Rozeshka Blitz and her daughter Zissel. He told Shlomo how Zissel had saved Sarah's life during the first child hunt in the ghetto, and how Mrs. Blitz had left shortly after, leaving Zissel behind. He described how Sarah had been smuggled out to a convent, how Zissel had left the ghetto, and how her mother had returned and been killed by the Nazis when he and his parents were rounded up for Auschwitz. David explained how he had jumped from the train, and how he had found Peretz and Mordechai dead on the tracks. And he told of Ivan Ivanovich, who sheltered and protected him for the duration of the war, and finally brought him to the Joint Committee in Cracow just a few days ago.

As Shlomo listened to David's saga, his soul was in a state of deep turmoil. There was so much to hear and understand and digest all at once. Now he knew that Sarah had been placed in a convent, but he did not know *which* convent. Nor did he know if she had remained there throughout the war, or whether she was still alive. He must also find Zissel, if *she* was still alive. Many Jews had been caught outside the ghetto and had met the same fate as their brethren inside. In the one day he had spent in Cracow he had already managed to hear stories of Jews with forged documents who managed to impersonate Poles. Many had survived, but many others had been caught and killed, either by the Germans or by the Poles themselves. He must search for Zissel, but where?

Shlomo decided that first he would try the Joint Committee lists in Cracow. He had already read the lists through several times and not seen her name. Nevertheless, she might arrive tomorrow or the next day. Cracow was the center for Jewish survivors and newcomers arrived daily. He would stay in Cracow for a while and wait for her. If she did not come, he would search for her in the other towns that served as refugee centers.

Shlomo was anxious to find Zissel for two reasons: to find out about Sarah, and to find Zissel herself. Here in Cracow Shlomo felt much more attached to Zissel than he had felt in Eretz Yisrael. The fact that she had lived in the ghetto with his parents and had shared their sad fate almost to the end, endeared her to him now more than ever before. And he remembered that she had followed him to Eretz Yisrael, even though she herself was no great Zionist. He remembered, too, the unspoken promise he had made to her. Now all these memories and feelings merged, compelling Shlomo to find her.

Shlomo was also busy with David. During the years that David had lived with Ivan he had not looked at a Hebrew letter. Now Shlomo must try to help David make up what he had missed during all those years. Shlomo found an empty room where he could teach Torah to David and his friend, Chaim Glick of Nachrovah. Chaim was a few years younger than David, but there was no difference in the scholastic background of the two. Neither had learned very much. Furthermore, Chaim was very bright, and his sharp mind belied his age. David and Chaim sat and learned for hours each day, absorbing all that Shlomo could teach them.

In his free time, Shlomo checked the lists of new arrivals at the Joint offices, searching for the name "Zissel Blitz of Chedalonova." So far it had not appeared.

One day Chasidova burst into the house. She ran straight over to Zissel, wrapped her arms around her and exclaimed happily, "Zushka, my dear, you are saved!"

"What do you mean — I am saved?"

"In town I have just heard that all the Germans have left Nachrovah. They are fleeing for their lives, back to Germany, and the Russians are pursuing them."

Zissel sighed and answered, "Yes, that is very good news, but it has come too late. There is no way to revive the dead."

"Good news, no matter how late it is, is still good news," said Chasidova firmly. "The dead will not come back to life, but at least those who are still living will no longer die."

"That is true. Nevertheless, there is no room for joy in my heart right now." She thought for a moment and then added, "Now that there are no more Nazis in Nachrovah, I have an important mission to carry out."

"What is that?"

"If there are no more Nazis, I need not worry about the nuns informing on me. Now, at last, the time has come to fulfill my mission with Sarah."

Chasidova looked down at the floor, too embarrassed to look Zissel in the eyes. "I doubt that you will be successful. There are rumors that the six Jewish girls from the ghetto are to be baptized in the convent tomorrow."

Zissel jumped up as though bitten by a snake. "No! I will not let them take Sarah away from me. I must go to the convent at once. I will demand that they return Sarah to me. Sarah is Jewish, and her parents sent me here to ensure that she remain Jewish."

"Although I am a Christian, I am ashamed of this forced conversion of the ghetto girls," said Chasidova. "Nevertheless, as a devout Christian, I cannot bring myself to protest against the Church for taking these girls under her wing. You, my daughter, go and try your luck; perhaps you will succeed. It is no longer dangerous for you to be identified as a Jewess."

Without undue preparation, Zissel picked herself up and went to the convent. As she approached the entrance, she saw Tzorerkeh standing at the gate watching her. Tzorerkeh waited until the uninvited guest had approached the gate and was about to enter, and then she blocked the way.

"I have come to see Sarah Sharfson," said Zissel.

"Didn't Maria already warn you not to come here again?" threatened Tzorerkeh.

"I have not come to visit today. I have come to take Sarah away."

Tzorerkeh looked at Zissel with surprise and asked, "Who authorized you to take one of the children out of the convent?"

"The child's parents," answered Zissel.

Tzorerkeh smirked. "In that case, let the parents come in person to get their daughter."

Stung by this cruel joke, Zissel replied, "The blood of those murdered cries out from the earth, and you mock them!"

Tzorerkeh slammed the door in Zissel's face and locked it from the inside, leaving Zissel standing alone on the street. "Well, there is no point in standing beside a locked gate," she thought. "They will never open it as long as I am standing here." She picked herself up and went back home.

She told Chasidova of her conversation with the nun whose name she did not know. Chasidova sighed, but said nothing.

"I must find out what time they plan to baptize the girls tomorrow," said Zissel. "Then I can go in together with all the guests. Perhaps I'll be able to catch Sarah's attention."

Chasidova sighed again and said, "I wish you success, but I am not very optimistic. The time is written on the announcement. Tomorrow morning at ten, the girls are to be baptized. The public is invited to attend the ceremony."

Zissel realized that it would be no simple feat to get Sarah back. She would be all alone among hundreds of Catholics, but she felt she must make the attempt. All the responsibility for Sarah now rested on her shoulders. She owed her own life to Kolonymos and Bathsheva for having sent her out of the ghetto. Now she must try with all her might to save their daughter.

The next morning, Zissel did everything she could to strengthen herself, and by half-past nine she was on her way to the convent. From afar she could already see a large number of men and women entering the convent. When Zissel reached the gate, a husky young Pole blocked her way.

"You stay outside!" he ordered.

"Why?" asked Zissel.

"You are a Jewess," he answered.

At first, Zissel was shocked that he knew she was Jewish, until she saw Tzorerkeh behind him.

"Sarah is my sister," she said. "I will not allow you to rob me of my sister!"

The Pole lifted up his hand and made a fist, threatening to strike Zissel if she didn't back away. A crowd was gathering and listening to the dialogue as they waited in line to enter the convent. Zissel had hoped that some of them would come to her defense and demand that she be allowed in, but she was disappointed. All eyes were turned upon her with open hatred. Just then someone grabbed her arm and pulled her away from the gate. Zissel looked behind her and saw that it was Chasidova. "Let's go!" she whispered. "You are in great danger here!" She pulled Zissel away, leaving the crowd and the convent behind.

"I was wrong," Chasidova said. "I thought that once the Germans left Nachrovah, Jews would be safe here again. Now, after listening to all the evil comments I heard outside the convent, I realize that much time must pass before the shedding of Jewish blood again becomes a crime. Meanwhile you must be careful. You are still in danger."

Zissel was also in despair. She had just been deprived of her reason for living. Would she ever be able to fulfill her mission?

That night Zissel couldn't fall asleep. She lay in bed for

hours, her eyes wide open. Over and over, she reviewed Sarah's plight, unable to think of any scheme for rescuing her from the Church.

Toward morning Zissel fell asleep. Suddenly, she saw Kolonymos standing before her, looking straight into her eyes, his face white as a ghost. He didn't say a word, but Zissel read the blame in his eyes—why had she, Zissel, allowed Sarah to be baptized? Zissel wanted to defend herself—to explain how hard she had tried and why she had failed, but suddenly she saw Bathsheva standing beside her husband. Looking at Bathsheva, Zissel saw the tears in her eyes. She was filled with sorrow for Bathsheva. She wanted to sit beside her and tell her the whole story, but Bathsheva said, "It is unnecessary to tell me. Go and tell Shlomo and David."

Zissel was shocked to hear Bathsheva mention David, who had remained behind in the ghetto with his parents. How could she tell David? She wanted to ask Bathsheva where David was, but she couldn't utter a word. She tried over and over again to voice the question, but could not. Instead, she burst into tears.

Chasidova got up and went into Zissel's room. Zissel was crying in her sleep. Chasidova gently put one hand on her shoulder and said, "It's only a dream, my child."

Zissel awoke immediately. She knew that dreams reflect one's daytime preoccupations; nevertheless she wanted to believe that her dream had a deeper significance. The fact that she had dreamed about David pointed in this direction. She might have subconsciously been thinking about Shlomo, but not about David. She would follow the command given her in her dream — to find Shlomo and tell him that Sarah was in a convent. Now that Zissel had this new goal to fulfill, she had not yet failed in her mission.

Chasidova had mentioned that there were still Jews alive in Cracow. Her neighbors in Nachrovah had told her about them. They were very surprised that after all the Germans had done to the Jews, and after all the help the Poles had given the Germans, there were *still* Jews in Poland! They would never have guessed that such a thing could happen.

"I must reach Cracow. There I will be able to find out how to go back to Eretz Yisrael, to Shlomo. I must find him and fulfill his mother's command to inform him about Sarah."

That very day, Zissel took her leave from the Chasidov family. It was hard for them to part. Both Zissel and Mrs. Chasidov were crying, and even Mr. Chasidov's eyes were moist. Zissel thanked them for everything they had done. It was only because of people like them that she could still go on living. They urged Zissel not to despair; better days would yet come.

The Chasidovs accompanied her to the train station and stayed with her until the train departed. Zissel stood inside, looking out the window, and the Chasidovs stood outside, looking back at her in silence. Whatever there was to say had already been said. As the train departed, Zissel waved goodbye, and the Chasidovs crossed themselves as good Christians do, saying something — probably good wishes — which Zissel did not hear.

Six hours later, Zissel arrived in Cracow. She knew the city well and had no need to inquire after the Jewish survivors. It was obvious that they would be in the Jewish Quarter — in that section which had not been completely destroyed during the war.

Zissel found the offices of the Joint Rescue Committee and after registering, she walked over to the lists on the wall and began to look for familiar names.

When she reached *shin*, she was shocked. "It can't be," she thought. "It must be a mistake. Maybe there is another Shlomo Sharfson. The Shlomo Sharfson I know is in Eretz Yisrael. But the city is listed, too — Chedalonova. There was only one Shlomo Sharfson in Chedalonova."

Examining the list a second time, Zissel found David's name. For some reason she had noticed only Shlomo's name the first time. Now she was even more puzzled. Hadn't David remained in the ghetto with his parents and been transported to Auschwitz? How had he been saved? His hometown was also listed as Chedalonova. The same city could not possibly have been mistakenly listed twice.

Zissel started walking all through the building, searching fruitlessly for David and Shlomo, but finding neither. Exhausted, she finally turned her thoughts to the two slips of paper the clerk had given her. One was her new address, and the other was a coupon for food rations. Zissel decided to go to her new lodgings and to rest for a while.

Walking to the address listed on her slip of paper, she found a small room, with a bed, a pillow and two green sheets. Opposite the bed stood a small table and a shaky uncomfortable chair. Zissel lay down. She was not hungry or in any hurry to receive her daily rations. Gradually, she fell asleep.

After Shlomo had finished his daily lesson with David and Chaim, he went to the office to scan the names of the new arrivals. In a few seconds he reached the letter *beith* and was astounded to see "Blitz, Zissel of Chedalonova." Shlomo was sharper than Zissel. Instead of searching haphazardly, he ran immediately to the clerk to get her address. Before going there, Shlomo walked quickly through all the public rooms and courtyards, thinking that she might be in one of them. When he didn't find her, he went to Zissel's room.

Shlomo knocked on the door several times until a sleepy voice answered, "Yes?" He waited for someone to open the door. Inside, Zissel lay in bed thinking, "I must have dreamt that someone is knocking. I must get up and go back to the office to look for Shlomo."

Shlomo knocked again. This time Zissel jumped up and opened the door. Shlomo and Zissel stood facing each other in the doorway, both of them speechless. At first neither could believe his eyes, but after a few moments Shlomo recovered enough to smile and say, "Don't you know me? I'm Shlomo!"

Beaming, Zissel smiled back. "And I am Zissel!" They both laughed.

Shlomo came into the room. "There is much to tell each other," he said, "stories that cannot be told while standing on one foot. We need hours, perhaps even days. I imagine you haven't eaten yet. Let's walk to the office so you can get your food and eat, and then we'll talk."

Zissel's face became serious. "First of all," she said, "before I tell you the whole story, I must tell you one important thing that cannot be postponed."

"What is that?" asked Shlomo.

"Your sister Sarah is still alive," said Zissel.

Shlomo's eyes opened wide with excitement. "Where is she?"

"Sarah is in the convent of Nachrovah," she answered softly.

Shlomo turned white and his face trembled, but a moment later he regained his composure and said, "As long as she is alive there is still hope."

Zissel was relieved. She had fulfilled Bathsheva's command, and now she would no longer be the only one concerned over Sarah's fate. Shlomo would share her mission. Could there be any better partner than Sarah's own brother?

"Where is David?" she asked.

"He is here in the dormitory. He will be leaving for Eretz Yisrael."

"I want to see him. We were together in the ghetto."

"I know. David has already told me part of your story, and you will tell me the rest yourself. You'll meet him soon. We'll pick him up on the way to the office."

Shlomo and Zissel left her room, locked the door, and went to the office. On their way, they stopped at the Youth Aliyah dormitory for David. David stared at Zissel, surprised and delighted to see her.

"You were probably very angry at me, David, when I left you behind in the ghetto," joked Zissel. "Now I have come to apologize."

"After you left, your mother came back," said David.

Now it was Zissel's turn to be surprised. Her heart

pounding, she asked, "And what happened to her?"

David hesitated and then looked down. "The Nazis shot her just before they put us on the train to Auschwitz," he said softly.

Looking up towards heaven, Zissel said, "Thank God!" and sighed with relief.

"You are thankful?" asked Shlomo.

"My mother left the ghetto because she thought that she could save her own life by becoming a Pole. She didn't want to share the fate of the ghetto Jews. It hurt me terribly to see this. Now I am happy to hear that she came back to the ghetto. She returned to her people and died as a Jewess."

Unwilling to cause Zissel more sorrow, David did not disclose the truth — that her mother had been forcefully returned to the ghetto; she had not returned voluntarily.

"Why should you be so bitter about your mother's desire to leave the ghetto and save her life?" asked Shlomo. "You yourself left the ghetto."

"That is part of the long story which I will tell you later," answered Zissel.

It was almost dark now, time for the evening prayers. A *minyan* of Jews assembled in one room of the Joint offices, Shlomo and David among them. It was only now that Zissel noticed Shlomo's *yarmulka*, although he had been wearing it the entire time. After the prayers, Shlomo returned to Zissel and said, "It's too late to walk through town now. The day is over. Tomorrow morning we'll meet here. While we're walking we'll tell each other the story of our wanderings since we last parted in Eretz Yisrael. Our stories may be long ones."

Shlomo accompanied Zissel to her room and then returned alone to his own. He needed no help in preparing his supper. None of the Joint's meals needed any preparation as they all came from cans: meat, fish, and vegetables. Food that could be eaten cold was eaten straight from the can. Food that had to be heated was placed on a metal plate over a kerosene burner that the Joint had supplied to each person.

Shlomo was the first to arrive at their meeting place the next morning. When Zissel came in, she looked rested and in good spirits. Yesterday she had been relieved of a heavy burden. Now she no longer bore sole responsibility for Sarah. Shlomo wished Zissel a good morning and asked how she had slept. "You already told me once that it is hard to sleep in a new place," Zissel answered.

Shlomo laughed and answered, "Then you told me that you had slept very well."

Zissel laughed. "You have a good memory."

"Now let's start our walk so we can begin our stories. It may take a lifetime to tell them all!"

Shlomo and Zissel began to walk through the Jewish Quarter of Cracow. Most of the buildings were in ruins. None of the synagogues or *Batei Midrash* that Zissel had seen on their first walk were still standing. Shlomo and Zissel walked through the ruins, telling of Birobidzhan, the forced labor camp, and of Rishakova; of the ghetto, outside the ghetto and the convent of Nachrovah; of David on the train to Auschwitz, and of Ivan Ivanovich.

As Shlomo and Zissel approached the famous Rema Synagogue, Shlomo could not believe his eyes. The synagogue had not been destroyed! It stood as if on an island, untouched by the war. What had prevented the Nazis from devastating this synagogue?

Shlomo stopped in front of it. "Do you remember this synagogue?" he asked Zissel.

"Certainly," she answered. "You went in to pray here on our first walk."

Shlomo stood there, still looking at the building. Finally he said, "This is where I would like to have the wedding."

"Whose wedding?" asked Zissel, her heart pounding.

"Ours," answered Shlomo.

Zissel blushed. "Don't you want to return to Eretz Yisrael?"

"Of course. How could one imagine staying here? There is no place in the world for a Jew except Eretz Yisrael."

"Then why should we have the wedding here? Wouldn't a wedding in Jerusalem be more beautiful?"

"This will be our revenge on the Poles and the Nazis. They wanted to wipe us off the face of the earth. Having the wedding here, so they hear the sound of our rejoicing, will be the sweetest revenge possible." He paused, then continued, "Here I've been talking about a wedding without even asking the bride for her consent."

Zissel laughed and said, "I already gave my answer a long time ago."

"Yes," said Shlomo. "But then you were speaking to a different Shlomo who no longer exists. Now there is only the Shlomo of the *Beith Midrash*."

"I once told you that even if you made me a *rebbetzin*, it wouldn't scare me away."

Two days later, Shlomo and Zissel accompanied David

to the train station as he and his friends from Youth Aliyah began their journey to Eretz Yisrael. Shlomo and Zissel would join him later on. Many refugees accompanied the group from Youth Aliyah; some went all the way to Eretz Yisrael, others only as far as the train station. Even those people who themselves planned to immigrate to America accompanied this group in order to ease their consciences, as if to say, "You see, even though we personally don't plan to live there, we, too, love Eretz Yisrael."

A month later, a *chuppah* was set up in front of the Rema synagogue in Cracow and the sound of wedding songs was heard. The groom, Shlomo, walked to the *chuppah* and stood there waiting for his bride, Zissel. Shlomo's face was wet with tears. The veil covering Zissel's face hid her tears. She, too, was crying.

The people who brought the bride and groom to the *chuppah* were strangers, not relatives or friends. It was not a very large wedding — a few dozen people, including two or three rabbis. One performed the wedding ceremony and two others recited the blessings.

After the cup was broken and cries of "*Mazal tov!*" were heard, two Poles passed by, looked at the wedding canopy and heard the rejoicing. They stopped to watch and one commented, "Not even the devil is a match for those damn Jews!"

"If Auschwitz couldn't do them in, there's not a chance in the world we'll ever get rid of them," said the other.

They spit on the ground and swore. "The nerve of those damn Jews!" Finally, they left. Shlomo had had his revenge.

A short time later, Shlomo and Zissel immigrated to

Eretz Yisrael. There was no point in their attempting to search for Sarah in Poland. Anti-Semitism was so rampant that they would have endangered their lives by trying to find a Jewish girl in a convent. But upon their arrival in Israel, the first thing Shlomo did was visit the Chief Rabbi in Jerusalem and tell of his sister in the convent of Nachrovah. He asked the Rabbi to contact the Polish Church and demand that Sarah be returned to her family. The Chief Rabbi traveled to Poland and made every effort to help both Sarah and her friends, but to no avail. The doors and lips of the Church were tightly sealed.

The years went by. Shlomo and Zissel lived in Jerusalem, where Shlomo was one of the rabbis at Yeshivath ha-Mathmidim. They had two children — Rachel, named after Zissel's mother, and Kolonymos, named after Shlomo's father.

David and his friend Chaim Glick both learned at the same *yeshivah*. They were serious students who were rarely distracted from their studies. There was only one thing that occupied their attention besides their studies, and that was the worry over their lost sisters. Sarah had been entrusted to Chasidova's care in Chedalonova and Brachah, Chaim's sister, had been given into the care of Marussa, a Polish woman from Nachrovah. Neither girl had returned after the war. David and Chaim often spoke of freeing their sisters from the clutches of the Church, but so far they had not found any practical course of action.

David's position was a bit easier than Chaim's, for he did not bear the sole responsibility for his sister's welfare. Shlomo and Zissel shared his worry. In addition, Zissel had personally assumed responsibility for Sarah. Chaim, on the other hand, bore all the responsibility for saving Brachah by himself, for he had no other brothers or sisters, and both his parents had been killed in the holocaust.

One day Chaim appeared in the *yeshivah*, overflowing with excitement, and rushed over to David.

"I have some very important news for both of us!" he blurted out.

David, surprised, looked up from nis *gemara* and waited.

"I found my sister Brachah!"

David's eyes widened as he listened to Chaim's amazing story. Chaim had discovered his sister, purely by accident, in a convent right here in Jerusalem!

"And," Chaim continued, "the Polish woman Marussa had put her in the convent in Nachrovah! When I told her that I have a friend whose sister Sarah had also been in the convent in Nachrovah, Brachah said that Sarah had been her best friend! I asked her where Sarah is now, but she doesn't know. She hasn't seen her in years.

"When the war was over, the Jewish girls were all baptized, and their names were changed. Brachah became Barbara and Sarah was called Silvana. They finished elementary school and the theological seminary and were then separated. Each was sent to a different school to work as a missionary teacher." Chaim had finished his story.

"This is not good news for me," David said disappointedly. "I don't know any more now about Sarah's whereabouts than I knew before."

"Nevertheless," rejoined Chaim, "it's easier to search for Silvana in the Catholic missionary school system than it is to look all over the world for Sarah! At least you know where to start."

Realizing that Chaim's words made sense, David said, "Let's tell my brother Shlomo."

"Maybe your sister-in-law Zissel remembers my sister Brachah from her visits to the convent," said Chaim. "Brachah doesn't remember Zissel. I asked her."

Just then Shlomo, now Rabbi Sharfson, came into the room. All the pupils rose in respect for their teacher, returning to their seats only after he was seated. He began the daily lesson, but David's and Chaim's attention wandered far away that morning. They were not to blame if all their thoughts revolved around the story of Brachah's return; nothing else concerned them that day. They sat in class, counting the minutes until the lesson would be over.

After class David walked home with Shlomo, telling him Chaim's story on the way. Shlomo said excitedly, "We must invite Brachah to our house and hear her story in person. I have a feeling that she can help us find Sarah."

As soon as he walked into the house, Shlomo told his wife Zissel about Brachah. Zissel's eyes lit up and she, too, said, "We must invite Brachah here."

David walked over to the rented room where Chaim lived. A girl was sitting inside. David called Chaim out to the corridor and delivered Zissel's invitation to Brachah.

"We will come this evening," said Chaim.

David returned home to tell Zissel that Brachah and Chaim were coming, and Zissel promptly started preparing for the guests.

That evening, Chaim appeared at the Sharfsons' house, accompanied by a lovely young woman with large, dark Jewish eyes. Rav Shlomo greeted Chaim and asked him to be seated. Zissel shook Brachah's hand, trying to remember if she had ever seen her before. Brachah had been one of the six girls who were in the corridor of the convent the last time Zissel had visited there. But many years had passed since then, and she had changed.

Brachah, however, showed visible surprise as she met Zissel. "Sarah told me you were a Pole and your name was Zushka!" she exclaimed.

Zissel laughed and said, "Sarah certainly knew how to keep a secret. I always told her she was a bright girl!"

Zissel invited Brachah to sit down and tell them her story. As she talked, her audience kept looking back and forth, from Brachah to Chaim and from Chaim to Brachah. They were twins, and even now, they looked as alike as two drops of water. Brachah noticed their smiles.

"The resemblance between us is what saved me. Over a year ago, I was sent by the Catholic Mission to Eretz Yisrael to serve as a missionary teacher. I taught in the Convent of St. Paul on 6 Inquisition Street in Jerusalem. Two days ago there was a demonstration of *yeshivah* students against the mission in the courtyard of the school, and my brother Chaim was there. When he saw me, he recognized me at once because I look just like him! He called me, but when I saw him, I fainted. Then the police came and removed the demonstrators, including Chaim.

"The next day, Chaim returned, hoping to catch a glimpse of me again. I kept going out into the courtyard, for I had a feeling he would come back. When we finally saw each other, I picked up and followed him home, without even a good-bye to my friends in the convent. No one there has any idea what has happened to me."

Brachah smiled again and added, "Had Chaim and I not looked so alike, we would never have recognized each other."

Brachah finished her story. Cautiously, Shlomo asked, "Why didn't you return to your people before the meeting with your brother Chaim? You must certainly have remembered that you were Jewish."

"No one raised in a convent and taught Christian doctrines can free himself of his own power. He needs help. When I came to Jerusalem and saw Jews walking down the street who looked just like my father, my Christian faith was shaken. And when a second crisis came along, in the form of a sudden encounter with my only brother, the only surviving member of my family, it was much easier for me to break my bonds with the Church and return to my people."

Brachah paused, then added, "I was sent to Eretz Yisrael because I was such a devout Christian that no one doubted the strength of my convictions. Sarah was not sent to Eretz Yisrael, apparently because she was less firm in her beliefs. It will be easier to rescue her from the mission's net, if only someone from the outside can get to her."

Not only did Brachah look just like Chaim; she was as talented as he and she made a deep impression on Shlomo and Zissel. When Zissel served her company coffee and cake, she noted that Brachah made a blessing before tasting anything.

The guests stayed for a while longer and then went home. When they had left, Zissel asked Shlomo, "What do you think of Brachah as a wife for David?"

Shlomo thought for a while and answered, "She makes a very good impression. I think she might make a fitting partner for David."

Zissel did not let the matter rest. She visited Brachah several times and invited her to their house frequently. David and Brachah were able to spend time together and to discuss many things. Finally, when the time was ripe, Zissel herself spoke to Brachah and to Chaim. Chaim was pleased. It would be a great honor for him to be related to the *Rav*. Brachah, however, objected modestly, "Perhaps I am not yet worthy of your faith in me. After all, I was completely cut off from the Jewish people for many years."

"We have all returned to our Jewish heritage," answered Zissel. "You are no exception."

Brachah thought that Zissel was referring to herself, since she had also spent several years in a Polish home. She didn't know that Zissel was also referring to her husband.

Not long after, an engagement celebration for David and Brachah was held in the Sharfson house. The *tenaim* were read; the traditional plate was broken, and everyone wished the young couple a heartfelt *mazal tov*.

After her engagement, as Brachah became a regular visitor to the Sharfson household, she became increasingly aware that Sarah's shadow was still haunting the family, robbing them all of their peace of mind. No matter what topic of conversation they began with, Sarah's name would inevitably be mentioned. Concern over her fate hung like a heavy stone on their hearts. No one could devise any concrete plan for finding Sarah and bringing her back, but they believed firmly that one day, she would eventually return.

Slowly, Brachah came to the conclusion that it was up to her to act. She herself would travel to Poland in search of Sarah. There was no one more fitting for this mission than she, as she had been Sarah's best friend and would be trusted. Also, she spoke Polish fluently and was perfectly at home in the missionary school system.

When Brachah told David of her decision, he was stunned. On one hand, there was nothing in the world he desired more than for Brachah to rescue his sister Sarah. On the other hand, he was concerned for Brachah herself. Would she be in any danger? Or would she be influenced in any way by her renewed contact with the church?

David talked it over with Shlomo and Zissel. After weighing the matter from all sides, Shlomo decided that they should give Brachah a chance. By now he knew Brachah well enough not to worry about her. With her strong character, energy and imagination, there was no need for any concern. Zissel agreed. They convinced David, and Brachah began to prepare for her trip.

She asked David for pictures of his parents. "My brother Shlomo has the only family photograph," he said. "My parents, Sarah and I are in it. It's the picture he took with him when he first went to Eretz Yisrael, and he still has it."

Brachah was pleased with the snapshot. She asked Zissel for her picture, too.

"I didn't save any of my old photographs," said Zissel.

Brachah laughed and said, "Well then, if you have no pictures of yesterday, let me have a picture of today!"

Zissel lost no time and had her picture taken at once.

Brachah packed all that she might need for the long trip in a small suitcase, including her nun's garb, her Polish passport, and the two pictures. She was ready to set sail for Poland. David, Shlomo and Zissel saw her off, their hearts and eyes directed to Heaven with a silent, fervent prayer for her success.

Two weeks later Brachah arrived in Poland. She traveled from one convent to the next, from one missionary center to another, searching fruitlessly for someone who knew of Silvana Borovsky's whereabouts. Brachah began to fear that her trip would be in vain. Nevertheless, she continued her search.

Finally, in the town of Tzlavka, she hit upon good luck.

There she was told that Silvana had indeed been one of their teachers, but had moved to France over a year ago. When Brachah asked why, she was told that there was no longer any work for missionaries in Poland. As long as there were still Jewish survivors of the holocaust or Jewish refugees from Soviet Russia in Poland, it had been a fruitful field for missionary activity. These poor, uprooted, homeless, jobless Jews were easy prey for the mission. For a loaf of bread and a few pieces of clothing, they were prepared to accept the Church's patronage.

But most of the Jewish refugees had all left Poland—some for Israel and others for America or other parts of the free world. Only Jewish Communists were left in Poland, and these had no interest in any religion. In France, however, there was still a sizable Jewish population, mainly Polish Jews in transit and French survivors of the holocaust. There was still work for the mission among these people.

"Perhaps you know Silvana Borovsky's address in France?" asked Brachah. They did, and Brachah left Poland with the name and address of a mission school in Paris.

The mission is a secretive institution and does not normally divulge such information, but Brachah, wearing her nun's garb and bearing the passport of Barbara Sokolsky, a missionary from the Holy Land, inspired their confidence.

In her seminary years, Brachah had learned to speak French, and now she reaped the profits of her education. She was as at home in Paris as she had been in Poland. Nor did she have any trouble locating the school. As a nun, the gates of all missions were open to her. Brachah walked into the office and asked for Silvana Borovsky.

"In half an hour," the secretary told her, "Silvana will have a break. You can wait for her in the teacher's room."

The secretary showed Brachah into an empty room, which contained a single long table with many chairs on either side. Brachah sat down and waited. When the teachers started coming into the room, Brachah stood up and walked over to the window opposite the doorway, looking hard at each nun who entered.

Silvana finally came in. Brachah recognized her at once. She smiled warmly and walked toward her. Without a word she stood opposite Silvana, smiling, waiting to be recognized. Silvana stared at Brachah for a minute or two. Then her eyes lit up. "Barbara!" she cried.

Brachah hugged Silvana warmly. "Well, you finally recognized me!"

"Barbara, what are you doing here? Where have you come from? Where have you been all these years?"

Brachah smiled. "You are not giving me a chance to answer you. How can I remember so many questions? Even if I do remember, the answers take more time than the few minutes you have now. Come to my hotel after work today, and then we can talk with no interruptions."

As she spoke, Brachah nodded toward the table where the other teachers sat chatting, hinting that this room was not a suitable place for them to speak freely. She gave Silvana her hotel address and room number and promised to wait for her that afternoon. Then she said good-bye and left. In the yard Brachah watched the schoolgirls playing outside. She saw many Jewish faces and many Jewish eyes, and her heart was heavy.

While she was looking for Sarah in Poland, Brachah had lived on bread and fruit. Now that she was in Paris she could buy a hot meal at a kosher restaurant. Nevertheless, Brachah stuck to a simple diet. She had very little money left and it had to last her. After lunch, she returned to her hotel and went up to her room to wait for Sarah. She had two more hours—enough time for a nap. As soon as Brachah lay down on the sofa she fell asleep. The Angel of Dreams spread his wings over her and brought her father and mother to her in a dream.

Her father Yudel and her mother Esther stood before her, beaming with joy. "How wonderful, Brachah, that you came back to us," said her father.

"I expected this all along. My hopes were not in vain," her mother told her father.

"It is not enough that Brachah has returned. She must bring Sarah back, too," said her father.

"Why, this is the very purpose of her trip," explained her mother.

Suddenly, someone knocked at the door, frightening her father and mother away. Brachah reached out to catch her mother's hand and beg her not to go, but instead her hand hit the wall and she woke up. Someone *was* knocking on the door. It was Sarah. Brachah invited her in and they sat down at the table and began to speak in Polish.

"Where should we start?" asked Brachah.

"You know better than I," smiled Silvana. "I came to hear you tell me your story."

"Well, then," said Brachah, "we will begin not with words but with pictures."

She took a picture out of her wallet and handed it to Sarah. Sarah looked at it and turned white. She dropped the photograph on the table and pushed it away from her.

"Is that the way a daughter treats a picture of her father and mother?" asked Brachah.

"They are no longer my parents...they are Jews!"

"Don't say 'they are Jews.' Say 'they *were* Jews' before they were murdered by the Christians."

Shaken, Sarah objected. "It was not Christians who killed the Jews. It was the Nazis."

"All right, let's say it was the Nazis with Christian support. The Poles aided and abetted the Germans in the name of the Church's traditional hatred of the Jews."

"But the Church teaches mercy!"

"That is in theory, but not in practice."

"I don't understand you, Barbara. You are talking like a Jew, not like a Christian."

Brachah ignored Sarah's comment and took another picture from her wallet.

Sarah looked at the picture and exclaimed, "Oh! That's Zushka Yosefova!"

Brachah laughed and said, "No, it's not Zushka Yosefova. It's Zissel Blitz."

Sarah held the picture to her heart and asked, "Where is she now?"

"Zissel is in the Holy Land. I, too, have come from there."

"What brought you to France?"

"I came to show you Zissel's picture. She wants to see you very badly. It would be an act of Christian charity for you to visit her." Brachah pronounced the words 'Christian charity' in a mocking tone.

Stung by her sarcasm, Sarah paused for a minute, and then replied, "You speak as if you have returned to the Jews."

"Don't say 'returned to the Jews.' Say I have returned to myself."

"But you were even more devout a Christian than I! How could you return to the Jews?"

"That's just the point. Let me be your example. If I, who was such a firm believer, could return to my people, it should be much easier for you, who are not so devout."

Sarah did not answer. Brachah too was silent. She must now give Sarah time to absorb all her comments and to argue with herself. For a long time Sarah sat there, motionless, as if in another world. Brachah watched her from the corner of her eye, fully understanding what Sarah was feeling. Finally, Sarah burst into tears, sobbing so hard that her whole body shook.

Brachah went up to her, stroked her head and comforted her. "It is not an easy job to break the bonds that our captors forced upon us while we were at their mercy. It was not easy for me nor is it easy for you. But no one should try to be what he is not. You are a Jew, not a Christian. You were made into a Christian against your will, but you need not stay that way."

For hours the two friends sat and talked. The next day they made reservations on a ship bound for Israel. Many ships left France for Israel, and any Jew who came and asked was given free passage. Sarah did not go to say good-bye to her friends in the mission school. She simply disappeared, just as Brachah had disappeared from the convent in Jerusalem.

Brachah sent a telegram to Zissel, announcing that she and Sarah were setting sail. When the telegram reached the Sharfsons, they found it hard to believe the good news. They read the cable over and over again. Their hearts overflowed with happiness. It was hard to wait two whole weeks. With each day that passed, they became tenser and more excited. It was almost too much to bear.

Finally the day came. The Sharfsons verified the time of the ship's arrival and they all went to Haifa to meet the boat. As they watched the ship cast anchor and saw the gangplank come down, it seemed to them that the beating of their hearts could be heard by everyone in the port.

Finally Sarah appeared. Zissel recognized her immediately and ran to her with outstretched arms. Sarah saw her and opened her arms in response. For what seemed an eternity, the two women stood there, holding each other in a tight embrace. The last of the family had completed her long journey home.

The Sharfson household looked as if it were having a holiday. Accepting Zissel's and Sarah's invitation, the Chasidov families from Nachrovah and Temyonovah had just arrived in Eretz Yisrael. Sarah and Zissel had invited them as a modest expression of thanks for all they had done. They would be honored with trees planted in their names in the Forest of Righteous Gentiles.

There were only four members left in the Chasidov family now. The only son of the Chasidovs of Chedalonova had fought with the Polish partisans and fallen in Yanovsky forest. He himself had not excelled in love for the Jews, but his parents had proved by their deeds that they, at least, were among "the righteous of the nations."

David and Chaim rented a car and took them sightseeing. When they returned to the Sharfsons' house, they were full of praise for all they had seen.

"If we hadn't seen it with our own eyes, we would never have believed it!" they exclaimed enthusiastically.

"No one who knew the Jews of the ghetto could have imagined that they would be capable of building a state like this. Although I have now seen it with my own eyes, it is still hard for me to believe that the Jews did all this by themselves.

"I didn't even recognize the Jews here. In the ghetto all the Jews looked as though they were born bent over and could never stand up straight, but here Jews stand upright. Their eyes are also not the same. The eyes of the Jews in Nachrovah were full of unending sadness, indelible as the color of their eyes. But here I have seen happy eyes. In short, the Jews here are different," said Mr. Chasidov of Nachrovah.

"No," disagreed Mr. Chasidov of Chedalonova, "they are the same Jews. Their troubles in Chedalonova and Nachrovah made them different."

There are new faces in the Sharfson house today. Not only are Brachah and David married; Sarah and Chaim have also found their life's partners. Three new Jewish families have been founded. Now they are all assembled in the Sharfson house, awaiting the return of Rav Shlomo Sharfson from the *yeshivah*. When he comes, they will all sit down to a festive meal with their honored guests.

Later that afternoon, they all went to the forest. The Chasidov brothers and their wives each stood bent over his or her sapling, covering it firmly with the warm earth. The Sharfson and Glick families stood to the side, watching them admiringly. When the Chasidovs finished, their eyes were filled with tears. They were deeply moved. Almost automatically, all eyes turned to Shlomo, to hear what he would say to the guests on this occasion.

Shlomo turned to them and began. "The people of Israel have a long history. Over three thousand six hundred years have passed since the first Jew was born. A nation that old should number billions of souls, yet there are only a few million Jews alive in the world today. Throughout the centuries, other nations have cut off whole branches of the Jewish race. Even Abraham, the first Jew, was himself thrown into a burning furnace. Anyone who smashes idols is bound to be hated by idol-worshipers.

"At Mount Sinai the people of Israel became the symbol of belief in one God. As recipients of the Ten Commandments, they became, at the same time, the object of an eternal hatred by all other nations. The rest of the world can never forgive the Jews for the message of the Ten Commandments which they brought to the world—a message to restrain Man's baser instincts. All those who desire to give free rein to their baser instincts must of necessity become the enemies of Israel.

"This forest was planted by righteous Gentiles. Look around and see how few trees have been planted here, and you will realize how universal anti-Semitism is. The world numbers billions of human beings, but very few righteous people. Their small number emphasizes their exceptional courage.

"If, in the vast sea of anti-Semitism, there are still a few scattered Gentiles who are willing to endanger their own lives to save the lives of Jews, there can be no greater spiritual courage than this. These few deserve our unbounded admiration and recognition."

Shlomo paused. The Chasidovs' eyes were lowered modestly.

"After all the world has done to the Jewish People," he

continued, "there are still Jews alive the world over, and they are gradually returning to the land that God promised our forefathers. This is nothing less than a miracle. God does not perform miracles for no reason. This miracle is the strongest possible proof that the God of Israel is true to His people. The nation of Israel is eternal; it will outlast all the wicked of the other nations. This is the source of our strength. This is the belief that has enabled us to bear such a heavy burden for so many centuries."

Shlomo paused again and then concluded, " 'I believe with perfect faith in the coming of the *Mashiach*. And even though he tarries, I will wait for him, day after day, until he comes.' "

another novel by
BENZION FIRER / *Saadiah Weissman*

In the first hectic years after the declaration of the State of Israel, as waves of Jewish immigrants converged from east to west upon the tiny, struggling country, great deeds and great tragedies took place side by side.

When thousands of Jews — God-fearing people all — arrived from Yemen on "wings of eagles" as promised by the prophets of old, each was ready to greet the *mashiach* in the Holy Land of Israel. But instead of the *mashiach*, they found the 20th century — a strange, bewildering world which left them vulnerable and disoriented.

One of the most disturbing aspects of those tumultuous years was the unaccountable disappearance of hundreds of Yemenite children who had arrived in Israel only to vanish from the face of the earth. Persistent rumors had it that they were given away for adoption to non-religious Israeli families or sent to non-religious kibbutzim. Saadiah Weissman is the story of one such child — one child and two families whose lives, although vastly different, were tragically intermingled.

This absorbing novel, with its nearly disastrous ending, cannot fail to move the reader as it portrays the period from Israel's founding through the next two decades.

Translated by Chava Shulman